BOMBSHELL

HOLLYWOOD A-LIST

BOMBSHELL

HOLLYWOOD A-LIST

NEW YORK TIMES BESTSELLING AUTHOR

CD REISS

Montlake
Romance

Text copyright © 2017 Flip City Media Inc.
All rights reserved.

Published by Montlake Romance, Seattle

www.apub.com

Amazon, the Amazon logo, and Montlake Romance are trademarks of Amazon.com, Inc., or its affiliates.

ISBN-13: 9781503943544
ISBN-10: 1503943542

Cover design by Shasti O'Leary Soudant

Printed in the United States of America

For my daughter.
If you want to know how incredibly smart, funny,
warm, and beautiful you were as a little girl,
read this book.
It's a love letter to you.

CHAPTER 1

CARA

—Wipes. Please say you have wipes—
—Now—

The two texts came rapid-fire. *Ding ding,* really loud in the waiting room. The walls, the floor, the ceiling, and the lighting were hard, cold white, and the sound bounced off them like a gong. The receptionist with the bun and black tailored jacket looked up at me disapprovingly. I made an "I'm sorry" face, then clicked off the sound. The five other well-groomed women in their twenties and thirties ignored me.

—What's happening? Where are you?—

—Hallway ladies room. Bring wipes. I'm out—

Everything about the text was weird. Why was Blakely in the bathroom? She was supposed to be on the other side of the glass doors, interviewing for a nanny job.

I smiled at the receptionist as I walked out. She knew me. I'd worked with West Side Nannies for years. I spoke French, navigated private school applications, wiped noses, helped with pre-calc homework, managed ancillary staff, and kept the little ones safe.

My last job had ended amicably but suddenly. My agent, Laura, shrugged it off and told me she could get me anything. So I made demands. I wouldn't work for absentee parents. No actors. No celebrities. No Hollywood hangers-on. Just vanilla rich. Or vanilla well-off. Glamour came at too high a price. A nanny didn't even have to sleep with a daddy to end up on the front page of some rag, and if there was anything that terrified me, it was seeing my face on the magazine racks at the grocery store checkout.

In an hour she found me something so perfect I nearly fell off my chair. Two gay bankers in Hancock Park. I'd met their son, had coffee at their house, and accepted an offer. I was at the office to sign the contract and keep Blakely company as she sat for her kid-meet with a family who wouldn't give their name.

Apparently, the meeting wasn't going well.

I could hear the screams and cries of a child from down the hall.

I knocked softly and the door swung open. I got hit in the face with a wall of poop stink and the teary screams of a little girl.

Blakely crouched on the tile surrounded by a ring of white-and-brown-streaked wads. The expensive toilet paper disintegrated when it was wet. Her hair had started falling out of her perfectly professional blonde chignon. She turned to me and stuck her hand out, snapping her fingers for the wipes.

She was an actress first, nanny second. Taking care of Hollywood kids was easier than waitressing, paid very well, came with rent-free housing, and sometimes—if you were lucky—the schedule was flexible enough to audition.

But she had a hard time finding work these days. Money was getting tight. Blakely had been my first friend in Los Angeles. We'd met at a birthday party and she'd taken me under her wing. So when her name got dragged through the mud, I was the one to grocery shop for her so she could avoid seeing her distorted face at the checkout and I was the one who defended her to the other caretakers at events.

Now I was going to bring her wipes because it was the least I could do.

The toilet seat was covered in brown streaks. The little girl standing by the throne with her stained pants around her ankles was crying so hard her face looked like a wet tomato.

Blakely was holding a wet wad of toilet paper with her fingertips. The door clicked closed behind me. She wiped the little girl's tears with a disintegrating piece of toilet paper and gently shushed her. The shushing didn't quiet her. I handed my friend the wipes and wet some overpriced hand towels so I could wipe down the poop.

"It's all right," she said in a gentle-but-firm nanny voice. "We're going to get you cleaned up in a jiff." Blakely stood, fell halfway out of her pump, and skidded on a soggy wad of toilet paper and poo, landing on her butt.

The little girl went from big-fat-tear-weeping to screaming in terror. I stepped over Blakely and kneeled in front of the little girl. I felt my chest expand as soon as I looked at her. My heart swelled and broke a bit. I'd do or say whatever I had to to soothe her.

"Are you all right?" I asked Blakely in a singsong so the little girl wouldn't get upset.

"I think I fell in poop," Blakely said from behind me. "Yuck. I did."

I turned back to the little one.

"Hi," I said, hoping she'd hear me through her wailing. "My name is Cara, what's yours?"

Blakely interrupted, "Nicole, it's—"

"How old are you?" I asked. She snarfled, making a massive effort to get herself together. I'd seen men dig ditches with less struggle. Good kid.

"F-f-f-f—"

Blakely broke in. "—Brad Sinclair's daughter."

Talk about grocery store fodder. The A-list Oscar nominee had had a five-year-old from a short fling dumped on his doorstep a week earlier. If I were this kid, I'd shit myself too.

"Five," the girl spit out.

"Five?" I acted surprised and impressed. The fact was, Brad Sinclair's bodyguards were going to bust in here in a minute and arrest both of us. This girl needed to calm down. "So big! Wow." I snapped a few wipes from the dispenser and handed them to her. "Do you want to wipe your eyes or can I do it?"

"You," she sniffled. I patted her cheeks. News of her had been all over the internet. Notorious Hollywood playboy Brad Sinclair had knocked up a girl six years before, when he was working in a little crystal store in Venice Beach. Right after he got cast in his career-making role. She'd put his name on the birth certificate but never told him. When she died in a freeway accident, the state contacted him, DMZ got wind of it, and no one had been able to talk about anything else for a week.

"Are you feeling sick in your belly?" I asked.

She nodded.

"And your head?"

"It hurts right here." She put her hand on the front of her head and moved it back. Top of the head. Not neck. That was good. "And it smells really bad in here."

Her face screwed up. She was about to cry again.

"You're right," I said. "It does. Should we clean up a little?"

"Yes, please!"

The mother, whoever she was, had raised her well so far.

Blakely cut in, "I have an audition in an hour." She tossed the wad of paper in the toilet.

"You smell like a colon." I looked at my watch. "And you don't have time to get home and shower." I pointed to the seat and addressed the

4

little girl. "Hey, great job cleaning up. My name is Cara. Do you want to tell me your name?"

She shook her head. Her face had gone from red to pink to normal, revealing brown eyes big as cups of black coffee and thin eyebrows. Her coloring was nothing like Sinclair's, but the lines and planes of her face were so similar, she could have been his clone.

"That's all right. You don't have to tell me. Let me see what we have back here." She bent over in the shameless way of children so I could see that the backs of her thighs were covered in brown stink.

"Not so bad," I said. "Blakely, can you toss these and grab me a fresh one?" I handed her the wad, keeping my eyes on the child. "This is a nice shirt. Who is this?" I pointed to a pink horse with kitten ears.

"Pony Pie. Her nature symbol is joy."

"We could use some of that."

"We could," Blakely said, handing me a wipe. "But this sweetheart really is a joy. Just having a hard day." She leaned forward to make eye contact with the girl and winked. Nicole wiped her nose with her sleeve.

"I agree," I said. I got to work on the girl's bottom while Blakely wiped down the bathroom.

Blakely whispered, "I'll never make it home to shower and get to Culver City in—"

She gulped her words back when there was a hard knock on the door.

"Blakely Anderson?" a male voice barked from the other side. My friend and I looked at each other.

"We're in here," I called.

A key slipped in the lock and the door slapped open, revealing two huge guys in dark shirts with radios squawking. The little one started screaming again, stamping her feet in poop streaks.

"Close the door close the door close the door," she shrieked. Blakely threw her hands up. The guys came for the girl, who was getting more upset by the millisecond.

What I should have done was step back and let them take her, shitstains and all. I would have had far less trouble. But I didn't have time to think it through. The bathroom was small, the guys were big, and the girl sounded irrevocably hurt and upset. I didn't have cerebral cortex time. Only lizard brain time.

I stood up with my hands out.

"Stop!"

They stopped. I had three seconds to talk over her screams.

"This little girl is upset because she's dirty. You two taking her out of here like this is going to make it worse so—"

My three seconds were up. Guy number one pushed me out of the way while guy number two picked her up under the arms just as she kicked off her stained pants, shoe landing in filth, ear-splitting screams. Blakely stood in the hall feverishly talking to someone. My heart fell apart for the little stinker.

"Whoa, whoa!" A male voice echoed above the din. "Can we all chill out for a second?"

Everyone froze except the child, who was upset past obedience.

In the doorway stood my agent, Laura, and Brad Sinclair. But honestly, Laura was a footnote to his presence. We all were.

I was used to celebrities and actors. Star power had no effect on me anymore.

But he was different.

Burgundy button-down and jeans. Blue eyes and brown hair that needed a brush. Six-two-ish. A jawline that may or may not have been geometrically possible. Sure. Those were all words that described what I saw, and I could have come up with a hundred more the next day.

But at that moment, with his shoulders filling the doorframe and Laura behind him, clutching a folder, he wasn't just a collection of perfectly fine features. He was action and motion. He projected himself outward, emanating heat. My ears turned red. Half a second turned to minutes. He was the hurricane and the eye of it. A constellation of angles and planes that curled around the world and complemented it.

Get a hold of yourself.

He was just stunning. One of a thousand like him.

Maybe a hundred.

A dozen.

Fine. You could count the number of men that gorgeous on one finger.

"Mr. Sinclair," I said, giving him my most authoritative tone. "There's no way out of here besides that door. I'm not going to take her. Just let me clean her up and bring her back."

"Who are you?"

I had to shout over the nonstop loop of the girl's screams. "My name is Cara DuMont. I was nanny to Ray Heywood's kids."

He knew Ray. Everyone knew Ray. Brad looked me up and down as if taking stock of my soul. I continued. "I'm not here for the job. But she's upset. I'm fingerprinted and background checked, and I'm not afraid of a little poop on the floor."

Brad looked at his daughter, the guys in the dark shirts, Laura, and then me, eye to eye. A man who projected star power like a lighthouse, but for the moment he was just a guy totally out of his depth.

"Okay. Thank you."

I reached for the child, and she fell into my arms. The screaming slowed as soon as I bore the full weight of her, and stopped completely when she was on a clean part of the floor.

I addressed my agent. "Can you grab some underpants and have housekeeping bring some towels?"

She nodded. The security detail backed out, and Brad Sinclair gave me one look, one burning look that took the breath out of me before I closed the bathroom door and kneeled down to face his daughter.

"Do you want to start over?" I asked the girl.

"Okay."

"My name is Cara. It's nice to meet you. What's your name?"

"Nicole Garcia." She sniffed and wiped her nose on her sleeve.

"Nice to meet you, Nicole. Wanna help clean this up?"

"Can we do my butt first?"

"Great idea." I liked this little one. Good thing I already had a job lined up or I could have fallen for her and her dad in a heartbeat.

CHAPTER 2

BRAD

"Buck up, son. Not a man born is ready for fatherhood when it comes. Best just to set yourself to getting it done."

My dad had a fucking positive attitude. Better than any of the "fruits and nuts" of Los Angeles with their pet therapists and white smiles. I grew up with "Stop yer bitchin' and get in the kitchen." I had no idea what the kitchen had to do with anything, but it was a good, solid southernism, one of many he launched like rockets right in front of the entire staff of West Side Nannies as if he didn't know I was a fucking superstar.

Dad had had his share of surprises, including knocking up Mom when they were dating for a week. He just put on his grown-up boots and started walking. And when he lost two fingers, pinkie and fourth on his right hand, to a circular saw at Redfield Lumber, he had it sewn up and went to work two days later. There was no patience in the Sinclair family for whining, bitching, or moaning. Slap a smile on your face and put your head down to work.

Like when your son discovers he's a father, you get on a plane within the hour and haul ass to Los Angeles. My parents were here so fast I barely had time to get my people in to clean the house.

I met Nicole at Protective Services after the DNA test was positive. She was crying. She was always crying. She was a bag of flesh, bones, and tears. I was sure she was cute. Hundred percent sure. But her mom had died while Nicole was reading (I confirmed, *actually reading*) in kindergarten and here she was, as if picked up and thrown over the fence with no way to get back in. I'd cry too.

The only time she wasn't crying, or almost crying, or breathing between sobs, was at West Side Nannies, in the bathroom behind a closed door. I told Laura there was no way she was in there, because I didn't hear sobbing.

But, lo and behold, Nicole was in there, not crying even though she was stick-dipped in her own feces.

It wasn't because she was sick of crying. It was because of the woman with the snotty tissue and the rock-steady mood ring eyes. The nanny . . . who was, I was told . . .

"Unavailable," Laura said. My dad grumbled disapproval and my mother *tsked*. They were really messing with my mojo. I couldn't be a celebrity and that-no-good-Sinclair-boy-who-spilled-paint-on-my-lawn-now-who's-gonna-pay-for-that at the same time.

"What's that mean?" I objected. "She's in the bathroom cleaning her up as we speak. What's she doing tomorrow or the next day?"

"We just signed her to a family full time. We'll find you someone, Mr. Sin—"

"I don't know if you know this, Miss, but I don't take no for an answer. That one in the bathroom is the one I want. She's the only one who's been able to stop that little girl from crying since she landed in my hands a week ago."

I'd never wanted a woman so badly in my life, and though she was definitely hot, my dick wasn't even involved.

I was going to have her. I needed her.

Two weeks earlier I'd been twenty-four hours into the most epic party of my life. My house was upside down, populated with a few hundred friends and a dozen security guys.

"Chill out, Gene," I'd said over the music, walking away from him. No one walked away from Superagent Gene Testarossa. Except me. "This is the same runaround as that girl last March."

"The one who said you gave her herpes?"

"Yeah. That one."

"You gave her herpes."

I spun on him. I poked at his Hugo Boss jacket with the beer bottle swinging between my thumb and the jabbing finger.

"The other girl gave her herpes, and it was oral herpes. I was clean. I'm still clean."

He shook his fat, pink-gold watch until he could see the face.

"Ken's on his way," he mumbled.

Ken Braque. Damn. I couldn't turn my back on my PR guy as easily as I turned my back on my agent.

I walked out to the pool. Everyone was dressed for summer except Gene, who always looked like a Wall Street banker.

"I have a month and a half off to do nothing but sit in this house and do what I want. I scheduled it. I made it happen. Moved heaven and earth. The mountain came to fucking Mohammed. And you're crashing it with what? Who? A girl named Brenda? *Brenda?*"

"Look. She died in a car accident two weeks ago and I came here as soon as I knew. Don't give me a hard time. If you're the father, you're the father."

"I always use a condom."

"You sure?"

"Because that's something I'd forget?"

"Six years ago? When you got that little horror movie and you were over the fucking moon because you were a nobody working in a crystal store? Yeah. You'd forget."

"This is serious," a voice came from behind me. I spun around.

"Ken!" I hugged him. When I signed with him I knew I'd made it as an actor. I had a career to spin. Boom. I partied harder that night than when I was nominated for an Oscar. Which was cool, but too surreal to drink over.

"Can you put pants on?" he said. I was in a dress shirt with a towel around my waist. I had no recollection of how I'd gotten that way.

"Hey, it's a party. I don't like feeling restrained. Crotches restrain me."

"You have a lot more to worry about than your pants."

"Is it this Brenda thing?"

"Brenda isn't a problem and she never was. This is deep and wide, Sinclair."

My agent was a douchebag, but my PR guy was the real deal. So when he walked back into my house, I followed.

The party had drifted into all four bedrooms, living room, office, den, billiards room, and the whatever room that I never figured out what to do with. We ended up in the laundry room. I hadn't even known I had a laundry room. Mom would be proud.

Gene had shuffled in. Ken closed the doors, then leaned on the washer and crossed his arms.

"Brenda Garcia. Remember anything about her?"

The question wasn't rhetorical. He was actually asking.

"No."

"You worked with her at a crystal store."

"I remember the store."

"Fine." He moved off the washer and stood on his own feet as if changing gears. "I'm not asking you to remember her or her daughter. It's irrelevant. I'm sure she was on a brain cell you killed already."

"My brain is fine."

I sounded defensive. Too many beers or too few.

"Right. Whatever. I don't care. You know what I care about? I care about what people think of you."

I took a mouthful of beer. Outside, someone was thrown into the pool. A woman, judging from the squeals. He might care what people thought of me, but I sure didn't.

"Now," Ken said. I listened to his voice, but not the words. What if I did have a kid? That made me a *father*. I'd played a father in *Verity*, but that was different than *being* a father. Right? I mean, that takes a ton of time, and time was one thing I didn't have a hell of a lot of.

"What were you saying?" I asked.

Ken sighed and pulled a yellow four-by-six envelope out of the breast pocket of his jacket. He opened it by pinching the edges.

"DMZ already found out by following the child protection agent into Gene's office and sitting next to her in the waiting room."

"Not my fault," Gene mumbled.

Ken continued. "Then they sent a middle-aged female reporter into the CPS office to pose as Brenda Garcia's aunt. Apropos of nothing. Because this is still real."

He took a picture out of the envelope.

It was a school photo of a girl. Maybe five? Six? Four? Who the fuck even knew? What was the age of maximum cuteness? Because that was how old she was. She had brown hair and huge, dark brown eyes. Big smile surrounded by dimples. Nose like a bell pepper.

I had blue eyes and light brown hair, but, despite that, the part of my brain that recognized faces calculated a visual equation and recognized hers. My mother's eyes. My sister's curls. My dad's chin.

Me. She looked exactly like me.

"Oh. Shit," I said. "No. Nononono. I wrap it up, Ken. You have to believe me."

"Okay, I don't know when you're going to get this through your head," he said. "It doesn't matter what I believe. It matters what the public believes. I have your clone, right here." He held up the picture. The more I looked at it, the more it sunk in. She was mine. "And Ms. Garcia put your name on the birth certificate as the father."

"Fucking bitch."

"You will speak of her with respect from this moment on," Ken roared. "First, because she's dead, and people do not like it when you speak ill of the dead. Second, she bore you a daughter and hasn't gone public. She was a single mom working behind a counter at the Coffee Chain. People are going to be on her side."

He was right. My mother raised me better than that. You don't speak ill of the dead or insult a woman. You don't give anyone a reason to think less of you. I tried to hear my mother's voice in my head, but it was hard to hear without also tasting her biscuits and gravy. With corn. And butter. And the smell of barbecue. Yeah. Dad wouldn't get mad at the messenger. Dad wouldn't turn his back. Dad would be Mister C3. Cool, calm, collected.

Okay. I was good. I had this.

I had to just breathe in. Man up. Breathe out.

"Where is she now?" I asked. "The kid."

"Her name is Nicole, and she's in foster care. Now, here's what you're going to do before this explodes. One, you're taking a DNA test. Two, if she's not yours, you set her up a college fund anyway."

"What if she is mine?"

"I light you a cigar and set you up with a staff. Because you're not ditching her. It's too late for that. You're not ditching her, and you're showing up in Thailand, on set for *Bangkok Brotherhood* like nothing happened."

"How's he gonna—"

Gene didn't get a chance to finish his sentence before Ken interrupted.

"He has no choice. If he bails on that shoot, he's never going to work again. And he has a kid to support now." He turned back to me. "Private school's no joke. You need the money. Staff up. You can't miss a single rehearsal or you'll be back in Arkansas. It doesn't matter how famous you think you are. You can disappear. And if you're not on set in Thailand on schedule, you will disappear . . . Poof." He kissed the tips of his fingers and spread them out.

I didn't want to disappear. Not back to Redfield. I'd worked too hard.

"I got this."

Gene made a huffing noise that was long on disbelief and short on actual humor.

"What, asshole?" I asked him.

"You? Man. This is a fucking disaster. What are you going to do with a kid? You're not even wearing pants."

"You," I poked him in the chest, "need to have a little faith, my friend."

I brushed past him to walk out, taking a swig from my beer bottle. It tasted like piss. I stepped on a pair of panties. I had no idea who they belonged to.

Shit. What the hell was I going to do? I traveled like Marco fucking Polo and worked like a dog. I partied like it was my job because my job didn't leave me too much time to party. And I was going to add a kid to the mix? What the fuck was I going to do?

Gene didn't need to have a little faith.

I did.

I was going to have to fake it until I made it. Act like I thought dads should act. Do all the things until they came naturally. I didn't know what the things were, but it wasn't like I was inventing anything, right?

———

The hot nanny in the bathroom had a gift, and I needed it.

Nicole had cried when she met my friend Mike's kids. She cried in my mother's lap. Sobbed when Mom bought her the sneakers with the toes that lit up whenever she walked, ran, stepped, or jumped. She even cried in her sleep.

I thought a little help was all I needed. Mike had given me the number at West Side Nannies. I held the card like a fucking magic sword, but I left there no better off than I had arrived.

On the way out from the bathroom incident, an insane pack of paparazzi had found the back door where the limo was parked. And by insane, I mean they were more aggressive than I'd ever seen in my life. I swore their lives depended on getting a picture of Nicole. One of them held his camera in front of her and flashed it in her face. She cried. Of course she cried. I would have cried too. I grabbed for the camera and missed because my dad held me back. Good thing. I was just about ready to peel that guy's skin off his skull.

In the back of the limo, Nicole wouldn't look at me. Too busy crying.

The only time she'd stopped crying was for the hot nanny.

My mom sat across from Dad and me with Nicole on her lap.

"Hard to miss her with those shoes," Dad grumbled.

"They're fine," I said.

"You tell her no, after what happened," Mom huffed at Dad.

"What do they want?" Nicole asked.

"Just a picture," Mom said, stroking her hair.

"They want a broken face," I said.

"Hush!" Mom made her stern face.

"I'm scared," Nicole sobbed.

I sat back in the seat and covered my face. I could smell the bathroom soap on my hands. Jesus Christ. Acting like I had this under control wasn't working.

"We should be home." Dad laid down the law, pointing at me with his three-fingered hand. "She needs family. Not staff."

"We'll do the interviews at the house from now on." I moved my hands away. Nicole was looking at me as if trying to figure out who was in charge. Too bad I had no idea either. My act was falling apart from the inside out.

"A man needs to raise his own children," Dad declared. "You Hollywood types delegate the important things and attend the nonsense personally. Well, it's—"

"The circumstances, Milton." The girl was limp in Mom's arms, head on shoulder, watching Sunset Boulevard pass by. "They're not normal."

"The hell they're not."

"Don't say a bad word," Nicole said, tears slowing down to little sobs.

Dad huffed and crossed his arms.

"Is the lady coming home with us?" she asked, picking her head up as if her head was clear for the first time.

"Which lady, sweetheart?" Kid talk still felt weird in my mouth.

"The bathroom lady. With the black hair."

What was I supposed to tell her? For the first time since she'd come home with me, she wasn't crying. She looked hopeful, like clouds parted at the mention of the bathroom lady or something.

"Maybe."

"Don't say maybe. Say yes or no."

"I don't know."

"Yes or no! Yes yes yes!" she shouted, and I could feel the tears coming.

"I'll try—"

"No maybe. Yes or no."

"Yes, okay? Yes."

Nicole nodded as if telling herself it was true. I'd said yes. Then she rested her head on my mother's shoulder again.

Next to me, my father covered his eyes and shook his head.

CHAPTER 3

CARA

The morning after we met Brad Sinclair he was still embedded in my mind. I couldn't get away from thinking about him in that bathroom doorway. He was a dude. A party animal. A fuckaround.

"I don't think I'm getting a callback," Blakely said as we climbed a particularly dusty incline on Griffith Park. "I was ten minutes late."

"But you smelled nice."

She shook her head, swinging her ponytail back and forth.

"Can't film a smell. But the face?" She drew her hand over her face as if she were on the floor at the Los Angeles Auto Show. "This face is instantly recognizable as the woman stupid enough to fall for Josh Trudeau."

"Everyone forgot that."

I was lying. No one forgot it. She'd forever be the face of a nanny who fell for a daddy. Fresh from the supermarket headcap.

"And I don't think I got the Sinclair job either," she said after swigging from her bottle. "Which, maybe it's a good thing."

It had started getting hot earlier in the day, so Blakely and I wanted to finish the hike up the hill by nine a.m. The mountain sloped and curved up to Dante's Peak, a copse of trees smoked out but not destroyed in the 2008 fires.

"It's kind of a disaster," I said. "The surprise kid? Nothing good can come of it. You can tell he's trying though."

"He has no choice."

"And what they say about him?" I said between gasps for oxygen, continuing as if I hadn't heard her. "All true. It's like so raw. The presence."

"I thought he was shorter." Blakely sucked on her water bottle. Her blonde ponytail swung behind her. She looked gorgeous even after two miles uphill. My bangs were plastered to my forehead, and my eyes were wet from the dust.

"Too good-looking to work for," I said, getting out of the way of a woman in a tight leotard and her dog. "And straight. Too straight."

"I know. And inexperienced. He'd probably think he was entitled to it."

"Too risky. I pity the girl he hires."

I shook my head. Brad Sinclair was a tabloid headline waiting to happen.

"I hope you get to pity me. I need the money."

I nodded. He wasn't going to hire her. He'd get talked out of it by anyone who cared about his reputation. After her affair with Josh Trudeau she became the nanny equivalent of box office poison. The rumor mill never stopped churning.

Raymond, my last boss, had cut me loose before the rumor mill had a chance to churn. We hadn't done anything, but when he got engaged to Kendall, she wasted no time turning me into a problem. Executive powers came with the engagement ring. Her first order was that the other pretty woman in the house had to go. I was young and cute, and you don't bring a time bomb into your home.

And that's exactly what a celebrity nanny is. Not only is she attractive but she's great with the kids. She does all the things the dad associated with his normal upbringing, which is likely the upbringing he promised himself he was going to give his children.

The nanny represents that failed promise. She kisses boo-boos, packs lunches, cooks what the children like, and sits to eat with them. His wife is usually in the business as well, and travels, works all hours, and manages a business team as well as the household team. She represents all the dad's failures as a father, because she's juggling everything but the children.

There were plenty of men who didn't fall for the high-priced, educated, young, beautiful nanny, but there were plenty who did. You could read all about them while your food was on the conveyor belt at the grocery store. It happened so often it was surprising when it didn't.

Despite Raymond's numerous failings as a father and human being, he never hit on me. He never even looked at me cockeyed. I appreciated that, and as time went on I took it for granted. He was based in Los Angeles because he owned a conglomerate of internet and paper tabloids that fed off the very people he called friends. But because he wasn't a celebrity himself, I could get him when the kids needed him, he respected what I did, and I loved Willow and Jedi.

"You had such a sweet deal with Raymond Heywood," Blakely said, voice rising and falling with her gait.

"Yeah. I guess. But two gay bankers? This new family is even better. They aren't interested in seducing women, they have no travel schedules, there are no paparazzi out front."

"Yeah. You lucked out."

She said it ruefully, and I understood why. She'd been caught with Josh Trudeau by his wife. Marsha Trudeau had recorded them from the bedroom closet and posted the video on YouTube. It was a mess. Blakely's career came to an abrupt halt, but the damage to her heart was worse. She didn't know he was a serial cheater. She'd confused a busy husband and wife with a failing marriage. She'd believed everything

Josh had said and let herself fall in love. He was never going to leave his wife. They rarely do.

She got an apartment and didn't leave it for months.

She worked as a dog walker and house sitter. She changed the name on her headshot to Sarah Colt and started over. Sometimes when she went on auditions she wasn't recognized and got a callback. Sometimes it wasn't that easy.

I thought about her a lot, because what happened to her terrified me.

I didn't want it. Anything but that. People looking at a picture and deciding I was a whore. Strangers making a judgment about me. My blood turned to ice whenever I imagined it.

"I heard Ray and Kendall went back to West Side and asked for a woman in her fifties."

When Ray Heywood let me go I moved in with Blakely. Her job prospects hadn't improved, but she could do her own shopping and seemed to be moving on.

"Menopausal women are the horniest," Blakely said. "And West Side doesn't do unattractive or older, sorry to say."

An old Korean couple in plaid golf visors waved and smiled.

Ruefully, Blakely continued. "I wish I could just change my face sometimes."

My phone chimed. Speak of the devil. My agent.

"Hi!" I said while Blakely polished off her water.

Laura sounded businesslike and positive when she delivered bad news.

"Matt and Dom fell through."

"What?"

"Sorry, Cara. It wasn't you."

"What do you mean it wasn't me?" I felt the world shifting under my feet.

"They love you, they just decided they wanted someone who speaks Spanish."

"I speak French! What's wrong with French? Willow Heywood is fluent because of me. Did you tell them that?"

"I'm sorry, Cara. We can send you out again. You're easy to place."

I wanted to throw the phone. Instead I just hung it up.

Blakely had heard everything. She put her hand on my back.

"You'll find something."

"Sure. I'll get hired and go in like a little puppy, all tail wagging and wanting to do a good job, then one of two things will happen. No. Three things. He'll look at me like I hold the keys to the life he wanted and missed, and I'll quit before I ruin their marriage." I counted off a second finger. "Or the lady of the house will start snapping at me every time he's in the room, or I'll hit the lottery and get a single mom who won't fire me until she gets a serious boyfriend. Then I'm out. And it's not fair. Because they only want pretty nannies. Having their kids toted around by someone unattractive or middle-aged is like a black mark on their records. And we're like inanimate household accessories until the person in the house with the dick feels sad or lonely."

"Wow. You need some ice cream."

I was frustrated and disappointed. I also had no business complaining about any of this to Blakely, who had it ten times worse.

"I'm sorry," I said.

"You were just speaking my mind."

"Let's go down to Cups and Cones," I said. "I'm buying."

CHAPTER 4

CARA

Things work out the way they do for a reason. Sometimes the reason is that the universe wants to screw you. For fun, maybe. Or because you getting screwed is in service of someone else's "things happen for a reason."

But the reason isn't always rainbows and unicorns. When my parents got reassigned to Paris the reason was so I could learn French, and when it was Pakistan it was so I could stay in the house all the time, and when it was Korea it was so I could fall in love with a boy named Shin who clumsily took my virginity two weeks before we had to move again. When The American School in Stuttgart was full, Dennis and I went to Lycée Français and stayed. The universe must have wanted our lessons to be rigorous and consistent no matter where we were. Certainly, Dad didn't mind that we were taught to always just be polite, deferential to authority, and keep our noses clean. But by fourteen, nothing about me was clean.

It's true, sometimes things happen for a reason. And sometimes the reasons suck.

Moving around that much meant I didn't have a chance to fall in love. And if I couldn't fall in love, I was just going to let my body have a party. Free birth control in Belgium and not being anywhere long enough to get a "reputation" meant I could do what I wanted. I just had to make sure I kept away from other girls' boyfriends and stuck to guys who didn't talk so much.

When I was seventeen I cost my father his security clearance. I was caught in a car on a desolate Scottish road with a rugby player. People talked. My parents, who kept their noses so clean they glowed, asked for a transfer so we could start from scratch yet again. We went back to the states in deadly tense silence. After that, I felt as if I couldn't do anything right. My parents made me nervous. My father in particular always seemed to look at me sideways, as if he was looking for me to get into some kind of trouble.

Once we settled in Texas I had a habit of not disclosing any information about anything. I got into and out of minor scrapes by being straightforward and respectful at the same time. I adapted easily to new situations and watched how other people behaved before I acted. I was a natural diplomat.

My peers and their parents may have been right. I might have been cold. I might have been unemotional. People and their judgments scared me. I was only really myself around children.

I went to college for child development and took on a teaching position for about five minutes before I was offered a ton of money to watch Jude and Karen McVino's twin toddlers while they shot a movie in Austin.

When they went back to Hollywood I went with them. I said goodbye to my parents. They got stationed in Argentina while I was gone and after a few phone calls it got too easy to stop talking to them. Then it got hard to pick up the phone.

I was fine. I felt like I had a new family because those kids set a light off in my soul.

Not every child I've watched did that. I've loved them all, even the most rotten and entitled kids in town. But a few were exceptional.

"Brad Sinclair wants to meet with you," Laura said on a call the day after the Griffith Park hike. Blakely and I were on the balcony of her cheap Los Feliz rental. She had a beer and a magazine. I had a book and a bottle of water.

"He's too famous."

"I told him you'd say that."

"Do you have anything coming up? Isn't Ken Braque's wife pregnant?"

"Three months. You might want to meet with Brad for a consultation. The poor guy's confused as hell and his parents are going back to Arkansas soon."

"Tell him how to parent? That never goes well."

"Just go meet him," Laura said. "As a favor to me. It'll look good for the agency."

"For you," I said. We said our good-byes and hung up.

Blakely put her foot on the railing. Her big toe poked out of her sock and the brand of beer she was drinking was a dollar a can. When I opened the screen door she held the magazine up.

"What do you think of her nose?"

I looked at the picture of Frida Julian. "Looks like a nose."

"It used to be huge. I was in acting school with her. Total honker. And she was stunning, even with that thing on her face."

"You have a nice nose." I sat on the chair next to her.

"Yeah. But if it were bigger that would be all people would see. I'd be unrecognizable."

I didn't feed further into her fantasy. I had to figure out if I wanted to step into Brad Sinclair's life.

"Maybe she was stunning *because* of it." Blakely considered this more to herself than me. I wasn't even in the room anymore. She needed something to do besides worry and wonder. If she could just get a job, she'd be all right.

I decided to see Sinclair. At the very least, maybe I could help out Blakely.

CHAPTER 5

CARA

The house was ginormous. The kind of house you got just because you could. Everything about this stank to high heaven. Everything about Brad Sinclair was wrong. From his travel schedule, to the way he partied, to the number of women he reportedly bedded weekly.

A guy in a white shirt and black jacket opened the car door. Probably a driver on staff. That was a good sign. But as signs went, the yellow Maserati with the scratched bumper parked by the garage wasn't as good.

"Thank you," I said, handing him my keys. I'd been briefed on how well-staffed Brad Sinclair was. So the house valet didn't surprise me. The guard at the gate didn't surprise me. The catering truck behind the house was likely some celebrity chef who kept the fridge and pantries stocked when the celebrity in question was home.

Which wasn't as often as people thought. I'd traveled with the McVinos, and the life they led was unfriendly to keeping a house, a family, or a routine. Unless they took their entire staff with them, a working actor or director spent weeks at a time eating in hotels in the middle of the night after a fifteen-hour day. They picked what they could off craft services tables, and if the film didn't have a huge budget, the only options on the table were fat, sugar, and salt.

Uncomfortable costumes, exposure to weather, long hours, tons of waiting.

I'd need a staff when I was home too.

The front door opened. I expected a housekeeper or butler, but it was the actor himself.

I hadn't forgotten how beautiful he was; I'd just chosen not to think about it.

"Ma'am," he said. Southern boy. Parents together. Christian elementary. Public secondary. Two years at USC Drama. Dates his costars for a month after the wrap party, then moves on. Poring through the trades and making calls, I'd discovered he'd spend at least eight of the next twelve months overseas doing action movies, but most had post-production in town.

"Mr. Sinclair," I said, holding my hand out. "Nice to see you outside a bathroom."

He shook my hand.

I'd shaken plenty of famous hands attached to gorgeous men, but my imagination was sparked by the way his fingers slid against mine to grasp them and the way our palms pressed together. My mind clouded over with ripped sheets, hard muscles, and soft skin.

"Pleasure's mine," he said and my brain skipped like a trip on a cracked sidewalk over the word *pleasure*.

He didn't give me the oversincere hand-over-clasp to show me how damn happy he was to see me, but there was something intimate about that half a second.

Just a consultation.

I followed him into the house. Dora Donovan had designed it. Looked like her with her faux-midcentury white couch and shag rug. That wasn't going to work with playdates unless he wanted to keep an upholsterer on staff.

We went through the living room to a smaller room with a pool table smack in the middle. It had a stained glass Budweiser lamp over it and was racked for nine-ball. Dora Donovan had nothing to do with this room, for sure.

"Wanna sit?" He held a chair out for me. The glass-topped table was just inside the open patio doors and was set with iced tea.

I sat.

"I'm not a date," I said kindly, indicating the iced tea setup. "Just so you know. You don't have to do things like hold the chair for me."

"Habit, I guess."

He sat opposite me.

"Chivalry is nice. But with the nanny, whomever you hire, it can be misconstrued."

He smirked a little, as if misconstruing his own thoughts. I cleared my throat and pulled my jacket closed.

"Where's Nicole?" I picked up the pitcher and poured him some.

"My parents took her to the park. She made the tea. My mother, I mean."

"I hear they're not staying?"

"No."

"And how is she?"

"My mother?"

"Your daughter."

He took a second to look out the doorway into the blazing sunset, then at his tea. He shook the ice down.

"I have no clue."

His honesty was refreshing. He earned my attention and respect with those four words.

He looked at the table, then up at me. The camera always caught his little imperfections: the scar on his forehead, the slightly crooked nose. In person, they were tangible indicators of his charisma, and were powerful reminders of the flawlessness of the rest of him.

"Laura said you have a photo shoot set up for you and Nicole with *Vanity Fair*."

"Yeah. So?"

"You need the money?"

"It's going to charity. A dyslexia fund. My sister has it so——"

"Cancel it."

I looked right at him. Didn't flinch. Didn't melt even though I wanted to. He knew I was right. In the millisecond pause and the way he broke his gaze, I knew I didn't have to explain myself.

"Will do." His voice was low and husky, like a growl turned down to one. As if he wanted to yell about not telling him what to do, but knew better. I could just about see the string he was tied together with.

"I think she needs as much consistency as you can manage. She was taking gymnastics. You should get her into classes."

"I can do that."

"Have you found a school for her?"

He took a sip of tea, then jerked his thumb southward.

"There's one down the Valley side."

"Laurence?"

"Yeah. There's another one on Wilshire. The public school's on Franklin." He shrugged. "Summer just started. We have a few months."

He wasn't prepared for this. Not even a little. Neither was I, because he seemed so vulnerable behind the cocky veneer that I wanted to help him, and that was the first sign I should run away.

I was there as a consultant, so I was going to consult.

"Nicole is a very together little girl. And I think, under normal circumstances she'd thrive in a tough, competitive school environment."

"She's going into first grade."

"It's also Los Angeles. It's a town of self-made strivers and their children. So kindergarten is the entry year. It's very hard to get a kid into first grade, even one as mature as Nicole. There's just no space."

"She's mature? She can read. Right? It's amazing." He beamed. I wanted to smile, but I couldn't be delighted for him. That was inappropriate.

"I know I saw her in tears, but once she calmed down she followed instructions and spoke clearly. She has great fine motor skills and when she cleans a shitstain she gets every speck off. At her age and for what she's been through, you're right. That's pretty amazing."

Flattering the child was a sure way to get the job, and even though I wasn't interested in working for him, per se, seeing him beam like a proud parent gave me hope for him.

"We had her reading tested. She's perfect."

He was really stuck on the reading. Most kids could read by the time they entered first grade, but he seemed happy in his bubble. I didn't want to pop it.

"She's doing great," I continued, trying to focus on Nicole and not the way his hand curved around his iced tea. "There's a school in Santa Monica called Crossroads. It's a great school, academically, but one of their core directives is the emotional health of the student. They have a grade-bearing course that focuses on each child's emotions."

He smiled that award-winning smile.

"Ma'am, I'm from the South. That hippy-dippy shit ain't gonna fly."

"And when your daughter breaks down because she never dealt with losing her mother, your good-old-boy shit ain't gonna fly neither."

I heard his foot tap, but didn't look at it. We were eye-locked, measuring each other.

Thank God I wasn't working for him. He was melting me from the inside out, and I had a feeling it was on purpose.

"You play nine-ball?" he asked.

"Sure do."

"You win and I'll go see your hippy-dippy school. I win and you go see the one on Wilshire."

"I don't see why it matters what school I see. It's your decision."

"You consulting or not?"

I hadn't considered seeing him after that meeting, but he had a point. A real consult on how to manage his daughter would take more than one meeting, and the pay was excellent. But I wasn't here for me. I was here for Blakely.

I stood up. "You break."

He handed me a cue. "Ladies first."

I took it and placed the cue ball in the middle of the table, about six inches from the headrail and lined with the center diamond. I had a break method shown to me by a hustler I'd dated in Paris. I always sank something in nine-ball.

I placed the cue on the rail wood and slid it back and forth, bridging high with my left hand.

"What the hell is that?" he asked.

"It's me breaking." I stood straight, getting the power from my hips. "Laura says you won't meet any other nannies."

"I don't want any other nannies."

I broke. *Clack tic tic tic pup pup pup* . . . the three threatened the side but bounced on the cushions. Nothing went in. That was a first.

"What's the problem with them?"

"Nicole doesn't like them, or I don't like them." He set up a one-three and sank it.

"Too hippy-dippy?"

"I don't like a woman who flirts on an interview to watch my kid." One-seven. Sunk. He was just going to run the one ball all over the table.

"I think you're seeing things."

He must have been. We were professionals, every one of us. Laura was damned serious about this sort of thing.

"I know women." One-five. Sunk. He was set up for the seven, and if he played it right, the nine would be next. I should have made a better break.

"I have someone," I said. "A friend. She's had some bad luck, but she's got experience and she loves kids."

"Really." He looked up at me from setting up his shot. "Where's she worked before?"

I didn't pause. Pausing was death.

"The Trudeaus."

He missed the seven. Stood.

"I'm not looking for that kind of help."

"It's not what you think." I leaned down and set up the one-nine.

"It never is. Take your shot."

"She's really great." I pocketed the nine. Game over. "So is Crossroads. I'll set up the appointment. Please don't use the phrase 'hippy-dippy' in the interview. The school doesn't need your money or the trouble."

"Good advice." He leaned down and retrieved the rack.

"You really should take my advice on this and just about everything."

I smiled at him and leaned on my cue.

He popped the balls back in the nine-ball diamond. "I don't want Josh Trudeau's nanny. Even without the extra services. I want you."

This is the kind of thing a single girl wanted to hear from a beautiful man. I was there as a professional. Despite that, I went a little jelly. I tightened my mouth into a line I couldn't let him see.

"So does Nicole," he continued, popping the balls into the shape. "She asks about the lady in the bathroom all the time."

"That's very nice."

"I'm not going to pretend I know what she's going through. I don't know too many five-year-olds in the first place. But you do know. Or you pretend well enough. Both your parents around?"

"They live in Fiji."

"Where the hell is Fiji?"

"Far."

"Do you visit?"

"No." I dropped my voice an octave. I hadn't spoken to my parents in years, and I wasn't in the mood to describe the slow, tidal drift that separated us. "Knowing what's going on with Nicole is a matter of human compassion, not pretending."

"And your friend? That human compassion too? Why are you coming around trying to place her?"

I felt trapped. Dug in deeper than I should be. I didn't know how it happened, but I never intended to tell him Blakely's problems. Now I felt as if I had to, or lie. I didn't want to lie.

"She's great. And she's not making the same mistakes again. She was devastated."

He lifted the rack off the diamond-shaped configuration of balls.

"Good rack," I said.

"You break. You sink the nine before my turn, I'll hire the two of you. You miss, you come work with Nicole for a month."

"Win-win for you."

"That's the only way I play."

I set up my shot and broke.

CHAPTER 6

CARA

The night after I beat Brad at pool, I dreamed of nine-ball. I made the shot over and over and every time it happened the same. I sunk it off the break, which wasn't what had happened the day before. The day before I sunk a ball on the break and the nine off the four.

In the real world it didn't matter how I won, just that I won. My dream life was more efficient. Nine off the break, and I was naked, because clothes would have gotten in the way of Brad Sinclair's dream body curved over mine as I leaned over the table.

He kissed the back of my neck, and his erection pressed against my backside. I didn't turn around, but in the dream I could see his body over me. Every bit of moisture in my body rushed between my legs. I woke up swollen and needy.

I took care of my business as efficiently as the dream told the story, turning Brad into someone, anyone else as I circled my clit with two fingertips. As I got closer to climax and my mind got weaker, Brad reappeared and I came fast and hard.

Fully awake, I promised to do a better job of controlling my fanta-sies. They were dangerous. Brad Sinclair was off-limits. I wasn't going to be a Daddy-toy. Not in this lifetime.

I didn't say that to Blakely as we got our things together for our first day with Nicole. We took separate cars up the hill to the ginormous house. I held my breath the entire way. I didn't know if I could even look at that pool table.

CHAPTER 7

BRAD

She'd beaten me fair and square. Nine off the four. She'd turned a loss into a win. Nice. I liked that. I also liked her ass.

"Don't talk about her ass. No one wants to hear it. Not even me."

My buddy Michael. Prince Squeaky Clean. He'd gone from famous kid to famous teen to the guy I met in college. Famous young adult. The guy never had a problem until he met his wife. She'd been a paparazza and a real problem. For a guy who spent his life worrying about what people thought of him, she was the last woman he should be with. He lay back in the sun by my pool.

"I'm just saying," I said. "And I have to say it to someone. My parents are cramping me. Every day's report card day, and I got rows of Fs and Ds."

"Tell them to go home."

"They leave today, but believe me, they can wave the report card at me from Arkansas."

"You taking Nicole to Blueberry's sixth birthday?"

The invitation had come that morning. I didn't know what it was at first. It was a cupcake in a basket tied to the bottom of four helium balloons. The delivery service had used a drone to float it over the mail chute. Then it followed the housekeeper into the house when she brought the mail in. That's what my mother told me when she handed me the cupcake. And that my dad almost shot it out of the air.

BLUEBERRY WOULD LOVE TO WELCOME NICOLE TO THE NEIGHBORHOOD.

I was being welcomed too. Somehow. To something. I had no idea what. To a world where birthday invitations came on helium balloons and kids had names like Blueberry.

Nicole loved the cupcake, and the balloons made her wild. I couldn't say no.

"You going?" I asked Michael. Stupid question. He had six kids now. He went to all the kid shit. "What should I get? For a present. I'm supposed to bring a present, right?"

"Let the nanny take care of it. They do research. Make calls. Ask the other nannies what the kid likes. Blah blah. No brainer. Just don't bring the blonde nanny."

I leaned back so I could see into the office off the kitchen. Paula, my right hand and easily half my brain, sat with the two nannies. Cara's hair was dark brown. The other one, the one who came with the deal, she was blonde. Blakely. She'd fallen for Josh Trudeau's line.

I did the Hollywood math.

Blueberry Trudeau was having a birthday. Her father was Josh Trudeau. Him in a room with Blakely was a no-go. Right.

"Dude. I'm bringing the other one. I'm not a fucking idiot."

"If you say so." He got up. "And the party, it's kids. It's not upstairs at the NV Room."

"You're worse than my parents. Every little thing. I'm not an animal. I know how to act, all right?"

"Good." He dove into the pool, splashing me. Asshole. I don't know what I did to make him think I couldn't handle myself at a birthday party, for Chrissakes.

"Bradley!" my dad called, as if his one goal in life was to prove my point. "Ten minutes! Stop lollygagging!"

Michael laughed and got out of the pool.

CHAPTER 8

CARA

Brad's personal assistant did what all PAs did. Everything.

When Paula opened the door to me and Blakely, she put her hand to her chest as if speaking from deep in her heart. She wore a smart linen suit and matching lavender pumps. Her skirt was a quarter inch lower than sexy and her smile was as wide as the Mississippi River.

"It is just such a relief to see you all here. I swear on a stack of peach pies she's cute as a button and wild as a dog without a collar. Come on in."

"I'm sure she's very good," Blakely offered.

"Well, bless your heart. My mother always told me I was more adult than kid, so no wonder I don't understand them."

She brought us to the office adjacent to the kitchen.

"We have about ninety minutes to get cozy," she said, indicating chairs with folders in front. "I know we're going to be the best of friends."

Through the back patio doors, Brad hung out by the pool with a man whose face I couldn't see.

"Bradley's parents are leaving today out of SMO. They are so dear. We got them to go charter for the flight, but they wouldn't agree to the expense of a helicopter." She made an absolutely adorable wrinkle-nosed smile. "Bless their hearts."

The man by the pool with Brad got up so I could see him. Michael Greydon. There was too much star power in this house already. Michael jumped into the water.

"Bradley!" called a deep-throated male voice from another part of the house, "ten minutes! Stop lollygagging!"

Paula folded her hands in front of her, ignoring the scene outside.

"A touch of history," Paula said, putting her thumb and forefinger half an inch apart. "The gentleman of the house and I were a thing in high school, but now it's strictly business." She handed us both folders. "And there's quite a bit of business. He's got a big old staff. On page one you can see all our names and cell numbers listed, including yours. Welcome to the team!"

The list was two pages long and included security, event planners, more security, caterers, housekeeping, and now—me and Blakely.

"That little bombshell sure threw him, but our goal as his helpers is to make sure he doesn't have to take even a minute off work. We're aiming for . . ." Her thumb and forefinger pressed together and she drew them straight across the space in front of her. ". . . seamless."

They all wanted seamless. Every celebrity and power hitter I'd worked for had scheduled their life twenty-four months in advance and if a child came six months into that, then seamlessness had to be achieved. Actors didn't get to cancel projects once preproduction started. One cancellation would be the last, no matter who they were.

"We can deliver very close to seamless," I said.

"I've seen your résumé," she replied. "I know you can. And between me and you . . ." Hand to her chest, she leaned in to Blakely. "Joshua Trudeau is a rake of the worst sort. I know you've learned your lesson, and luckily, while Mr. Sinclair might be busy with the ladies, he's nothing like that awful man."

I stiffened. Blakely was sensitive about Josh, and I didn't know what she'd come back with.

"I was young and stupid," she said, making jazz hands. "Now, check it out, I'm old and bitter."

Paula made a wrinkle-nosed smile again. I doubted she'd ever get Blakely's humor.

"Can I ask you a question, Miss?" Paula said.

"Of course." Blakely tried to sound upbeat, but I feared a personal question about Josh was coming. Judging from the way she tapped her pen on her knuckle, she was waiting for just such a question.

Paula whispered as if she wanted to know a dirty secret. "Is that really your name?"

"My real name is Blair. But I hate it. It tastes like lemons."

"Bathroom lady!" a little voice shrieked. Before I knew it, I was nearly impaled with a rhinestone-encrusted magic wand as Princess Nicole climbed onto my lap. Her hair was bunched in knots on one side of her head.

"Good morning, bombshell!" Paula said with a thick coat of sugar.

Nicole twisted to face me. "What's a bombshell?" She patted both my cheeks with each syllable.

"A fun surprise. Who brushed your hair?"

She whipped her head around to Blakely, pointing her finger as if she'd had something to say for a long time and now was just going to spit it out.

"Do not wet the toilet paper. It falls apart."

Blakely saluted her. "Never again. I promise."

Paula cleared her throat. "Nicole?" Her voice was impatient, tolerant, teeth-grindingly annoyed, and an eggshell-step away from timid all at the same time. "We're working."

"Uh-huh." She twisted in my lap until she faced the table and folded her hands in front of her. "I can work too. Then I can go to the airport after."

Brad appeared at the patio screen door with his sunglasses flipped to the top of his head. They messed his hair up just enough to make him look casually flawless. The dream at the pool table and the feel of his fingers between my legs came flooding back.

"Hey, ladies. Welcome to Chez Sinclair."

All three of us said hello. All but Nicole.

"Hush, Daddy, we're working."

"Can I brush her hair before you go?" I asked.

"It's fine. She looks like Amy Winehouse. Come on, princess," he said, opening the door and stepping inside. "Time to take Gram and Gramp to the airport."

"Then ice cream?"

"Sure, kid. Sure." She clambered off my lap, blew us a kiss, and took her father's hand. Paula didn't say a word until they were out of earshot.

"Let's go through our folders, shall we?"

I opened the folder again and put the staff list aside. Right side. W9s. Passcodes to the back house, the back gate, the side door. Parking instructions. A boilerplate contract. A Non-Disclosure Agreement. All standard.

Left side. A few pages that included a daily schedule and Brad Sinclair's schedule for the following month.

"I thought he was between pictures?" I said. "Ten hours a day blocked out for 'script?' It's—"

"No one in the business works harder than that man," Paula said. "They all say he's a mindless party animal, but I will kindly beg to differ."

That may be well and good, but I didn't see a minute in there for him to be a father. Not that it was any of my business. Naturally.

I changed the subject. "If he needs to schedule a school tour or interview for her, do I go to you?"

"Yes," Paula said, back to baseline. "It's for everyone. By my heart, it's not to create any distance between you and him. But he's awfully busy so we worked out a system. I'm your go-to for schedule changes and requests. You can speak to him anytime. Open-door policy is what he said, but just please ask me first all right?"

Blakely and I nodded. We'd seen this before. If I was being honest with myself, the farther I was from Brad Sinclair, the better.

Paula moved to the next sheet in the folder. "We have a lovely two-bedroom pool house on the property with a really nice kitchen. You'll each have a room. Now, if you look on page three, I worked out a schedule I sure hope you like." She pulled the last sheet out of the left side of her folder and Blakely and I did the same. "I set it up like my daddy's. He was a fireman. Forty-eight hours on, forty-eight hours off. During shift hours you're on call from ten at night to six in the morning. If you need to switch between yourselves, I say . . . let's keep it friendly. Just switch it. Except . . ." She drew out the last "e" and pursed her lips. "You ladies are going to be living with us so let's not have anything be uncomfortable. We're all girls here. Right?" She flipped her wrist at Blakely.

"I pride myself on my girlishness," Blakely said in a very not-girlish way.

Paula jumped right in. "Blueberry Trudeau's birthday party fell on your shift. That has to be switched. Don't you think?"

"I understand," Blakely said flatly. Crap. This wouldn't be the last time Nicole's and Blueberry's fathers crossed paths. Hopefully, Brad would keep a two-nanny rotation after I left so she could dodge stuff like this.

"That sure is a load off. Now, Miss DuMont, you can cover it, right?"

"Sure can." I tried to match her sunny enthusiasm and came up short.

Paula leaned down and retrieved a short, neatly folded pile of new clothes in plastic bags. She slid them to me.

"What's this?" I asked, flipping through the pile of clothes. White polo. Khaki pants.

Paula rolled her eyes and waved away more concern than I actually had. "All the nannies at the party have to wear this. It's Marsha Trudeau. She's got some sort of 'problem' so we just go along to get along. Well! Do you want to see the pool house?"

"Down to the socks?" Blakely exclaimed. "I mean, sheesh. I guess I can't blame her. Sorry, Cara. I'll make it up to you. Think big. A cruise. A condo in the hills."

"I've worn worse. Ute Maven made all the nannies wear those mechanic pantsuits with a zipper up the front. She delivered the whole getup right down to the underpants."

"This goes down to the bra, actually," Paula said, standing up. "I hope I got you the right size." She looked at her watch. "Brad will be back around two. He usually has friends over in the evenings. If you could make sure we're bombshell-free by seven, that would be just great."

With a big smile and a snap of a stack of folders, Paula ended the meeting.

CHAPTER 9

CARA

I liked beautiful men as much as the next girl, but I was around them all the time so their effect wore off. I thought Brad would be no different.

I kept having pool table dreams about him, and it was disconcerting. I sunk the nine on the break every time. I was naked every time. After that, they changed.

Sometimes they incorporated a gesture or word from the last time I'd seen him. Sometimes not. It was a couple of days into the job before Dream Brad penetrated me. He got me on my back on the table and stood over me. Like half of America, I'd seen him naked before. In Technicolor. In the dream I had every detail of his chest with its dash of hair across it, the drum-tight abs, the blue eyes eating me alive. I throbbed. He spread my legs and thrust into me.

I woke mid-orgasm.

He always made me wetter than I'd ever been, and, most disconcerting, I'd stopped pushing him out of my waking fantasies. I didn't have the mental control in the morning, and I figured if I just let it be, he'd wear out his welcome in my head.

It didn't work out that way.

CHAPTER 10

CARA

I felt solidly settled in after six days at Brad Sinclair's. I shouldn't have gotten settled in at all because it wasn't a permanent job, but I couldn't help it.

I blamed Nicole. She had an exceptionally slow large intestine and was afraid of the sound of toilets flushing. This gave us plenty of time together in bathrooms, and I did what I always did.

I got attached. Just a little. Nothing I couldn't handle.

She crossed her ankles when she settled in for a good number two, which could last upward of eleven minutes. Her sneakers lit up when she swung them and they hit the side of the bowl.

"Done yet?" I asked on day seven, not that I was counting.

"Two more." She held up two fingers and hummed a tune about Thumbkin. I joined her, standing by the window. Two stories below, in a little alcove with a wooden picnic table, Brad sat across from Paula. She wore a pastel pink suit jacket, but I couldn't tell much else about her from my angle. She had a movie script in her hands.

Anyone in Hollywood could see a script a mile away. Stack of three-hole paper fastened with brass brads or a brightly colored agency cover.

Courier font. The text was arranged toward the middle of the page where dialog was formatted. Action stretched across the margins and long chunks of it were unheard of. Movie scripts didn't look like TV scripts. They were fatter and the paper was all white instead of color coded for last-minute revisions.

So. Movie script, folded to the middle. Paula's voice lifted to the window. It had no inflection or accent whatsoever. She sounded like a machine.

Brad had his elbows on the table. Even from two stories up I could see his right leg bouncing. His entire body thrust forward in laser-like attention.

Then he said something. I was too far away to discern his words. Possibly a repetition of what the blonde said, but also completely robotically.

Not in years of working for producers and actors had I seen this method, and I thought I'd seen everything.

"Can I tell you a secret?" Nicole said from the bowl. I crouched down in front of her.

"Yes."

She motioned me to come very close, so I leaned forward. She cupped her hands over my ear and whispered.

"I like my daddy."

"Really? Well, that's good. I like him too."

I didn't mean any more than that, but hearing myself say it in my own ears made me think a little harder about it.

Did I like him?

Besides the obvious stuff. The stuff you could see and hear. Did I like him, and did it matter?

"It's a secret," whispered Nicole. "You can't tell."

Who did she worry I'd tell? Brad? Her mother's ghost?

"I won't tell."

She put her thumb and pointer at the corner of my mouth and drew it across.

"Zip it, lock it, put it in your pocket," she said, locking my mouth and putting the invisible information in an equally invisible breast pocket.

"Done," I replied with a nod.

"I'm ready!" Nicole singsonged with her arms out. I helped her off the bowl.

We cleaned up, and I held her up so she could wash her hands. We'd need to get a stool for her bathroom. I usually came in after a consultant, or the parents had some experience with children. I'd never been in a house where so many of the little things had been missed.

"Where do our bones go when we die?" she asked, rolling the soap between her palms.

Perfectly normal question, but I had to tread lightly. She was asking about her mother.

"Back into the earth where they make flowers and fruit."

"And what happens to our skin?" She put the soap down and rotated her hands under the running water.

"It goes back into the earth to make trees and grass."

"Does it hurt?" She held her dripping hands out.

"No." I snapped the pony towel off the rod.

Nicole rubbed her hands on the towel.

"Are we lonely in the ground?"

"We're not inside our bodies anymore."

This was going places I shouldn't be taking her. Brad had been raised Southern Baptist, so though he and I hadn't discussed it, that was the theology I was going to spoon-feed Nicole.

"Where do we go?" The expected question, delivered like a train into the station on time. I crouched to her. She was so beautiful and guileless. She didn't understand her own pain, what had happened or why. And it wasn't going to get any clearer when she got older. All she wanted was to know her mother was all right. To make sense of it.

"She's in heaven playing with God."

"Playing what?"

"I don't know." I smoothed her dress down. "What did she like to play with you?"

"Ponies. She made them talk."

"Then I bet she's playing that with God right now."

It felt like a lie. I didn't think Brenda Garcia was doing any one thing or another. I had no idea, but I couldn't tell this little girl that. I cared about her more than I wanted to admit. She was thoughtful, graceful, kindhearted, and methodical in anything she touched. If I could have a little girl of my own, she'd be just like Nicole.

Stop. That's enough.

"There are flowers outside," Nicole said, rescuing me from my own thoughts.

"Yep. Want to go look at them?"

"Yes, please."

CHAPTER 11

BRAD

"He can tell me what to do," I said. "He can send me a thousand miles away. He can put as many pounds on my back. Take my land. Take my home. He can break my back . . . hell, he can break every bone in my body. But he can't tell me where my heart lies, and my love, it lies deep inside you."

Paula didn't move a muscle, but the air played at her hair, teasing out a few strands and waving them. When we'd been in high school she kept it in a ponytail with wispy bangs. After we moved to LA she made it more like Redfield than before. The bangs got thicker and the rest of the hair stayed a noncommittal shoulder length as if her way of being hip was to be so unhip it was cool.

I tried to gently break up with her before I came to Los Angeles, but let's just say it didn't work out that way. She was a very persuasive woman. We came to LA together, but she knew it couldn't last. Not when the business and all the women in it were ready for me. We broke up cleanly. She dated. I dated. She came back as a friend a year later, when my career became 50 percent acting and 50 percent shit-I-didn't-want-to-deal-with—her accent and manner were too comforting to resist.

I needed a personal assistant. It was taking me too long to learn my lines, and she knew enough about me to give me the help I needed. I got the studio to pay her. My first taste of privilege. The rest wouldn't fall into place for almost a year.

"Your line," she said. "Inside you."

"That makes no sense," I objected.

"I'm sure their million-dollar script doctor would love to hear all your thoughts, honey. But then they'll change it."

"How can he be worried about his own heart if it's somewhere else? If it's with her, his life isn't what he's talking about."

"My mommy is the yellow flowers!"

Nicole's voice rose above the birds and breeze for the third time in as many minutes. She and the birds made fusion jazz in the garden. If it got humid enough, I could pretend I was in Arkansas for sweet minutes at a time.

"You do this every time." Paula leaned over and put her hand over mine. "You're so hard on yourself. Just get the lines."

"I want a pink one!" Nicole's voice again. "We can make it live in water for Daddy."

Paula took her hand away and leaned back, making that smile that looked like sunshine and waterfalls but actually signified a deep annoyance. "How about we go inside? Maybe if it's quiet you'll be able to concentrate."

"I don't have ADD. Concentrating isn't a problem."

I wasn't being obstructive. I really didn't mind distractions.

Paula was usually cool and unflappable, exactly what I needed, but she was acting as though one kid caused world chaos. I'd been raised with kids everywhere, so I knew what chaos looked like and seen adults ignore it.

She leaned forward, ice blue eyes sharp with intent. "I'm sorry. I was just thinking about you. I worry. You know that."

Nicole ran onto the patio with a bunch of flowers that looked like they came from the boxes on the edge of the fire pit. I never gave the flowers a thought. I had people who took care of that sort of thing. But when she came running to me with a fistful of yellow, I was glad I'd hired gardeners.

"Here!" she cried, pushing them into my chest. "These are Mommy!"

"You mean *from* Mommy?"

"No!" She screwed up her eyebrows and crossed her arms.

"Just go with it," Cara said from behind the girl. "I'll explain later." With the sun behind her, she was just a silhouette softened with glare. She shifted until my eyes were in the shade and I could see her.

Paula was constantly between us with her big Arkansas smile and her way of taking care of everything. But even with Paula's obstruction, I could feel Cara a room away. I'd been fantasizing about her since she leaned over the pool table to miss the four. My fantasies were frustratingly generic. I couldn't hear her voice in my head because I didn't talk to her enough to recreate it. I had no way of knowing what she'd say or do. Yet, I couldn't stop thinking about her.

I sniffed the flowers with a big sucking sound.

"Mommy smells great," I said. The nanny smiled at me. I got stuck in that smile for a second. It was the first time she'd smiled *at me* and not *in spite of* me.

Nicole climbed into my lap. "What are you doing?"

"Working," Paula said, closing her script and smiling. "Cara, honey, be a peach and go swimming or something with Miss Bombshell while Daddy works."

"Come on, Nicole." Cara held her hand out. "Let's go have a snack. We can put those in water."

I tilted the yellow daisy to the side and spoke in a high-pitched voice.

"Water, please, Nicole, put me in water. I'm so thirsty."

"Aw, poor flowermommy." She stroked the petals. Cara smiled.

I put my fingers in Nicole's hair. It was well brushed and smooth. I caught on a knot and gently pulled it apart. I searched for another tangle. Found one.

"Does she need a haircut?"

"No!" Nicole exclaimed. "Mommy liked it long."

"Well, far be it from me to interrupt family time." Paula stood up. "I'm going to use the facilities."

"Okay, bye, Paula. Drink some water for me," I made the flower squeak. Nicole loved it, and Cara laughed, hands folded in front of her. Paula disappeared into the house. Cara watched her go, then glanced at me.

She cast her eyes down when they met mine. It was weirdly demure. Then she tucked her hair behind her ear. I couldn't take my eyes off her. She was so sharp and smart, but there was something about that pose, the tilt of her head, looking down at my daughter, fingertip barely touching her hair.

Nicole addressed the flower. "Mommy, do you think Cara's pretty?"

I thought . . . well, no. I didn't *think*. I *knew*. I just couldn't *say*. Unless I hid behind the voice of Brenda Garcia, who I'd barely known. I felt entitled to speak my mind in that disguise.

"Very pretty," Brenda's voice said from the flower.

Cara's face turned pink. Shit. What was I thinking?

"Is it okay if she's my new mommy?"

"Peanut butter and jelly!" Cara exclaimed before I could answer. "Let's eat lunch!"

Thank God, because I almost said yes.

"Yay!" Nicole shouted.

Cara didn't make eye contact with me. She held her hand out and Nicole hopped off my lap. I gave her back the flowers and they trotted away. A second before they turned the corner to the house, Cara looked back at me and smiled as if she forgave me.

That felt absolutely perfect.

CHAPTER 12

CARA

I'd done a French braid on Nicole for Blueberry's party, which should have taken three minutes, but she fussed and pulled it out. Brad commented that his daughter's hair was a mess before I could fix it.

He was trying. I kept telling myself he was trying.

In the hours before Blueberry's party, the Greydons came by Chez Sinclair for a playdate. They brought their six kids, four nannies, and lunch.

If Brad Sinclair was an A-list actor—and he was—Michael Greydon rose above the alphabet. The A-lister's A-list. He was such a star he could quit to adopt six children with his wife, a notorious paparazza. I was even a little starstruck, and I was never starstruck. But when he and his wife came for a pre-party iced tea, I noted his low-wattage glow and sane approachability. It was hard not to stare.

The ride to the party pulled up promptly at two. Kids and nannies herded into a shiny black bus lined with video screens and games. Brad, Michael, and Laine went in a separate car. Apparently, our destination didn't have a helipad.

All four Greydon nannies were from West Side, so they were fit and attractive. Pleated khakis and a white polo couldn't hide a thing, even in my case, with a shirt that was three sizes too big and a bra that was a cup size too small. The pleats in my chinos seemed designed specifically to create dual pouches over the crotch, and the legs were so long I had to cuff them.

"It's a thirty-day job," I said. "Then I'm leaving. So if you hear of anything—"

"You're leaving? Why would you leave?" Helen interrupted in French. The children were engrossed in a highly anticipated movie that was still two weeks from release. "There's no wife to judge you all the time. It's perfect."

Helen had come from France to au pair five years before and stayed for the sun and easy work. She held the Greydons' six-month-old while the other nannies entertained the children or gossiped.

"It was always temporary," I answered in French. "The celebrity lifestyle isn't for me."

She *tsked*. "All the perks! Nice clothes, tags still on. Food from the best restaurants. All the people you meet. You can live the life without having the life. No?"

I just shook my head, but I didn't tell her the other reason I had to run away as if my shoes were on fire.

I'd had another pool table dream. And another. It was a good thing Paula was my go-between. I was starting to blush whenever I was in the same room with Brad Sinclair and he hadn't even touched me.

CHAPTER 13

BRAD

Michelle Novatelli held court at Blueberry's party even though it wasn't her house.

"Wait until you get to middle school. You're going to want to put a bullet in your head."

She put her pointer and her tall finger together and mimicked blowing her brains out. She was straight outta Brooklyn. Worked her way up to studio head at Overland and never looked back, unless she was doing her Bensonhurst schtick. Then her accent got thicker than a brick and she talked faster than a jackrabbit fucks.

"Five schools. Two events each. Application had essays. Dude. *Essays.* They know who I am. They know what I make, but I couldn't get in without essays. Don could buy and sell these assholes, but I still had to wear heels to the interview."

We were surrounded by money and fame, but Michelle just kept on like a middle-class Italian girl shocked at the private school system. Everyone else was amused by the act, agreeing enough to keep her going, nodding because they'd either gone through it or would soon. I should have nodded too. But I wanted to take her two fingers and blow my own brains out.

"And then after she asks a twelve-year-old what she wants to do when she graduates college, (eye roll) she asks her . . . the *next question* . . . is 'What do you want to be doing in ten years?' So my daughter says, 'Isn't that kind of the same thing?' So we crossed that one off the list."

Laughter.

My glass was empty.

Fuck. I wanted to jump off a tall building. I was supposed to care, but I'd already forgotten what school she was talking about.

I knew these people. I saw them all the time. Ken Braque, my PR guy, was there with his wife. Met her once. Couldn't dig her name out of my mind. She was five eight with long red hair. Three months pregnant and looked like she'd maybe eaten a big dinner. That was all I knew about her.

But this was who he was. This was what he did with his beautiful wife and his two kids when I wasn't around. When he was doing family things. He was talking to Michelle Novatelli about middle schools.

I felt like an intruder on the most mind-numbing underground culture ever.

I looked out to the backyard. All the kids were riding ponies and eating sugar. I wanted to ride ponies and eat sugar. Nicole ran across my field of vision, pulling Cara by the hand.

That smoking body in a white polo and pleated chinos. Want to talk about injustice? It was right there. What was wrong with these people? They hid what they couldn't handle.

I was dead. Curling up and dying on the corner of Boredom Blvd. and Tedium St.

And to think, I was the guy who wouldn't leave the club with only one girl. It was two, sometimes more, or why bother?

"They're really progressive, and they have a ceramics studio." I didn't even know who was talking anymore.

The kids had the party, and I got to die of boredom, remembering the good old days like an old man. What were their names? The girls? It was something funny. I'd laughed all the way to Mike's house, because I let them have my fucking pants.

"No, but they give a ton of financial aid, so you really don't know who the kids are going to school with."

Two hot women came up to the glass doors. Twenties. One had curly hair. One with hair blown straight. One curvier than the other. They sat down in front and lit cigarettes. They couldn't see inside. Good thing too, because I recognized them. Two years ago, they'd spent a morning fighting over my pants. I'd slipped out and gone to Mike's place in my underwear. I smiled to myself. That was fun.

"And there's a real drug problem. Blow jobs in eighth grade. You gotta be careful."

What were their names? I flipped through the files in my head where I kept the clutter I was too busy to think about. The stuff I intentionally forgot so I could function.

"Unless you like blow jobs," Ray Heywood said, and everyone laughed.

Jenn and Jennifer.

They were right there. Pants girls. I needed to say hello, at least. It was like kismet.

I tapped the window with a fingernail. Jenn or Jennifer leaned back and focused past the window, full lips opening into an O when she saw me. She grabbed her curly-haired friend's elbow until she turned around. I waved and jerked my thumb to the side door.

I put my drink on a coaster and slipped away.

Ken caught up to me as I walked through the family room.

"How's it going?" he asked.

"Good, good."

Jenn and Jennifer stood on the other side of the door, waiting. I remembered these two. It came back to me and I smiled a little. Yeah. They were fun until the catfight, then they were even more fun.

"You canceled the *Vanity Fair* shoot with Nicole?" Ken asked.

"Yeah, she's scared of paparazzi. I don't want to freak her out."

"People want to see her," Ken said, "She's the most coveted shot in town right now."

"I don't need the money."

What I needed was to get away from buzzkill conversations. Period. What I needed was to be Brad Sinclair.

"The publicity is priceless." Ken tilted his glass to me. "Look. I'm not trying to work in social situations, but this is a crossroads for your image. It's a golden opportunity to move from young talent who stepped in shit to seasoned professional. Let's find a way to make it work. Okay?"

"Sure, sure." I clinked glasses with him without connecting the dots between Nicole and my reputation as an actor. I had two girls waiting for me and if I recalled right, they could suck a golf ball through a garden hose.

And that was what Brad Sinclair was about. I wanted to be *me* again.

CHAPTER 14

CARA

The party was pretty standard. A team of horses and miniponies had been brought in for the kids. Nicole's face lit up like the Vegas strip when she saw them. She was barely contained, and she spent the entire time thanking Blueberry each and every ride.

Blueberry, who was made of sugar and spice and curly blonde locks, took to Nicole almost immediately. Everybody likes being thanked.

The lowdown on birthday parties for girls named Blueberry is this.

Yes, it's a show of money, but everyone in this world has money. So from the outside, the staff, the organic gourmet food, the trucks of décor, and world-class performers all look like a pissing contest that's about money.

It's not about money. It's about showing the child how much they're loved. Mommy's shooting six days a week for twelve hours a day and Daddy's on the phone during dinner, and these things needle Hollywood parents.

So, once or twice a year they shower the children with exactly the things they like. Horses. Superheroes. Princesses. And of course, their friends. Anything goes because that one day is about the kid. Once

I realized the intensity of the events was about love, I got a lot less uncomfortable.

The kids, however, have parents and if they're staying, they need to be entertained. Some parties are drop-offs. Bring us your child and we'll show them a good time. We'll pour them into your driver's car sugar-sticky and wiped out. Some, like the Trudeau party, are sleepovers with a big grown-up component. Open bar. Separate buffet of complex adult dishes. Sea bass. Tri tip. Quinoa salad.

Nannies and kids ate at a separate table. We whispered news in hushed voices and made sure the little ones on the other end of the table had what they needed. I kept a careful eye on Nicole. She was new, after all, and though little girls don't get truly awful until fourth grade, she was sensitive. I'd advised Brad to be prepared for her to skip the sleepover part of the party. Actually, I'd advised Paula, who said she'd let Brad know. She seemed more interested in making sure his work wasn't disrupted than anything.

The gossip was good at the nanny table. A few divorces, which meant the need for help would be adjusted. A couple of pregnancies. Some rumors.

"And then she . . . Grace . . . she catches him drinking from the baby's bottle," Brandy, a Cornell-educated nanny for the Greydons, said as she picked at a French fry. She was passing on a rumor about the famously dysfunctional Grace and Thomas Dresden. A.k.a. Gromas.

"Oh my God," I whispered. "Does he have a breast milk fetish?"

She leaned all the way forward and the rest of us leaned in too.

"No. He's in outpatient rehab. Alcohol."

She paused for effect, making eye contact with each of us.

"Mayra was spiking the night bottles with Baileys. When he found out he drained them."

"No."

"Yes."

"What did she do? Grace?"

"Stopped breast-feeding. Obviously. And threw out the Baileys."

We all groaned. Heidi handed me my phone, where she'd navigated to the online Baby Naming Pool for Ken Braque's kid.

"That's crazy," I added. "That's why no one decent will work there."

The name pool was about half full. On the y-axis were name types. Boy. Girl. Androgynous. We weren't guessing the sex of the child, but the gender of the name, since a boy could easily have a girl-sounding name and vice versa. On the x-axis: Fruit. Occupations. Nature. Vintage. Pop Culture. Places.

Pilot, Scout, Governor, Poppy, Pepper, Cayenne, Sequoia, Jupiter, Happy, Beautiful, and Vancouver had been hand-typed in. The payout on getting the name exactly right was enormous.

The Heywoods' new nanny sat downtable, since Jedi was in Blueberry's class. Their nanny was stocky, with a silver bun and a gruff demeanor. She had a thick accent that could have been Hungarian.

"Which box did you buy?" she asked. "I took Nature. Boy name."

"I can't even think of any boy names after nature. Maple? Pine?"

"These people will think of something." She waved a meaty hand in the general direction of the adults.

"I think Nature. Girl. That's Bluegrass, Hibiscus, Flower . . ." I claimed my box and put the phone down. "Speaking of, how are Willow and Jedi?" I asked.

"The boy is fine. Doesn't notice anything." She pushed away her French fries and chicken. "The girl. Always so crabby?"

"No. She's usually pretty upbeat."

She shrugged. "Maybe there's a boyfriend."

Maybe. Willow had had fleeting crushes since she was five. At twelve, it was time for one to stick.

"How is Brad Sinclair doing?" Petra asked. She was a young au pair from Madrid. "The golden boy? Has he adjusted?"

"It's only been a little more than a week," I replied. "His parents just left. He likes Nicole, and I have to say, she's a great kid. And he wants to do it right. But his schedule is set a year ahead. It's not like he's had time to make any changes. So we're working on it." I shrugged. I didn't want to give anything away, but not saying anything at all about the biggest story in town would alienate me.

"He's so beautiful," Petra whispered. "And single."

"Hush!" Helen said. "We are professionals here."

Petra and the other girls exchanged glances. I didn't want to confirm or deny what I felt for Brad. My dreams around the pool table had gotten more vivid and arousing as the days had gone on. They were ridiculous, of course, and probably had more to do with the fact that I needed a boyfriend than anything.

"I'm going to go check on Nicole," I said, putting my cloth napkin on my plate. "Can I take anyone's stuff to the kitchen?"

I gathered some plates and silverware and went to the kitchen with them. Looked for Nicole at the dessert table. Not there. Went to the art table, the photo booth, the bounce house. I finally found her kneeling on the grass with Blueberry, playing with a stack of cards with illustrations of, shockingly, ponies.

Brad was by the bar, holding one of the party's signature drinks and talking to two girls. Women. Ladies. Whatever.

I didn't care.

He was my boss, and I didn't know the guy.

Not really.

One of the girls was tall and had her hair swept up in a loose bun. She was fit and tall. Looked like a runner, which reminded me that I hadn't run in too long. The other was full-figured and had curly hair. They both had the most perfect skin I'd ever seen, and were hanging on his every word.

Which was none of my business. He put his arms around them and whispered in the tall girl's ear. She giggled and nodded, then he said something to the curly-haired one, who got mad and pushed her.

"Miss Cara!"

Nicole and Blueberry were at my feet. Nicole's big brown eyes pleaded as she held up a pony card.

"I left Pony Pie in the van and I want to show Blue."

I wanted to thank the little one profusely for giving me an excuse to get away from whatever her father was doing.

"You want me to go get it?"

"Yes, please!"

"Okay, you go play and I'll check the van." She and Blue ran back to their little grassy spot with the cards between them.

I turned and found myself face-to-face with Josh Trudeau.

He was an actor and a legit heartthrob. He never marketed himself as a good man. He always had a dark streak and the devil in his blue eyes. His mouth was made of sex. So when his affair with Blakely went public, no one was surprised, least of all his wife.

"She said she wanted a magician," he said with a touch of Australian accent. "And she's sitting in the grass with the orphan girl instead of watching him."

"Her name is Nicole."

"She seems nice. Not much for magicians though."

"Do you want me to take them over to him? I can do it pretty easily, but I promised her I'd get her toy out of the van."

He looked at his drink pensively. "What's your name again?"

"Cara DuMont."

"Have we met?"

"I used to work for the Heywoods."

"Ah. Let me guess." He looked me up and down in my Mrs. Trudeau-approved chinos and polo. "Kendall found you threatening."

"I work for families. The whole family. If one person in the family thinks I'm not going to work out, then I move on."

He nodded as if truly and deeply understanding every nuance of my troubles. I knew why Blakely had gone down the dark path with this guy. His attention was spellbinding.

"Of course," he said, then motioned back through the kitchen. "The van. It's in the alley. Let me take you."

As much as no married Hollywood daddy wanted to be seen alone with Blakely, I didn't want to be seen alone with Josh Trudeau. I hadn't seen Ray and Kendall, but Jedi was probably somewhere, and I didn't want to prove Kendall right about my intentions.

"I can figure it out," I said.

He held out his hand to me. "The gate has a code. Come on. I won't bite."

It wasn't biting I was concerned about, but I had to go with him or risk getting labeled as difficult. It was his party. His house. He didn't want to be seen with me any more than I wanted to be seen with him.

As if proving my point, he took me around back, away from the party.

"Where are you from, Cara?" he asked. Small talk as we walked the length of the high wood fence.

"Everywhere. I'm a military brat, but mostly French-speaking countries. My parents did some intelligence liaison work."

"Like spies?"

"Not that glamorous."

"*Parlez-vous français?*"

"*Oui, je parle français. Le faites vous?*"

"You just heard the extent of it."

I laughed with him as he punched numbers into a keypad. The lock clicked and I opened the gate. The van was there, wide open with matte black flat-screen TVs covering the interior walls. I could see Nicole's little pink pony on the seat. I grabbed it.

When I turned, Josh was clicking the gate closed. I moved the stuffed toy from one hand to the other, then back again. A nervous gesture, because I was suddenly uneasy.

"You're really a beautiful girl."

"Thank you."

He stepped toward me, and I stepped away. My back hit the side of the van.

"You have a real presence," he said softly. "More than looks, presence is what's important."

"Mr. Trudeau, I—"

"I can make things happen for you. A girl like you . . ." Another step, and I could see where his lips were ever so slightly chapped. ". . . you have something."

"I don't need anything." I put my hands on his chest, pony between them. "I'm fine."

He opened his mouth to say something, but a titter of giggles and shushes came from the other side of the gate. Josh didn't move. Jesus Christ, what did he think he was going to do? Force himself on me? I was perfectly willing to bite a chunk out of anything that got close enough to my mouth, I didn't care how gorgeous it was. I looked right into his eyes, leveled my intention on him.

"Back. Up."

He smirked.

Behind him, the code beeped. The smirk faded, but he didn't move until the gate scraped open with a cheer from a couple of female voices and a "hey-ho!" from a male voice I recognized, but couldn't see because this asshole was in my way.

I gave Josh another shove. He took a step back, and there was Brad, an arm around each girl he'd been with at the bar.

"Uncle Josh?" said the one with the bun.

"Jennifer," Josh said, rubbing his lips as if I'd gotten my lip gloss on him. What an unbelievable fucker.

"Dude," Brad said, glancing to me. He was clear-eyed and sober. He pointed to Josh. "What the fuck are you doing?"

"Hey, bro." Josh flashed his most winning smile and held his hand out to Brad. "You know how it is." He jerked his head to me. I could only stand with Nicole's pony in my hand, mouth open in shock. He was accusing me of something I'd taken great pains to avoid. Motherfucker. And no way I'd be believed. Not with friendship and careers in the mix.

It looked like Brad was going to shake his friend's hand, and the asshole relaxed for a split second. Which is all it took for Brad to punch him in the mouth.

The cracking sound was immediately followed by an *oomph* and a *thup* as Josh's head hit the side of the van. Brad stood over him, getting his body between Josh and me.

"Oh. My. God," one of the girls said.

"Do not try and bring that shit in my house," Brad said, pointing at Josh as if he was ready to drive a hole into him.

"Are you serious?" Josh seemed totally incredulous. "This is my house."

"Totally fucking serious. She takes care of my daughter. She is off fucking limits."

Josh got his feet under him. "You have no idea what being a father means, you twat. You've been at it a week."

Brad turned to me. "Come on." He took my arm and led me through the gate. He smelled like expensive vodka, but he seemed as sober as I'd ever seen him.

"You have to know I didn't initiate that."

"We have to get Nicole together." He didn't even look at me, just talked through his teeth. "I don't want you walking around here alone right now."

"I was just going to get her pony and he insisted on coming. I'm not trying to seduce Josh Trudeau."

"I'll call for the car."

"Did you hear me? It's important."

He stopped at the back door to the house, holding his hands up.

"I heard you. I believe you. He's known for this shit. Women who take care of kids turn him on. It's his thing."

"And Blakely got all the blame."

"Well, knock me over with a tea bag." He was dripping sarcasm and rage. I didn't think it was even possible for this laid-back dude's dude to get this intentional about anything.

I took a deep breath.

"Nicole was on the lawn last I saw."

"Let's go." He walked around the house, through the brick garden path so fast I had to quicken my steps to keep up. "I gotta get out of here before I hit him again."

"He didn't actually touch me."

Brad didn't answer, but stalked onto the grass where Nicole sat alone with cards splayed in front of her. The French braid was crooked, half out of the knot, creating a halo of loose hairs.

"Thank you, but don't ruin your friendship over me." I was minimizing it, and of course I shouldn't, but the stakes were pretty high for him. He had to keep company with these people. "It doesn't have to be a big deal."

He spun on me as if I'd said he was stupid and his mother wore army boots. I'd seen that face before, in movies. It was even more gorgeous when he was acting angry or pained. But those were movies. This was real life. Yes, his face was still beautiful, but with the addition of something fearsome it became unearthly.

He pressed his lips between his teeth, as if biting back his words I knew for sure I didn't want to hear.

CHAPTER 15

BRAD

You know. I'm not that guy. I'm not the guy who gets all weird and intense about anyone or anything. Maybe about work. I'm intense when I'm on set. But when it comes to people I'm not related to, easy come, easy go. Win some, lose some. All cool.

I shouldn't have hit Josh. Probably, that was the most intense response outside killing him, which occurred to me. Once I did it, I had to split. Get Cara and Nicole out of there, back home, away from that whole weird scene. But I just kept on burning. Like the coals deep in the campfire. The ones ten guys can piss on and they still stay hot.

Too hot for words, until she made a little comment about what Josh *didn't* do and how I didn't have to be mad. Man, the white hot got turned up to white hotter, and I had words. Two words. I shouldn't ever say these words and thank the good Lord above I bit them back.

You're mine.

Now, like I said I'm not that guy. But when she said he didn't touch her and I should let it go like some hippy-dippy-one-love-bullshit, I nearly lost it. I nearly went back, found Josh, and cracked his head against the corner of a cabinet for good measure.

She was mine and Nicole was mine and he'd stepped on that. He'd stepped into my house and tried to take something that belonged to me.

I was being unreasonable. Not only was she temporary help, she was *the help*. She had her own life and I was taking it too far. I was making it personal. It wasn't personal.

Right?

"Hey, Brad!" a woman's voice called from behind me. A young woman. I turned.

Jenn and Jennifer, running across the lawn toward me. Jenn in front. Jennifer grabbed her shirt and yanked her backward. She fell.

"Crap," I said.

"I'll get Nicole," Cara said as Jenn swung her arm out and tripped Jennifer, who took two giant steps and righted herself. Cara couldn't leave me alone with these two. I didn't know why, but I needed her.

"Stay."

Jenn bounced up and the two of them headed right for us. They were five steps away when I realized why I needed Cara there.

To prove I wasn't sleeping with either of them.

I'd been five minutes from having both of them at once. Just normal shit. But something about me changed between the agreement to take our threesome out to the van and seeing Josh with Cara. As if the adrenaline dump had changed my cellular makeup, I felt weirdly, oddly, inexplicably . . . *guilty.*

They reached us, huffing and puffing as if they'd gone uphill instead of across a lawn. I glanced at Cara. She had her eyes on Nicole.

"Hey, Brad," Jenn said, starting a give-and-take between her and her cousin.

". . . If you want to . . ."

". . . We're around . . ."

". . . we can meet you . . ."

". . . upstairs?"

Cara's head snapped around to them. Now was my chance to prove I was better than she thought. Golden opportunity. So perfect I didn't have a minute to ask myself why I cared.

"Nah," I said. "We have to go."

"Next time," Jennifer said, elbowing Jenn.

Cara went to Nicole before they finished, and I followed at her heels.

"Hey, sweetheart, how's it going?" I said when I got to Nicole. She was stacking her cards in a neat pile.

"Blue said I could have these."

"Where is she?" Cara asked, scanning around the party. The breeze flicked her hair around her face. She looked like a warrior.

She's not yours, Mr. Weird Impulse.

"She went to see the guy with the rabbit and the big hat." She held her hand out to Cara. "You have Pony Pie?"

Cara crouched down and gave Nicole the doll. "Are you all right?"

She waited for an answer that didn't come. Out of the corner of my eye, Jenn and Jennifer approached again.

"Let's go," I said, holding out my hand for my daughter.

"I want to stay for the sleepover."

"Not tonight."

"Why not?"

"Because I said so." I sounded exactly like my father, for the love of fuck.

Nicole's face got rock hard. Eyes squinched. Lips tight. Chin puckered. She wrapped her arms across her chest and locked them.

"I said," Nicole stated as if I didn't hear her the first fucking time, "I want to stay for the sleepover." She even enunciated more slowly.

"Sweetheart," Cara started but never finished. I didn't have time for nicey-nice. Explaining shit to a five-year-old wasn't on my to-do list. I picked my daughter up, slung her over my shoulder screaming, and carried her the fuck out.

Car and driver were close.

"Her overnight bag," Cara said.

"Leave it. She has her pony."

The driver closed the door and we were off. Nicole had tears on her cheeks. They were as big as golf balls and her lips were extra red and swollen as she wept. She wouldn't even let Cara touch her.

I felt like a first-class asshole.

"Don't do this on my account," Cara said.

"Your account is my account."

You're mine.

Everything was confused and backward. I felt like someone else. Like the guy who wears a gray suit and a red tie with his shiny black shoes. A guy who drives a Buick to work every day and trades it in every two years for a new one. Eats dinner at the same time every night, fucks his wife twice a week, and drinks his rage with the football game on. It did not feel good to be that guy, but he was the only guy I could be in the back of that limo.

"Here's how it's going to be," I said to Cara as much as myself. "From now on, I'll take her where I want. She's mine, and I'm not hanging around these people. She's going to have to live my life with me, not part of this crowd of idiots. Second, I'm not hiding Blakely. She's coming where she needs to be. Third. If he touches you again, I'm going to break his face. Let's see how Redfield stacks up against Encino in a fair fight."

Cara patted her leg absently while she spoke. "I'm sure you could take him in a fight." Her smile challenged me to make an ass of myself by getting into a fight at a kid's birthday party. I was just about ready to see how that worked out.

But no.

I was a father. Fathers didn't do shit like that.

Right? I wished someone would tell me.

Nicole was still mad, but had worked her way backward to a few sniffles and tear-dampened sleeves. She crawled onto Cara's lap so she could get her sulking puss right in front of me. She crossed her arms tightly and scowled.

What did my father think when I looked at him like that? What did *any* father think? Was I supposed to discipline her or wait it out? Tell her what's what? Who's in charge? How it makes other people feel? Talk sense?

I didn't know how I was supposed to do this, and Nicole didn't make it easy to figure it out. She just curled up on Cara, who was pretty damned firm with her. All the times I'd seen them together, Cara was setting out rules, or correcting her or listening. I hadn't done any of that.

In all the time I'd spent with . . .

Wait.

Not much time at all.

Dad didn't take us anywhere, and he fell asleep in the green chair most nights. But he'd had us the first five years. Right? He'd had a chance to develop *feelings* where I hadn't.

Maybe that would explain the thing I was most embarrassed about. I hadn't had some lightning bolt of emotion when I met my daughter. Just a little voice that told me she was cute and another that said it would be fine. Another voice said she was my responsibility and another answered that meant I had to get the best staff on it.

But no little voice with a *feeling*.

My mother's voice scolded me.

You never tell a soul you just had that thought, Bradley. Why, look at that little nugget! They'll say you're a sociopath.

I answered the voice in my head, sulking like a twelve-year-old.

I don't care what people think.

That quieted my mother for half a second while Cara stroked Nicole's hair, dividing it into strands for a new braid. Then she came back like a vaudevillian poking her head from stage right.

You zip it, lock it, put it in your pocket.

"You know what's funny?" I said before I thought about it, "I have a staff and a house as big as a palace, but I never felt like the king of my castle. Not even with Nicole there."

I felt like an asshole before I even finished the sentence. That was too much information. She was an employee. She wasn't even supposed to be in the back of the limo with me. But I wanted her there. I wanted her to stroke Nicole's hair when my daughter was mad at me, and I wanted to talk to her about . . .

What?

Nothing.

"You never had a proper coronation," she said before I could finish the thought, snapping the rubber band off Nicole's braid. "Most men get time to prepare mentally. Pregnancy or the adoption process. You were kind of thrust onto the throne." She unraveled the braid. "And the little princess too."

She surprised me. I thought she was going to tell me I wasn't the king of anything. I had no business using old-fashioned terms. I was backward. Stupid. A caveman.

But she didn't. She got what I was saying.

In an oversize white polo and beige chinos, she was the least regal person I'd ever seen, and maybe I wasn't much of a king in sandals and shorts, but we understood the kingdom and how fucked up it was.

I was glad I'd gotten her for a month, and I knew I was going to lean on her more than I should. And I was glad I'd gotten away from Jenn and Jennifer before I made an even bigger ass out of myself.

Nicole made me want to do better and Cara made me want to prove it.

"I'm going to the SAG thing tomorrow night. Nicole's coming."

Cara looked at me darkly. "Her bedtime's eight."

"Yeah. I know. But people want to see her, I have to go, and life goes on. I'm not like those people. I'm not my parents. I'm not those parents back there either. I'm me. This is the hand we're dealt. We gotta play it."

"I'll go then. I have a dress."

CHAPTER 16

CARA

When you see pictures of celebrities at events with their children, you can bet there's a nanny for each kid hanging around the sidelines. We exist on the fringes, just outside the camera's field. We wear simple black clothes, easy shoes, and a little makeup so we don't stand out. We know where to take the kids when they act out and how to manage a room full of power hitters without being seen.

No one wanted to see us. We prove that Hollywood is full of people who aren't magical or perfect, but human beings who need help juggling twelve-hour days and family responsibilities. I liked it on the fringes. I liked my anonymity.

Blakely didn't have that luxury. She'd be seen and photographed. The entire episode with Josh Trudeau would be dredged up and she'd be unemployable all over again.

Blakely sprawled over my bed, swiping her iPad. I needed to tell her about the incident with Josh, but I was too nervous. I considered putting it in a note, an e-mail, anything but face-to-face.

"I'm not saying I mind getting the night off," she said. "But this sucks."

"Are you on Tinder again?"

"See this guy here?" She flipped the screen so I could see a guy holding his phone up to a mirror.

"I don't understand the picture-in-the-bathroom-mirror thing. Don't these people have friends?"

"Here's what he wrote me. 'Hey. You're pretty hot. You look like that nanny that slept with Josh Trudeau. LOL.'"

"Swipe left on him. Or right. Whichever." I pulled a simple black dress out of the closet and threw it on the bed.

"Why didn't I know he was a player?"

"Because you didn't know and you respected him enough to keep it a secret. So none of us warned you."

"Wrong. Because my mother supported me by sleeping with married men so I have it in my head that it's normal, which it's not. Ever." She knocked her head with her knuckle as if she could tap the right way of thinking into it.

I got my shoes out. Black. Low heel. Unobtrusive. Easy to run after a kid from the dressing rooms. It was the perfect moment to tell her, but I didn't.

"Look." She tapped on the screen and showed it to me again. I recognized her headshot but she looked *off.* "Higher cheekbones. A little pouf in the lips. Brown contacts."

"What happened to the huge nose?"

"I found out that's harder than making it smaller."

I took a deep breath and spit it out.

"He made a play for me," I said. "At the party yesterday. In the side drive. I'm sorry."

She fell back on the mattress and covered her face with my pillow.

"I'm so ashamed." Her voice was muffled.

"Don't be. I get it. He's not my thing—but I get it."

She threw the pillow at me. I caught it.

"Stop saying that. If you forgive me, I have to forgive my mother, which I don't."

"Brad says Josh is hot for women who take care of kids." I tossed the pillow on the bed. "He's a dick. He should get that hard-on for his wife."

Blakely shot up to a sitting position. "You told Brad?"

"He saw it." I snapped the dress up. "Josh is an asshole. End of."

"Wait. He didn't fire you?"

"No. He got . . ." What was the word? It wasn't simply *angry*. ". . . protective."

I realized I was staring into the middle distance with the dress draped over my arm, remembering my boss with a fire in his eyes. Like he wanted to rip Josh Trudeau's face off with his bare hands.

Over me.

Me.

I was important.

"And?" Blakely asked.

And I liked it. Which is wrong. Everything about how it felt is wrong.

"And what?"

"And are you all right?"

Blakely knew how wrong it was. She'd been dragged through the mud for months.

"I'm fine," I said, looking at my watch. "If you could get Nicole ready, I think we're leaving at seven."

She bounced up.

"Yes. Okay. Man, I like our boss."

She kissed me on the cheek and dashed to the front house to get Nicole ready.

I had to admit, I liked our boss too.

Shit.

I didn't move for too long. I didn't even know what I was staring at. The way he'd protected me, left those two girls behind, slung his

78

daughter over his shoulder, and took charge? I could see him as something more. Something real and stable.

All of it sent warmth from my heart to the fold between my legs. The twisted logic of dreams had clicked together unrelated ideas. Sex. Brad Sinclair. Security. Stability.

In the real world, nothing said instability like Brad Sinclair. He and security didn't occupy the same room comfortably. He was less stable than my parents. More likely to move. Less emotionally accessible. But in dreamland, when I was bent over the pool table working up to an orgasm so strong I woke up, all those puzzle pieces clicked together and made perfect sense.

In the real world, I could dismiss dream logic, until he nearly broke Josh Trudeau's face. Then it came together. It became real, and it was more arousing than just about anything I'd ever felt.

You've lost your mind.

Truly, I had. I peeled off my jeans and shirt and headed for the shower, arguing that I needed one anyway, then arguing that I only had to soap up, rinse off, and get out fast, then that I wouldn't be able to function with a constant throb between my legs, then that I should take the shower cold.

Nah. I put the temperature all the way up. I wanted to feel every drop. I got in and was engulfed in the water's soothing heat.

I wanted a real home. A stable person to spend my life with, and they were in short supply. I hadn't given up; I'd just stopped looking for a man.

In my fantasy he said—

Spread your legs, baby. I'm going to lick you.

Pretending he was someone completely different when he bent down and put his face between my legs. When I put my hands on my body, I felt his hands. When I touched my nipples, I did it the way I thought he'd do it. The way I wanted him to.

Take me take me take me . . .

I wasn't supposed to think of Brad Sinclair. I'd had an excuse that morning. I was half asleep and coming off a dream. In the shower, I made that tiny tiled room a safe place where it was acceptable to put one hand on the wall, one hand between my legs and tease my clit until I thought I'd explode. Just this one time. Make it last.

Are you close? I'm going to come in you.

In that voice. That magic voice. Not too high or low. The rhythms of it. He'd spread my legs while his hips thrust, looking down at me. His eyes on me while he ripped me apart with his dick. Fast then slow. Pushing in all the way to the root. He'd tell me not to come. He'd ask me to wait for him. He'd *demand* I wait for him. I slowed the motions of my fingers as I got closer.

Imagining his orgasm. His gasp. His groan. Losing control because of me.

That did it. I came so hard I had to lean on the wall.

CHAPTER 17

BRAD

My father made fun of me when I bought my first tux. Called me a fancy-ass.

"I think you need an update come fall," Paula said, straightening my tie. "I'll call Max and have him come for a fitting."

"They all look the same."

I stood in front of the mirror. I looked like a clown. I yanked the tie off. Nicole appeared in the doorway.

"Can I wear the sparkle-toe sneakers?"

"Sure."

She called down the hall. "Daddy said yes."

Blakely stepped into the frame and addressed me.

"They won't fit in at a black-tie event," she said. "But your call."

"Whatever she wants," I said. "I don't care what people think."

Paula put her hands on her hips.

"Stars! You're bringing the bombshell?" she asked. The nickname was funny the first fifteen times.

"My daughter? Yeah."

"Brad, honey. No one's bringing their kids to this. Now I'm not trying to tell you how to be the father—"

"Hell you aren't."

"Bring her to the . . . what's it called? The associated event."

"She's coming. Let them get their pictures. I want to hang out with her and if I can't get downtime to do it, she can come to work with me."

Paula made the face where she tightened her lips and raised her eyebrows. Disapproval. She was the gauge for when I went over the line, but ever since Nicole, the dial on my barometer had changed.

And I was in charge. No one ever told my father how to raise us.

"I'm going. I'm taking Nicole, and you know what else?"

I didn't wait for an answer. I leaned out the door and called down the hall.

"Blakely!"

Her disembodied voice called back.

"Yeah?"

"Get dressed to come with us."

"What?"

I didn't repeat, but turned to Paula.

"I don't care if people talk. My daughter can wear whatever she wants. This is my house. This is my business. I'll tell Cara to stay home."

I left because I didn't want Paula to talk sense into me. Everyone in the business could kiss my ass. I went to the pool house with all the righteous anger of a man doing what he wanted without asking permission for a damn thing.

———

A neighborhood where you didn't have to lock the doors was a cliché. Small-town nostalgia. Small towns sucked. You couldn't dream in a small town. But the unlocked door thing was real. I never knocked to go anywhere. I walked in and out of every house on my street because that was what we did.

The pool house was on my property. I owned it. Sure it was a private space, but I was a product of my childhood. The glass doors in the back were wide open, so I just went in to tell Cara she had the night off.

When I heard the shower running I should have left. Obviously. But I went into her room. Peeked. I was making sure it was the shower and not just a faucet.

Yes, that was it. If it was a faucet, I could go in and talk to her. So I was checking.

Her jeans were stretched over the floor in the shape of the letter W. And the water sound was definitely coming from the shower.

A gentleman would leave.

But I hadn't been a gentleman since I crossed into LA County in my 2003 Chevy Cavalier. Nope. I was ruled by my career and my dick. Right then, my dick was doing the decision-making, and the door to the bathroom was ajar, and the door to the shower was glass.

Oh, Jesus Christ.

Yeah.

The water and steam obscured my view from full porn-site clarity, but that made the scene even sexier.

If that was possible.

She had one hand on the wall in front of her and the other, God help me, between her legs. I could see the shape of her tits and her ass sticking up.

Head thrown back.

Ass rotating.

Skin slick and shiny.

My dick was at full attention.

I could smell her soap and hear her just over the sound of the water.

I'd stepped close to the door without realizing I'd done it. That was the dick doing the thinking.

She groaned. I saw her mouth open. A dark oval behind the wet glass.

I was really going to have to go jerk off immediately.

Then she came, bending the arm that was on the wall until she was pressed against it. A long groan bounced off the tiles.

Fuck fuck fuck.

I wanted to see her come for me.

Like that. For me. Yeah.

I wanted to fuck her blind. Fuck her open. The dick told me to go into the shower and take her. The dick hadn't been refused in years. The dick got what it wanted and right then it wanted Cara DuMont so bad I thought the blood rushing to it would break it.

I had a moment of sense. A moment where I could have turned around and waited in the living room, or outside, or on Mars. And that sense wasn't overwhelmed by the dick. Nope, I was going to get in my rocket ship and go to fucking Mars, but probably the living room. I was going to leave.

But the shower door clicked open.

And my brain felt all the shame you'd expect, but the dick? The dick just saw her soaped-up tits and the length of her slick thighs.

Did I mention I left my jacket in the main house? I had nothing to hide the eight-inch boner pressing against my leg.

CHAPTER 18

CARA

I was recovering from my orgasm when I realized I needed shampoo and it was under the sink. I was going to be late if I didn't snap to it, so I opened the door without taking another breath and there he was.

I didn't scream because I sucked air in so fast.

"Shit!" he cried, putting his hand over his eyes like a kid in a scary movie.

Oh my God, he had a tent in his pants.

Not a tent. A tour bus.

"What the hell?"

I was too stunned to close the shower door. It was glass, so what was the point?

I covered myself, one arm barely covering my breasts and the other the triangle between my legs.

"I'm sorry! I was just—" He took one hand off his eyes to point over there, wherever that was.

"Are you serious?"

"Nicole! I was going to—"

"Get out!"

I took my arm off my chest and reached out to slam the bathroom door. But even with him out of my sight I felt him. His eyes. How they'd gone from my body and shot up to my face before he covered them.

My clothes were on the other side of the door.

I was embarrassed and angry. I didn't want to think about what he'd seen me doing.

How about that boner?

I was also tingling from the prospect of him seeing me with my hand between my legs. Everything about this was uncomfortable and weird and arousing.

I was shaking as I put the towel around me.

To hell with it.

I tucked the edge of the towel under my arm and walked out, leaving water footprints behind me.

He was in the living room, sitting on the couch with his legs crossed.

"I didn't see anything," he said, hands up.

"Don't you knock?"

He lodged his tongue in his cheek and looked away.

"Look, I'm sorry," he said. "But like I said, I didn't see anything."

A second little voice told me to mention the inhuman size of his erection. That would include me admitting I was looking at his crotch, which reminded me that he was starring in my fantasy. So voice number two told me to shut the hell up. Don't acknowledge it. Don't even think about it. The state of his penis was an inappropriate topic of conversation.

"You always get hard when you don't see anything?"

So much for voice number two.

He looked me right in the eye, leveling his gaze in utter seriousness.

"I'm sure I don't know what you're talking about, Miss."

Now it looked like I was suffering from wishful thinking. He was infuriating.

"You're a dick." I said it with enough venom to kill an elephant.

He looked at his watch. "I came to tell you Blakely's coming tonight. You have the night off."

"Well played, Mr. Sinclair."

I shut the bedroom door so I could get dressed without his eyes working me over.

"I'm sorry!" he said from the other side of the door.

I didn't answer. Eventually he left.

CHAPTER 19

CARA

You should quit.

I was still on severance from the Heywoods. Money wasn't the issue. This was borderline harassment. I lay on my bed in the dark, looking up at the ceiling.

You should quit and sue him.

Blakely had come back at a quarter to ten and gone right back out, leaving Nicole's monitor with me. Brad had stayed at the event.

I didn't tell her about the shower. I wasn't afraid, but I didn't want her to think badly of him. I didn't know why it mattered to me. Maybe I didn't want her to think he was another Josh Trudeau.

Really, what did I want out of him?

I must have fallen asleep at one point, because I had another Brad dream. I had my hands on the shower wall and he was fucking me from behind.

Get it deep. Harder. Give it to me.

There were pool balls on the floor, and I tried not to step on them, because they'd roll under my feet and I'd fall, but the closer I got to orgasm the harder it was.

He tapped on the shower glass in my dream, loud enough to wake me up. The feeling of his shaft between my legs disappeared, and the sound of rain and tapping continued.

"Cara, waaaakeeeee uuuuuppppp . . ."

His voice far away, but real. Not dream real but real real. I bolted to sitting.

He was tapping on my bedroom window.

"IIII'mmmm knoooockiiiiiiingggg . . ."

It was 2:17 in the morning. The rain was the sound of the sprinklers.

"Jesus Christ." I shook the sleep away. Was I dressed? Yes. Sweatpants and black T-shirt. I got out of bed and slapped the window open. He practically fell through it. I swallowed a laugh. He was adorable in his wet tuxedo and red eyes.

"I am so sorry," he slurred, reaching his whole arm in the window, finger pointing aimlessly. "I . . ." He put his hand on his chest. "I am an asshole. I should have knocked. And I should not have enjoyed the view so long. I am a—" He swayed. Gripped the windowsill. "—I am a pig."

"You're drunk."

"I'm sorry sober too."

"Drunk apology accepted. I'll accept your sober apology in the morning."

"Okay. I like you. I don't want you to be mad at me. You should be mad at me, but I don't want you to be. I want you to like me."

"Go to bed."

He leaned back out the window, paused. "Do you like me?"

"Against my better judgment, I do."

"Okay."

He was so drunk he could barely stand.

"Please go to bed."

"Okay. I will apologize tomorrow. And the next day. And . . ." He swayed. "And the next day. I wasn't raised like that."

"Go. To. Bed."

He gave me a salute and walked right through a sprinkler, toward the front house. I closed the window.

This job was the worst I ever had. I really should quit.

But I couldn't. I didn't know if it was Nicole, or Blakely, or Brad that kept me there, but I felt a pull to see it through. Or at the very least, decide later. I went to the bathroom, did my business without turning the light on, and walked back to the bedroom. I could hear the sprinklers, and the motion-sensor light was still on. I reached for the drapes to shut out the light.

Brad was lying in the grass facedown, arms and legs in a big X, getting sprinkled on.

I could leave him out there.

The sprinklers turned off.

I could, he deserved it. But I couldn't.

I put on sneakers and a hoodie and went outside. He was face-first in a mud puddle.

"Brad?"

He didn't move. I'd moved big drunk men before. In Scotland there had been a boy who had no idea when to stop drinking. Then in college, more than one boy, more than one time.

I pulled his arm until he was on his back, then pulled both wrists and pulled forward. If I'm making it sound easy, it wasn't. I slipped and fell in wet grass, and grunted like a tennis player. But I got him to sitting. Half his gorgeous face was dotted with mud.

"Brad?"

No answer. I slapped him. Nothing. Slapped again, harder. He groaned.

Then I pulled my arm back and really hauled off and whacked him.

"Ow."

"You have to wake up. I can't carry you."

"That hurt."

"You deserve it."

I crouched, getting my shoulder under his arm.

"Okay, I'm going to count to three. On three, stand up."

"Do you know you're beautiful?"

"One."

"And you smell like a fruit cup."

"Two."

He looked at me, the weight of his head tilting his face at an angle to mine. "You're the queen of the house."

"Three."

We lurched up. Took a step left. Adjusted. Stood steady.

"Can I just sleep here?"

"No. Nicole isn't going to find your drunk ass on the lawn in the morning."

"Shit." Despite his alcohol saturation, that word held a ton of meaning.

I forgot I had to think about my daughter.

I didn't think about her finding me.

I'm going to have to change.

No one should count on the authenticity of drunken emotion, yet there was something so deep about the tone of that word. Even if he didn't remember how he uttered it the next morning, there was something inside him that knew he had to fix this.

"Lean on me," I said.

We took one step forward, then two. I held his wrist with one hand and his waist with the other. The front of his tuxedo shirt was brown with mud. I got wet wherever his clothes touched me.

"Thank you," he said when he stumbled.

"No problem. Step up here."

He stepped up to the pool patio.

"You hurt my feelings," he said without hurt in his voice. As if he was just stating a fact. "When you called me a dick."

"I'm not sorry."

"I don't blame you. Do you have fantasies, ever?" He ran the question into the statement as if they made sense together.

"Like about what?" I asked. His arm around me, his breath soft in my ear. Even his dependence was kind of a fantasy.

"You know what bothers me about fantasies?"

"Watch this chair here. Whoa." I pulled him left, narrowly missing tripping over a lounger.

"You never know if you're getting it right," he said.

I turned to him, and found his eyes taking up my entire field of vision and my nose two inches from his.

"What do you mean?" Up ahead, the screen door was wide open. He must have come out that way.

"Like when I fantasize about fucking you."

We almost tripped on the entrance. I swallowed my lungs, stomach, and heart in one gulp. He was drunk. He didn't mean it. He never thought about fucking me. Not Brad Sinclair.

And he was my boss.

"Step up," I said, turning back. My face burned red hot.

He stepped up. We were in the back room. I was never going to get him up the stairs to his room, so I pivoted toward the guest room.

"Do you come with a dick?" He slurred, but I wasn't mistaking the words or meaning. "Just a dick? Or do you need a little help?"

"Brad, really?"

"I have this one fantasy where you come without help and one where I touch you."

"This is totally inappropriate."

I kicked open the guest room door.

"I want to know which one's right, then I won't ask again. And what do you call your . . . you know . . . girl parts?"

I ducked and let his weight drop. He fell to a sitting position, soaked clothes sticking to his beautiful body. White shirt exposing his nipples and the hair on his chest, eyes a third lower, seriously asking me what term I used for my genitalia.

"I'm assuming you talk dirty," he said. "I shouldn't assume. But it's my fantasy and I'm keeping it."

A drop of water fell from his cuff onto the wool carpet.

"The jacket has to come off."

He nodded and went for his lapel, but even that messed with his balance and he nearly tipped over. I grabbed him and pulled him up.

"You know the best part of them?" he said. I tugged his cuff so he could get his arm out. "The part when I spread your legs."

I sucked in a breath. My nervous system fired, dropping all sensation and urgency to my core. I had to pause to breathe before I pulled the other cuff.

"I'm looking in your eyes and you say *yes*," he continued. "You bend your knees."

I tossed the jacket over a chair.

"And I . . ." He put the backs of his hands together and moved them apart. "God."

I didn't have to take his shirt off. Didn't even have to stay in the room with him. I could have left. But maybe this was a little bit of my fantasy too. Maybe his attention was something I craved, even if he wasn't supposed to be drunk or muddied.

He looked concerned for a second.

"Do you shave? Landing strip? I don't care, but I want to get it right."

I undid the top button and took the studs out of the front of his shirt. I had to kneel to get to the bottom buttons.

"Tell me," he said.

I got to the last button. His head tilted down to me, and I looked up at him.

"Just tell me that."

I reached for his cuff links, but he pulled his arm back and did it himself.

"My fantasy is about you." He pointed to me. "If I don't know this stuff, it's about some random woman."

He dropped the cuff links on the carpet.

"How I manage my hair depends on my mood," I said, grabbing his cuffs. I pulled his wet shirt off and put it over the jacket. "I'm not attached to any one way of doing it. I really hope you forget this tomorrow."

"I still have to memorize the third act," he said. "I bet you taste like strawberries."

I pushed him back, and he fell like a sack of potatoes, arms out, bare chest breathtaking in the moonlight. I wanted to put my hands on it. Claw at the skin. Feel the nipples get hard under my fingers. Talk filth until he got hard.

I got back on my knees and took his shoes off.

"Thank you for taking care of my daughter," he said as I picked his legs up by the ankles and swung them around until he was straight on the bed.

Only a guy midblackout could go from subject to subject like that. It meant he was forgetting things as soon as they were happening.

"I talk during," I said matter-of-factly as I put the blanket over him. "And dirty. And dick. And even though it's inappropriate and against all the rules, I'd love for you to bury yours in me so hard it hurts. I dream about you fucking me like an animal three nights a week, and the other four you fuck me like you own me." I patted the blanket.

"I'll never work again," he mumbled, half inside his drunken dream world. He couldn't have been talking about burying his dick in me. "No one will want me if I don't show up. Everything will be gone. All sad faces."

"Good night." He murmured a response. I kissed him on the forehead.

When I came back to put a glass of water and aspirin on the night table, he was passed out.

CHAPTER 20

CARA

I got up early and went to the gym. I ran, climbed, did sit-ups and a spin class, but nothing worked Brad's words out of my mind.

He fantasized about me. That was the bottom line. I imagined his voice telling me what he wanted to do to me and replayed it over and over while I pedaled myself into a mass of sweat and burning muscles. On the screens above, DMZ flashed Brad on the red carpet with Nicole in his arms.

They were adorable, and Nicole hadn't been out that late. Blakely wasn't in the photos. I would have called the entire evening a success if he hadn't shown up at my window in a wet tuxedo.

It was Blakely's shift until after dinner. When I got back from the gym, Brad was working with Paula by the pool, doing whatever the thing was that they did. Nicole was underfoot with her toys; the space under the table was her own unique world. The ponies lay among Brad and Paula's feet. Nicole made one of the ponies kick a ball, and it rolled out of the protection of the table. She went to get it. In the meantime, with the girl's back turned and her father reciting a line, Paula lifted her leg and quietly crunched the Lego horse stable under her heel, dislodging the lilac plush pony that lived there. With a flick of her foot, she brushed it toward the wet drain on the other side of the table.

When Nicole got back she gasped in horror. She'd spent a ton of time on that stable.

"Hush," her father said, oblivious.

Nicole had been well trained in hushing. From her days in the coffee shop cabinet, when her mother couldn't get a sitter, she knew she had to stay quiet when a parent was working, so she did.

I stayed quiet too. For now.

When I got to the pool house, Blakely was curled up on the couch with an iPad. Her hair was cut short and dark brunette.

"Your hair," I said.

"Like it? I look different, don't I? Would you recognize me?"

"Yes. And Paula's a bitch," I said without preamble.

"You mean Miss Mint Julep Ladygirl Fiddle-dee-dee? Yeah. Screw her. Every time Brad wants his daughter around, she looks at me as if it's my fault I have an hour off."

"How was last night?" I asked.

"Boring. I was with her for an hour, then I stayed in the limo for the next two hours waiting for him to bring her back out."

"Was she scared of the cameras?"

"A little. Not too bad." She looked up at the clock. "I have to bring her to gymnastics at two. I'm testing the hair. See if the guy at the desk thinks I'm a stranger."

We were interrupted by a knock on the front door.

"When you get back we'll switch," I said, opening the door. Brad was on the other side in aviators and a white T-shirt. The previous day came back in a flood of skin-tingling hormones. The shower, the fantasies, walking with his arm on my shoulder, me undressing him.

"I'm going to take Nicole," he said without a greeting, then pointed to me. "You should come."

It was Blakely's shift, but she just shrugged.

"Okay," I said. "Let me get my shoes on."

CHAPTER 21

CARA

Celebrities living in Los Angeles drive more often than you think and do everything else less than you think. Driving is an entitlement. It means you have control. And Brad I-Didn't-See-Anything Sinclair was trying to prove he was in control.

Nicole sat in the backseat humming. She had a book on her lap and her leotard under her summer dress.

Brad leaned on the wheel of the Range Rover, arms toned and tan, sunglasses glinting, looking disaffected and in charge. It was hot, but for my part he needed to cover himself all the time, every second of the day. With a tarp. Because the night before came back to me full force. Starting with the dream of him in the shower, the imagined feeling of his skin against mine. The erection on my soft bottom. His lips on the back of my neck . . . all the way up to his very real questions about how I like to fuck.

"Yesterday . . ." I started but couldn't finish. I knew what I wanted to say, but the thought of him watching me froze my tongue.

"You know, the steam coming out of that bathroom, I thought the place was on fire."

Jefferson Avenue at midday was clear, and we were going to be at the gym in ten minutes.

"Mr. Sinclair. Really?"

"Oh it's Mr. Sinclair now? Listen. I didn't see anything, ma'am."

"I need you to really not just come in the back house again," I said. "Where I'm from, when you come to someone's house, you knock. You put your fingers together in a fist and—"

"Where I'm from," he started with full good-old-boy accent, "we don't leave the doors unlocked unless we want people running through."

His tinge of Arkansas accent implied a superior upbringing with traditions buffed with time.

"Knock anyway."

"Believe me," he said, flipping his blinker and changing lanes for no apparent reason. "I'm never going in that house again without an engraved invitation."

"Okay. Good. No more peeking."

So. What do you remember?

"I wasn't raised like that."

"You keep saying that."

"When did I say that?"

He'd said it last night, at my window. But if he didn't remember, I didn't want to remind him. We'd crossed a line. If he blacked out, then what had happened the night before was mine and mine alone. If he remembered, then between the shower and the fantasies? I'd have to resign.

"Some interview, I think. Did you have fun last night?"

He smiled and made a *pfft* sound. "Sure. After I sent Nicole home I had a few drinks and woke up in the guest room."

Did he remember the water and aspirin? Did he assume Paula had left it? Or was it just an empty glass when he woke?

"Daddy told jokes the whole time!" Nicole chimed in. We both turned. She bounced her little light-up toes. "Like . . . Ask me if I'm a tree!"

I obeyed, reminding myself to keep it clean in the front seat. "Are you a tree?"

"No!" She laughed. "What's brown and sticky?"

"I don't know."

She and Brad answered together, "A stick!"

Nicole was beside herself with laughter.

"Where are you from, anyway?" Brad asked me.

"Everywhere. Nowhere."

"You trying to get mysterious with me?"

"I grew up on air force bases. Diplomat housing. That kind of thing. There really is no, 'Where I'm from the gates are locked and the doors are open,' because it changed all the time. But mostly we were behind big walls with guards. I needed an escort in some places. Pakistan. That was crazy."

I shook my head and looked out the window.

"How crazy? You get kidnapped?"

"No. I wore a head scarf whenever we left the base because I wanted to fit in. There was no Lycée so I didn't go to school. I had this nowhere feeling. I guess that doesn't sound very crazy."

"How old were you?"

"Twelve. I bet you were doing something completely different when you were twelve."

He laughed to himself.

"Shit. Yeah. That was my first summer working at the lumberyard. Hot as f—heck. The sawdust stuck to me everywhere. Every night I had it in my butt crack."

I laughed, but it was only to cover up the fact that I was envisioning his gorgeous ass filled with sawdust. Nicole had her own reasons for cracking up.

"Daddy said *butt* again!"

"Again?" I said. Brad shrugged and Nicole just kept laughing. At least they were getting along.

He pulled into the lot and put the car in park.

"I'll get her," I said, opening the door. "You lay low before the paps find you."

"Cara," he said, taking his sunglasses off.

"Yeah?"

"It won't happen again."

The way he looked at me—he meant it. Every word came from a deep well of sincerity and regret.

"I know," I said, dealing with my own well of regret.

CHAPTER 22

BRAD

Cara got out and unbuckled Nicole. I twisted around to look at her. She was freaking cute when she smiled. If I could harvest those dimples and sell them on the open market, I'd be richer than I already was.

"Turn around," she said. "I need to fix this hair. Who made this braid?"

"Daddy!"

"It was perfect when we left," I defended myself from the front seat.

Cara rearranged Nicole's stray brown strands and dangling bobby pins into a tight ponytail.

"I'm going to do the balance beam all by myself," Nicole said, patting her hair to make sure it was flat. "I won't even be scared."

A bobby pin popped off. Cara leaned over to get it. I could see down her shirt, and the way her naked body looked in the shower came back to me. I turned around to face the front.

"Hop down," Cara said. Nicole jumped to the ground and pushed the door closed with both hands. Had to do everything herself. Was the self-sufficiency from my family or Brenda's?

I didn't know, but when my daughter turned and waved at me, I could put money on where she got the smile.

I hadn't even known Brenda, really. She'd had a nice smile. The kind of smile you wanted to look at all the time because it was so warm. When customers came into the store, the girls came to me and everyone else went to Brenda. Everything about her had been inviting, but the smile was more than all that put together.

See, you do remember her.

I did. Not much more than the smile came to me though. I didn't even remember our night together. Or nights. There may have been more than one. She was from a time long ago when I needed a comforting smile.

I watched Cara's ass sway in her jeans as she went toward the double glass doors with Nicole's hand in hers. She was something. Not my type. Too serious. Too bossy. She was an art film that had a SAG waiver. I liked big summer tentpole girls. Cleaned up and produced. Bigger than life. I could work them quick and move to the next without ever thinking about it again.

But that shower scene. Open mouth when she came. I shouldn't have seen it, but I did. I walked right into it. I'd had a good thirty seconds where I could have turned around and gone into the other room, but I was turned on like a thirteen-year-old.

What kind of man stays and watches?

It was a shit time to assess my life, but it wasn't like I had much of a choice. I'd gotten drunk the night before, but the escape had been short and painful.

I was a single dad.

The papers had already told everyone that. Ken made sure he used the phrase whenever he opened his mouth. I hired people to help. I painted a room in my house pink, but the words *single dad* still sounded like I was talking about a character I was playing. Like when the hosts on the morning shows say, "*You're* a single dad when the spaceships land on Los Angeles. How did you prepare for the part?" And I say, "Well, Tammy or Joan or Christy or whatever, I just got myself this really cute kid. You should meet her. She's the bee's knees and my parents love her."

This wasn't a part I was playing, but I couldn't shake feeling like it was all fake.

Cara held the door open for Nicole. My daughter deserved better, but she didn't have better. She had me.

CHAPTER 23

BRAD

Arnie liked having a cigarette in his mouth when he shot pool even though the ashtray was right fucking there.

I'd brought a few guys from Arkansas with me. They'd all found their own life or found their way home eventually. Not Arnie. Arnie was kind of an asshole. And by "kind of" I mean "completely." My buddy Michael wondered why I kept him around. He said stupid shit, had a sense of entitlement that put people off, zero work ethic, and a very small constellation of talents. His gold chain was so heavy it made creases in the skin of his neck and he wore his sunglasses inside because he'd spent two hundred dollars on them.

He was the asshole who had nowhere to go. No one else wanted to be his friend. I felt sorry for him. In fifth grade, he'd given Ray Borden a shiner for calling me a pansy. In eighth grade, he didn't tell Maryann Jonas that I was the one throwing pebbles at her window that certain night, even though her dad really held his feet to the fire. He'd let me copy his homework most days and corrected the spelling on my essays, never asking for a thing in return. The list went on.

So maybe he wasn't a complete asshole. Maybe he just had a narrow worldview and no filter.

He was great at pool though. Geometry hadn't been his thing in tenth grade, but somehow it came together for him when he shot nine-ball. He shifted a little, lining up, the gold rope curving along the edge of the cue.

"The nanny's on her way out, right?" he asked, threading the cue through his fingers. I was sure he had the whole table figured out already. "Then I can go for it, right?" He looked at me over the top edge of his blue wraparounds.

"We'll see."

"We will." He took his shot, sinking the eight off the one.

We'd agreed on a month, and time was up. It was going to be me, Blakely, and Nicole soon enough. Plus some mystery nanny the agency was searching for. I needed one who could travel.

"Might keep her," I said, chalking my stick. "If I do, you're sidelined indefinitely."

I said it as if it was an option, but Cara had been clear she wanted to move on.

"Come on, man." Arnie circled the table, eyes on the balls, still in sunglasses and with cigarette. "If you're not going to tap that body, at least let me do it."

"No and no."

He pulled his smoke from his lips and wedged it between two fingers he held up for me. "Just twice. I wanna see how those tits shake when she's taking it from behind."

"Shut the fuck up, Arnie."

"Then I wanna see her face with my dick in it."

When I was twelve, Grady Markham had made a crack about my sister's face. Something about how it would look with her knees on each side of it.

I'd been deeply offended. That's what I told the sheriff when he was in the principal's office. "Deeply offended." Which was southern for "So fucking mad I had no problem breaking a soda bottle on the table and slicing Grady's cheek open."

That was my sister. He was insulting my family.

Arnie saying shit about Cara wasn't anything like that, because she wasn't family. No, my feelings weren't brotherly, but the rage was the same. Arnie put all the things I'd thought about Cara in the most disgusting and disgraceful words possible.

Which made *me* disgraceful.

And this was the woman who took care of my daughter.

So it was family.

But it wasn't.

But it was all confused and I was mad as fuck.

My hand, my left hand, oddly, considering I was right-handed, swiped at Arnie's blue wraparounds. They went flying, exposing Arnie's fox-colored eyes and thin eyelashes.

"Fuck? Dude?"

"I mean it. That's my daughter's nanny."

What does that even mean?

Fuck that. I didn't know what that meant and it didn't matter. I only had a debt to white-hot rage. I put my finger in his face.

"Any single human being who takes care of my daughter is off-limits for tit-shaking and face-fucking."

Nice going, using Nicole like that.

Arnie put his hands up like some wronged party. A guy who'd stepped into a pile of shit from someone else's dog.

Maybe he had. Maybe what I felt had nothing to do with him.

"You know what?" he said. "You want me to keep it in my pants, hire an ugly one, yo. Don't be dangling some bombshell bitch in my face and say I can't even talk about touching it."

"It? You forget where you're from?" I admit I carved off a little of my voice coaching to make the point. "No Redfield boy talks like that. Your mother didn't raise you to call a lady *it*."

"Don't you tell me about home. When was the last time you went home? Buddy redid the bar, and you didn't even go see it. You have nieces and nephews telling all their friends Uncle Brad's famous, and I bet you don't even know what they look like. I bring them presents when I go. No." He wagged his finger at me. "Don't you tell me shit. I love this life as much as you, and I still make it back home."

You know how that hit?

It hit below the belt, right where Faye Sweeny kicked me in fifth grade and I passed out. Arnie wasn't Faye though. She sent me a handwritten note apologizing. Arnie went right back in.

"Buddy fixed Margie up." *Slap*. Sunk the six. "Your nephew's graduating high school. He can act, you know? Biggest talent in Redfield since you." *Slap*. Sunk the one off the seven. "And how about taking your daughter around?"

"You know what, you fuck? You sit around here telling me what to do? Want to live my life? I have a three-hundred-page script to memorize and a fucking kid. Sure, let me take a vacation in Arkansas. Great idea."

Arnie threw his hands up. "Fuck this shit." He took a step away from me and swooped up his glasses, then pointed them at me like some community college professor. "I'm your friend. Until you die, I'm your friend. With or without the house. I don't like outsiders and I like the life here. But you gotta take care of what's yours."

Fuck him. I couldn't get home. I didn't have long before I was shooting on location in Asia, and you don't just leave a movie in preproduction. It wasn't the money. Not my money, at least. Hundreds of people had planned the shoot and without the lead actor no one had jobs.

I wondered if I had time to talk my nephew out of acting.

Did I have time to go back? If push came to shove, could I visit? Bring Cara and Nicole?

I didn't want to go back. I didn't want to see the street I grew up on, because it was still fucked up. My parents wouldn't move. Fixing up their house and my sister's just made them nice houses in a town that was like a prison.

And I was different now. Leaving was frowned upon. Sure, my friend Buddy was happy for me, but he was going to give me shit that I thought I was better than him. He married his eighteen-year-old girl-friend when he knocked her up and here I was with a secret kid. Party boy. California dude. Shot down from the sky.

Since when do you care what he thinks?

I didn't care, and I never judged him or anyone.

I should have brought Nicole first thing. I didn't care what they thought, but they'd think I lost my manners. And they'd all ride me because I'd knocked up a girl. Like Buddy did. Like Dad did.

They'd forgive me because I was like them. No matter what I said, the thought of that bothered me. I'd worked too hard to be better. Do better. Make more of myself.

And I didn't care what they thought—but I did.

I couldn't pull it apart. I was getting tense. I hated being tense.

"What's on your fucked-up brain, Brad?" Arnie asked after missing the seven. I'd taken too long to think about it.

"I forgot your birthday," I said.

"It's tomorrow."

I leaned down to take my shot.

"Party, then. Right here." Sunk the seven. "But swear, Arnie. You keep your hands off the help."

"On my honor, dude."

I nearly laughed out loud.

Nicole's voice came from the kitchen as she ran into the billiards room.

"Daddy!" She said the word like a demand, both feet planted. She had an open blue Sharpie in one hand as if she'd been in the middle of drawing.

"Yeah, sweetheart?"

"Miss Blakely says we got invited to Sam and Bonnie's?"

It took me a second to remember Sam and Bonnie were two of Mike and Laine's kids.

"If she says so."

"I want to wear the suit with the flower right here." She pointed to her neck, getting a blue dot on her chin. Arnie laughed and bent over the table. I put the pool cue down.

"Can I have that?" I held my hand out for the marker. She twisted her whole body to keep it away from me. "Nicole. Sharpie doesn't come out. Give it to me."

She pursed her lips and held her chin out like a weapon. Did she get that stubborn pride from my side or Brenda's? I'd never know.

"Do you need help?" Blakely asked from the doorway, reaching for the marker. "If you take it, the waa-mbulance is going to pull up."

I held my hand out to stop her. "I got it." Flipping my hand around, I put it out to my daughter. "The pen. If you want to wear the bathing suit with the flower right here." I poked where she'd left the blue dot. She softened a little, but not much.

"Miss Cara and Miss Blakely hid it."

Blakely cut in. "It's a size eight. It looks like a shopping bag on her."

"I grew!" she shot back at her nanny before turning to me and holding her hand up as far as it would go, the Sharpie wedged between thumb and forefinger. "I'm so big. So so big."

Behind me, I heard clacking balls and the hollow sound of one of them sinking. I lost interest in nine-ball and Arnie. I just wanted to see how big that suit was.

"Okay, big girl. Give me the marker and let's go take a look at the suit."

"Pinkie promise I can wear it."

I held my pinkie out and Nicole hooked hers over mine. How bad could it be?

She passed me the marker and I gave it to Blakely.

"Nice work negotiating the hostage, sir," she said, snapping the cap on.

I winked at her and took Nicole to her room. I went to her dresser, but Cara and Blakely were lousy at hiding things, because Nicole knew exactly where the bathing suit was. She scrambled under her bed and pulled out a blue zip-up bag with a handle.

"It's in here." Pulling the zipper around the top, she opened the flap. I recognized all the things my parents had bought before they met her and figured out her size. Too big. Too small. Wrong color. Wrong cartoon.

Kneeling next to the bag, she stuck one hand deep into it, wiggled, and came up with a pink, white, and blue one-piece with a poufy three-dimensional flower at the neck.

"This one. See the flower? I want this one. It's not too big."

I held it up.

"It's fu—" I caught myself. "It's huge."

"It is not." She snapped it away and stood so she could put it up against herself. The leg holes were halfway down to her knees. I took a closer look at it. It hadn't been in the stuff my parents bought. I'd remember.

"Where did you get it?" I asked.

"Mom bought it for me on sale. She said I could wear it."

Nicole hadn't come with much. A plastic bag with Pony Pie and some clothes. I'd never inventoried what was in the bag, but at that point, I would have let her wear a size-eleven men's shoe if it came out of that bag. It had been all she had, and I wasn't going to deny her a single item.

"Well, if your mom thinks it's all right, I guess we'll figure it out."

She clapped and jumped up and down, then flung herself around me, squeezing for all it was worth.

"Mommy said I had a nice daddy! She said it and she knew it and I knew it!"

"Oh, she did?" I sat on the bed, ready to hear more.

"She did!" She put her hands on my cheeks and pressed in. "She said you were nice."

The worst word in the English language. I didn't remember if Brenda was subtle enough to know that *nice* could be a compliment or an insult. I didn't remember anything about her besides her smile.

"What else did she say about Daddy?"

"You lived far away and you were the handsomest."

Harmless little lies. Right? But inside them, I wondered if Brenda thought I was unfit to raise Nicole, and wanted nothing to do with me because I wasn't stable enough. She would have been right. She'd been right about a lot and still, I didn't know her.

I could have said a few dozen things Nicole wasn't ready to hear. That a lot had changed since I'd been with her mother. That I might have come for her, eventually. That I was actually not nice. Not nice at all, but I could be if I tried.

"I'm glad I met you," I said. I meant it. I was glad I could be there for her. I wouldn't be half the parent her mother was, but at least I could buy her bathing suits that fit even if she didn't wear them. That had to be worth something.

"You too, Daddy. Can we try it on? The suit! Let's try it on!"

She ran to the bathroom to try on the huge bathing suit her mother promised she could wear.

CHAPTER 24

CARA

"We had a pool," Nicole had said to the lifeguard. "In number thirty-four!" Thirty-four was apparently her old apartment number. She wore a pink, white, and blue one-piece halter with a flower applique at the neck. She and her father insisted it fit. It didn't. Blakely and I jury-rigged an elastic belt from another suit, a few safety pins, and tight swim shorts into something weird but functional.

"My mom taught me. Watch!" She jumped in, wiggled underwater while I held my breath, and popped up, doggie-paddling her way to the edge. The lifeguard gave me the thumbs-up, but I stayed in the water to watch anyway.

Blakely and I were at the Greydons on a playdate.

"Her mother was really on top of it," Blakely said.

"Yeah. Like Superwoman. Did you know she took her to work?"

"At Coffee Chain?"

"She'd stay in the cabinets if her mom couldn't get her a sitter. Honestly, her mother must have thought Brad was the worst of the worst. Which is totally unfair, if you ask me. He's all right."

Blakely peeled her socks off and put her feet in the pool. Behind her, Michael and Laine Greydon sat at the patio table with another couple.

"Not for nothing." Blakely stretched her legs. "You're falling in love."

"She's a nice kid is all." I backed away from the kids to let them have fun. "She asks the most wonderful questions and—"

"I'm not talking about the kid," Blakely said softly. "That was expected. You're powerless against children. It's Brad Sinclair."

Being in the same house with that man was getting difficult. He constantly did an end run around Paula to sit with Nicole and me. He had a way of moving that made me think of sex. His good-old-boy routine hinted at a set of core values I could relate to, even if he didn't live those values, I could almost, sometimes, in slivers of moments . . . kind of . . . see it.

Unless I was making it up in my head.

"He's attractive." I didn't look at her. She'd know I was lying. "Any woman in America will tell you that."

My denials felt hollow. If I couldn't convince myself I wasn't attracted to my boss, I wasn't going to convince Blakely. Once she heard about the shower (*Oh my God, that is so tacky*) or undressing him while he asked me how I liked to fuck (*Oh my God, that is so hot*), I went for broke and told her about the dreams and morning fantasies (*Oh my God, you've got it bad*), and she decided something was going to happen between us no matter how much I denied it.

"Just don't end up on the cover of a tabloid." She kicked a little spray of water. "Not for screwing your boss. It's awful. Really awful."

"I'm a professional," I said, catching myself too late. "I'm sorry, I didn't mean to imply you aren't."

"No, you are. I'm not. I sat in the limo last night thinking. I want to be an actress. I got sucked into this world because the money's good. But I can't do this anymore."

I got up on the step.

"What do you mean?"

"I think I have to quit."

I don't know why I was surprised. Maybe it was the time and place, or the fact that she was telling me and not Paula. Maybe it was the fact that she wasn't reacting to getting a part, or a callback, or even a meeting.

"Are you sure?"

"No-yes-no?" She cringed as if she thought I'd be mad. "I know you went out of your way to get me this gig and I appreciate it. But I saved up enough to get some stuff done. Just enough so I look different. Now I have to go do it."

"This plan you have? It's nuts. Totally crazy."

"I'm in a crazy situation."

"You're disfiguring yourself."

"Cara. Don't be that way. Haven't you ever wanted anything so bad you'd do anything to get it? Ever?"

"You should leave your lips alone. You have great lips. I'd kill for them."

"Fine. No lips."

I had the sneaking feeling of being left behind. I was about to become what my friend Blakely "used to be" before she "realized she wanted more out of life."

Was it wrong that this was all I wanted? Taking care of children was fun. I enjoyed it. I enjoyed Nicole and her father, even if he was the most slippery slope I'd ever tried to climb.

"I'm sorry," she said. "I need change. A lot of it."

"Don't be." I sat on the ledge next to her. "I'm a big girl."

I couldn't be angry. Not outwardly. I couldn't blame her or demand more than she could give.

"When are you going to tell Paula?" I asked.

"When I'm sure. Who even knows what she'll do."

"I don't trust her."

"If she calls Nicole a bombshell one more time, I'm going to break her face."

"Blakely, now . . ." I cautioned her but kind of agreed.

"In a nice way."

"Miss Cara! Miss Blakely! Watch!"

Nicole was perched on the side of the pool. She bent her knees and dove in hands first. I clapped loudly for her.

That little girl made it all worthwhile. I didn't know if I could leave her. Not if Blakely was going. And I didn't know if I could stay.

CHAPTER 25

CARA

We pulled up Brad's private street in the hills. The cars blocking the way irritated me more than they should have, and the music coming from the back may have seemed louder and more abrasive than it would have if Blakely hadn't just told me she was leaving.

"Paula said party," I said. "But this is nuts."

"It's nothing. Come on. You've seen this before."

I had. A million times. What surprised me was my own disappointment. I'd thought, based on small gestures and efforts, that he was trying. Obviously, I was wrong.

A security guy approached my open window.

"Can I see your ID?" he asked. I was ready to be annoyed, and his demand just did it.

"How do you work for Brad Sinclair and not know who we are?"

Blakely leaned over me. "Ignore her. Here's my license. And this is Nicole Sinclair in the back." She turned to the backseat. "Say 'hi,' Nicole."

Nicole held up Pony Pie and waved her. "Hi!"

A Maserati pulled up close behind me, but the guard wasn't moving. He looked at Blakely's license, then her. He flipped through his clipboard while she tried to hold back a smirk.

"Hang on." He went to the booth.

"It's the hair," she said.

"Maybe you don't need plastic surgery."

"Or it'll just make it so much easier."

The security guard checked Nicole against a photo on a different clipboard, then me and Blakely before he let us in.

Deep breath.

I breathed deeply getting out of the car, getting my bag out, locking the door. It wasn't helping. I didn't know why I was so wound up.

"I'll take Nicole in," Blakely said, hoisting the girl's swimming bag. "Then I have an audition. I'm staying out tonight."

"All right. I'll meet you."

I went in the side entrance, all pretense of calm shattered completely by the sound of grunting behind the hedge separating the parking spaces from the service entrance.

"Bitch! Let go!"

I ran around the hedge.

Two people. One female in a silver matte skirt and burgundy hair. One male in skinny jeans and tight white T-shirt. Both involved in an epic battle to the death.

The woman, who I realized was a young girl as I ran down the service drive, had the guy's hair in a death grip. She growled as if the only part of her brain that was functioning was way in the back of her head, where the lizards lived.

I got between them. She let go, but only after twisting her body around so hard he landed against the wall. He had four long scratches on his cheek.

"She's fucking crazy!" he shouted.

I turned to the girl.

"Willow?"

She was underage. I knew that for a fact. Not to mention out of breath. Red-faced. Lipstick-smeared.

"Miss Cara?"

"Button your shirt."

I spun on the guy. He pulled a clump of bloody hair out of his scalp.

"There is no way you mistook this person for eighteen."

"I mistook her for female. Fuck. Look what she did!"

I took out my phone. "You're right. We'll let the cops sort it out."

He ran like his ass was on fire. When I turned back, Willow had buttoned her shirt. I took her chin in my hand.

"Look at me." She did, and through tears I saw bowling-ball pupils. "What did you take?"

"Just a little ex?"

"The fact that you think you can tell the difference between a little and a lot speaks volumes." I let her chin go.

"Don't tell Daddy," she sobbed.

"It's five o'clock. Who's supposed to be watching you?"

"I'm in middle school. I don't need anyone watching me."

I'd spent most of my career watching much smaller children, but I knew all about teen faux-logic.

"I can't even begin to answer that. Come with me."

"I don't have to."

She was making a last-ditch effort to maintain her autonomy and stay out of trouble. Fortunately for her I wasn't impressed with how she handled either. I picked up the silver clutch that had fallen against the wall. Opened it. Checked for the phone and snapped it closed. No self-respecting LA teen was going anywhere without their phone.

"Willow," I said. "You're a smart and funny girl with a bright future. That guy needs to be in jail. He was in the wrong. But this is a grown-up party, and you don't belong here."

I walked toward the front, knowing she'd follow. But she didn't. Not right away. She called out from behind me.

"You left us!" she cried.

I didn't turn around, but I stopped.

"One minute you were there and the next Dad had this old lady cooking and Kendall's trying to buddy up to me and share fucking makeup tips." She ran up to me and got in front where I could see the veins of mascara down her cheeks. "What about our Wednesday lunch? Have you thought about that once? Huh? Because I've thought about it for three Wednesdays and you didn't even call me."

"This is the drugs talking."

"Oh, bullshit. You are such a bullshit liar."

I had to take a deep breath. I was the adult, and I wouldn't be baited.

"It would be inappropriate for me to make plans with you. I'm sorry about that. But I miss you too, Willow. Ever since I was fired I've missed you guys."

The muscles in her face went slack, and her jaw dropped enough to leave her lips parted.

"Fired?"

"You thought I quit?"

She looked away, staring into the middle distance, as if watching the movie of the past few weeks on the big screen in her head.

"They said you left."

"It doesn't matter. Come with me."

She came, suddenly a kid again, docile, obedient, and overdressed.

I found a security guard. He hurried over to me. I plastered a smile on my face and gave him Willow's bag. "Can you make sure this young lady gets home?"

Willow didn't say a word to me as she was led away. Good chance her driver was waiting at the bottom of the hill. She'd get home fine. I was going to have to call Ray and tell him what happened. I dreaded it. I dreaded talking to him and getting Willow in trouble. But she was still a child. She didn't have any rights yet, and thank God for that. She wasn't ready for them.

Now to deal with the other adolescent in my life. This one had his own house and a new daughter, and he was my boss.

CHAPTER 26

BRAD

"I don't want anyone in this part of the house. Off-limits. If I find anyone but my daughter or her nannies back here . . ." Paula and the security guard waited for me to finish. I'd gotten the biggest, scariest-looking one to stand at the hall to Nicole's room.

"You got it," he said. "No problem."

People had started arriving. Music had started playing, and I had a feeling I was going to regret this.

"The bombshell and the nannies are on their way back," Paula said when we got to the kitchen. It was bare. One drawing stuck to the fridge. Me, Nicole, and Cara. Blakely was a little to the side. Nicole had written all the names on the top. I was so happy she could write them I nearly had the thing framed.

"Who's on tonight?" I knew Cara was on because I counted the days, but sometimes they switched.

"The dark-haired one. It'll be fine. Don't you worry your head about it. I have it all under control."

"Thank you, Paula. It means a lot to throw this party for Arnie. I couldn't do it without you."

She blushed a little. Sometimes I thought she still had it for me, and sometimes I thought I should just up and tell her it wasn't going to happen. But I couldn't afford to lose her. Couldn't risk being right and shaming her into quitting or being wrong and offending her into walking out.

"You just have fun tonight." She patted my chest. She was from the South. We touched each other. I didn't think anything of it until that night when her fingers lingered a little too long.

"I'll try."

The script sat on the counter. I'd wanted *Bangkok Brotherhood* so bad a year ago I'd auditioned for it. I just wanted it. There hadn't been any bad consequences to getting it. Only upside. Now I had a daughter and a schedule to keep. I had to be in Thailand prepared or, as Ken liked to remind me, I'd never work again.

I put the script in the silverware drawer and slapped it closed.

I needed to get back to the script when I was fresh, but in the morning I was going to get sidelined by calls and daily bullshit. Questions. Decisions. I'd seen three schools and in the end I was going to do exactly what Cara said I should have done in the first place. She was competent. I couldn't say the same for myself. The enormity of my responsibility made me want to give it to someone else. At least when Nicole was out of the room. That was when I decided I wasn't making another decision for or about her ever again. Then she showed up with those dimples and that sense of humor. Or she'd make a bratty demand, and I knew I could handle her because I figured it wasn't so bad. The little crises like a bathing suit or a pair of shoes were kind of fun.

I kind of wanted to hang out with her more than I wanted to throw a party.

A little.

Maybe the party could go on, and Nicole and I could go get ice cream or something. I'd get back by the time stuff started rolling and—

"Mr. Daddy!" Britt Ravenor came in with a bottle in each hand and hugged me, landing big lipstick kisses all over my face. Her girlfriend piled on, and I forgot I wanted to hang out with my daughter.

CHAPTER 27

CARA

It wasn't uncommon for an A-list actor or studio head to have staff constantly move in, out, and about the house. Housekeepers, assistants, cooks, nannies, and security moved around freely during assigned hours. But the party I walked into was beyond what I'd seen before. Too many people in the house. Too many bikini bottoms. Too many nipples. Too many drinks. What the hell was he thinking? The music was thumping the entire house.

Nicole and I hung out for a while building block towers and knocking them down. Doing a puzzle. Playing pretend princesses. I got her bathed and put to bed. Luckily, the swim had exhausted her. The party had become a low rumble. I didn't realize the power of it until I got to the main part of the house. By then, I was white-hot, scanning the laughing, beautiful faces for Brad.

Waste of time. The man had his own magnetic field. He was talking to some stunning young girl with his bare foot on the coffee table. All smiles and charm, exposed legs, and tanned hand on a beer. Sunglasses flipped to the top of his head.

"Sinclair!"

I couldn't have yelled louder, but he barely acknowledged me until I was two feet away. Then he looked over.

"Yeah?"

"What are you doing?"

The stunning young thing looked me up and down with an unmasked sneer. What a waste of a pretty face.

"Throwing a birthday party." He shrugged.

I was dismissed.

I had no right to do what I did next. I was an employee. I was not the mother of his child, nor was I the head of the household. I was nobody. Infinitely replaceable. Exactly nothing. Stating my opinion of him, his action, his attitude was so far out of my contractual obligations that I expected to be thrown out as soon as I finished.

I pushed him. Literally.

"You're an asshole." I had a moment where I could have paused, or run away, or calmed myself. But he looked so stricken, I saw an opening, and in my anger I went right into it. "You should have given her up for adoption if this is what you're going to do. Because I've seen this go down before. I've seen how this shakes out. You make this her normal and she's going to be snorting coke by middle school. In Malibu. With a driver and a Prada bag, yeah, all that. And she's not going to know where she ends and the paparazzi begin. She's going to be a target for the media unless you protect her. You're the only one between her and . . ." And what? Getting pawed at by an older guy behind the hedge? "Look at you! *Look at you!*"

I could have said it ten more times.

We'd earned an audience, and though the music hadn't stopped, all conversation had. Paula stepped between us, facing me, and held her arms out.

"We're all going to take a deep breath and—"

"You want to look at me?" Brad shouted past Paula as he slapped his beer on the coffee table.

"Look at how you're acting!" I leaned around Paula, even as she shifted to block me. "You have a child in the other room."

He unbuttoned his pants. When everyone gasped, she turned and saw him over her shoulder.

"Bradley!" Paula scolded. "Do not—"

"Get a good look!"

He spun around and dropped his drawers, mooning me with his perfect ass.

The room went into uproarious laughter, hoots, and shouts. Camera phones were out. Brad shook it for me. I wasn't angry anymore. I was humiliated. Cowed completely.

Paula made a show of covering her eyes. "Oh my good Lord Jesus what are you—"

For the third time, she wasn't allowed to complete a sentence.

"Daddy! Your butt is out!" Nicole cried in her pajamas. She obviously hadn't been as exhausted as I thought.

Maybe I would have gotten angry again. Maybe I would have found a way to stay and protect her. Maybe my heart would have softened another ten degrees if one of the caterers hadn't been holding up a tray of glasses. She didn't expect a five-year-old still in her pajamas and bare feet. She only tried to dodge a chair and tripped on Nicole.

For a second, time stopped.

The server kept the tray aloft while keeping her feet under her, but weight plus momentum plus the slippery wet platter resulted in a show-stopping *crash*.

Nicole stood in the center of a minefield of melting ice and broken glass.

"Don't move!" Brad shouted.

"Get her out of here!" Paula pointed at me with one hand and Nicole with the other.

Before I could tell Paula that nothing would make me happier, Nicole melted into loud, blubbery sobs.

Brad tiptoed through the glass and lifted her to safety. The staff descended on the mess with towels.

When he turned, he and I were face-to-face, Nicole crying on his shoulder. The music rose. The chatter came back, and he and I were still locked, not speaking.

Not with words, at least.

His anger was still all over his face, but it veiled something else. Something deeper. Regret? Understanding?

He just mooned you to make a point.

"I'll pack my things," I said.

He didn't answer, and though I should have just walked off and done what I said I was going to do, he held me fast with his stare.

"Your résumé said you have a first aid certificate."

"So?"

He looked down. I looked down. A pool of blood spread beneath his foot.

"You're a mess," I said.

"Can you fix it, doc?"

"Only if you promise to never show me your butt again."

"Can't promise that, sorry. I'm just going to have to rely on the kindness in your heart."

I should have politely refused, because I couldn't be in that house another minute. But what was it about mistakes? Why were they so sticky? They rolled along, picking up other mistakes, growing into a ball of unstoppable bad habits on an ever-steeper incline. A dozen people could have looked at his foot, but I had to do it because he challenged my kindheartedness.

"Lean on me," I said, about to enter into my eleventy-millionth mistake. "I put the kit in Nicole's bathroom."

He put his arm around my shoulder, while his other arm held his daughter. He smelled of pool chlorine and alcohol, leaning on me to hop to the bathroom as he fist-bumped his buddies, promising to return to the good times. When we got to the private part of the house, his hand cupped my shoulder instead of hanging off it. Like the waterline creeping forward on the beach, the dreams seeped into my mind. The pool table. His hands on me. The way I came when he entered me.

Remember the part where he pulled his pants down like a child?

I did. And this was a symptom of being a heterosexual woman of childbearing age who hadn't had sex or male attention in too long. But his hand felt good on my shoulder, and after yelling at him in front of a room full of people, I needed to feel good.

CHAPTER 28

BRAD

Nicole's bathroom looked like a bloody crime scene and Cara was a sadistic fucking criminal. I sat on the purple kid-size chair. Cara sat on the pink-and-green plastic stool we kept by the sink so my daughter could reach the faucet. My foot rested in her lap as she dug tweezers into my skin. She'd put Nicole in bed and closed the door behind us.

"Big one coming," she said. If it was so big, why did she need the goggles? Was she trying to look like a fierce fucking human-torturing alien from Venus?

"Ow! Jesus!"

She held up a bloody shard, smiling.

"Are you all right, Daddy?" Nicole asked from the other side of the door.

"I'm fine, pumpkin."

Clink. The shard went into a tray. Sadist.

"You have nice feet," she said, angling the tweezers to grab another piece of glass.

"Thank you."

"Can't say the same for your ass."

"My ass isn't nice?"

I was actually offended. Deeply hurt. I'd been called worse, but coming from her it cut deep.

"Nope." She pulled at the skin on the bottom of my foot to expose the glass. Or to turn me on a little. Just a little. Between her hands on me and the way she stuck my heel between her legs, I was turned on just a little.

A lot. If I had to split hairs, she was turning me on a lot, and I had no idea if she intended it or if this was just Cara being Cara.

"I get paid good money for that ass."

"Well, it's not nice."

"You're making some comment about the circumstances."

She pulled the goggles to the top of her head. Her eyes were ringed red from the edge of the eye gear and her hair made crazy spikes around the strap.

"The *circumstances*?"

"You came at me like a wild banshee."

". . . and so you mooned me?"

"You treated me like a child in front of people I work with."

"Then you acted like one?"

"It's my job to make the story fun. That's what I did."

She slid her goggles back down and inspected my foot, wielding the tweezers with her mouth pressed tight. She must be stung from losing the argument. I wouldn't rub it in. I liked having her attention on me. Liked her hands. I leaned back on the plastic chair, soaking in my victory. I was going to take it easy on her. I was drunk on pain and forgiveness. Her thumb along my skin. Yeah. Gentle and confident. My dick woke up a little and I was just relaxed enough to not give a god damn that she was off-limits.

The music still came in loud and clear from downstairs. I was torn between missing my own party and settling into the way she touched me.

"I have a comeback for that, you know," she said. With her eyes not grabbing all my attention, I got a chance to really look at those lips. The top one was slightly bee stung, and the bottom one was trapped under her teeth as she bit it in concentration.

"Oh, yeah?" I linked my fingers together over my stomach. "Tell me your comeback."

And if it involves those lips around my dick.

She pulled a piece of glass out of my foot. No pain.

"That it's my job to protect Nicole, and by yelling at you I was protecting her. It's a pretty good comeback, as they go. But then you'd come back with, 'No, it's her father's job to protect her,' and I'd say, 'Nice job, Daddy,' and I'd win the battle but lose the war."

Too-fucking-shay.

"No one told me there was a war," I said.

"There is." She dropped the tweezers in the sink and took off the goggles, plucking a little spray bottle out of the kit. "There's a war for Nicole. And you win. No matter what. You can and should do whatever you need to. It's my job to make sure she doesn't die on my shift."

She sprayed my foot and I jumped. She held the ankle steady while she burned the fucking skin off. All I could say was *ah ah ah.*

"But I'm sorry I came at you like that. You could fire me for much less. Probably should."

"I guess we're even then, from the shower."

She stared at my foot, but not really *at* it. More *through* it.

"That night, you came home from the SAG event late."

"Yeah?"

"Do you remember anything? How you got in the bed?"

Oh, shit. My mouth, my throat, my guts went dry.

"My pants were on." My only defense.

"You're welcome."

"What happened?"

Her eyes darkened and I panicked. I'd wanted her, but had I taken something I shouldn't have?

"Nothing. You talked a lot of nonsense. I got your shoes and shirt off and put you to bed."

"Thank you."

She squirted the open wounds again and I shouted.

"Daddy?" Nicole's voice came from the other side of the door. "Are you okay? Really?"

"He's fine!"

"She's killing me!"

Cara cracked a smile. It was a gorgeous sight.

"Hey! Don't kill Daddy!"

Nicole wasn't kidding. Her voice was soaked in terror. We looked at each other. Right. Death should be off the table.

I leaned for the door and swung it open. Nicole trotted in with a little drawing pad in one hand and a pencil in the other. She nearly impaled me with it as she hopped onto my lap and turned to face Cara. From my vantage point I could see her point the pencil at her nanny. I had to imagine her tough little face.

"Don't. Kill. Daddy."

"I won't." She split the paper off the back of a Band-Aid and stuck it on me. "But if he keeps it up, I might have to hurt him just a little."

"Okay," Nicole agreed.

"*Okay?*" I objected. My dad had always complained there was a female conspiracy in the house, and I started to think he might be right.

As if she wanted to confirm the conspiracy, Nicole turned to face me, practically kneeing me in the groin. Even though she was on my lap she waved her fingers at me to get me closer. She whispered in my ear.

"I like Miss Cara."

"Okay."

She put her finger to her lips.

"Shush." She ran her fingers over my lips.

"Zip it. Lock it." She opened my chest pocket and dropped the little pad into it. "Put it in your pocket."

"I'm zipped." I looked past her and saw Cara smiling. Nicole fished her little pad back out and sat frontward. I took her hair in my hands, separating strands.

"You always make these pretty braids," I said, crossing one strand over the other. Then another. It made a mess. "You need to teach me."

"It's easy," Nicole said, as if she'd ever done it.

"What are you working on?" Cara pointed to the little pad before she got another Band-Aid from the box. I settled into the painless part of the process.

Nicole flipped through the little spiral notebook until she found her page.

"It's a unicorn." She showed me with her pencil as a pointer. "And that's her brother. He's a Pegasus."

"Wow," I said. "It's kind of really good." I held it up for Cara. "Is this normal?"

"She's ahead in fine motor and verbal skills, if that's what you mean."

"And she can read." I kissed her nose. "You're amazing."

She waved her hand in front of her nose. "Daddy, you smell bad."

My phone beeped and buzzed. I got it out. Arnie.

—*Dude*—

Right. I had a life I was living. The music seemed louder once the spell of these two was broken. I had friends downstairs and things I was doing. I had a movie to make and a staycation to take. I'd gotten distracted from my distractions by my favorite distraction.

He sent me another text right after.

—*Are you fucking the nanny?*—

133

Fuck. What a douchebag.

—NO!—

I put the phone away and slid Nicole off my lap.

"I have to go."

I had to prove immediately that I wasn't fucking the nanny. And not because I cared what anyone thought about me. Shit, I'd just pulled my ass out in front of twenty people with camera phones and DMZ's e-mail. But because it wasn't good for anyone to think Cara was doin' the daddy.

Nicole flipped a page and held it up.

"This is my pony."

"Nice." I looked to Cara. "You're on tonight?"

"Yes," she said with a hint of suspicion.

"You need to buy me this pony," Nicole said with flat seriousness.

"Okay." I patted her head. Literally. I patted her head and promised her a pony. That was how much I wanted to get downstairs in less time than it would take me to hop out of the nanny's bed and get dressed. "It might get loud tonight, so bring her to the pool house if you need to."

Her reaction was swift and angry, and she held it back. I saw it. One nanosecond she gritted her teeth and the next she smiled like a game show host.

"Sure."

I left, gimping on the sliced foot, smoothing my hair down so it didn't suggest a just-fucked-her look. I was halfway down the stairs before I thought about that.

Why did it matter what people thought? Why was I protecting her? She was a big girl. She was doing her job, and I was keeping my hands off her. Done and done.

CHAPTER 29

CARA

—Cara. It's Ray—

As if Ray Heywood wasn't in my contacts. As if I wouldn't know his number straight off or I'd wiped him from my phone. Nicole's room was getting dark, and the freshly bathed little girl had gotten to sleep while I reclined next to her.

—Willow says she saw you? Can you call me?—

If I called him, he'd hear the music and the party downstairs. I didn't want him to. And I didn't want to wake up Nicole, who was sleeping on my shoulder. And I didn't want to navigate the minefield of Willow's word against mine in real time. I had no doubt she lied. She was a good girl, but there wasn't a sane eighth-grader in Hollywood. Puberty was a gateway drug to adolescence, and everyone overdosed.

—Can't talk now. Sorry—

—She's still pretty shaken up—

I had no idea what she'd told her father. I was sure it was all my fault. Maybe it was. Maybe I'd been too much of an employee and not enough of a leader. I looped one arm over Nicole, and I held up the phone with the other hand so I could type.

> *—I don't work for you anymore. So I'm just going to come out and say what I think.—*

Was I going to do this? I hit Send but still . . . I could backtrack. Soften it. Right?

As if in direct answer, a bottle fell downstairs. Nicole's room looked onto the pool, and as the party had continued into the night, my disappointment in humanity had grown deeper.

> *—She was at Brad Sinclair's party this afternoon. No friends. Just her. Not appropriate. Total cry for help. You're lucky. It could have been real bad—*

More? Was I going to go for it? You bet I was.

> *—You and Kendall aren't her buddies. She's a good kid, but she needs supervision and guidance. Parents.—*

I waited for the long-winded reply defending his parenting and his daughter. Instead, I got something much shorter.

—Call me when you can. I want to talk—

———

My job with Ray Heywood hadn't been terrible. Actually, it had been great. Maybe that's why it hurt to lose it.

Ray Heywood was a single dad living and working in Los Angeles. He never looked at me as an available bed buddy or gave me a hard time about how I managed the house. He was just completely disengaged, and as Hollywood parents went, that was as good as it got.

My last day on the job started like every other day. The kids were at school. I'd made them their breakfasts, packed their lunches, made sure Willow had her homework, confirmed the robotics tournament for Saturday, and piled them into my car. I'd dropped them at two separate private schools across Los Angeles, promised to come back at two thirty and four thirty for pickup, and driven back to the house where I'd intended to pick up Jedi's toys, then make annual doctors' appointments.

When I'd gotten back, Raymond was on the couch in his linen suit, looking as if his dog just died.

But he hadn't. Frisky was at his feet, slapping his tail against the Mivondo rug, waiting for me to get back so I could feed him.

"Hi," I said, glancing at the clock. Ray was never home at nine a.m. Not unless there was a parent-teacher conference, and sometimes not even then. He was rarely home for dinner or bedtime either. He was a "quality time" parent. A week in Disney with all the trappings. Summer in Aruba. Skiing at the Aspen resort. Parenting as if cramming for a test. I couldn't complain. I liked Aruba and I liked his kids.

"You all right?" I'd asked, hanging my coat. I lined Jedi's shoes up with Willow's. Jedi's special talent was laughter. He wasn't detail-oriented, and I chased him around all day, picking up, straightening, putting away as he laughed his way through life.

"I'm fine. Just wanted to chat."

He'd indicated I sit across from him, which was awkward. I'd sat in any chair I wanted for the past two years. I'd sat with him and worked on middle school applications for Willow. I'd briefed him for the interviews and done research on which schools she'd like. She'd get into all of them, of course. Not only could she go wherever she wanted on her own steam, but her father was a household name that was feared and respected.

I'd been immune to his white teeth and swoopy little coif. He wore a big silver ring on his middle finger and a leather strap thing on his wrist.

"Okay." I sat across from him. "Teacher recs go in this week. I think the administration's going to call Jeannie at Harvard Westlake for her, but she really likes Marlborough. They won't push her for both, so—"

"This isn't about Willow."

"Oh. Okay." That was all we'd talked about in the past month as he got in late from his girlfriend's place and left early for morning call. So it could be anything.

"I think you're probably the best nanny I've ever seen. All my friends are jealous."

He'd smiled with his big white Chiclets as if he got personal pleasure from the envy of others.

"Thank you."

"The kids. They love you. I think . . ." He tapped his thumbs together. "I think they think of you as more mother than their mother."

Their mother lived in Humboldt County. When her acting jobs dried up and the divorce went through, she'd moved there with a boyfriend and grew weed full time. Raymond had done the impossible in the state of California and gotten primary custody. The kids Skyped with their mother once a week. It was uncomfortable, and Willow got sullen whenever the call came through.

"I'm not a replacement," I said, citing the nanny mantra. "Just a supplement."

"Right, well, that makes this really hard, is what I'm trying to say."

Ah.

Crap.

The surface of my skin had gone cold.

There was only one conversation an employer started that way.

"This? This is hard?" I asked. He was going to say it. I wasn't saving him the trouble because I still didn't believe it.

"I have to let you go."

There it was.

"Why?"

"I'll give you references anywhere you want to go."

"Why?"

"I'll say the kids got older and—"

"Do not make me ask you again."

I used my bossy voice. The voice that dropped an octave. The voice that meant business. Jedi picked his shit up and Willow did her homework when I used that voice. Raymond's tan went gray and his jaw slacked a little. God, I didn't know whether to slap him for being a wuss or crawl under a rock for pole-vaulting my boundaries.

I held my breath and my tongue. Those references were important.

"It's Kendall," he'd said, opening his hands as if he were presenting a gold box full of high-quality motives instead of yet another relationship with yet another actress. "She's . . . you know she's a Hollywood girl. She sees someone . . ."—he made an open-handed vertical hand motion toward me—"a woman living with me."

"It's not like that. Did you explain that it's not like that?"

"I did. But you have to admit, Cara, there's no hiding." He made that motion again, up and down my body.

"I dress modestly."

"I know, I know. You're a professional. But, look," he shrugged, "she's worried. And if she's going to marry me, she wants to know there isn't a second beautiful woman down the hall."

Oh, they were getting married. At least he was buying the cow that was dropping shit all over the house.

His house.

Now Kendall's house.

Not my house.

"I debated whether I should tell you the truth, but I think I owed you that much."

Again, he wasn't being an asshole. God I wanted to be so mad and I couldn't be.

"Thank you for the references."

"I'll cut you a check for six months' severance."

"Thank you. I'll pack."

I shot up and walked to the stairs.

"Do you want to wait for the check?" he called from behind me.

Did I want to wait for money?

Yeah. I did. I also wanted to call Kendall and explain to her that her future husband was not attractive to me at all. I'd heard him fight with his ex-wife. I'd seen him ditch his kids for a screw. I'd never seen him hand either of his children a morsel of food when they were hungry. He doled out compliments like potato chips, but they were brittle and slippery and nutrient-free. He was a grotesquerie of trending fashion statements and in his eyes I could see the bitter, entitled old man he was going to become.

I wanted to tell her I wasn't a threat to her, but she wouldn't believe it.

I'd dug my suitcase from the back of my closet. I'd been with the Heywoods since I was twenty-two. Two years. I'd gotten a master's in child development in that time. It had been worth it, but I wasn't ready to leave.

"You don't have to pack so fast." Raymond stood in the door, his face and body stiff with concern.

"I don't want Kendall to think I'm going to try and get you in bed before I go. What your fiancée thinks is important. Seriously. You need to show her you care about her feelings and you'll do what she wants. I don't want to mess with what you have with her."

I was being disingenuous. I believed what I said, but I didn't think giving Kendall what she wanted would ever satisfy her.

I plopped a pile of clothes from my drawer into the suitcase. "I can come by a few times to help with the transition."

"I don't have anyone to pick up Jedi today," he said. "The new lady isn't coming until late this afternoon, and I have to get to work."

The pile of jeans hovered over the suitcase. I'd stopped thinking about packing when my brain overloaded.

He'd already hired someone.

And he was asking me to pick up Jedi, who got out of kindergarten at two thirty and not Willow, who got out of robotics class at four thirty, because he already had someone for later in the afternoon.

"Did the kids know?" I asked.

"No. I'll tell them later. You should just drop him off."

He hooked his thumbs in his front pockets and tapped his fingers on his thighs.

"Let me pick up both kids. Let me talk to them. Let me cook for them one more time and eat with them so I can answer their questions. Have whomever it is start after dinner."

"No. We're doing it this way."

This is why you don't get attached to the kids. This is why you do your job and think about something else and try to have your own relationships. You protect your heart as if your life depended on it. And you fail, but you try.

I snapped the suitcase shut.

"I'll take that check now."

———

Nicole wasn't generally a deep sleeper, but I had to get out from under her. It had gotten dark an hour ago, and I had to use the bathroom. Carefully, inch by inch, I slid out, tucked her in, and did my business.

When I got back to the bedside, I looked out the window. I could see the pool house, where my own bed was, the pool itself, the people surrounding it, mellowed by the night. The music had slowed too. It would be harder to slip back to my room without being noticed.

I wasn't cut out for this.

What did Ray want? What was happening with Willow? What would happen to Nicole if I left?

She'd be fine.

They'll all be fine.

I had no power. No control. No say in any of it. And I could be wrong about anything because they weren't my kids, and I'd never have my own.

Let it go.

On the patio, Brad bro-hugged some guy. On ground level, in the daylight, I could probably identify him. But from Nicole's room he was just a guy talking to my boss, a loyal man with huge talent, a relaxed demeanor, and an earnest sense of humor.

He was just another thing I wanted but wasn't allowed to think about wanting.

Self-pity tasted worse than a hangover. I hated it.

I left, walked down the hall, the steps, through the living area, the floor wiped to a sterile shine. The screen door was open. I closed it behind me and skirted the outer edge of the pool area, taking my powerlessness with me.

CHAPTER 30

BRAD

I was at the mellow stage of the evening, but the evening hadn't caught up. I sidelined at the pool watching everyone dance and swim. The bartender flirted. The security guys made themselves scarce. The DJ I hired at the last minute was famous in his own right, and shit was going nuts.

And I was Mr. Pensive holding the same warm beer for twenty minutes. I didn't fight it. Mellow was all right.

I saw Cara slip out the back door and make her way around the pool fence. Walking quickly, her hair bobbed in the rhythm of her steps. Sensible flats for chasing a kid around. Jeans and blouse that would have looked dumpy on any other woman looked sexy as hell on her.

If I was thinking about settling down, which I wasn't . . . but if I was thinking about it, she was exactly the kind of woman I'd look for. Even without Nicole. It wasn't about that. She wasn't afraid to speak her mind, and her mind was really on point. She could shoot a mean game of nine-ball.

None of that was even on my radar, if I was being honest with myself. That was after-the-fact shit. And the fact was she turned me on.

She wasn't supposed to. But man oh man, something about the canned peaches scent and the body she tried to hide.

I knew what she had, and it was perfect. Even through the steam on the shower doors.

I didn't realize I was deep down the rabbit hole until Arnie crossed paths with her. Said a few words with a laugh. Shit. Nothing that came out of that guy's mouth was anything I wanted Cara to hear.

She said something back and as she walked away, he slapped her ass.

I was halfway across the yard before I consciously decided to move.

"Arnie, you stupid fuck."

He had his hands out as if to say, "What did I do?"

Fuck him. I could deal with him later.

I chased her.

"Cara," I called.

She turned.

"I'm sorry, for him. About him. Whatever. Not whatever. Fuck!"

I hadn't felt inadequate since I moved to Los Angeles. I got breaks few of my friends got. Girls worshipped me. Look, that's the fact. I could sugarcoat it in humility, but you wouldn't believe it. I was a king and a hero as far as I could see.

Well, right then I felt two dollars short for the ninety-nine-cent lunch.

"It's fine."

"No, it's not."

She leaned on one foot and looked up.

"Okay it's not fine. Just keep him away from me, okay?"

"I will."

"I have the monitor." She indicated the pool house but didn't look at me. Like she *couldn't*.

"Sure, sure."

Dude. She wants you. Do you see how she can't look at you?

I was making stuff up in my head. And it didn't matter. She was an employee. The most beautiful employee I had. The most essential. The warmest. Biggest pain in my fucking ass—

She went through the obstacle course of people and furniture, taking the most direct route to the back. I followed her as if she had me on a string.

I couldn't let her go. She drew a circle of sanity and caught me in it. I needed five minutes of her time. She relaxed me. Made my life seem just a little less crazy. I didn't know what I wanted out of her, but I couldn't get that mellow back while I wanted her against reason.

I got to her at the gate to the pool house.

"Have you ever been to Thailand?"

"Yes," she said, still walking fast. "Why?"

"I have this movie—"

"*Bangkok Brotherhood.*" She put her hand on the gate as if she was about to push it open. Behind me someone dove into the pool.

"How did you know?"

"It's my job to know." The music was lower past the pool. I wouldn't have heard her otherwise. She still hadn't looked at me. Fast-fleeting impressions. Her black lashes as she looked down. The rippling turquoise light from the pool on one side of her face and darkness on the other. A woman laughing in the house. The crickets on the pool house side of the gate. The creak of the earth grinding up against my life.

"I don't know what to do," I said. "I'm confused every day. But I can't go without her. And I can't go without you."

"My thirty days is over during that shoot."

Was she being hostile? What was with the pointed look, or the way her head tilted so her hair fell along her cheek? I needed her. Her presence made Nicole's life easy and my responsibilities bearable. But there was more to it. She drew me in. Her competence wasn't comforting. It fueled a desire that all the wild girls in the world hadn't.

"I'll double your rate," I said.

"You don't think you're bringing her, do you?"

"Pardon me?" I said, reacting before thinking. I was trying to be polite, but she countered by holding her hands up as if fending me off.

"Never mind. Sorry. You're fine. Your call, totally."

She stepped back, spun, opened the gate to the pool house. She was going to go to bed. I didn't want to be alone in my overcrowded house. Didn't want to end the night on that note.

"Wait." I leapt to her side, closing the gate behind me. She erupted in light. Motion sensors. I'd had them installed all along the path to the house.

She spun on me.

"Mr. Sinclair. I have no say in where you take her or what you do."

"Let me hear your say anyway."

She crossed her arms. Paused. Thinking before she spoke. I liked that. A woman who engaged the engine before putting the car in drive was a rare thing in my world. Or maybe not. Maybe I just enjoyed her engine a little more.

"You sure?" She looked up at me suspiciously. Her eyes changed color constantly, and at the back door they were navy blue with brown flecks. I had a strange and inappropriate thought about what beautiful children she'd make.

"I'm sure. Spit it out."

She didn't. She took another second to look toward the pool where the party was in full swing, then back at me.

"Anything I say is said because I care."

"Got it. Moving on."

"And because I want you to succeed."

"Train's pulling out of the station, miss. Better get on it."

"Okay. First off. You really haven't dealt with this at all. Not that I blame you. Having a child dropped in your lap out of nowhere is an

146

adjustment even for people who are prepared. But you haven't stopped the partying or the working one iota since she arrived."

I bristled, but acted like I didn't. Good thing I was an actor.

"I've cut the partying by a lot, I'll have you know."

"Well, I'll trust you on that. But all these people make it hard for you to get to know each other. And the work. Whenever Paula's over, you chase Nicole out, and Paula's over ten hours a day."

"I have to work. I'm not the only one in town working."

"You're the only one in town with a kid you never met."

Man, she was so close to the line where I'd tell her to pack up. She was right on the fucking thing. But the other side of that line was a cliff. She had no idea what was at stake—everything I ever worked for and wanted—because Nicole had shown up.

"Your parents did a great job while they were here, but they're from a different world and all their kids are adults. They didn't set you up with routines. Habits. Events she can count on. And now you're going to take her to Thailand with you?"

"What am I supposed to do? Leave her here?"

"Stay home."

Stay home. Sure. And let a $120 million movie fall through. Tell them to just cast another bankable guy who happened to be available right now. Because anyone who's bankable isn't scheduled a year in advance. Yeah. That was going to work out great when I couldn't get another picture because I was a flight risk.

I think I laughed, or some snide version of it.

Her face went soft, dropping from hard truth to a malleable reality I didn't understand.

"I can't watch this. It's too much." She paced across the dark path, tripping the lights as she walked.

Jesus. She kept moving that god damned line.

"You're not supposed to get emotionally involved, you know!" I called out.

She stopped and stayed still long enough for the lights to flick out. I held my breath. The moonlight fell blue on her hair, and she looked like she could just fold into the darkness.

I kept my breath. Didn't need air. Wouldn't know what to do with it.

She turned so slowly the lights didn't register it.

"You're right," she said. "That's why this is temporary. That's why I didn't want to work for a celebrity household. Because I can't stand seeing kids getting dragged all over the world or orphaned by their parents' jobs. I've seen it done well and I've seen it done right, but it's not often."

She walked down the path and the lights followed.

This was bullshit. I ran out and got in front of her.

"Lady. You have no idea what you're talking about. I've done the best I can. I was going along pretty-as-you-please before this bombshell dropped—"

"She's not a bombshell. She's not a problem to solve. She's a human being you made. You don't see her. You don't see how hard she's working to deal with what happened."

"What about you?"

"What—?"

"What are you dealing with?"

"As your consultant, I advise . . ." She stopped talking, letting her advice hang midair. I wanted it. I wanted to pluck it out of dead space and take it, whatever it was.

"What?"

"I advise . . ." She took a deep breath. "You seem all right."

"What kind of advice is that?"

"What do you want for her? For you? What were you hoping for?"

The idea that I was hoping for anything was ridiculous. I laughed. It had a sardonic edge, what my grandmother would have called "laughing outta two sides of your face."

"I ain't had a chance to hope for much, ma'am. I was just going about my business. I was a happy guy, you know? All I had to do was work and be nice to people. So you'll excuse me if I have to adjust."

"You never thought about it? When you saw your friend Michael Greydon adopt six kids, what did you think? Anything?"

I didn't know if she was implying I was deficient. Would she? And what *did* I think of my buddy marrying a lady-pap and adopting six kids?

"Figured it would happen at some point. The normal way. Girl, then wife, then baby. And I think he's crazy. Fucking nuts. He can't go out without asking his wife. Can't take a dump without having a kid banging on the door. He had a career . . . a real career. Now he's doing one movie a year and spending the rest of the time in legit theater so he can be home. What the hell is that? Is that me? Is that Brad Sinclair? Mike didn't work his way out of a lumberyard in Arkansas, all right? He was born royalty. That's not even an option for me, so this little girl? She's gonna have to roll with it."

Cara tapped her finger against her bicep and watched me as I had a mini meltdown. Didn't move. Jesus Christ, she was so in control. How did she do that?

I should have been ashamed of having a tirade. Mom had a way of making me so embarrassed of my tantrums that I stopped. *How do you like that now? Everyone seeing your insides? Pretty as a wild boar, I'd say.*

Somehow, Cara didn't make me feel like that. I felt safe. Weirdly safe. Uncomfortably safe.

"What?" I asked.

"I was an afterthought. My parents love me, but they didn't know what to do with us. We were an inconvenience. That was how I felt. And when I see other kids having to bend their lives around their parents' careers? It makes me sad, and I want to solve it for them. But there's no solving it. And here I am again."

"Wow." That was more information than I ever thought she'd give about herself, and I wanted to answer every word. I wanted to tell her that she wasn't anyone's inconvenience. Her parents loved her. They had to. Who wouldn't?

"Do all the nannies talk like that?"

"Only the ones with thirty-day contracts."

She was leaving. I kept forgetting that. Figured it would work itself out so she'd stay. Obviously, that hope was one-sided.

I wasn't used to chasing women. They chased me or appeared right and ready where I needed them. But this one was different in every way. One, not a woman in the strict sense because she was staff. I was paying her to do a job. She wasn't a hanger-on or a costar. She wasn't available. I wasn't supposed to go near her. Not in that way.

But, man. Shoot me in the face. The way she ran her fingers through her hair to get it out of her face, and the way it just flopped over it again? And the crickets? And the smell of bluegrass like home. It just looked right.

For the first time, it made sense.

And fuck sense.

"You're a time bomb," I said. Filter-free Brad in full effect.

Her jaw set, and for the second time we stood still long enough for the path to flick into darkness. Her lips parted, and before another word left her mouth I was in motion.

I kissed her. I didn't know why. To smash the barrier of her hardened jaw. To sweep away the bullshit talk of consulting. Whatever. It was wrong. But at the time it seemed like the only thing to do.

She pushed me so hard I fell back a step. Disappointing, but not unprecedented. She stood back, panting. Took a gulp. I had to work hard not to smile.

I still had it.

CHAPTER 31

CARA

His lips were heaven. His hands on my face were Planet Dream and Planet Real crashing, fusing, pulling both out of orbit. I couldn't breathe, couldn't think, couldn't even groan how good he felt touching me. Better than the dreams, better than the morning orgasms he inspired.

Oh God, I was falling for this. In half a hot second, my defenses dropped with a *clang* and I let myself get hurled into deep space by that kiss, spinning and twisting, reality and fantasy joined into a single burning body.

Cara.

You're not supposed to do this.

A single, small voice threaded through my consciousness.

Then regret.

Then anger.

At him. At myself. At my body. I had to push him away violently or the push was going to turn into a caress. He took a step back and I caught my breath.

"Jesus Christ, Sinclair, what do you think you're doing?" I didn't feel bad about pushing him because the anger was still in my veins. I had to stop myself from pushing him again. I didn't think I'd be able to walk away. "Do you think I want to end up on the cover of some magazine? You think I want to get dirty looks up and down Sunset?"

This guy could ruin me. He had all the tools to do it. He was gorgeous and laid-back. He listened when I spoke and had a daughter who was just about perfect.

But I'd be on the cover of tabloids. I'd become an ugly stereotype. I'd get ditched with nothing but a bad reputation to show for it. I'd cry. I hated crying. Children cried and I soothed them by not getting all weepy myself.

There he stood, with the pool party behind him. A movie star. The most eligible bachelor in Hollywood and to me, he was an overwhelmed father with no clue how to manage his daily tasks, but formidably lit by stars. An awe-inspiring display of power and presence with a magnetism that led right to him.

Hollywood stars weren't stars just because of their light. They had a gravity generating mass and unbearable heat. Something coded in their genes, like hair color or height. I'd seen it before from the diplomats I met when I was a kid to the moms and dads I worked for in Los Angeles, and having identified it, I resisted it. Easy.

He was different. His heat seemed made for me.

It wasn't.

It was a trick. That kiss, as short and inappropriate as it was, had vibrated every cell. His taste, his scent, the feel of his lips.

I had to pack. Just pack and go. This job was tainted. Everything was tainted now. Head down, I walked to the pool house, my sexless shoes pumping in and out of my vision.

I had to go.

Never see him again.

Maybe once.

Stopping dead in my tracks with my hand on the doorknob, I laughed.

"What's so funny?" Brad asked from ten feet behind me. He held his shirttail to his lip, exposing a flat, tight washboard stomach and that god damn muscled V-thing at the waist of his low-hanging shorts.

"I've lost my mind, that's all."

"We have something in common."

"No. Let's not do this. Look—"

"Look, I—"

He stopped himself when we said the same thing at the same time . . .

"I'm sorry."

What was I apologizing for? Being kissed? Being watched in the shower? What the hell was wrong with me?

"You keep having to apologize for inappropriate behavior," I said, then I opened the door and walked in. He stood just outside, backlit by the front light. It came to me that we were alone. It was dark. He'd just kissed me in a moment of weakness. I could claim weakness too, because I *was* weak. My knees barely held me, and my body gushed with desire.

"Don't be done," he said, his voice stroking under my clothes. Which was all in my mind. The result of a year without a date. But I couldn't breathe right, and my nipples got hard under my cotton bra.

My feelings were as inappropriate as his actions, and I had no control over either.

"I don't know what to do," I said. I was being too honest. I was about to cross into unprofessional.

"Tell me what to do then."

I don't know where I got so bold. Something in me was pushing him away because he scared the hell out of me. Or I scared the hell out of me. When he raised his eyebrow as if I'd crossed a line, something in my chest shrunk. I didn't want him to be displeased, even though I wanted him to make it easy for me and throw me out right there and then.

"Kick everyone out," I said.

He didn't hesitate to take his phone out, which was unexpected. The light shined in his face as he tapped and swiped the glass, the light casting shadows from below and lighting his blue eyes to light gray. He put the phone in his pocket, and the light under him snuffed.

"Five seconds." He didn't explain further. If he'd been unsure of himself, he wasn't now. His feet spread apart, arms crossed, chin high, music thumping behind him.

Five. Four. Three. Two. One.

Nothing changed.

"Ten, then."

Five seconds later (give or take) the music abruptly stopped. A chorus of *aw*s went up, but still, we didn't move. The pathway lights flicked out. Then the voices and splashing were over. Then the undulations of the turquoise light slowed. Still we said nothing, just regarded each other. I didn't know what he felt. Couldn't have guessed at it. He could have any woman he wanted, any time he wanted. The most glamorous, sophisticated women in the world were at his beck and call.

But maybe the things he didn't remember saying were true. Maybe he did want me.

I took care of children for a living. In order to do my job, I had to wear sensible clothes and speak in a lilting singsong voice. Nothing about me could have been desirable to a man like him.

Yet, in those seconds, with his eyes on me in the darkness, I tingled everywhere my skin was covered, as if his vision burned through my clothes.

"You have the monitor," he said, fully stepping into the house. In the new silence, his voice resonated against the sound of the crickets and the pool filter.

He stood still, bare feet spread, arms crossed.

"I'm sorry," he said. "I'm not making this easy for you."

"It's not your job to make it easy for me." I shifted the little speaker from one hand to the other nervously. It hissed and crackled when it moved. "You need to start looking for new staff."

I held the monitor out. He put his hand over it, but didn't take it.

"Stay. You should really stay."

"I can't—"

I was interrupted by an ear-splitting scream from the monitor.

Nicole.

Brad spun around and bolted. I was right behind him. Out the door, running faster than the motion sensors could react, he took two long steps and vaulted over the fence. I went through the gate and skidded on the wet tiles around the pool, while Brad kept his bare feet on the grass, running across the patio, through the kitchen, past tipped bottles and a bra and a sock from somewhere. He and I ran up the stairs, down the hall, and through the white door where—

Nicole. Tears streaming, curled in a ball of pink ponies and white ruffles.

Brad scooped her up, and she screamed.

"Cara! Miss Cara!" She wiggled out of his arms, and he dropped her in mine. She wrapped her legs around my waist and her arms around my neck like a hungry boa.

She smelled of soap and powder, and she fit in my arms like an egg in a carton. There was something decidedly uncomfortable about the comfort, especially with her father standing there like a right fielder in a Little League game.

He gave half a nod and turned to exit the room. This was too easy. It was too easy for him to walk away; it was too easy for me to hold Nicole in my arms while she calmed down. It was all too facile, and it was the start of a downhill slope that led to him not being the parent he needed to be.

But that was none of my business, now was it?

Many people say that children are very intuitive. Another easy assumption is that they just know things that we don't know, and they sense what they need without ever verbalizing it. It's all too easy . . . but then something happens and all of the assumptions seem incontrovertible.

"Daddy," she cried, lifting her head. "Stay here please."

I could believe he wanted two things at once. He wanted to get out of that room and let me handle it, and he wanted to stay there just as much. The conflict wasn't in his face, because I couldn't see his expression, it was in the resigned slouch of his shoulders and the quickness with which he turned to walk back into the room.

He laid his hand on her back, and she returned her head to my shoulder.

She yawned and pointed to the bed. "It's time to sleep now."

Brad and I looked at each other in the dark room. Nicole just waited. And when we did not react quickly enough, she picked her head up and pointed to the bed again and said exactly nothing.

"Say good night to Daddy," I whispered.

"No," she demanded. "He needs to stay. You need to stay. I had a very scary dream. I am not joking."

I held my mouth tight so that I didn't laugh at her fear, but she spoke like a little adult and it was so damn cute.

"It's a twin bed, sweetheart," Brad said.

"We can fit," Nicole insisted. "Miss Cara is skinny. I'm skinny. Daddy, you can take up more room." She pointed to the bed. "Go go go, Miss Cara. Just go!"

I didn't look at Brad. I didn't even want to know what he was thinking. I just had a job to do.

I laid Nicole on the bed and tucked her under the covers. In my peripheral vision I could see Brad standing on the other side of the bed, hands in his pockets. Still couldn't see his expression. I guess I was okay with that. I had every intention of wiggling out of this.

I laid next to Nicole right on top of the covers.

"See?" Brad said. "There's no room for me."

"Miss Cara has to get under the covers." She said it as if the space between the sheets was actually some alternate dimension where I had a third of my actual mass. "We can be like a real family."

I glanced up at Brad, with his arms folded and half a smirk on his face. The perspective from below made him seem taller, broader, more confident and cocky than ever. Maybe it was having a woman in a bed, any bed. Or seeing that I was about to obey a five-year-old when I'd been so eager to tell him what to do.

I got under the covers.

Nicole scooted over, tucked her hands under her cheek, and said, "See, there's plenty of room." Her face was so close to mine it looked as if she had one big brown eye with broomstick lashes.

"I don't—"

My protest never landed. The sheets flew up as if a monsoon hit. The bed creaked and tilted to one side as Brad wiggled himself under the covers. I shifted. Nicole shifted. We fit like tablespoons nesting in the teaspoon slot. I put my arm around the girl because it had nowhere else to go. He had to do the same and I could feel the hairs on his arm so close to mine.

I picked up my head just enough to see over Nicole. He was smiling at me. When our eyes met, he winked. I put my head down. Smug little prick. Gorgeous, charming, surprisingly authentic yet unsurprisingly smug little prick.

The desire to touch him was overwhelming. I could smell him. A combination of beer and partying and something I couldn't pin down. Something *him*.

In seconds, Nicole was breathing evenly. I didn't dare speak. I didn't want to wake her. But I wanted Brad to know that once she was asleep, he could leave.

Right?

That would make sense. But he didn't leave. Even after his daughter was deep in dreamland and I could tell he was awake, he stayed. So did I. I didn't have any sleep in me. I felt his thumb graze the skin of my arm and I shuddered.

"Should I go?" I whispered.

"She expects us to stay. Both of us."

"She won't even remember in the morning."

"She's half southern. She won't forget."

"You're all southern and you forgot."

His thumb still touched my arm. I didn't move away, but I knew it wasn't right. He shouldn't be touching me, but if I moved, he'd stop.

"Did I forget something I should remember? Tell me."

I told myself a sudden movement would wake Nicole, but that wasn't the real reason I kept my arm where it was.

"Your pants were on. But you said things you didn't mean."

"About?"

The tip of his thumb stroked my arm. He wanted me. I'd dodged a hundred tabloid-shaped bullets. I'd never wanted one of my kids' fathers, and when they made a move on me, I politely declined and resigned before they could fire me.

But Brad Sinclair was different. Between getting chased to the pool house, his admissions on the steps, running to Nicole and lying here together, something had changed. *We* had changed. We'd been softened and molded. We might wake up in the morning and go back to who we'd been, but there was no morning in the dark room. Just the places where we fit and the soft voices of confession.

"I need to change the subject," I whispered. "Please."

"How are you so good with kids? It's like you know what to say to them."

"They're just people. Little, new people."

He didn't answer right away. Nicole shifted, facing him, and he stared at her sleeping face.

"I don't know what to do," he said. "I thought . . . last night I thought I should put her up for adoption. It seemed totally sane and reasonable. I had my publicist's number right there, at my fingertips. I was ready to tell him to find her a good home. Figure it out, you know. Just get out of this because I know what I have to do. I had eleven cousins. I've seen people raise kids. People without a pot to piss in. But I can't do it. I just can't. What the hell? Right? But it's not all money. I can't buy myself into being a good father. And I can't change my life. Not that much. Not unless I want to go work at the lumberyard in Redfield for ten bucks an hour, and what then? My parents and my sister would end up raising her anyway."

"You're not going to work in a lumberyard in Redfield."

"You don't know."

"You have two Oscar nominations."

He didn't seem convinced. I could have gone on about his prospects, but the lumberyard in Redfield wasn't about manual labor, or minimum wage, or long hours breathing wood dust. It was about some greater fear that had followed him to Los Angeles.

"I don't feel anything, Cara. The thing you need to be a father, I don't have it. I'm just going through the motions. She's cute and cuddly. Yeah, I like playing with her and hugging her, but on a day-to-day? She's like someone else's puppy. I mean, look at her. Who couldn't love her? Me."

I'd seen him try. Seen him show real affection and act like a father with stakes in the game. I didn't agree with every one of his choices, but it looked to me like they were made because he was trying to be the best parent he could.

"I worked for Rachel Fitzsimmons," I said. "I took care of one of her kids while she was in delivery and right after. She had postpartum real bad, and she wouldn't take any medication for it. She wanted to breast-feed. It was hard for her, because emotionally she wanted nothing to do with the baby. But every day for three months she went through nursing until she felt like she could take the medicine. And so I know this isn't the same. But sometimes you just go through the motions until you wake up and realize you loved the kid all along."

He'd moved his hand to rub his lip, as if the friction helped him think. It sure didn't help me think.

CHAPTER 32

BRAD

Until we were in bed together, I hadn't thought seriously about making Cara mine.

That was a lie. I had. I just hadn't thought about the consequences.

That was a lie. I just hadn't decided to ignore them.

Until I was in that bed with my daughter between us, I chalked desire up to being around a hot woman. But I was around hot women all the time. They were like sand crabs on the waterline. You didn't have to dig too far or too long before one crawled into your hand.

I was tired. Half hungover. It was dark and the edge of the bed was an inch away. If I moved I'd fall, and if I didn't move I'd fall. All my defenses against myself were down. I told her things I'd made up my mind to keep to myself. That I didn't know how to love my daughter. That I was uncomfortable and unhappy. I was relieved to have it off my chest. I didn't realize I'd been suffocating under the weight of it.

I touched Cara over my daughter's sleeping body. Just her arm. The kiss on the path was so fast I hadn't had a chance to taste it, but that arm? I felt it. I drew my fingers down the soft length of it. She didn't pull away for a long time. When she did, she tucked her pillow and kept away.

"She's sleeping," she said. "You can probably get out now."

I hadn't been rejected by a woman since middle school. And Doreen McCody's rebuff didn't last more than a week before I had my hand up her skirt.

"You're so sure?"

"Yes. Just keep it quiet and go slow."

I had to see if she was right. So I moved my arm off my daughter and got one leg on the floor, slipping off until the bed didn't slope on my side.

And that did it.

Nicole picked her head up.

"Where are you going?"

I made eye contact with Cara over Nicole's mat of hair. She was smiling as if she was trying not to laugh.

"Just going back to bed," I said. "Miss Cara's gonna stay."

"No. You stay."

She threw her arms around my neck and put all her weight on them. I was trapped.

"You should go," Cara said. "If she gets used to you being here, it's going to become a habit."

"I'll be scared again," Nicole said, voice still thick with sleep.

Cara tried to pull her off me, but the little stitch was tenacious as hell.

"She's a Sinclair," I said, lying down. "She's gonna protect her habits. Right, Nicole?"

"Shh," she said, tucking her hands under her cheek. "I'm sleeping. Close your eyes. Go to sleep too."

"Okay." I put my head down. Nicole put her arm over me to make sure I didn't leave, and Cara stayed still on the other side of the twin bed. Maybe she slept. I sure didn't. I couldn't get the knowledge that Cara was a foot away out of my head.

It was a long night. I suspected Cara was awake, but I didn't want to talk.

I could have gotten up, but the bed smelled like her, canned peaches and flowers. Her breath came at a shallow, long pace. She was sleeping. Fuck it. I didn't want to leave. The house was a mess. And I didn't want to get into my own bed. For what? I was fine half on, half off the twin mattress.

I relaxed. I just wanted to think in her presence. Ask her what the fuck was happening without saying anything. I had a list of things she didn't do. She didn't judge me. She didn't presume even when she did. She didn't make eyes at me.

The things she *did* do were uncomfortable.

She made me comfortable, which was uncomfortable. She had a soft, seductive voice that never tried to seduce me. Around her, I wanted to make a go of the daddy thing. A real go. Not a sideshow. She made it seem possible. I didn't know how she did that, or why, or if it was intentional. But when I thought of trying harder, she was the second thing on my mind, after my daughter.

CHAPTER 33

CARA

The dream that night was the same, but different. We were kneeling on the pool table fully clothed, kissing. Just kissing. I tasted him. Heard him. Smelled the pool chlorine and rum. I woke slowly, still feeling his pressure on my lips.

Last night.

Things had happened. Nothing in the grand scheme, but in my little universe I woke to new boundaries. I'd gone from having a nocturnal secret crush to letting him kiss and touch me.

I felt bad about it. I felt confused and ambivalent. I felt Nicole's breath on my shoulder and kicked myself for putting myself in a position where I'd have to leave her.

I opened my eyes. Brad was gone and Nicole was poking my cheek in time to a pony song, each finger down the line.

"Good morning," I grumbled. "How did you sleep?"

"Okay. Daddy left."

"Do you want breakfast before Miss Blakely comes?"

"Little bun and cream cheese, please."

"Let's get dressed."

I fed Nicole and got her in a dress. She came to the pool house, where we played a noncompetitive, oversimplified version of chess. Right outside, two ladies in smocks were picking up beer bottles in the back, and a pool guy was skimming the water.

—*Ray Heywood wants to meet you?*—

It was Laura, my agent from West Side. I didn't answer personal calls when I was with kids, but could usually text.

—*We didn't make exact arrangements, but yes*—

—*How's tomorrow?*—

Ray had called Laura to make an appointment with me. That meant he was paying me, and it meant he wasn't just asking for personal advice. He wasn't just going to thank me or yell at me.

—*What does he want?*—

—*I think he wants you to keep quiet about Willow*—

There were a few words for exactly how insulting that was.

—*When have I ever disclosed anything that goes on with a family?*—

—*Never. I know. Just meet him. Hire you back at the best. Free lunch at the worst*—

Nicole was making the black king kiss the white queen.

"I love you, Mr. King," she mimicked with the piece. "I love you too, Mrs. Queen." She made smacking sounds.

—All right. He's buying—

———

We got back into the main house at about eleven. Nicole wanted another cream cheese sandwich.

Brad was already in the kitchen underlining things in a script. He looked as though he'd gone out and come back already.

"We'll be out of here in a minute," I said when Nicole and I hustled in.

"Wait!" He let the script flop closed. "I've had a lot of time to think."

"Side effect of a kid forcing you into a twin bed." I pulled the tub of gourmet cream cheese out of the fridge. The little slider buns were in the bread drawer. Knife. Plate. Little girl on little bench.

Brad leaned over to Nicole. "How would you like to go to Disneyland?"

She gasped and covered her mouth with brows arched over wide eyes.

"That's a yes, I'll take it," Brad said with a big stunning half-moon of a smile.

Nicole clapped. "When?"

"Day after tomorrow. Two days of nothing but fun."

He glanced at me. I was supposed to say something.

"I think that's a great idea."

Nicole bounced as if her chair was a trampoline.

"I hate to bring this up," I said softly, looking at Brad. "Have you arranged security?"

He snapped his fingers. "Under control."

That was what I was afraid of. His version of under control wasn't mine. Not when it came to Nicole and not when it came to where his lips landed. I was pretty sure we'd keep spontaneously combusting in moments of weakness without making any decisions about whether I should stay or go.

"I think we need to talk," I said. "A lot happened yesterday. We crossed lines."

"I hate lines," he said, smiling. God damn that face. "Listen. I thought about it."

He paused long enough to refill his coffee.

"Go on," I said while Nicole drew Minnie Mouse.

"Coffee?" he asked. Nice stall. I'd give it to him because I needed coffee.

"Yes."

He took his time pouring and pulling the cream out of the fridge. When he handed me the cup I made an effort to take it without touching him, and failed. His finger brushed mine, and I remembered the way he'd stroked my arm the night before. The perfect amount of pressure.

I put the cup to my lips.

"Go on," I said.

"Before I start, do you have anything to say? I'm sure you have an opinion."

"You'd been drinking."

"Not that much."

"I'm trying to give you an out."

"If I wanted an out, I'd be out. I want in."

My mouth went dry. I swallowed, but I had nothing to go down. Nicole was singing to herself at the counter, and I wanted to die or jump up and down in joy. Both. Neither.

I started to say something, but never decided what, so I just stood there with my coffee circled by both hands, mouth half open. He met my gaze and held it.

"Here's how it is," he said, finally breaking the silence. "You don't want to work for me anyway. Ride out your time here, then all bets are off."

"What bets are off, exactly?"

Now I was the one stalling.

He jerked his thumb to Nicole. "You don't want me to talk about what I'm going to do to your body in company."

I had the professional demeanor thing down to a science until then, because I wanted to hear what he was going to do to me in fine detail.

I cleared my throat and focused on my circle of coffee.

"It's not appropriate. None of this is. We shouldn't even be talking about it."

"When your time's up, that talk's getting real. Mark my words."

He took a swig of coffee that had a serious finality.

"I do a lot wrong," he said, rinsing out his cup. "But when I decide something, it happens."

"Do I get to decide?"

It was a rhetorical question. Of course I got to decide. And I was going to let him tell me what he was going to do, and then I was going to let him do it. I could barely breathe thinking about it. I hadn't thought about the bulge in his tuxedo pants by sheer force of will, but at the counter with his promises heavy in the air, I let that vision move me.

Yeah. I got to decide. And it was yes. All the way yes.

I must have been wearing my feelings all over my face, because he smiled at me in a way that made me blush, and I had to work not to smile back like a teenager.

He came around behind me, and I remembered the first salvo of dreams where I couldn't see him. I could only feel him behind me. He leaned over and whispered in my ear. "See you in a couple of weeks, Miss Cara."

CHAPTER 34

BRAD

This was a setup. Mike didn't go to Ken's office unless he had a good reason, and the reason this time was Mr. Fuckup. Me.

Ken had called me to his office to talk about security at Disney, which I admit, I didn't call him about until Cara left for the day, because it hadn't occurred to me until she mentioned it. I bolted to my publicist's office downtown, around the back way where I wouldn't be seen by anyone who wanted an autograph or a picture, and up to his office, which was decorated in about forty-nine shades of gray.

Ken told me he'd take care of security in one sentence on the way to his office. Then, once I stepped in, he closed the door. Michael Greydon was on the couch in a navy jacket and white shirt. Mr. Neat. My friend. Didn't call. Didn't text. Just sitting there with an iPad on his lap. He hugged me and slapped me in the chest with the tablet.

That was where I saw the cell phone shot of me by my pool. I had a beer, but I was wearing pants, so fuck them.

"Tell me why I care," I said.

"Because I care," Ken said, snapping up the iPad.

"And you brought this asshole in to talk sense into me? Dude married a paparazza. A hot paparazza . . . but still."

Ken flicked his finger over the screen. Another picture of me with my shirt open. My pool. Geraldine Mancuso in a green bikini bottom. Her tits had been blurred, but the blur was flesh color, not green. She held a long glass bong in one hand and a cigarette in the other. Behind her, another topless girl had her back to the camera.

And of course, me mooning Nicole's nanny.

You know what I thought?

I didn't think *fuck them*, even though, fuck them. I didn't care what the public thought. Didn't care that my publicist was about to use my friendship with Mike as a way to get me to be someone with a more manageable life.

My first thought?

Cara was out of the frame. I was relieved.

"Fuck this. Tracey Shim got busted doing lines at the Thelonius Room."

"And she hasn't had a magazine cover since," Ken interjected.

I handed the iPad back, but Ken didn't take it.

"Read it."

I froze. Michael took the tablet and read from it.

"*And The Father of the Year Award Goes to . . . Literally Anyone but Brad Sinclair.*" Michael paused, looked for my reaction, and continued. "*His press release has him so graciously taking a strange child in, but instead of devoting himself to the foundling, he retains his playboy ways. Just last night, he was photographed amid a stunning constellation of alcohol and string bikinis. Where is the baby? Right in the same house with the nannies, of course. To make the whole situation more deliciously complex, there are actually two nannies. One's a classic Hollywood daddy-jumper, vaulting from Josh Trudeau's bed to Brad Sinclair's House of Debauch. The other is fresh as a daisy. She's managed to not have a single printable scandal in her entire career. Let's see how long that lasts, shall we?*"

He put the tablet down. "There's more. But you get the idea."

"This?" Ken said, "I can't fix this for you. If people think you're partying in the house, they're going to start wondering why Child Protective Services isn't at your door."

"Let them wonder. I don't care," I said, but I didn't believe it. Nope, just heard Cara's voice telling me how hard it was. How I had to pick a god damn lane or get off the highway.

She'd never said that exactly. But when I said it to myself it was in her voice.

"Is this where I talk?" Michael asked Ken.

"Go ahead. Talk your little heart out. But fix him." There was a knock at the office door, and the shadow of Ken's executive assistant appeared through the frosted glass.

"I'm sorry I personally offended you," I snapped, because screw Ken and his busy little life with the kids his wife took care of 24-7.

"Nothing's personal. Do you understand? As far as I go, I don't have a *personal* to get offended about." He pointed to Michael, then me, while looking at my friend. "I have to take a call. Fix him."

He left with the phone to his ear as if he'd already moved on. The glass door clanged then clicked.

"And I'm stuck in the office with Dudley Do-Right," I said, flopping onto the couch. "You gonna lecture me, I'm right here."

"Isn't Dudley Do-Right before your time?"

"My mother used to say that. Was he a real guy?"

"I have no idea." He shook his watch down until it was below his cuff, then checked it. "Listen. I don't care about your image."

"Good."

"Or your career. If no one hires you anymore, you can just move back to Arkansas. Your parents would be glad to have you."

"I'm not moving back."

"I know. It was just a worst-case scenario. For you. Your daughter's living her worst-case scenario."

"Dude, give me a break. She has everything a kid could want."

"I promise you, she doesn't care."

"You know what?" I stood up. I'd had enough and he hadn't even started. "Six foster kids a few months ago doesn't make you an expert. Not by a sight. It makes you crazier than a shithouse rat."

"Maybe, but—"

"No. No but. I worked my whole life so I could do what I want. Then I get here, and I gotta slice out weeks between pictures. There's no life of leisure. It's a lie. You make it, and you don't get to do what you want. You get to work like a plow horse. You knew this. You weren't surprised. Your dad, your mom, your second cousin on your mother's side . . . you all knew. Well, I didn't. I worked to get out and I get here and it's more work. I can't breathe, Mike. I can't breathe, and now I have to be a daddy? What the . . . *what the fuck?*"

"What do you want me to tell you?" His fingers tented between his spread knees.

"Tell me I can have a life."

"You can have a life. But not the one you planned."

How many parents did a guy need? Did I hit a hive of them or something? I felt as if I was being swarmed by people telling me what to do.

"That's what you came down the hill to tell me?"

"Give or take. And that you need to slow it down. This is big. It's not method. You're not prepping for a part. This is it. This is all you get."

Fuck this. Fuck this till Tuesday. Fuck everything about this.

"No pressure, right?" I grumbled and started for the door. I was being a brat. I knew it, but I felt like a justified brat who had plenty to be bratty about.

"And the nanny?" Michael called out just as I got to the door. My heart froze like Blomer Lake in January. Solid ice. Ready to crack if it was touched.

"How did you know?"

"Everyone knows." He looked at me as if I were a mint leaf short of a julep. Maybe I was. Maybe I was losing my fucking mind. I almost asked him why. I almost got angry because it sounded as if he was going to insult Cara.

But he was Michael Greydon. He didn't insult people. It was beneath him.

"I want her and I'm keeping her, Mike. I just haven't figured out how. And don't try to talk me out of it."

"You're joking."

"I'm not. She has this way. I want to do right by her, and then I want . . ."

To make her scream my name.

To fuck her so hard she's sore for days.

I couldn't say it. I was raised better than that. Weird enough to be thinking that way. I'd gotten rid of the southern gentleman bullshit and learned to live and fuck and party the LA way. No rules. I loved that life. I earned it.

"She did this thing to me," I said more to myself than Mike. "She makes me want to burn the house down. I don't know what it is."

I rubbed my eyes. I couldn't get the sight of her just before I'd kissed her out of my head.

"Well, I guess we know what Josh saw in her," Michael said.

"Josh who?" I must have sounded enraged, because my blood reacted. Fuck him. Whoever he was. Fuck him.

"Josh who?" If Michael's look was a guide, I was stupid as well as crazy. "Trudeau. Who did you think?"

I laughed, shaking off the adrenaline.

"Right. Never mind."

"What's going on?"

"The other nanny. Not the one Josh had an affair with. Not Blakely. Cara. I want her and it shouldn't be a problem. I can't help being an asshole and just taking what I want because it's there. I don't care what they think of me. But I care what they think of *her*."

He didn't answer. He just leaned back on the couch.

"Can you stop looking at me like that?"

"Like what?"

"Like you're a doctor and I'm the patient."

"Tell me about your mother," he said with a distinct Freudian lilt.

Fine. If I was going to be an emotional ass I was going to be an emotional ass.

"So, you know the time at Strasberg? When we were doing the game with the golf ball?"

"No."

"You douche. Yes, you do. There were six of us. Britt too. And we passed the ball between us. Every time we got it we had to tell a truth about the person we passed it to. Right? And I passed to you and I said you were a Hollywood prince who had it easy and you got mad, so you threw it back hard and said I was a golden boy because I had all the talent and didn't have to work at it. I sent it back to you and said you were going to waste your life worrying about what everyone thought about you. Then you sent it back and said the truth about Brad Sinclair—he's worried everyone will know that he cares what people think so he makes sure everyone thinks the worst. Remember that?"

"Trevor took the ball away after that, right?"

"Yeah. But you were right. I was too, because you were a fucking prince."

"I still am."

"Thank you for admitting it. And right now? Sitting here in Ken's office, I want to be you. I want a reputation I can be proud of. I want to look at what I've built and say, 'That's mine,' like it matters."

"Having kids will do that to you."

"Can you stop being a dick for a minute?"

"Fine. Let me get this straight. You want the nanny. But if you have the nanny, you're going to have a shit reputation that you don't really care about except you do, for the nanny's sake. And you want to stop being the Hollywood party boy for your daughter. But if you start screwing her nanny, it's going to screw with her?"

"Something like that."

Michael stood up and fastened the top button of his jacket. Cary fucking Grant had nothing on the guy.

"I can tell you one thing."

I stood up too.

"What's that?"

"You don't have small-town Arkansas problems anymore. You're almost a Hollywood prince. But not quite."

"Watch your back, buddy."

"You gave me some advice once. You said to do what I wanted because it was what I wanted and not pretend it was something else. So, what do you want?"

The simplest question in the world. I wanted Cara's body and her time. I wanted to be a good father and do good work. The parties and the clubs came in a distant tenth on the list. I'd done all that. There was nothing new about it.

What did I want?

"Everything," I said. "All of it."

CHAPTER 35

CARA

I didn't know what to expect from Ray Heywood, but he couldn't do anything worse than give me a hard time in front of everyone at Kate Martello's.

I had a feeling it was going to work out all right. My Brad dream had come like clockwork, and I woke up not just turned on, but happy. He and I were a terrible match, but once I wasn't Nicole's nanny, I could at least prove to myself that these dreams and feelings were misguided. I was hungry for sex and affection. Not Brad Sinclair particularly.

Yes, once I wasn't his daughter's nanny, I could kiss him again, and it would be . . . sad.

I parked the car myself and crossed over to the back entrance of the restaurant.

Brad and I were going to have some kind of short-term fling that proved we were incompatible and then what? I'd fallen in love with Nicole.

Do not fall in love with the children.

I had a fantasy. Ray hired me back. I let Brad do all the things to my body he ever imagined.

But I didn't have enough of an imagination to make the relationship permanent. So what happened to Nicole? I couldn't be the first of many that drifted in and out of her life. I couldn't break her heart.

The standard-issue dog pack of paparazzi hung out behind the velvet rope. They usually ignored me, which worked out perfectly, thank you.

I didn't even look at them or look down when I passed. My mind was on Nicole, who I loved, and Brad, who was the worst kind of person in the nicest kind of package, berating myself for giving up one so I could have the other. I couldn't see a way around it. Couldn't see a way to have them both. Or even one without the other.

I approached the guy in the suit who let people in (or not) and was about to say my name when I heard it, loud and clear.

"Cara DuMont!"

I looked to the source of the call, and never found it, because it was drowned out by the entire dog pack calling my name and the uncomfortable sight of black lenses pointed in my direction.

"Miss DuMont!"

"Where did you get those shoes?"

"Where's Brad Sinclair?"

"What did you say when he mooned you?"

"How was that kiss last night?"

I swallowed my heart and lungs in one gulp, but they lodged in my throat.

The kiss.

On the path to the pool house.

Of course someone had seen it, but I hadn't seen anything on the web about it. No pictures had surfaced. Had I missed it? Who knew about it? Everyone? Insiders? The public? What were they saying? Was I a whore? Was I a curiosity? Who was I? I couldn't hear, taste, feel anything outside the fracture in my sense of self.

"Miss DuMont," the man with the dark suit said. I looked at him. Forties. Kind face. Tablet tucked in the crook of his arm.

"Yes." I could barely get my voice past the organs stuck in my throat.

"This way."

He led me through the doors, through the packed, loud room with the high ceilings. I recognized Fiona Drazen and Neville Rage without taking my eyes off the maître d's back. I didn't want to know if they were looking back at me.

Ray stood when he saw me. Next to him, Kendall smiled with her long, shiny hair and bangly earrings. The maître d' held a chair out for me, and Ray sat after I did.

Kendall tucked her hair behind her right ear with her left hand. The stone in the engagement ring was the size of a lightbulb and twice as bright. She was my age. Taller. Richer. More sophisticated but not more worldly.

I didn't know why I felt as if I had to compare myself to her. My name on the lips of a pack of paps had left me exposed to my vulnerabilities.

"Thank you for coming," Ray said.

"I'm happy to. I'm sorry about what happened with Willow. I didn't know what else to do."

"It's fine—"

"We want you to know," Kendall interrupted Ray, "that we don't approve at all. She's too young, for goodness' sake."

"She was supposed to be at volleyball practice."

They jumped on each other's sentences. It was kind of cute.

"And we spoke to the mother of the girl she was supposed to get a lift from."

"The nanny was supposed to drive them home."

"Never told us Willow wasn't in the car."

"Said it wasn't her job."

"And the woman we hired lost track completely."

"And we thought you'd never do that."

"Never."

"Never, ever."

They ran out of story. I let the end hang there. The waiter came and we ordered.

I didn't know what I wanted out of these people. I'd come in hoping they'd offer me a job so I could leave Brad with another job ready, but sitting there, wondering what inconstant parenting had to do with Willow's troubles, what they'd mean for Nicole, how much I wanted Brad, and what a fool I'd been to think we could keep it under wraps, I doubted everything. I was falling into the cracks between all the things I wanted.

"And Willow?" I asked. "She's old enough to be held accountable."

"Of course!" Ray said.

"I took her phone away for a week," Kendall said with finality.

"Did she tell you to go fuck yourself?"

I even flinched from my filterless comment, but Ray laughed.

Kendall didn't look amused.

"She'll live," Ray said. "My lovely bride-to-be might not." He put his arm around Kendall, and she pushed him off playfully, but without any real humor. She was mad. Willow must have sparked quite a row. I could only imagine the screaming, and Jedi hiding in his room with his Legos.

"I think you'll be fine," I said. "I honestly . . . I don't know what you want out of me. I've never gone to the press with any kid's problem."

"We were worried," Kendall said.

"Not really," Ray interrupted.

"You didn't work for us when you saw her. The NDA didn't cover incidents after we terminated you."

"Oh, Kendie," Ray said, exasperated. "You don't get it."

"Look, this is business, honey."

"Yes and no. Mostly no."

She flipped her wrist at him and her bracelets bangled.

"There's money involved," Kendall insisted. "It's business."

"It's more complicated—"

"You didn't have her sign anything to earn the severance."

"You guys are making me nuts," I broke in. "Can we get to the point?"

Kendall leaned back and crossed her arms, her body language deferring the entire matter to her husband, who looked as if he now wanted to crawl under a rock and die.

"Just say whatever it is, Ray," I said. "I won't walk out. I'm hungry."

Ray put his elbows on the table. His cuffs hiked to show off a thick gold bracelet I hadn't seen before. It was no more than another stylish bauble, but it reminded me how much money and power he had. How many connections.

"Willow's young, and her mistakes can follow her for a long time."

"You know I'm not going to start calling people."

"Maybe not now. But if something else happens and it goes public, people are going to come to you for background. She's not covered with this incident. Legally, you could talk and we don't want that."

It was my turn to lean back and cross my arms. How many ways could I tell this guy I wasn't going to hurt Willow?

"So," he said, pulling an envelope from his inside pocket. "In here is an agreement to not disclose what happened and where you saw her. It's the same NDA, give or take, as you signed when you were hired."

I took the envelope. I could sign it just so these two could sleep at night. It didn't matter. I wasn't going to say anything anyway. I opened the envelope. Ray picked a pen out of his inside pocket.

"And if you sign it," Kendall said, "it's ten thousand for you."

I didn't know why I found that aggravating.

No. Once I froze in place with my hand out for the pen, I figured out why every hair on my body stood on end. The payoff implied I'd ever hold insider information about a child over that child's head. It questioned the very basics of my integrity.

I closed the envelope.

"I don't want your money," I said, sliding the envelope to Ray. "And I'm not signing it. I'd never, ever hurt Willow. And thank you, but I'm not hungry anymore."

I left, walking right out the back as if there wasn't a pack of paparazzi waiting for me. I didn't care. Maybe they were going to say I was storming out because Ray and I were having an affair. Sure. Why not? Let them see me. Let them think what they wanted.

Apparently, Ray didn't care either because he caught up to me right inside the door.

"Cara, I'm sorry."

"It's fine."

I just wanted to get away from him. He represented a failure I couldn't control, and he was a passive-aggressive sad sack. I didn't know how he managed to run an office staff of dozens, much less a household staff you could count on one hand.

"We really miss you," he said.

"Say 'hi' to the kids for me."

The maître d' held the door open for me. The dog pack was shouting to Wanda Cravitz, who was doing a three-point turn and waving before coming in for lunch.

"There's no one like you," Ray said from behind me. I looked back at him.

"You trying to get in my pants?"

He smiled at the joke I wouldn't have made when I worked with him. It made me wish I'd lightened up a little when I was in his house.

"We thought about hiring you back."

If I could have chosen my feelings, "hopeful" wouldn't have been on the list, but that was how I felt. The door might not have been open wide, but it was ajar, or unlocked maybe. The Heywood house had been an enviable job, and if Kendall was on board, all the better. I assumed I knew what the obstacle was. I could crush it.

"I'm only with Brad a limited time."

"I had to put the kibosh on it when pictures came across my desk this morning."

Forty thousand pictures came across his desk in a day. One of them had to do with me. I gripped the shoulder strap on my bag so tightly my knuckles went white.

He got his phone out, and the maître d' let Wanda Cravitz in. I stepped to the side in the whoosh of her entourage, knowing well and good what was in the pictures, but hoping against hope that I was wrong. I hadn't seen them, and I would have.

"We bought all of them, and we're not printing them. Everyone knows about them. The rumor mill. It's real."

He handed me the phone. "That's the first. There are four more." He cleared his throat as I flipped through. "If Kendall ever saw them, she'd flip on you. And me. She'd assume things that aren't true about us. She's a beautiful woman, but she's been hurt before."

They all looked black except for a blotch of light illuminating two sets of legs standing close together. One had a blur of light by the faces. Brad and I could have been any couple kissing in a dark backyard, but with the right copy, I'd be tarred.

I handed the phone back.

"Thank you."

"I felt like I owed you."

"You didn't. But I'm not signing that thing."

I could have left, and I probably should have gone to the door faster, but Fiona Drazen was on her way out with Karen Hinnley and I couldn't walk through the traffic they caused. So I had to hear his short, painful speech in its entirety.

"Listen. You've given me plenty of good advice about kids. Let me give you a little about men. Stay away from that guy. The only two things he's ever loved are a good time and getting what he wants. You're a challenge to him, and you deserve to be more."

"Yeah." I agreed so I could get out of there. I didn't want to be trapped in the industry eatery for another second. The paps could photograph me and call my name. I didn't care, as long as I wasn't kissing someone I worked for while they did it. It was the crowd making me feel like a caged animal. The noise from the high ceiling. The bustle of the lunch hour. I couldn't think. I didn't know if I had to.

"Thanks, Ray. Again. I meant it when I wished you the best."

We shook hands and I weaved around a TV reality star and a pack of paparazzi who ignored me in favor of the reality actress. I got in the front seat of my car as if I'd just robbed a bank, but when I turned the key, I didn't drive away.

I didn't move. The Hollywood sign was in front of me, three miles away on the horizon between two billboards, letters barely legible from the far western side. One of the billboards was for *Broken*. Brad's blue eye was ten feet high. The laugh lines around his eyes hadn't been smoothed over, and his pores were as big as a fist. Intentional. Appropriate to the story. He looked exactly like that kiss-close, and I shared the view with millions.

I felt violated by that eye.

I'd told myself I didn't want to be a part of celebrity culture. I'd said I wanted to just be around children. I'd told myself a lot of things and right then, I didn't believe any of them.

CHAPTER 36

BRAD

She was gorgeous. They'd all been complete knockouts. Girls like that moved out of their hometown as soon as the captain of the football team turned his back. Tall. Tight. Shaped like lingerie models. They all sat in the agency conference room as if it was a casting call, but with buttoned-up blouses and ponytails.

"Why did you come to LA?" I asked the fifth one. Maybe fifteenth. Who the fuck even knew. At interview number two I had the feeling I wasn't going to find someone to replace either Blakely or Cara.

"My agent said I had to move here if I was serious about acting. So. Here I am. I have a degree in child psychology from Michigan, and I love children."

Since time was short, Laura had set up a full day of interviews. She said they should meet Nicole, not me. Like we did the first time. I brought her and we did it that way in the morning, but I didn't like strangers looking at my daughter and trying to get her to like them. What was she supposed to make of all these pretty faces? She was five and she was mine. I'd get a short list together. We could go from there.

I put Nicole in the playroom with Blakely, who gave me the moon eyes as if she wanted me to know she felt guilty about chasing her dreams. She shouldn't feel guilty. I wouldn't.

The girl from Michigan had a nice résumé. Seemed to come from a nice family. And it was all very nice. She looked exactly like her headshot. I got no feeling from her at all.

"My daughter lost her mother. She gets attached."

"I'd love to meet her."

"You're auditioning on your days off?"

"Probably." She smiled. Skin like butter. Had to say, she was knockout material.

I hadn't shaved that morning, and I rubbed the stubble. I liked the feeling on my palm. It woke me up.

I was comparing all of them to the nanny I was losing. Who was perfect. Who I wanted to fuck so bad my balls ached. I wasn't comparing their fuckability. I swore it and I meant it. But my wires were all crossed up. I couldn't look at them without knowing I didn't want to fuck them as bad, and seeing that as a good thing.

My dick wasn't supposed to be in the reckoning. How much or little I wanted to bed the nanny wasn't supposed to matter. The interviews were for Nicole. What was best for *her*. Not me.

After nanny number ninety, I found Blakely still sitting at the kid-size table with Nicole. I wanted to be sitting at that table. I wanted to draw crazy-ass unicorns. So I sent Blakely home.

"This would be easier if they met your daughter first," Laura said from the doorway of the playroom.

"She doesn't need to be confused," I said. "Too many nice faces trying to get her to like them." I held a marker up for my daughter. "Is blue next?"

She peered at my paper and pointed to the orange stripe on top of my rainbow.

"No, silly Daddy." She snapped the blue marker out of my hand and handed me a yellow as if she were handing me an Oscar.

"Here's what I want," I said as I made a yellow rainbow stripe. "I want the best. I want two ladies. At least one should have so much experience nothing shocks her. I'm thinking she'd be with the same family twenty years and she'd be bored now because the kids go to Harvard. If she has my mother's values, even better."

"What are your mother's values?"

"Good Southern Baptist."

"Great. You sure you don't want to keep Cara DuMont? I'm sure she can be convinced."

I was about to dismiss the idea, because I did want to keep her, and the only way to do that was to replace her. But Nicole, bless her heart, had ears like a fucking rabbit. She handed me the green marker and didn't say a word. Didn't look up at me. Actress. She heard everything. Every damned word.

I thought I'd gotten away with trying to replace Cara. Even though I was replacing her so I could keep her, there was no way to explain it to Nicole.

Blakely was easier. The news went down with vanilla fudge swirl ice cream.

"Are you going to live in another city?" Nicole asked as Blakely wiped her face.

"No," Blakely balled up the napkin. "I'm staying in Los Angeles."

"Daddy," Nicole said matter-of-factly.

"Yes?"

"Miss Blakely should stay with us. She can go to additions in daytime and sleep in her regular bed at nighttime."

Nicole Garcia-Sinclair. Solver of all the world's problems.

"We need that bed for your new nanny."

"What new nanny? Not Miss Cara. Miss Cara's staying, right?"

"Yes," I said without thinking. Blakely shot me a look. "Mostly." Then Nicole shot me a look. Jesus Christ. These women. "Yes. Miss Cara's staying."

Nicole asked about Miss Cara the whole way home. Over dinner, she asked if Miss Cara was coming to Disney the next day. When I tried to twist up a French braid and made a huge mess, she suggested I learn from Miss Cara. And when Miss Cara herself showed up to do the night shift, Nicole ran to the door.

"Daddy was talking to a hundred pretty ladies today."

"Really?" She crouched to Nicole's eye level and looked at me sidelong. Half a smile. "A hundred?"

CHAPTER 37

CARA

Brad stood back a bit, arms crossed.

"Ninety-nine hundred!" Nicole spread her arms wide. "But none were as pretty as you!"

"I don't believe it."

"Miss Blakely's leaving! She's going to be an actress!" Nicole squealed as if Blakely's dreams would come true just because she'd freed up her schedule. I hoped she was right. "Do you like my dress?" She held out the pink cotton stripes of the skirt. "I like your shoes."

I was wearing new sneakers. I thanked her, complimented her twinkling light-up shoes, and we continued the exchange into the hall. Brad waited, leaning against the doorframe, looking at me as if I was the only woman in the world. My heart sank. I had no chance against him.

I decided right then I wasn't telling him about the pictures. I didn't want him to tell me it wasn't a big deal.

"You were at West Side today, I presume?"

"Yeah. It's bad out there."

"You're coming tomorrow, right?" Nicole swung my hand back and forth and made a please please please smile.

"To Disney?"

"Yes, please!"

Brad didn't move. The assumption was that since it was my day, I was going. That was going to have to be renegotiated. Everything was going to have to be renegotiated. He changed the subject as if he knew.

"I'll read her books tonight. We picked a few."

"Really?"

"Really. Why?"

"You never put her to bed before."

"I'm down to one nanny soon. You people are so unreliable."

"Don't even." I looked down at Nicole. "What are you wearing tomorrow?"

"Grandma sent me something!" She pulled me to her room. I looked down before I turned at the landing, and he was there at the bottom, watching me silently with a level of determination I hadn't seen from him.

Then in a split second, he winked and playful Brad was back.

CHAPTER 38

CARA

I approved her outfit for the theme park and handed her off to Brad for the bedtime ritual. Everything seemed to go smoothly. Bath. Dressing. Kiss for Daddy. Reading in bed with Daddy, which was more singing-and-making-things-up than following the story. Kiss good night. Lights out. Apparently bedtime went all right. I even heard him brush her hair and teeth.

Brad came to the kitchen with his beat-to-hell white T-shirt and jeans. My hormones rushed through my blood like marauders setting the village on fire.

"If she's down, I'm going to the back," I said. "If you need me—"

He was on me in half a second with that mouth, those hands. I was utterly powerless against his kiss. His tongue found its way into my mouth. He tasted like a bad decision. He tasted like the thing you always said you shouldn't have done, but didn't regret anyway. A little bit of starlight. The tart sting of the forbidden and the sweetness of a sin you think you're getting away with.

Every inch of my skin came alive, and I felt heavy and swollen between my legs. One big undeniable throb set to the rhythm of his kiss.

We stumbled into the hallway, and without the sound of Nicole's patter, we became unhinged. Desperately, wildly irrational. I was leaving, and once I wasn't in the house caring for his child it wouldn't matter. I'd be a target for the paparazzi, but not as the nanny.

He pushed me against the wall. Something rattled. Me. I rattled. He yanked my shirt up, getting under my bra and pulling it over my breasts. It happened so fast, his mouth on my nipple, testing its limits, his hands pulling my jeans open.

I whispered his name, and he shushed me by putting his mouth over mine again. I groaned once, and when he put his hand over the crotch of my jeans and pressed it hard, I groaned again.

"I've wanted you for weeks," he said between his teeth. "Now *this*." He pressed his fingers against me hard, and I gasped with pleasure. "I'm going to have it."

His eyes were so blue, so intense, and his voice wasn't the laid-back party boy I'd met. He was a guy who didn't take no for an answer, and I was a girl who wanted to say yes.

He picked me up and deposited me on the kitchen table. I wrapped my legs around him, and he pushed me down, grinding his erection into me, mirroring the motions of his tongue in my mouth.

"Yes," I said. No time for another word. Joined below the waist like magnets, he carried me down the hall, kissing faces and necks, all tongues and lips, my hands under his shirt. He was hard everywhere. Taut. Skin stretched over lean muscle.

He pushed his dick against me and I pushed back. Pure heat. Friction fire. The flame of potential of what was coming. I couldn't get enough of him in my hands. They were too small, clawing at clothes and skin.

"You ever been eaten out by a southern boy?"

I had to think. There hadn't been many, but no one from Los Angeles was from Los Angeles.

"Southern England."

"Doesn't count." He hooked his fingers under my jeans and started peeling them off. "You're in for a treat, sweetheart. Us southern boys eat pussy like pie. And I like pie."

Yes. Yes and yes. *S'il vous plaît* and thank you too. The world could take these last weeks in his employ and shove them right where the sun don't shine because—

"Daaaaaadddeeeeeee . . ."

———

"I have no idea how this happened," Brad said softly. He was lying down in the dark on the other side of his daughter's sleeping body. I could see him over the edge of her soft round cheek. Her arm was draped over me, and her legs were thrown back to hook his to her.

"You're spoiling her, that's how it happened."

"She's afraid of having a nightmare. Then she became one."

I'd never seen him say a negative thing about his daughter or show signs of a short temper. I was glad to see he was finally getting involved enough to get grouchy.

He reached over her and touched my hair.

"You're real pretty on the kitchen table."

"We should wait anyway."

"Not interested."

"We agreed."

His voice got sharp with urgency, but not unkind. No. Just ferocious.

"There is no way I can stand seeing you and not fucking you."

I pointed at Nicole, raising my head a little to make a face, mouthing the word *language*. Nicole groaned and opened her eyes halfway.

He and I waited in silence for her breathing to get regular again.

"What's the difference?" he whispered.

What was the difference? People.

"I had lunch with Ray Heywood today," I said. "There was a dog pack outside Kate Martello's, and they wanted to know how you kissed. Ray showed me pictures from the party. It was us in the yard. It was dark. It could have been anybody . . . but they all know it's me. And he knew it too. He was going to offer me my job back but couldn't because of the pictures."

"What did you say?"

"I thanked him for not printing them."

"About how I kissed. What did you say?"

I picked my head up. Nicole didn't stir.

"Brad, really?"

You're a challenge to him.

"Well that was a real short one the other night. Just now? Before the little nightmare? I think you got a better sense of what you're refusing."

"I'm not refusing. I'm postponing."

Nicole scooted down in sleep, nuzzling her head into my neck and her body into her father. She wasn't between our faces anymore, and I could see him in the half light. I could have leaned up and kissed him with the slightest effort, except for what that would have led to.

He reached for me, touching my cheek. I couldn't breathe when his finger moved to my chin and stroked my lower lip. My mouth went dry.

"Did you always play it so safe?" he asked.

"Yes." I answered too quickly. "No, actually." He smiled when I changed my mind, pulling my bottom lip a little. It would take the slightest movement to take his finger in my mouth. I wanted to taste it.

"Tell me." His whisper was a seduction. "Tell me everything."

The night was so dark, and I felt so safe in our little cocoon that I decided to tell him.

"My parents were in the military so we moved around all the time, but we moved to Austin when I was fourteen. Just another school where I was the new girl. I had no friends. I never had time to keep them. I never fit in because by the time I figured out what I had to do to fit in, we moved again. But this time I talked my parents into sending me to the regular school instead of the Lycée. I just wanted to be a regular kid, and the difference between the French school and a regular public school in Texas? Planetary. I'd traveled all over the world at that point, and that Texas school was like nothing I'd ever seen."

"How?"

"Everything was football. It was like a religion. Except for the religion, which was second."

"My mother would argue with that."

"Well, she'd be right, I'm sure. But from the outside, where I was? The high school players were treated like kings. The girls whispered their names. And there was one. Tyler Stokes." I said it with the same fascination I heard it.

"Let me guess. The quarterback."

"Yes. A senior. With a girlfriend who was the biggest bee-eye-tee-see-aytch in the school. I could tell it the minute I saw her. So I steered totally clear of her and hung out with the kids in the French club."

"You had a French club?"

"Four of us, actually, including Tyler."

He chuckled.

"His mother made him join because he'd failed before. She wanted him to go to Texas Tech, and he needed a language."

"And he hit on you," he said as if it was a fact he already knew damn well.

"Yeah." I didn't continue right off, remembering that moment in the hall after school. We were outside the library. The other girls in the club had practically done his French homework for him, and he cornered me. I'd felt short and vulnerable, yet emotionally aroused. "I felt like I had this big opportunity. I could really fit in. I could live where I was as if I was from there. You know? Like he could validate me or something. I played coy for a week, but when he broke up with his girlfriend and came for me an hour later, I couldn't even pretend I'd say no. So, yeah. It went on for about a month. And I didn't play it safe because he didn't want to. I wanted to fit in so badly. I dreamed of a big stupid wedding and a big dress. A party. All of it. So stupid."

I wasn't crying outright, but enough moisture had gathered under my eyes for him to wipe away with his thumb.

"I got pregnant. Naturally, right? And he wasn't so nice. He asked me how many guys I'd been with, only he didn't even say it that nice because I wasn't a virgin at all. And he told me to take care of it, but it wasn't his problem. I didn't know what to do. If I told my parents, they'd take me out of the school, and it was the only chance I had to be normal. And I had no friends to talk to or ask what to do. In Texas they have all these rules about getting an abortion. The clinics are so far away, and there're waiting periods. So I begged Tyler for help. He got an address from one of his friends and took me. He didn't wait because he had football practice. It wouldn't have changed anything if he had anyway. It was some lady's house. I sat alone, waiting, thinking that's what I get for dreaming about a big wedding. As if I could be normal and have all the things everyone with a real home had."

"You can have—"

I cut him off. I wasn't done and the next part was critical.

"The lady was nice. She was a nurse I think, and she meant well. I'm sure she did. But it was a mess. A real mess."

A bloody mess. A mess of tears and tubes and needles. My parents surprised me with their understanding and love, but none of that could heal what had been broken inside me.

"Anyway," I said, swallowing a bunch of gunk. "It all went wrong. I can't have my own children."

Brad leaned back and snapped a tissue out of the box on the night table. I reached for it, but he held it away and only when I put my arm down did he hold it over my nose to wipe the sobs away.

"That's a crime," he said tenderly.

"I guess. Tyler surprised me by not being a dick about it. We stayed together until the end of the year, but he cheated on me a week before he left for Tech."

I'd surprised myself by not caring.

"Yeah, well," I continued after clearing my throat, "now you know why I play it safe all the time. You shouldn't need the universe to tell you twice."

He pulled me to him and put his forehead to mine.

"That's quite a story, Cara-bean. I'm sorry that happened to you."

Before I could answer, he kissed me gently, tenderly. I breathed it in. So good. Everything about it was a comfort. A temporary, facile, convenient comfort I couldn't get used to, because it didn't change anything.

Nicole stretched and Brad and I separated, laughing quietly. She turned around and nuzzled her father as if she was afraid of him leaving. She was the most perfect safety net.

"She's right." He patted Nicole. "I think I met a hundred pretty girls today." He brushed hair from his daughter's face. "Some were even qualified for your job. But I didn't want them. I'm not even talking about fu—" He stopped himself before dropping an f-bomb in front of her. Good man. "They all had one thing in common." He looked up at me. "They weren't you."

I didn't breathe. I was too confused. I couldn't stay his daughter's nanny. It was a trap. He was wrong for me. Too much partying. Too busy with his job. He'd never be faithful or stable. But I wanted him, and I'd never have him if I stayed.

I was aware of the contradiction, but I wanted him.

"This is a mess," I whispered. "If I stay with Nicole, this is off-limits. You and I. We don't exist. We can never exist. And I can't be here with you guys and be around you anymore. It's too hard."

"We'll figure it out."

"I don't see how."

"You have to trust me." He touched my cheek again. "I have it under control."

"You're pretty confident." My eyes fluttered closed. I didn't know what I was saying; I just wanted him to keep stroking my face and neck all night long.

"I'm going to find a way to have you," he said. "I don't do halfway. Ask anyone. I'm all-in, all the time. And it's you, Cara DuMont. I want all of you. You feel right to me. Everything about you. Your voice, your face, that body. That body."

He bit his lower lip. I wished I could photograph the moment I felt like his world. No one else. Nothing else. Just me. I spent so many days being an invisible force in people's lives that his full attention was as uncomfortable as it was arousing. We spent long seconds doing nothing but looking at each other in the night light. He became something more than the player, the partier, the brilliant but unmoored talent.

"If my daughter wasn't in this bed, you'd be moaning so loud."

"Let me find another job."

"And then?"

"You'll have to make good on those promises, southern boy."

"You've got yourself a deal."

We were up hours after that, sharing jokes, touching what we could safely reach. I think I slept a little, but for the first time since I took the job, I didn't have a vivid dream of his body next to mine.

CHAPTER 39

CARA

"I told West Side Nannies I'd take anything," I said to Brad while braiding Nicole's hair at the breakfast table. "So I have to get over there."

Brad wore shorts and sandals. Nothing extraordinary except the shape they covered. His sunglasses were already pushed to the top of his head, and he hadn't even left the house yet.

"But, today? You had to jump so fast?"

I was annoyed that he was annoyed. He'd seemed so urgent about it the day before, and now I couldn't tell if he was vacillating or if he just didn't get it.

I didn't want to seek clarity in front of Nicole, so I just braided her hair while she ate her cereal and hummed to herself. He watched me. Full eye contact. Tapping his foot.

"Daddy," Nicole said matter-of-factly as she pointed at the top of her head, "watch Miss Cara. See how she does it?"

Perfect time to change the subject.

"Look," I said. He stood hip to hip with me, his foot pushing against mine, shoulders touching. "You start at the top with three strands and gather more as you go."

"You sure have nice fingers," he said with a thick southern accent.

"Watch the hair." I went quickly. "Over. Catch. Over. Catch. See?"

"Are you going to take a picture with the princesses?" Nicole asked. Neither one of us answered. Nicole looked up at me, almost pulling the end of the braid away.

"I'm not going today." I finished off my work with a little blue elastic.

Her face went from excited to distressed.

"Why?"

"I have to meet some friends."

I waited but got no help from Brad. He could be a real jerk sometimes. Like when his daughter wasn't going to get what she wanted. Note to self.

Nicole put on a sulk, turned to her dad, then back to me.

"Why can't they come?"

"They won't fit in the helicopter," Brad said. Well, that was an answer at least. It wasn't going to work but he tried.

"Get another one." An obvious solution to any self-respecting five-year-old. Grown-ups were so stupid, and I smiled in spite of myself. Brad did the same.

That smile hit me broadside. It wasn't about his power or his ability to control his daughter. It was about a moment's delight in a child's logic. I liked him again. He was likeable for a hundred reasons he got paid good money for. But there was more to him. He was genuine. He listened. He was open to change yet stalwart in his beliefs. He spent his money on things that pleased him or minimized inconvenience, not status objects. He never pretended to be more than he was but didn't suffer from insecurity or false humility.

He was who he was. Utterly and authentically.

His smile lasted less than a second, and in that slice of time, I pivoted.

"What are you looking at?" he asked, smile gone. The effect of it lingered in the form of a skipped heartbeat.

I'm looking at you.

Really.

Just you.

I swallowed the words because I didn't even know what they meant, crouching in front of Nicole so I could look away from him.

"You get to spend the day with your dad. Do you know how many girls want to spend a day with your dad?"

"You need to come too." She folded her arms in a righteous huff. "Or I'm not going."

"You're going to let Daddy go by himself?"

She nodded decisively.

Brad glanced at his phone. "The car's ready."

Nicole tightened the tension of her arms and mouth, pointing her chin up just enough to display proud intransigence.

I started to explain, "This is a you-and-Daddy day."

"Miss Cara has to come," Nicole interrupted. "Or I'm not going. I don't want to sleep in the princess hotel or ride the spaceships or *anything*," she whined, nearly in tears. "Please please please come."

"I can't."

I looked up to her father, hoping for a little backup. What I got was a guy with his arms crossed and half a shrug on his shoulders.

"It would be a hell of a lot easier if you came, I gotta say."

"Do you want to do this or not?"

"What if she has to pee?"

"There are family bathrooms."

"She's going to be bored without you."

"She's never bored."

"What does she eat? Do I have to feed her?"

I wanted to kill him, but then I'd have to touch him. And if I touched him, all the violence would flow right out of me.

"Can we talk?" I growled.

He just smiled at me and followed me onto the back patio.

"What are you doing?" I demanded.

"Nothing?"

Had I felt a shadow of admiration and desire cross my heart thirty seconds before? Had I melted at his genuineness and sincerity? God. There must have been drugs in my breakfast. I put my hands on my hips. Sometimes, an authentic person can be an authentic ass.

"You're changing your mind."

"If you know what I'm doing, why are you asking?"

"You. Are. Infuriating."

"You know what's funny?" He pointed as if formulating the idea. "I see you with her, and you never lose your temper. She's a real thorn, but you're a saint no matter how bitchy she gets. But with me? You're blowing a gasket here. Why is that?"

"She has an excuse."

"So do I."

"What's that?"

"You're not going to tell me all about what's wrong with me?"

"Go to hell." I spun to go in the house, but he stepped in front of me.

"I want you there because I want you. Okay? I like you. I like being around you. I want you to come because it's more fun with you. And I want a shot at getting on top of you. That's it."

There it was again. Full-frontal honesty. No smile this time. No delight. Just the brutal reality of who he was. He took a step in my direction—just a half step too close. I put my hand on his chest and pushed just a little against the hard muscle.

"We were waiting until I wasn't on the payroll. Remember?"

"I hate waiting."

"You—"

201

He kissed me and I swore the kissing thing was going to have to stop.

Tomorrow.

Because on the morning of Disney Day I was weak and unprepared. I was shocked at feelings I didn't have time to process. And we'd kissed already, and no one was around—so I let him. And not only did I let him, I tasted his tongue and said whatever. Whatever whatever. I didn't have to worry about where we stood or what our roles were because he was with me and it felt good. So good.

"What are you doing?"

Nicole's voice came from the house, two feet away, where we'd stupidly left a girl who didn't like to be alone. She was on the other side of the screen, smiling so wide her face looked as if it was going to break into an explosion of dimples.

Worse than a thousand paparazzi seeing us together.

CHAPTER 40

BRAD

I didn't know what Cara's problem was. Like a kid never saw two people kiss before. But she froze worse than the first time I kissed her. She went totally fucking silent on me. Not a sound. Not a word.

I was the one who had to tell Nicole to get her jacket on. I was the one who had to tie the bow on her princess dress. It was like Cara had stage fright or something. I tapped her and asked her if she was all right and she said she was fine but man, I didn't believe her. Something was up.

She'd kissed me back. Couldn't be that. She was totally into it. I promise you I know when a woman wants to be kissed and when she doesn't, and Cara wanted to be kissed. One hundred percent into it. Until Nicole asked what we were doing and I said "kissing" because it was pretty obvious what we were doing. What was I supposed to say?

And Cara turned her back on me as if I were a stranger. Complete system shutdown.

I mean, come on. The three of us had shared a twin bed. Couldn't be any closer. Why was one thing okay and not the other?

"Please reschedule," I said. "I'm begging you. Don't hold what's going on between us against Nicole."

She slowed, resting her hand on the wall. She had beautiful fingers. Each one was engaged, tense, revealing her emotions just by the way they rested.

"You're good," she said. "You know just where to get me."

"I figure it's not going to work forever."

She stepped back into the foyer. I didn't hear what she said, but Nicole clapped and jumped up and down. Ten minutes later, we were at the helipad.

Nicole was scared of the helicopter. She clung to me like a spider, cringing the whole time. Cara was still in shutdown, but when she looked at Nicole she smiled. The smile was bullshit. It would fool a five-year-old, but me? No. I was not fooled. Not at all.

CHAPTER 41

CARA

I wanted to explain this to Brad Sinclair.

His daughter was cute as a button. Sure. She was also strong. She was in the process of withstanding something few children her age ever had to deal with, the loss of life as she knew it. She did it with good humor and curiosity. She was worthy of his pride, but she was still a kid.

She longed for stability. Adult guidance. She longed for completion and permanence. The reason she wanted us to be in her bed with her was because she wanted us together. And what we'd done by letting her see something was send the message that the stability she wanted had been achieved.

But it was more complicated than her young mind could grasp. And when the day came that Brad and I didn't work out, or I was no longer her nanny, or I continued to be her nanny but not her father's kiss-partner, what would happen?

I took the helicopter ride to Disneyland in silence. Nicole watched the land below in fascination and screamed when we dipped or swerved while her father laughed and held her tight. He snuck his fingertips to my arm when he could, but I was so deep in panic I couldn't even look at him.

Willow had lashed out after I left. While I was there, she never got all made-up and showed up to a grown-up party with a man who had no business taking her out. Plenty of kids that age pulled stunts like that so frequently they stopped being stunts, but I knew her. I knew her friend's caretakers. We talked. Willow was pretty well behaved, and it wasn't until I got fired that she lashed out.

Now Nicole. How would she lash out? And when?

I felt like an agent of chaos instead of stability. I did more damage than good.

Everything felt upside down. I wasn't even supposed to care this much.

We landed on the Disney helipad, which was shaped like the silhouette of a big, white mouse head. I was going to have to put a good face on this if I was going to function the rest of the day.

CHAPTER 42

BRAD

I should have invited Mom and Dad, but it happened so fast I didn't even think of it. Fuck it. I'd bring Nicole around after Thailand. Maybe I'd fly my parents into Bangkok. Or not. Maybe I'd just give the fuck up because I couldn't do a damn thing right.

"Cara," I said as we walked off the helipad. I had Nicole wrapped around me. "You're freaking me out."

"Why?" She smiled. Fake as shit. But I couldn't kiss the phony thing off her. And she needed to be kissed. By me. A lot.

"Because you've turned into an icicle."

She smiled again, but there was something sad about it. At least it wasn't fake.

"Let's give her a nice day and we can talk later."

"Good idea."

Four people in dark blue suits got out of a red-and-white polka-dot golf cart and greeted us. Three men and one woman.

"Hi!" the middle-aged woman in a blue suit said through a toothy smile. "My name's Erin. You must be Nicole!"

My daughter nodded and leaned into me.

Erin crouched to eye level. "I brought you something special."

Nicole hugged my leg tight but looked at the woman deeply enough to give her the time of day. Erin pulled a little pink bag from her satchel and held it out. Nicole looked at me, then Cara, then Erin.

"Take it," she said. "It's a gift from us."

Gingerly, Nicole took the bag and said, "Thank you." She held the bag up to me. It had fluffed pink tissue paper coming from the opening. "Can I open it?"

"Sure."

Erin helped her with the tissue paper, and Nicole pulled out a headband with two huge, pink-sequined mouse ears at the top. Eyes wide, smile the shape of half a peach pie, she hugged it to her chest, then handed it to Cara, patting her head and saying, "Can you put this on me?"

Cara did the honors while Erin held her hand out.

"Mr. Sinclair," she said, shaking my hand. "This is Steve, John, Bob." I shook hands all around. "We have everything set up for you. As we discussed, we can't prevent you from being photographed since it's a regular session today. We can keep other guests from getting too close to you or your daughter, and we are pleased to let you know you'll have access to all our rides and attractions without any wait times, as long as you let one of us know where you're headed next. This cart is at your disposal all day, and we're happy to show you through our VIP areas to all attractions and events."

Her excitement was palpable.

"Erin," I said. "You forgot to introduce yourself to Cara."

I stepped to the side.

"Of course," Erin practically exclaimed with delight. Fake. What was with the fake today? "I'm Erin."

Cara shook her hand, and we all got into the golf cart. Nicole was as excited as a puppy on a new hambone. Hopping on my lap, then

Cara's, then insisting on sitting between us, then at the edge where she could see.

Cara wasn't looking at me. She was sweet as sugar to my daughter, which is what mattered . . . but to me? Snow queen.

"Did I do something wrong?" I asked Cara.

"You don't introduce the nanny."

"Before that."

"Hey Nicole!" she said, "Do you see the castle? It's that way!"

Nicole squealed and climbed over me to get to the side of the cart where the white castle poked over the tree line.

"Careful," Steve or John or whatever said.

I held her in the seat and leaned in to Cara so only she could hear.

"The next time I ask you something and you use my daughter to change the subject, I'm going to kiss you, and I don't care who sees it."

Her head snapped around. Eyes sharp. Mouth tight. She was mad. I liked it, in a way. Fire was better than ice by a lot.

"You better not let your daughter see again."

"Why's that?"

"What happens when I'm gone?"

"When you're what?"

"I mean it."

Gone?

Did she mean dead?

You're thick as grits that set too long, Bradley Sinclair.

Gone meant gone. Out of our lives personally and professionally. I'd always figured she'd find a reason to stick around. I thought the whole "I don't like working for celebrity families" thing was a front. But no.

She wasn't lying. She meant it, and she was getting real about it.

I was going to get real about it too. I was going to admit to myself what I always knew.

She wasn't going anywhere. Personally or professionally.

One adjustment. It wasn't going to be easy. She wasn't going to stay just because I was doing whatever I did. I was going to have to work for it.

"I mean it," she repeated, then whispered, "keep your lips to yourself."

That made me want to kiss her more. Not because she was telling me not to, but because she was so whipped up. I could have stood on my head and spit nickels, and she wouldn't have budged.

No. She would have budged if I kissed her hard enough and long enough. Those tight little lips would have softened right up. No nickel-spitting required.

And working for it turned me right the fuck on.

I leaned closer.

"Don't you worry. There's not going to be any kissing today. Even if you beg me."

Nicole squealed and the cart came to an abrupt halt right in front of the pristine white castle. The cart wasn't the only thing that came to an abrupt halt. A family of four with a stroller and a little boy in a yellow T-shirt stopped dead when they saw me. I smiled at them. I expected a little holdup, but the security guards got in front of me.

Cara picked up Nicole and started for the castle. She knew where the VIP entrance was, because that sweet bottom knew exactly how to cut the line with the row of security guys behind.

She looked back at me, half a smile. A four-ton bag of shit and nerves lifted off me.

Just that. A smile to let me know she wasn't so mad anymore. She was trouble. Bad trouble. And somewhere in my guts I'd decided that she wasn't leaving when she said she was. She was leaving when I said she was.

I was going to have an easier time standing on my head and spitting nickels than letting her go.

CHAPTER 43

CARA

I'd spent a few weeks with Kevan Delight's kids, including a VIP, drive-the-cart-around trip to Disney. I had no idea how it was done any other way. I'd gone to Euro Disney once with my third-grade class, but barely remembered anything besides the lines and a really good hot dog.

Nicole was beside herself. She wanted to do everything at once. Haunted Mountain, the baby roller coaster, the games, the candy apples, the go-karts. And Brad was game. He went on every ride with her. Whatever junk she ate, he ate and they discussed the relative merits of kettlecorn to its buttered cousin with utter seriousness.

Security kept a nice zone around them. Brad ignored them and focused on his daughter. This was going to become her normal. A buffer zone from the public and a free pass from inconvenience.

I tried to keep a step or two away. It wasn't my day. I was just there to help, but Nicole kept pulling me close and checking to make sure I was within arm's reach.

I always thought of her first, but her father made it hard to keep a professional distance. If he wasn't talking to me, asking a question, or inviting me to join the Great Popcorn Flavor Debate, he was eating me alive with his eyes. He was totally inappropriate. He was exactly the dad all the nannies talked about over coffee. The one you had to watch, because given the right moment he'd pounce.

But he wasn't that dad. Not wholly and not indiscriminately. Blakely hadn't been on the receiving end of the inappropriate-daddy vibe. It was just me. I hoped none of the people photographing us with their camera phones or shouting his name for the gift of a wave or a smile saw the way he looked at me.

"You need to go on one ride," he said, folding a tuft of cotton candy in his mouth. He and Nicole were on a bench by a cluster of shade trees. I crouched in front of her.

He wore sunglasses, but I knew he was looking at me. I could feel his eyes burning through my clothes. We'd stopped for strawberry pie just ten minutes before. He'd speared his pie, watching me with one message.

Us southern boys eat pussy like pie.

Turns out, Nicole didn't like strawberry pie. I had to finish her piece.

"No," I said, wiping sticky pink strings from Nicole's right hand while she licked the paper cone she had in her left. "I don't like rides. And it's not about me today. It's your day."

"My day means you do what I say."

"Forcing me onto a ride might be fun for you—"

"It is fun for me. Completely fun."

"I'm here to facilitate. No more."

He leaned up, elbows on knees, dropping his voice to the exact timbre of my spine's vibration. "You're a professional. We get it. Now loosen up, buttercup."

"Has any woman ever resisted you?" I asked. He shook his head ever so slowly. I wasn't surprised I didn't have company.

"Teacups!" Nicole pointed back the way we came. "Come on! The teacups!"

I looked back that way for no particular reason. I knew where they were. I just had to look away from him. But if I could resist him, Nicole had other equally powerful talents against me. She hopped off the bench and pulled me down the path.

"Teacups," Brad announced to John/Steve/Bob, and the entire entourage trundled down the brick path. We hustled past the line, through the back, and were seated in our own personal lavender-and-white cup with purple and pink flowers.

Nicole pulled me close to her, then Brad, until we took up half the cup. She held one of our hands in each of hers and giggled uncontrollably.

"Was she like this on all the rides?" I asked.

"Yep. She knows how to have fun."

"Oh, like I don't?" The ride started churning. Slowly at first. Almost pleasantly.

"I want you to spend the next three minutes on this ride not worrying about something."

He slipped to the spot across from me. The world behind him zipped out of focus with a smear of color.

"I have to worry."

"I admire the way you think you can take care of anything that comes along. But now you've gotta put that away . . ."

His last few words were drowned out by the whipping wind and Nicole's delighted cries. I lost control of my body, sliding around before I could grab on. Brad had his arms on the backs of the seats, and Nicole hung on to the edge for dear life, her smile a point of stillness in the swirl.

Was this a kid's ride? The force of the spinning was incredible. I slid into Brad and landed with my head on his chest and he laughed, arm casually draped behind me. I tried to straighten up, got halfway, and laughed with him as my face got pushed into his.

I didn't worry.

Not for a second.

He put his arm around me and held me fast. The torque threw all the worry and anxiety out of me. The laughter dislodged it and inertia flung it away to a far corner of the park. We had now. These two wonderful people and me, in a purple teacup, screaming with music I could barely hear over the whooshing wind in my ears.

I let the ride push me into him and we laughed together, squealing with Nicole at this silly spinning teacup. Even when my stomach lurched, it lurched up to a smile. Even after I knew I was going to lose the handful of blue-ribbon strawberry pie, I didn't worry. I was happy. Centrifugal force was like a drug that separated body and mind.

I puked midlaugh. It landed on Nicole, whose squeals of delight turned to screams of horror. My stomach flipped again and a stream of bright red pie made a circular pattern from my mouth to, well, everywhere.

How much pie did I eat?

The volume of pie puke far outweighed the piece, but it kept coming, splattering the back of the teacup, Nicole, and my shirt.

Brad got a little on him, but he was more worried about me. The arm that had been coolly behind my seat grasped my shoulders and held me still.

I can't say I wasn't happy. In a way, because my mind was there while my body was here, the carefree minutes stuck with me. But I was certainly sick to my stomach.

The ride came to a stop after about a dozen more turns and body and mind snapped together again.

"Oh my God," I said. "I'm so sorry."

Puke everywhere. Brad gathered up Nicole. I covered my mouth as he crouched by me with his crying daughter on his knee.

"Are you all right?"

"I'm so embarrassed."

"That's not gonna kill you."

You know what was funny?

I wasn't embarrassed. I just thought I should be. By the time the team of suits got to us, I was chuckling behind my hands and Brad was laughing as if I'd just done a world-class sight gag.

I was a part of something. A little triangle of people. I didn't stop to worry about inappropriate intimacy or attachment just then. Didn't stop myself from naming it and accepting it because Brad had me. Stupid party boy Brad Sinclair in sandals and shorts. He had me.

And he had Nicole, who was beside herself.

"My dress! We have to clean my dress!"

Brad helped me up with his free hand. "Are you going to be sick again?"

"No. I'm fine." I stood, hands hovering over my puke-soaked shirt.

"How much pie did you eat, woman?" Brad joked.

"Don't say pie."

Even the blue suits laughed as they led us off the lavender cup of hell. Nicole kept her hands a few inches from her sides, sobbing softly, saying "my dress my dress."

Once we were on the golf cart, I peeled her dress off. She folded her arms across her chest and made a shivering motion. Brad took his jacket off and put it over her shoulders as the polka-dot golf cart whipped around the park.

"You should take yours off." Nicole wrinkled her nose and pointed to my puke shirt.

"I agree." Brad wrinkled his nose like his daughter. "You'd smell better. Not to mention look better."

"Be good."

Brad smirked. Nicole curled up close to him, breeze in her hair, and he put his arm around her. They were so damn cute.

Erin twisted around from the front seat.

"I called ahead to the first aid station."

"No, really. It was just motion sickness. I'm fine."

"I'm sorry, but park liability. You know how it is. If we let you go, you have to sign a waiver."

"I'll sign—"

"Just go," Brad said. "They'll take your blood pressure and look at your pupils. It's a free checkup."

"Brad . . ."

I had a list of good, solid arguments. But the way he looked at me stopped me from finishing my thought. He didn't care about the free checkup, he cared about me.

"You don't have to worry about me," I said.

"I'm not."

The cart came to a smooth halt at the first aid station.

"Was that the first lie you ever told me?"

He shrugged, letting a little smile curl the edges of his mouth. He hopped off the cart.

"We're going to keep her company, right, pumpkin?"

"Yeah." She held up her pink pony and made a squeaky voice. "We'll go with you."

Brad helped me off the cart while Steve led me through the glass doors. They opened automatically, but he still guided me as if I could trip over motion sickness.

Inside, the room was decorated to brighten the mood of injured children, with a train chugging along the perimeter of the room just below the ceiling and heavily branded toys and decorations everywhere. No corner was left uncheered.

A young woman with a pixie cut and pink scrubs met us at the door. Her stethoscope hung around a long neck, and she spoke to Brad before she even looked at me.

"Hi! I'm Dr. Barnes. We heard you were coming! Welcome!" Her gaze lingered over him 20 percent too long. She finally looked at me. "How are you feeling?"

"I'm really fine."

"You'll be out of here in no time. We get this a lot with the teacups. Come on in!" Back to Brad. "Mr. Sinclair, we have a VIP waiting room for you and your daughter."

She led me to the exam room and pressed her back against the closed door and took a breath. It was only a moment, but the way she put the clipboard to her chest told a long story.

"He is magnificent," I said. She seemed relieved I'd broached the subject.

"How do you even sit next to him?" She shook her head, pulling the pen from the top of the clipboard.

"I don't do much sitting, to be honest. His daughter's a handful."

"I bet. Okay, sorry. That was terribly unprofessional."

"He has that effect on people."

"Yeah. Phew. Okay. Sit over here, and we'll just make sure this was an isolated teacup incident."

The brightly colored paper crunched when I sat on it, thinking about how Brad Sinclair had utterly crushed my professionalism.

CHAPTER 44

BRAD

When we got back to the hotel, Nicole chose a new set of clothes. She'd latched on to a DVD about bows and a blue submarine with squeaky little animal creatures. I'd tried to pay attention, but the text from Ken, my PR guy, came in just as I realized I'd never care about finding all the bows in the submarine.

Ken didn't bug me about what happened on social media unless I needed to do damage control. That was rare, since my reputation was so borderline bad even mooning an employee barely registered a blip. I never explained why I didn't do social media. Everyone assumed it was because I didn't want to say anything I couldn't deny later. They were right. Partly.

I skipped over the tiny words and went right to the photo Ken sent. Me and Cara on the teacup ride and the headline in bold yellow. ZⱵMORNI Ɐ TƎϽⱯՈ.

Shit. It was going to take me a few minutes to figure out what that said. I didn't have a piece of paper either.

I knew it was already going to take some effort to keep Cara past her thirty days, but if this headline was bad, and I had to assume it was if Ken was texting, then I was going to have to bust my ass to keep her.

"What's that say, Daddy?" Nicole asked. I didn't even realize she was looking over my shoulder.

"Grown-up stuff," I said. "Can you read it?"

She knotted her brows and sounded out the letters slowly, but quicker than I'd do it.

"SSSSStttttttt . . . what sound does O make?"

"It depends. Try the 'oh' sound."

I was so proud of her. I knew what people meant when they said their hearts melted. I hadn't before, but that phrase was exactly what it was. It hit me all of a sudden. Not just that she was a cute, little puppy with a big "awww" factor, but that she was mine. My little girl. My own creation. My responsibility. My joy.

And all those words were inadequate. The change was that big and overwhelming. It wasn't about thoughts or even emotions. The feeling was a part of my body.

All at once, my heart turned liquid for my daughter.

"Stoooooo . . ."

When Cara came out, I put the phone away. She stood in the doorway wearing a knee-length XXL T-shirt with a neck-to-waist graphic of thirty or so happy characters.

I tried not to laugh and failed.

CHAPTER 45

CARA

Brad didn't focus on his phone much. He didn't spend time on social media from what I could see, leaving it to his fans to talk about him behind his back. I didn't wonder about that. Some stars didn't engage that way.

So when I'd walked into the VIP waiting room and he was staring at his phone with his lips straightened in concentration, I'd been tempted to ask what the problem was.

But whatever was on Brad's phone simply wasn't my business. He put it away as soon as he got a good look at me, and cracked up at my new, clean, horrible T-shirt. So I'd forgotten about it.

We'd chatted about the DVD and my shirt on the cart ride and in the limo until we pulled into the hotel driveway.

"Everything okay?" I said, giving in to temptation.

"Yeah. It's cool." He smiled a big movie star smile that I didn't trust at all.

We stopped in the circular drive in front of the hotel.

He and Nicole had a suite with a grown-up bedroom and bathroom while she slept in a princess-themed room with a separate bathroom done up in castles and rainbows. I was in the studio next to them. There were only two suites and two studios on the floor. The nanny setup was obvious.

"I should give her a bath," I said, holding my arms out. Nicole yawned and tucked her head in her dad's neck.

"You need to give yourself a bath, teacup." He flicked me my key-card, and I snapped it out of the air.

"But—"

"I'm perfectly capable. Go on, now." He shooed me.

"All her outfits are in little bags, set up together." I stepped backward down the hall.

"Are you joking?"

"She was supposed to wear the frogs tomorrow, but she might need them today."

"Yes, ma'am. Shoo."

I backed up another step, turned, and went into my room.

He was capable in small doses. I knew that. I was being too sensitive to his inconvenience. He'd live. He might even get closer to his daughter.

The room was small but luxurious, with pillows galore on the queen mattress, a down comforter, a TV as big as a dinner table, and a glass-enclosed shower separate from the tub. There were perks to being a nanny to the rich and famous. I pulled off my pants and soaked them in one of the two bathroom sinks. Brushed the yuck out of my mouth at the other one. Peeled my underwear off, set the water to scalding, and got under it.

I had vomit chunks in my hair. Gross. That's what I got for puking into the wind. Ugh. What a weird scene. What a weird, fun scene. I'd laugh about it in ten years. Hell, I'd laughed about it five seconds after it happened.

I'd never had so much fun with a family. Not even my own. We never went anywhere because we lived everywhere. When you live in

Paris for eight months, where are you going for vacation? That's how my parents thought. Maybe they were right. Their lives were crazy. The last thing they needed was to block out fun time with my brother and me. They couldn't even plan a week ahead because they never knew when we'd be packing to move.

I never felt like I'd missed out on anything until I rinsed the shampoo from my hair in a Disneyland hotel shower. I'd missed something, but I wasn't dead yet. I had plenty of time in life to puke on all kinds of rides.

"What are you laughing about?"

I jumped. An indistinct yet unmistakable man's form stood on the other side of the wet glass, in the center of the bathroom. Fully dressed. Bare feet.

"Brad!"

He snapped the door open, looked at my naked body up and down.

"I knocked. You didn't answer."

He stepped into the shower. His tan shirt got dark under the water, sticking to every curve and angle.

"Jesus! You boiling crawfish in here?" He put his hand on the knob, and I pushed it off.

"Go away."

"Say it again and I will."

My mouth made a shape for the G sound, but a rivulet of water flowed down his cheek and changed direction, following the path of least resistance to his lips, and dripped down. It enchanted me. Like the crystal droplets between his eyelashes and the steam rising off his shirt. They glistened as if infused with magic.

"Where's Nicole?"

"Cleaned up and passed out."

His lips. The way they moved. Just like on screen, but bigger, better, wetter. Every second that passed took my breath away.

Was he waiting for something?

Me, perhaps?

I didn't know what I was supposed to do. I was frozen. He didn't belong there. We didn't belong in the same shower. He didn't ask first. Why wasn't I mad? Why didn't I scream and throw him out?

Because my nipples were tight even in the hot water. Because his body called to mine. Because I was made of flesh and blood.

And common sense. I was made of all the sensible thoughts I'd ever had.

"This can't be a thing," I said. "This is now. And it's a secret."

I didn't do things like that. I didn't have one-night stands or booty calls. Not for any moral reason. They just didn't interest me anymore. Been there, done that, puked on the T-shirt. Until now, and now was all I had.

"That's a yes?" he asked.

"Yes," I said. I didn't know what I was agreeing to, exactly, but I was okay with it, whatever it was. As long as it was now, when I wanted it, not when I could make excuses for it.

He crashed his lips into mine.

Without his daughter between us, away from his property, far from Los Angeles, I let myself feel the things I'd forced away.

You're allowed.

It was such a conscious decision to let go. I had to tell myself I was allowed to enjoy his mouth, his hands, and the pressure of his body against mine. But once I did I was flooded with the agreement of mind and body.

Go ahead.

I kissed him back fully. His hands went down my back, over my ass, grabbing it and pulling me into him.

"How long does she nap?" he whispered in my ear.

"Forty-five minutes."

"Turn around."

He turned me gently until I faced the wall with the shower head.

"Let's get this soap out. Come on. Head back."

He stroked my hair, letting the water run through it, running his hands over my body in tandem with the superheated water. I groaned when his hands drifted low, slipped between my legs, pressed down where I throbbed most. I bent my knees and spread my legs so he could get all the way down.

Losing my mind. I was losing my mind.

"Do you want me to fuck you?" he said into my ear.

"Yes."

"Now?"

"Yes. I can't believe I'm saying it, but . . ." The last word dropped into a groan as he stroked my clit. My legs wouldn't hold me.

"Not just once. This isn't a one-time deal. God, you're so fucking sexy. I need more than forty-five minutes."

"We can't be a thing. Say it's not a thing. I can't be a thing."

"Not a thing." He pulled moisture from inside me and ran it along my clit.

"Zip it. Oh, God, lock it."

"Put it in your pocket."

He punched the shower knob, shutting off the water.

"Not standing in the shower," he said. "Not the first time."

He picked me up, both of us soaking wet, and carried me out of the shower with my legs wrapped around him. He dropped me on the bed and stood there, hair dripping wet, shirt sticking to his utter perfection. I got on my knees and he gently pushed me back down.

"I want to look at you, teacup. We don't have a hell of a lot of time."

He peeled his shirt off and tossed it. His wet shorts hung heavy and low on his waist. Past the line dropping below his navel. Past the V at the top of his legs and bottom of his abdomen. Way past propriety.

"Time, Brad. We don't have a lot."

"Yeah—and I've wanted you too long. What a good girl you were. Stayed on the subject. Never looked at me. Never flirted."

He took me by my knees and opened my legs slowly. That action alone sent shock waves through me.

"I saw you look at me."

"And?"

He put his lips on my inner thigh.

"I wanted you, but—" I gasped and stopped when he nipped the sensitive skin.

"But?"

"No but." Saying the truth was hard, because I hadn't let myself consider it fully, not when his mouth was near me and his hands pulled my skin so he could see where I was most tender. "I want you to fuck me."

I could barely breathe it. I hadn't let words like that leave my lips for a long time, and they felt so good.

He wrestled with his fly and his pants dropped with a wet slap. His dick was long and, God help me, so hard the skin stretched.

From the other room, his phone dinged. He didn't even pause for it. I felt like the most important woman in the world. Just for the moment, his world was mine.

"Tell me how you want me to fuck you," he said, moving to the inside of my other thigh, making me crazy with lust.

I was out of practice, but his lips inspired me. And his hand, stroking my folds ever so lightly, yes.

"That day you saw me in the shower?"

"Mm hm."

"I was thinking about you deep inside me so hard. I was sucking your fingers as you took me."

He looked up at me and kissed my mound. "I had no idea."

"What?"

"That you had such a dirty mouth."

Oh, he didn't, did he?

"Eat my pussy, Mr. Sinclair. Like a southern boy eats pie. I want to come in your mouth."

"Before I make you come, you need to agree. This isn't the last time. I'm not finished with you."

But how?

How will that work?

I pushed all the questions out of my mind when his tongue ran from clit to opening and back. My mouth opened and he reached up, putting his finger on my lips and I sucked it, digging my fingers in his hair.

Sometimes Nicole woke early, and with the overstimulation of the morning, it was possible she could get up. I prayed for that nap, sucking his finger harder when I thought I'd burst. I didn't make a sound. Bit it back. Sleeping child. So close.

He stopped. That was when I gasped.

He looked up from between my legs, a smile touching the corners of his eyes. Laugh lines and pores, just like the man on the billboard, only better.

"You close?" he asked.

"God, yes."

He got up on his knees, stretching magnificence over me.

"Have you ever tasted yourself?" he asked, lips on mine, not kissing. Not yet, just touching me with them.

Had I? I didn't even remember. I couldn't even stir up a particular memory of another sexual encounter. I kissed his lips, his cheek, tasting myself on him. Tart sex and musky water. In my world, the relationship was so forbidden that I was more uninhibited than ever, putting my tongue on the lips that had been between my legs.

"I was telling the truth." I felt the head of his dick on my inner thigh. The lower half of my body gravitated toward it. "I can't get pregnant. We can skip a step."

He didn't answer right away, but cast his eyes down to my lips. He'd skipped a step before, and it ended with a little girl. Why should he trust me?

"Or not," I added quickly. "But I don't have anything. And I don't know if you brought protection into the shower."

"I've been around. I always wrap it up."

"Except the one time." I smiled a little to take the accusation out of the words. I didn't think he was lying. He was remembering with a scalpel.

"You don't have to trust me."

"I know I don't." I spread my legs wider in answer.

"Go ahead, teacup. Put it where you want it." I tingled. Filthy. Raw. He moved his hips, grazing it over me.

I swallowed. Reached down. Stroked him. My thumb found the drop of wetness at the tip and rolled it around.

I wanted it immediately, and I wanted to make it last. I pulled him close and ran his tip along my seam. I groaned. He'd gotten me so close with his mouth. I wanted to make this the fuck of his life, but I didn't know how.

I put his dick at my opening and pushed forward.

"All the way," I said, and he thrust all the way in. Stopped. Closed his eyes. Sucked in air. I yelped in pleasure. And he went in to the root, full friction against my clit. "Hard. Hard, Brad, hard."

He gave it hard enough to hurt, fast enough to please. I was reduced to gasps and vowels. I clawed at his chest and he drove into me with power and precision, angling himself to rub me where I needed it.

"Come. Come for me. Let me see you fucking come." He growled it, and I yelled for him, overtaken with an orgasm without boundaries. A toe-curling, back-scratching, muscle-tightening climax.

And then he came, and my God I hoped I'd remember it the rest of my life. I touched his face to remember it, how he was even more beautiful when he lost himself.

I did this.

CHAPTER 46

BRAD

Lying in bed next to Cara, I felt a wave of guilt. I could forget about the texts I'd gotten on the way to the hotel for only so long. But once we were done, the texts poked me like a sharpened dowel.

—I suggest you come back to LA right now and do some damage control—

Ken had texted while we were talking about puke smells in the limo. Supposedly there was a picture from the teacups, and I was waiting for it.

In the meantime, Cara's body was directly responsible for the smile on my face.

I hadn't had skin on skin in a long time. She was wet and tight and supple everywhere. She came like a fucking storm. If I hadn't had something on my mind, I would have exploded on the third thrust, and I could have forgotten my stupid reply to Ken.

—What? I got some puke on me? Big deal—

—They're prepping headlines that have nothing to do with puke. What are you doing with the nanny?—

It was dishonest to fuck her after I saw the headline, and more dishonest to not take sixty seconds to decipher it.

—Nothing—

"I took it easy on you," I said, getting off her. I'd told Ken it was nothing, but she wasn't nothing. I wasn't sure what she was or what we were together, but it wasn't nothing.

"Next time you're going to come so hard you're going to have to slap yourself out of it."

Up on her elbows. Knees bent. Tits pointing right at me. Nipples still hard. I wasn't interrupting that moment with the picture that was about to be published. Not before I handled it and fucked her at least one more time.

At least. Once more from behind. Her on top. Bent sideways. And that mouth.

"Promises, promises," she said, rolling over. That ass.

My shorts were a soaked, ten-pound pile on the floor. I wasn't putting them back on. She got up on her knees, back to me, and I wasn't letting that pass. I grabbed a fistful of hair and pulled until she was bent, looking at me. I wrapped my other arm around her and got my fingers between her legs. She gasped. The way that made me feel. Like a fucking lion.

"I say what I mean and I mean what I say."

"That a southern thing?" She moved her hips against my fingers. She liked it. That cold, emotionless professional liked my fingers on her pussy. Every thought in my head was filthy.

"You're never going to forget me."

"One more time." She whispered it. I could make her beg. The thought got me hard again. "Can we?"

Could we? Shit, she was already begging. Sure we could. I kissed her hard. Let that be her answer.

"Daddy? Miss Cara." Nicole called from behind the door to the suite. I'd closed but not locked it. "I'm lonely!"

"Coming!" Cara jumped off the bed like a shot, leaving me kneeling on the mattress naked, dick at half-mast.

As far as I was concerned, she hadn't even started coming.

CHAPTER 47

CARA

I wiggled into sweatpants and a T-shirt, totally commando. I went into the suite and closed the door behind me. Nicole stood in the middle of the living room with her dad's phone in one hand and Pony Pie in the other.

"This beeps too much."

"Did it wake you?" I took the phone from her and put it on the side table, scooping her up. She rubbed her eyes with her fist, dislodging a huge sleepy bit from the corner of her eye.

"I was dreaming about the ride with the log. The one that goes down the river like this?" She dropped Pony Pie to flatten her hand and move it down diagonally.

"Maybe after lunch we can go." I rubbed her sleepy crust away. It was only late morning. We'd left very early, and that's how fast the park goes when there are no lines.

Behind me, I heard Brad creep up to the door. His clothes were wet, and I didn't have to turn around to know he hadn't gone to get a hotel robe and he was as naked as a stunning male jaybird. "Let's go to the potty."

I took her down the hall, and she wiggled down. I assumed she was going to run to the bathroom, but she went in the other direction.

"I forgot Pony Pie!"

"Wait!"

I chased her, but it was too late. When I turned the corner into the living area, Brad was in the middle of the room, stark raving naked, holding his phone over his magnificent—

"Daddy! How did you get naked?"

"He was taking a shower." I picked her up, but she was too big to get picked up if she didn't want to be and I was trying not to laugh. So she got herself back to the floor.

"Why were you taking a shower in the living room?"

"I'm not. Go on, now." He took a hand off the phone to shoo her away.

The scene was entirely too delicious, but Brad looked as if he wanted to die a quick death and I couldn't watch him suffer.

"Come on, Nicole, let's go potty."

She hopped toward me and took my hand, ready to drag me down the hall. I copped one last glance at Brad's naked body, ready to give him a look that would let him know how I didn't mind the view. My eyes met his. He winked at me. I drank in his entire body, right to the core of him, where he held the phone between me and perfection.

—ORM IN A TEACU—

The letters his fingers didn't cover glowed yellow and huge on the phone. I froze. Nicole yanked on me.

"What?" he asked.

"Storm in a teacup? What is that?"

"Come on, Miss Cara!"

But I couldn't move. The font was blocky and tall. Headline font. I'd seen it a hundred times when I was turning supermarket magazines backward for Blakely.

"Later," he said.

"Brad."

"Go on, now."

He was serious, and he was right. I took Nicole to the potty, but a cloud had settled over me.

CHAPTER 48

BRAD

Coming right off a really nice fuck, the last thing I wanted to deal with was Ken. Didn't want to deal with my daughter either, but there wasn't much I could do about that. At least she was cute.

And now it was final. I'd fucked Cara five minutes before her life went tits up.

I had a hard time reading from a screen on normal days, and if I was anxious or distracted, forget it. And of course, in the new text, the headline was embedded in the image so I couldn't use the voice app. So I grabbed the pen and pad from the night table, copied the gibberish like a grade schooler, and deciphered it from there.

STORM IN A TEACUP

Not a big deal. Not worth a text from Ken. So I focused back on the photo. There was the problem.

The picture was ridiculous. The angle and the movement lied. I hated liars, and I hated that picture.

All the pictures. Someone had the shutter on repeat, and all of them were pasted together and posted like a fucking flip book.

The motion sickness was in full Technicolor, and yeah, she'd be ashamed, but we could laugh at that. What we couldn't laugh at was the movement before it, where she slid across the seat and it looked as if she was kissing me. The tilt of my head. The position of our mouths. My arm around the seat, then her. Nicole watching.

Then she puked and wasn't that just hilarious as a water bug in a june bug suit.

I followed Ken's link to the trash rag that had posted the little flip book of bullshit. There were comments. Three digits' worth. Something between 129 and 921. I knew enough. There wasn't enough ink in the pen or time on the clock to help me figure out what they said. I used the voice app on one and in a flat monotone a female voice said:

Another slut masquerading as a caretaker for children. I feel sorry for that little girl.

It took every bit of effort not to throw the phone across the room.

I wanted to wipe these assholes off the earth. Draw a line around Cara and destroy anyone who crossed it. I'd do it or I'd pay someone to do it.

I dictated a text.

> —*You get this shit down it's bullshit. It's camera angles. Tap my fucking lawyer what's his name*—

I'd sent the text to Ken without thinking. I was exploding from the inside. I hadn't been that angry since I didn't even know when. I pulled the auto-read down to the lowest volume.

—*Working on it. Get back here*—

Where was laid-back Brad who didn't give a shit? I had to take a breath. If Cara saw me like this, she was going to get upset.

I could make light of it, but Cara wasn't stupid. And she wasn't inexperienced with this bullshit either. Hollywood wives have long memories.

In the time it took me to think about Hollywood wives, the video of the tacked-together pictures was linked 170 or 701 times.

The comments. My God. So many. I couldn't read them. I felt the anger roil all over again.

And I'd just fucked her. That wasn't going to help.

But it couldn't be undone either. Couldn't unfuck the situation. Couldn't unfuck her. This was going to contaminate everything. I was gripping my phone so hard my knuckles were white.

"Can you put some clothes on?"

I looked up. Cara was standing in the doorway with her hand over Nicole's eyes.

"Yeah, sure." I rushed into the bedroom and closed the door.

There, I did something I didn't think about long enough. Something I never thought I'd do.

I set up a lie.

If I showed her, she'd never feel safe with me. Of all the reasons to hide what I knew, one terrified me the most.

I needed to see where it went with her. Just to see. I didn't know why. We were going nowhere, but it was a compulsion. If she knew about this, my compulsion would never be satisfied.

I wasn't an intense guy. Not normally. But this was real. I needed to protect her and whatever it was we were doing.

Just to see.

I took a screenshot of the website when the flip-book video of her puking was on. Did it a few times until I got it right. I deleted the link to the website and Ken's text. Deleted my cache and history so the social media links would disappear. It took twice as long as it should have because I was stressed and everything was jumbled.

That wasn't going to hold up for long.

I e-mailed the front desk. Told them my daughter was in trouble and needed the Wi-Fi password reset so she couldn't get on her iPad.

"It's improv," I told myself. "Just say yes."

CHAPTER 49

CARA

Nicole wanted to watch TV, so I let her while I read a text from Blakely.

—Where are you? I have to tell you something—

—Disney—

—I thought you weren't going?—

—Didn't you have something to tell me—

—I GOT A CALLBACK!—
—Also there was something that just showed up on Twitter—

—Congratulations!—
—What?—

Brad came out of his room with a spring in his step. In pants. And shoes. I was immediately suspicious. Even Nicole, who was watching the pony show with a little bowl of O-shaped cereal in her lap, noticed.

"I like your shoes, Daddy."

"Thank you. I like your barrette."

They were tennis shoes, but they were newish. I wondered if I had inspired the switch from sandals and shorts. I turned my phone off and put it facedown on the shiny dining room table.

"Did you want to get lunch?" I asked. He came to the table and leaned over.

"You're the only thing I want to eat."

"Cute. Your daughter needs more than dry cereal. And then we should head back out. We didn't see half the park before I launched my cookies."

He chuckled, then turned to Nicole.

"Nicole, honey, how would you like to see Grandma and Grandpa?"

She bolted upright. "Grandma!?"

"Yeah."

"They're coming?"

"No, we're going there."

I felt powerless. He was leaving Disney early, and I couldn't help but think it was because of me.

"If this is because I puked, I'm sorry."

"Don't be. Forget it. I think we can squeeze ten days in before we have to leave for Thailand."

"My thirty days is up during that shoot."

"It's perfect, listen." He held his hands out as if they could contain me. As if I already had one foot out the door . . . which, maybe I did even if I didn't realize it. "You and I have this problem. You work for me," he put his right hand to the right side, and his left to the left as if weighing gold dust on a scale, "and we have a personal relationship. So you go to Arkansas as Nicole's nanny, and you come back from Thailand not her nanny."

He slapped his hands together as if getting the dust off them.

That was a lot of travel for a kid, and his solution solved nothing between us.

I started to object, then remembered my place as far as Nicole went. If he wasn't harming her or making poor decisions, I didn't have a thing to say. As far as he and I went, I didn't have a better solution. So I'd go with him to his parents and then to Thailand, where I'd metamorphose from nanny to "not her nanny." Nothing. Zip.

"Should we eat first?" I asked, trying to get back to business if not in my mind, at least in my actions.

"We'll get something on the way." He smirked at me, gorgeous thing. I never thought it would last, but I never thought it would be so short.

"I'll pack up."

I went into my little studio. The bedsheets were wrinkled, and there was a damp spot where my wet hair had been.

I collected my toiletries from the bathroom, swiping the soft soap and little bottle of conditioner.

"Are you all right?" Brad said from the doorway. He'd put on a sports jacket. I didn't know he even owned a sports jacket.

"Yeah. Confused. But I'll be all right."

"What are you confused about?"

I blurted it out, running the words together. "We have about ten days left and then Thailand and then I'm nothing except what I'm not so I don't want to think it's me or what just happened here that's making you leave but I do have to think that."

He stepped forward, and I held my hand up.

"Don't."

"What?"

"Don't kiss me or anything."

He took out his phone. "I wanted to show you this away from my daughter."

STORM IN A TEACUP

It was the headline I'd just seen.

"Scroll," he said. I put the shampoo down and drew my finger across the glass. A picture of the teacup ride appeared. I was throwing up on Nicole.

I hadn't ever wanted to see myself in the paper. My perverse imagination built the scenario into the thing I thought about when I wanted to horrify myself. To be flat, oversexualized, called names, and surrounded by strangers who hated me.

Now it was right in front of me. I was in the paper, and laughter was the only appropriate response.

Without sexual connotation it was just funny.

"All right? That's the reason. I just want to get out of here until this blows over. I mean I know it's funny, and you can stop laughing now."

"I can't. It's too good."

"I'm trying to protect you from embarrassment here."

"I know, I know. I feel like I have no control. I mean—" I waved my hands between us, trying to swat away misunderstanding. "I go where you go because I work for you, and after that what do we call it? And what do we tell Nicole because we can't say we're just . . . you know."

"What happened to the dirty mouth?"

"I'm on duty."

He pocketed the phone. "We're going in half an hour."

I got my stuff together in five minutes and went to Nicole's room to pack her up. I passed the dining room table so I could text Blakely and let her know I was going to Arkansas.

"Have you seen my phone?" I asked.

Brad and Nicole were on the couch watching a show about cheetahs.

"Nope." He popped an O in his mouth. "Look in the foyer."

"I had it here."

He shrugged.

I figured it was in my bag, and went to Nicole's room to get her ready to go.

CHAPTER 50

CARA

I was Nicole's primary caretaker by default, and I was going to be harder to replace than ever.

Sex complicated everything about this. When I was gone, was I really gone? If Brad and I were working toward something, then I'd be around Nicole and the new nannies. Would I have a say in what they did? I'd be the girlfriend. Girlfriends didn't raise their boyfriends' children.

This is why you don't fall in love with kids or daddies or families. This is why I did this in the first place, because I loved children but didn't get close. And here I was. On a train between stations, going too fast to stop. In the car. To the helipad. Over Orange County. Landing in Santa Monica. Getting on the charter plane.

When the laughter over my teacup ride died down, what would the media say?

Stop worrying.

Nicole looked a little green on the helicopter. I gave her seasickness medicine. We didn't need two people puking in a day.

Brad focused on Nicole, who regaled us with tales of a land of ponies made of pasta and their queen of tomato sauce. We deduced she was hungry, and I rummaged around the galley for snacks. It was a long flight, and he'd arranged the plane on short notice. We had no attendant and no catering.

"I found some stuff."

I dumped juice boxes, bags of peanuts and chips, two sugary granola bars, and an apple on the little table between leather couches. Nicole reached for the juice box and held it out for her father, who was sitting across from her.

"Open, please."

He cracked open the box and pulled out the straw. I sat next to her and handed it over when it was open. Brad pulled open the peanuts, glancing up at me.

"How you doing, teacup?"

"Fine."

"I realized something as we were taking off." He passed the open bag of peanuts to Nicole. "I never hear you saying you have to call or visit your parents or anything."

"I've never been to Arkansas."

"Where's your mommy and daddy?" Nicole asked, immune to my subject-changing strategy.

"Far away. And we don't talk much at all."

"Why?" Nicole placed a peanut on the center of her tongue and closed her mouth around it. I sneered at Brad.

"Because sometimes people drift apart. It happens. Sometimes there's so much wrong between people it makes talking to them hard, so you don't talk anymore."

Brad's eyes narrowed as if he didn't trust my answer.

"What?" I ripped open a fruit roll.

"No big fight or nothing?"

"We're too polite for that. My father resents that I got him in trouble with the State Department. I resent getting dragged all over the earth. I can't tell him to turn back time and be a different parent and he can't tell me he wishes I'd been a morally upright daughter. So we say nothing."

I wedged the granola bar between my back teeth and tore a piece off. Nicole made a smiley face out of peanuts.

"If you're not going to eat them, just don't eat them," I said. "Don't play with them."

Nicole pushed them into a pile.

"That deal you got with your dad sounds real productive," Brad said.

"I don't want to talk about it. Tell me about Arkansas."

Under the table, Brad's bare foot found mine. Over the table, he opened a granola bar and a bag of chips for Nicole.

"It's home."

"I like the sound of that. More. Tell me more."

He popped a peanut in his mouth. "I can walk down Dickson Street any time of day and see someone I know." His foot crawled up my leg. "Everywhere you look is family. Every face. Even the cousins you don't like, they'll come when you need them."

His foot pressed the inside of my knee and pushed it out, opening my legs under the table. I jerked my chin to Nicole, who was eating a strawberry yogurt bar and drawing on her iPad. He was undaunted, running his toes inside my thigh. I swallowed hard, letting my body decide for me. I had pants on. It was all right. Even if she saw, she wouldn't understand.

"Redfield Lumber is right outside town." He popped another peanut, perfectly calm above the table while his foot pushed my other knee out. "Few miles. My dad worked there from when he was seventeen. Supported us with just that one job. I was in high school, just fu—messing around. I cut a few classes in my day. I worked in the yard in the summers. So I figured I'd just work there once I graduated. School didn't matter. I had to show up for tests, and sometimes I did."

He put his foot flat between my legs.

"Brad."

He didn't stop. I looked over at Nicole. Her head was on the table. The seasickness medicine did that to kids. She'd be out for two hours and not sleep at night.

"The day my dad's fingers got cut off, my sister came to class to tell me. But I wasn't there. I was smoking behind Sweetzers's Candy and messing around with Ginger Halley. I didn't want to be found. Well, my sister Susan, what did she do? She didn't panic. Didn't put out an APB. She told three people she needed to find me."

He pushed against me, straightening his knee, the ball of his foot finding the warmth on the other side of my jeans. I slid down to increase the pressure. I couldn't help it. He was rubbing me in the exact right place with exactly the right intention.

Above the table, he counted off on three fingers. "A cop. The garbage man. And Mrs. Liston, who knows where everyone is, all the time. Twenty minutes after my sister went back to the hospital, Buddy came around the back of the store and told me what happened with my dad, and he wanted a pack of cigarettes while I was at it."

I heard him, but I couldn't create intelligent questions or make a good joke. I had nothing but the friction of my body against him.

"You should see your face," he said.

My lips parted. "I can't." I glanced at Nicole. Even sleeping, her presence was going to keep him from finishing me.

He put his foot on the floor. It felt like he was ripping off a Band-Aid, and I gasped in disappointment. He leaned forward.

"You have two choices."

"Yes?"

"Behind that curtain is a sleeper. Behind the door is a bathroom."

"Nicole in the sleeper."

We vaulted into action. He scooped up Nicole, who didn't wake, and I headed for the bathroom. It was small, but not as small as on a commercial flight. There was room for two, and it was clean and warm. I was barely in when he followed, snapping the door behind him, and suddenly the space was half the size and twice as hot. He pushed me against the counter, face smashed to mine, popping my jeans open.

He took his lips away from mine. "I want to see you. Lean back, beautiful." I leaned back, putting both hands on the counter behind me. He slid his hands down my pants, unceremoniously finding my wet clit. I vibrated everywhere.

"Yes," I whispered. "Like that."

He pulled one of my legs up until my foot was on the opposite wall.

"Go on," he said. "Come on my fingers. And look at me."

"I want to tell you something," I said. Barely.

"I'm not stopping so you better start talking."

"I'm with you. You. Small-Town Brad smoking behind the candy store. That's who's touching me right now."

"Ain't that the truth."

The sensations got harder and hotter, growing into a ball of pleasure bigger than my body. I kept my eyes open for him, letting his face fill me.

"I'm going to—" I stiffened and came, open mouth, no sound, eyes closed. With his free hand he held my jaw, rubbing past when he should.

"Stop!"

He didn't.

"Look at me this time," he growled, putting two fingers inside me, pressing my clit with the heel of his hand.

"God, fuck," I said through clenched teeth as another orgasm pushed through. My hips jerked. I kept my eyes open, letting him own me fully. I was blind with pleasure, but I could see the satisfaction in his expression in the warm lights.

I pulled my body forward and I fell against him.

"Thank you," I said, chest heaving.

"I had no idea you were so hot. I need time to figure out just how hot you get."

I pushed away and went right for his fly, popping the button open.

"Let's start with the next ten minutes."

"Oh, yeah?"

I unzipped him with one hand and pulled his dick out with the other.

"I really like what you have here, Brad." It fit in my hand like it was made for me. It put me in control. I licked my lips and put my mouth close to his. "Kiss me now. The next time you kiss me I'm going to taste like you."

He grabbed me by the hair on the back of my neck and smashed his lips on me, open mouth, tongue tasting me. Then he yanked me away by the hair.

"Start sucking then," he said through his teeth.

I kneeled. Took a breath. Been a long time. I licked the length of it, tongue flat, making it slick and wet as he gripped my hair.

"You're teasing me," he groaned.

I looked up at him, mouth poised on his tip, holding it by the base.

"Make me take it," I said, then opened my mouth.

His eyes went to surprise, then to heat as he gripped my hair even tighter and pulled my head into his dick. I opened my throat and took him, fighting the urge to gag, still pushing forward. He went down my throat and I let him push my head forward until my nose was pressed against him.

He pulled me off him and I breathed.

"Jesus." He was in pure shock. Then he smiled and I had to smile back up at him. I didn't know how much longer I could surprise him, but I loved the ride.

"Keep calling him and he might show up. I'd hate for the second coming to be anywhere but my face."

He tried to keep a straight face, but laughed anyway. Then I laughed. Me and Small-Town Brad. I was sure I'd like him with or without the fancy career.

"All right," he said, weaving his fingers in my hair more tightly. "You asked for it."

I sucked in a deep breath and took his dick. Sliding, sucking, breathing him in. He thrust harder and faster, letting me breathe when I yanked back. I went into a zone, using his rhythms, groaning deep inside. I was wet again for him, throbbing with every thrust. I wrapped my hands around his shaft, sliding along the length when he pulled out.

"Come in my mouth," I gasped before I opened up and took him again, using my spit as a lubricant for my hands.

A long, deep groan escaped him, and he pulsed as he came down my throat.

When he was done, I swallowed and dropped back against the cabinets. He slid down the wall until he was sitting on the floor with me.

"Fuck." He shook his head in fascination. "You've got a whole other side."

I rubbed my aching jaw. "I was out of practice."

He leaned forward and kissed me.

"No one at home's going to understand you."

"I'm not that complex."

"I mean that you're a nanny. What that means."

"And the fact that we're fucking?"

"That should probably stay under wraps. They don't care you're the nanny, they care we're not married."

"I think that's all right. I still don't want to confuse Nicole. So I'll just be your employee out there."

He stroked my face right there on the bathroom floor.

"The shoot in Thailand. It's in ten days," he said. "Are you guys coming? I'll have her back in time for school. And I'll have you back so sore you won't be able to do anything but beg for it again."

"Can't wait."

I couldn't. Even knowing it was all going to end soon enough, I wanted him. Impractically, foolishly, shamelessly, I wanted him.

CHAPTER 51

BRAD

Dad drove us from the airport, just like he did when I didn't have money for a cab. He and I sat in the front, Nicole and her nanny in the back. Cara rooted around her bag for the first few miles.

"My phone. I swear it was on the table and now it's nowhere."

"When we get home you can call the hotel and see if they have it," I said.

"So frustrating." She kept looking at the bottomless pit of her purse. She didn't know the meaning of frustrating. Frustrating was leaving it under my pillow in the hotel and feeling like a shit heel.

"So," Dad looked at Cara in the rearview, rubbing the spot where his right pinkie used to be, "what are we calling you?"

I wanted to kick him. I knew he didn't like the idea of me getting help with Nicole, but if he was going to be an asshole about me bringing Cara, I was going to kill him.

Cara didn't seem to mind.

"Cara's fine. Nicole calls me Miss Cara."

Dad nodded. "Good. Children need to have respect. This first name business really puts me off."

"What should I call you?" she asked.

"Grandpa!" Nicole chimed in.

"He's your grandfather, sweetheart," I said. "Not Miss Cara's."

"Milton's fine," Dad said. "My wife's Ermine. Everyone calls her Erma."

"Okay. Thank you."

"You got any . . ." He waved his hand as if trying to clear the dust off the right word. ". . . whaddya call? You a vegetarian or anything?"

"Nope. I eat everything."

Dad turned down our street and nodded as if she'd just told him everything he needed to know.

"Good. That works."

Mom and my sister, Susan, waited on the porch with a passel of grandkids. We weren't even all the way up the drive before they were banging on the car. Worse than paparazzi. Nicole freaked out, hiding in Cara's armpit.

Once she got out and saw Grandma, she laughed and clapped. Dad picked her up and swung her around. Susan shook Cara's hand. My brother slapped my back. Aunt Janie pinched my cheek and told me I was skinny. My old Uncle Walter, who was six three and 160 if he was an ounce, agreed with her, grabbing at my waist to feel the love handles that weren't there. Nicole ran to the porch with her cousins, holding up her stack of pony trading cards. Cara tried to catch her, waving twinkling sneakers.

"Nicole! Put your shoes on!"

I grabbed her arm. "Leave her. If she doesn't get dirty, we're doing it wrong."

"We?"

I didn't have a chance to make up an explanation for a slip of the tongue. Buddy from next door, who ate his boogers every day at lunch until third grade, who knocked up and married Vicki Sommer before he left high school, tackled me. He smelled like motorcycle grease and sweat.

"You didn't bring Paula?" he asked.

"Nah, I'm not here to work."

In third grade, when Buddy worked on the seven and eight times tables he got a look on his face that was half twisted out and half relaxed fugue. It had meant things weren't computing, and rather than work it out he usually just accepted a D and moved on. He got that look when I mentioned Paula's absence, then shrugged and took his D.

"You have to see Margie." He punched my arm. "Man, she's gorgeous!"

Margie was his Harley. He'd been fixing her since he was seventeen. He never looked twisted and fugued with his hands in an engine.

"You been fucking it?" I waved my hand in front of my nose. "You stink, bro!"

"Bradley James Sinclair!" Mom shouted. "You got a mouth like a cesspool."

Buddy threw his arm around Mom. "I'm glad you're back. Now she can get off my case. Come check Margie out. She roars and purrs."

I didn't look to my parents or my siblings, but to Cara, who was talking to my sister about I-didn't-even-know-what.

"Hey," I said, and she turned. "I'm going to go next door for a minute. You'll be all right?"

"We'll be fine. Have fun."

I trotted over to Buddy's garage to see his bike and glanced back at Cara talking with my sister on the way to the house I grew up in. I didn't feel anything. Nothing.

Just at home.

CHAPTER 52

CARA

So. Many. People.

The oldest person I met looked as though she wasn't a minute under 150, and the youngest had just been born a few weeks earlier. I caught as many names as I could and tried to keep an eye on Nicole, but I got pulled in a dozen different directions before being placed in front of a pile of carrots and a cutting board.

"Nanny?" his sister asked. I repeated her name to myself. Susan. An uncle or two came in for beers, but the uncles were indistinguishable from cousins. The gender rules seemed set in stone. All the women got dinner on the table, all the men sat outside. Everyone helped with the children.

"Nanny," I replied.

"What kind of word is that?" She cleaved an onion, and it opened into two rocking half-spheres.

"Shorter than caretaker?"

"Leave her alone, Suze." Brad's mom, Erma, was in constant motion.

"I'm being interested." Susan had her brother's jawline, which was both disconcerting and striking on a woman.

"You're talking without saying anything."

Susan rolled her eyes and sliced a thin crescent of onion. "Seems all right's all I'm saying. Taking care of kids? I don't get paid." She bit the edge off the onion slice, then munched it down to her fingertips.

"It's great," I said. "I have the best job in the world."

Because my boss has the dick of a god.

"Is Paula still around?" Susan tried to look casual as she cut the rest of the onion.

"Yeah." I was conspicuously silent. Not another word would pass my lips.

"She and Brad still doing it?" Susan ate another sliver of onion and looked at me intensely with her gray eyes.

"Susan." Erma punctuated the name by slapping a slab of raw meat on the island. "Why are you poking this woman?" She put her clean hand on my shoulder. "Ignore her. Paula gave her grief when she went to visit. Acted like the queen and someone's looking to take her down a peg."

"She treated me like a servant. Then she told me not to bother my brother when they were working and don't ask questions. Like I don't know his 'big secret.'" She froze with air quotes suspended and the onion hanging from her mouth half-eaten. She glanced at her mother, who shook her head and put her attention back on tying the meat.

"She cares about him is all," Erma lilted. "Bless her heart."

Aunt Rochelle, who didn't express anything beyond nonverbal reactions, snorted derisively as she measured out two cups of rice.

"Sure does," I said, cutting my carrot. More words about Paula were going to pass my lips despite my best intentions. She hadn't done anything wrong. Not technically. Not outwardly. Not to me. "And bless her heart for it."

Brad had his mother's smirk. She didn't look at me when she tried to hide it, but I saw. He looked just like her.

Susan was less circumspect. She laughed and clapped. It sounded just like him.

She stopped abruptly when the windows started shaking. LA earthquakes shook the windows. If it was strong and you were in the hills, you could hear an unnerving rumble. The blubbering engine fart that rattled the side windows was much louder than that.

"Buddy!" Susan shouted with an offhandedness that could only come from issuing the same warning hundreds of times. "Get that thing off our property!"

Brad's mother opened the window over the sink.

"Bradley! You know better!"

"Where's Cara?" he shouted over the rumble. "I can't find her."

I abandoned my carrots and leaned over the sink, knife still in my hand. Brad sat on a Harley that barely fit in the driveway. In the night dark and the flood of the headlight, he looked like James Dean, but sexier, sweeter. With sneakers instead of boots and hair unweighted by grease. I didn't realize I was biting my lower lip until it hurt.

"Let me take you for a ride," he shouted.

I loved the feel of his attention, and I let myself enjoy it before I answered. I was the nanny. The staff. Not the first person he should be thinking of when he wanted company on a motorcycle ride.

"Nicole would love it," I called out the window, deflecting the attention.

"Oh no!" Erma shouted. "You are not putting that little girl on that monster." She plucked the knife from my hand. "Go. Please. Before he gets exhaust in the roast." She shooed me away exactly like her son shooed.

"You sure?"

"I need to give Susan the carrots before she eats all the onions." She squeezed my forearm. "Please."

She pushed me out. Literally pushed me.

I took the hint and ran outside.

CHAPTER 53

CARA

The last wedge of sun had slipped below the horizon five minutes earlier, and the sky darkened to teal on the east and glowed orange on the western horizon. Margie rumbled between my legs and my arms wrapped around the hard tight shape of Brad's waist.

He hadn't been wearing a helmet, and hadn't offered me one. The safe cocoon of his family must have already formed around me, because I thought nothing of it. Rounding a highway, through a wooded area, down a main street, I was lost in five minutes. I pressed my cheek to his back, smelling the leather and the wind, and let him take me wherever he wanted to go.

He turned at a wooded road and stopped where the road ended. When the engine cut I could hear the trickle of a creek and the click of the kickstand going down.

The headlight flickered out. When the bike was stable I got off.

"How you feeling, teacup?" He swung a leg over the bike.

"Fine. That was a nice ride."

"I was worried you'd toss your cookies."

"Take me for a ride on the teacups again. You'll see some cookie-tossing."

He took my hand. I hesitated. It was too dark. I couldn't see a foot in front of me.

"I have you." He pulled me forward, telling me to watch my step when a root jutted up, until the trees cleared and I could see the edge of the starry sky above and hear the rustle of the brush and trickle of a creek.

Brad pulled off his jacket and laid it on a boulder on the bank, then took my hand again. He helped me to the ground and sat behind me, legs around mine, arms around my waist, chin on my shoulder.

Words to describe how that felt. None in English. Best thing ever with a shade of this-is-wrong. Comforting and disconcerting.

"Your family's very nice."

"I feel like I live on another planet," he said. "They don't know why I can't clean my own house as it is. They don't understand why I brought you."

"I don't blame them."

"And there's something else. It's about Paula. Buddy clued me in."

"Okay?"

"Paula's from around here. She's been in the habit of suggesting I was just having my fun until I settled down and married her."

"Really?" I said sarcastically. "She's open-minded. If you were promised to me, I would have put a cowbell on your dick."

He laughed. I heard some relief in it, as if he expected me to be mad.

"Word got around and, well, people don't take to being lied to. She's gonna be embarrassed. No telling what she'll do."

"Are you going to ask her about it?"

"Nope. Doin' it the southern way. Keeping it courteous. No fuss. But I thought you oughta know in case someone brought it up."

"Noted. I'll zip it."

"Lock it."

We said together: "Put it in your pocket."

He kissed me in the dying light of the day. I felt nothing, heard nothing, tasted nothing but his lips.

"We needed to get away from everything. Just change geography. Go where no matter what, I'm me and even if they don't get it, they love me. I think this trip was right. I've done everything wrong, and this feels right."

"What have you done wrong? You conquered Hollywood. Five years ago you were nobody."

He didn't reply right away.

"There's a lot you don't know."

I shrugged. Of course there was.

"Well, I know you like to peek into a girl's shower."

"True."

"And you like to show off your ass when you're losing an argument."

He laughed and squeezed me.

"You're a voyeur and an exhibitionist already. How bad could the rest be?"

"Well, now you know where I'm from. I should have warned you first, but I was afraid if I did, I'd chicken out. It's rednecks and old Harleys. My house ain't much, but I paid off the mortgage. Dad hasn't mowed the lawn, and it looks like a weed farm. My sister's got four kids from three guys. I guess that's the worst of it."

"I think that's the best of it. You're so real, Brad. I think you're better equipped to handle fame than most people. You're whole."

He tucked a bit of hair that the wind had taken on a ride. The wind immediately reclaimed it.

"I'm not," I continued, "I wanted you to know. I was meant to have children and I can't because I rejected the first one."

I'd never said that out loud. I had to turn away.

"Seeing your family . . ." I continued. "Even for a few hours . . . I like you even more, but I know this isn't a permanent thing we have, and I'm okay with it. I can't offer you what you need. So you don't have to try and impress me or prove anything to me. You need to have a full life, and I'll keep you from that."

Maybe most women would have been afraid he would have agreed and reiterated that temporary was the best kind of relationship. But not me. I was afraid that he'd deny it. He'd either say I was whole and fine because he didn't want to think of us as temporary, or because he was lying just to make me feel better.

He did neither.

"A full life's not just for people who don't have problems, teacup." His phone buzzed against me and plinked a banjo tune. "That's Mom," he said. "We'd better go."

He stood and pulled me up. It was night already, and the crickets squeaked loudly, competing with the ringing phone. We kissed for a moment, softly before I pushed him.

"Answer when your mother calls."

He took the call.

"We're coming back now," he said without preamble.

He listened, rubbing his eyes. His body went slack. "Okay, I'll take care of it when we get in. Bye, Mom. I love you too." He tapped off. "Gotta get back."

"Is Nicole all right?"

"Yeah. She's fine." He sounded distracted and unsure. "It was something else. Come on. Let's go."

CHAPTER 54

BRAD

"I had to go. I had no choice. No. Fuck this. I had a choice. Stay and wear you down until you were nothing but a fucking piece of a woman or . . ."

I stopped. Mom had texted that Paula had been calling. We'd had a session I'd forgotten about. I couldn't keep putting the script off.

"What?" Paula said from the screen. The Skype from my parent's old computer was delayed and grainy, and I could hear dinner happening through the door, but I had to take an hour out to review the script or I was going to make a fool of myself on set. Too bad my brain was everywhere it shouldn't be. I was out of my element. I was distracted. I wanted to be at the dining room table more than I wanted to be working.

"I forgot it," I said. "Can you—?"

Nicole burst in with a paper crown and a donut.

"Daddy, I brought you a dessert."

She jumped on my lap and stuck the donut in my mouth. I took a bite and gave it back.

"Thank you, pumpkin."

She tried to put it in my mouth again, but I turned away and gave her a stern look. I wanted to get back to work.

"Yes, thank you." Paula smiled a mile wide from the screen. "You're cute as a bug in a banana split. Is Cara there to help out?"

Nicole aimed the donut for my mouth again, making airplane sounds.

"Enough," I barked. She started crying.

A little square at the bottom of the screen held the image of me with my daughter on my lap. Behind me, Cara stood in the door.

"Is she all right?" Cara asked. "I can take her."

"Daddy doesn't want my donut!" She held up the arc of crumb-dropping cake.

"Save it for me," I said, wiping her tears away with my thumb.

"Cara, honey," Paula said from the screen.

"I have her," Cara said, getting her hands under Nicole's arms, but I wouldn't let go. If she was crying, I wanted to be the one to tell her it was all right. She was my job, and I needed to be the one to wipe her tears.

"Both of you are going to have to cool it!" I said to the other two adults in the room. Cara stood behind me, and Paula pressed her mouth closed while I spoke to Nicole.

"You." I pointed at my daughter. "Sometimes you have to let Daddy work. Sometimes you have to save the donut for later."

She sniffed and nodded. "Okay. Can we play the card game after?"

"Yes. Now go with Miss Cara."

After a tiny pause she held her arms out to the woman behind me. Cara picked her up, and with the child on her hip she patted my shoulder.

Absently, I squeezed her hand before it slipped away. The door closed behind me, and I turned my attention to Paula.

"All right, we were on page eighty-seven?"

She didn't answer. She didn't move. Her face was full and round and expressionless.

"What?"

"Are you . . . I hate to have to ask this. It's terribly impolite."

"We're past that, Paula."

"Are you having physical relations with that woman?"

She smiled when she asked, as if she were on an interview show asking the president what happened with the intern. It took me a second to catch up to the fact that I'd squeezed Cara's hand on the screen because it was almost as if Paula wasn't there. But she was, and I'd been stupid.

"Are you on page eighty-seven or not?"

"I'm serious, Bradley."

"I'm sure you have your own business to mind."

"You don't mean that," she said. "I know you don't. You tell me everything and if you try and distract me again, it's as good as a split-tongued lie. And you . . . you can't lie to me. I've given you everything so don't. Just don't you lie to me, Bradley Sinclair. I deserve better."

I couldn't see much detail on the crappy screen, but I could tell she was upset.

"It's not about lying. I'm not ready to talk about it. I'm ready for page eighty-seven."

A last-ditch, pathetic attempt to salvage the session and my friendship. But I'd pushed it off a cliff before I mentioned the page number. I'd carelessly touched Cara's hand in front of Paula.

"You're a liar," she said. "I have a list as long as my arm."

They say the truth hurts more than a lie.

This hurt bad. More than Paula's uncharacteristic rudeness, her words hurt me. There wasn't any subtext to them. They just went right for the throat, and I reflexively put up my defenses.

"Tell me why it matters," I said. "It never did before so tell me why it matters now."

She closed the script.

"You brought her home. To Redfield. She's going to meet Buddy and Susan. She's going to Warren's drugstore. The creek. The high school. She's going to see all of it. They're going to know her."

"Why is that a problem?"

I'd baited her now. Smooth move, asshole.

"I can't tell you without opening my heart."

She flipped the edges of the script absently, looking just off camera. Maybe looking at her own little square in the corner and wondering if she could see herself telling me the problem.

"You don't have to," I said, trying to protect her from herself. I knew what she was going to say, and I wanted to protect her from my response. She wasn't going to like it.

She either didn't hear me or didn't believe me. Maybe she needed to get it off her chest.

"Those are our places, and I don't want to share. You trot her out all over Redfield and you sully them."

"I'm not understanding." Maybe I expected something more straightforward.

"I don't know what's not to understand unless you're thick as a brick. We have that place together. You and me. All them girls only know one part of you and the other was mine. You bring her into my town, and that just says something about you. It says you don't care about propriety or what people say about us."

"Us? Paula, there hasn't been an *us* for years."

Her face fell again. I thought she couldn't look any more upset, more angry, more sad, all jumbled in a bunch of bright dots.

"Not to you. But I was the last one you were with there, and that was mine. I was the girl they talked about, now I'm being replaced by what? A *nanny*? How am I supposed to show my face at Warren's come Christmas? All them feeling sorry?"

"Wait a minute—"

"You don't know people. You don't know what a star you are there. You don't have any idea what they all think. Now I have to quit or the talk is going to burn my ears straight off."

"Were you telling everyone we were together? That's a lie."

"They all asked when you were gonna wake up and marry me, and what was I supposed to say?"

"That you can do better."

"That's a lie."

She could do a ton better than me, but instead of hanging my argument on her intrinsic value, which would have saved the friendship, I got more aggressive.

"And saying I was waiting to marry you isn't a lie?"

"Don't you talk to me about lies, Bradley Sinclair."

Her arm moved and the screen flicked to black.

I shut the computer. I was shaking because she and a few others protected a lie I told every day.

I stood up to get away from the computer. I depended on her friendship and support, and she'd depended on me for hope. Having removed the hope from her life, I would have to live without the friendship and support.

CHAPTER 55

BRAD

Any fourth-grader will tell you lies are like snowballs rolling down a hill. But I was told early on that if I was honest about my dyslexia, no one would hire me. I'd be too much trouble. It was hard for me to manage on-the-fly script changes. I couldn't read dialog without struggle.

If someone read it to me and I repeated it, I could learn it easily, but I was no one in the business. I was broke, inexperienced, anonymous. One of a few million flowing in and out of the city every year. Casting directors were looking for reasons to disqualify talent so they could narrow down to the winner and move on to the next. Dyslexia made me unemployable.

So when I had auditions, I recorded someone else reading the sides and listened until I had it. Paula did it first, Michael did it when he was in town, and then Paula again. I trusted them to keep it under wraps. And when I got my first full-length feature, I still didn't tell the director. I wanted to just do the work. Then I'd tell them.

But I got my next picture before shooting had wrapped on the first, and I didn't want to lose that.

So, there we were.

"And here we are," I said to my father on the front porch. Almost everyone had left. Cara was with Mom and Susan in the kitchen. Nicole and her cousins were watching TV. Dad sat in the aluminum and blue plaid chair he always sat in, and I was on the swing. Our beers were mostly empty and warm as a hand, but we held them like security blankets. "I'm really good at memorizing. And I can flow with changes on just a few repeats. But fuck if I didn't lean on Paula. I don't even know if I have a flight to Thailand. I have forty messages on my phone from the preproduction team, and all I want to do is sit on the porch and drink beer."

"You'll figure it out. You were always real smart."

"Is that why everyone called me retarded?"

A spark and *zzt* came from the blue bug zapper that hung from the ceiling beam.

"We don't use that word no more."

"Never took you for PC, Dad."

He shrugged and put the bottle to his lips with his three-fingered hand. "Things change. If you don't get on the train, it just leaves without you."

"I liked the way things were."

Zzt. The humidity was cloying, thick, a heavy density against me.

"God doesn't care what you like, but he will send you what you need to figure it out. Like this girl you brought. She helps you. We can see that. You needed her and God sent her."

"Yeah." I tapped my bottle on the edge of the swing.

"And you love her."

"No. Jesus Christ, Dad."

"Watch your mouth. That particular train hasn't left the station."

"Sorry." I felt as if I was ten all over again, rolling my first cuss around my mouth before letting it fly. "I was surprised you said it."

"I know you live different out there. You all have your nannies and staff for your family and handle the career yourself. We always knew

Paula wasn't your future, no matter what she said or didn't say. You came home one Christmas with her, and all you did was work. But this one." He jerked his thumb inside. "You love this girl no matter how much you cuss our Lord over it."

I don't know what made me think I could hide anything from my parents. These are people who found out I was cutting school even though my grades were no worse whether I went or not. Neither Buddy nor Arnie ratted me out. Mom and Dad knew just because they *knew*.

"I do, and I have no idea how to make her mine."

"You could start by telling her you love her."

"You have no idea how complicated it is."

He planted his feet wider and leaned back, putting the beer to his belly.

"How complicated could it be?"

"She'd have to stop doing what she loves. So what, right? She'd just . . . what? Take care of Nicole because she's my daughter? And if it doesn't work out, what then? Nicole loses her. I lose her. She loses her career. She loses her anonymity. I can't be with her and protect her at the same time. But I have to be with her. I have to. She's like glue. She holds everything together."

He nodded, looking out into the front yard. The crickets were loud, and the bug light zapped more mosquitoes than it had ten minutes before.

"First, you better tell her about the reading problem."

I shook my head and sipped my beer. "She thinks I'm this really honest guy."

"Then you better get to it."

"Yeah. Before we leave for Thailand. Or before *I* leave."

"Atta boy." He tipped his beer to me and we sat in silence, listening to the *zzt* of sparking mosquitoes.

CHAPTER 56

CARA

Brad got more disconcerted as the next two hours passed. He said he had a fight with Paula and acted like it was nothing. He drank a little, laughed less, hung out with his father on the porch but kept looking into the middle distance as if his mind was back in Los Angeles.

I helped clean up the bottles and dishes. Brad's mom washed and I dried. Apparently, the dishwasher worked but was still not trustworthy with the good china.

I was just hanging up the house phone with the Disney hotel. They'd confirmed they'd mailed my phone to an Arkansas address for an ungodly amount of money. Erma fiddled with the silverware and asked a question that must have been on her mind.

"Is he a good father?" she asked.

I hadn't thought about it. I didn't think of parents as good or bad. They did their best or they didn't. So I took my time answering.

"I've worked with a few dads in the business, and I have to say . . . he's great."

She didn't respond. I hoped she believed me, because when push came to shove, he tried harder than the rest of them, and that mattered. He made plenty of mistakes, but Nicole would grow to see a man who was present for her.

"I had a feeling," she said warmly.

———

His parents had set up Susan's old room for me and Nicole, putting their famous son on the couch for the night. His childhood room was now his mother's sewing room, and his room as a teen had been in the garage. It was used for storage.

"Honestly," his mother said, "why would you come back here with that mansion you live in?"

"But that couch is for midgets," he complained.

"You're not too big for the floor, young man," his dad replied with an eyebrow raised. "Unless you want to get one of your fancy staff to make you a reservation over at the Sleepytime Motel on Route 46."

Brad snapped up a pillow and tossed it on the floor.

"I sleep late, Dad. Don't step on me in the morning."

So we settled in. I slept in Nicole's bed.

"Where's Daddy?" she whispered in the dark.

"Downstairs."

"Is he coming? I can't sleep without him and you. I'll be scared."

"You'll be fine."

"No! I—"

As if on cue, the door opened and Brad slipped in. I got up on my elbow, adjusting to the hallway light.

"Daddy!" Nicole sat up and turned down the sheets on his side.

"Shush," he said, getting in fully clothed.

"You're going to get in trouble," I said.

"What are they going to do? Ground me?"

We squeezed into the twin bed, as usual. With his daughter curled up against him and the blue light on his face, I knew I hadn't lied to his mother while drying dishes. We stayed silent for a few minutes, sharing a long pillow, existing in space together, until Nicole's breathing got slow and regular.

"Is everything all right with Paula?" I asked.

"Yeah. I mean, no." He paused and took a deep breath. "We'll figure it out."

"Was it what we talked about? What she'd been saying about you?"

"I don't want to hang too much on that. Just that she knows I know, and I'm sure she's pretty mad at herself, which won't make her easy to be around."

"Do you want to go back and work it out with her? We'll wait here."

He turned his whole body in the tiny slice of space left on the twin bed, and looked at me over Nicole's head.

"Really?" he said. "You'd stay here while I went back to make up with her?"

"Yes. It's not that big a deal."

He reached over Nicole and stroked my cheek.

"You trust me?"

"To what? Negotiate a reconciliation? Or keep it in your shorts?"

"Yes."

"I'm sure I can find a cowbell around here somewhere."

He smiled in the shadows. No cinematographer could have captured that moment better than my heart did.

"I bet," he said. "If we got out of bed, she wouldn't wake up."

I slipped off the bed. He gently moved away, practically falling off. Nicole shot up, looked at me with eyes half closed, then her dad.

"Where's my pony?" she asked. I found it on the floor and gave it to her. She collapsed in a heap and was out like a light.

"I think we turned a corner here," Brad said.

"I think so."

He took my hand and pulled me out of the room. Down the hall, tiptoeing past a room where a man snored so loudly it sounded like a saw. We got to a door to the outside at the end of the hall.

"I'm in my nightgown," I said, as if he couldn't see my hips and hard nipples through the thin cotton.

"Not for long."

He opened the door and took me to a rickety set of wooden stairs along the outside of the house. *Clap creak clap clap,* he didn't say a word and didn't leave me an opening to ask a question.

When we got to the bottom he picked me up, taking my breath away, saving my bare feet from the cold stones.

"Are you all right?" I asked when we got to a padlocked door. "What's going on?"

"That house is too damned small."

He turned the black disk on the padlock and popped it open. Swung the hinge and opened the door with a jerk. He dropped me inside.

The overhead light was dim, but I could see cobwebs and old movie posters on blue paint. Cardboard boxes were stacked everywhere, but I could discern the shape of a bedroom under them. A desk with boxes under and over. Loft bed with no mattress. A dresser with boxes on top and in front.

"When they said it was storage they meant it," I said.

He faced me, and I knew why he wanted to be away from the house. Bathed in intensity, glowing with desire, he was a man on a mission.

"I'm not spending another night in bed with you unless you're naked."

I felt naked already, the way he was looking at me. My nipples stuck out of the nightgown, and my clit had just started to throb.

He brushed his hands over my breasts, feeling the tips. "All day, I wanted you. You sat down by the bluff, and I saw that little bit of skin over your waistband."

"You were a gentleman."

"Not anymore." He pinched a nipple through the nightgown, and I groaned. My spine turned to jelly. It was easy for him to turn me around so I faced a stack of boxes. My body had no will of its own when he bent me over. I even hissed out a "yes . . ."

He picked up my nightgown in one swift motion, exposing my ass to the air.

"This is mine." He ran his fingers over my slickness, slipping two inside me. I groaned. He took them out and put a third finger in, stretching me. "You ready to get fucked?" He pushed inside me as deep as he could.

I couldn't see him take his dick out, but I knew he was, and I felt it on my cheek as he stroked my lower back.

"Take me," I said. "Please."

"You're so hot. Such a sexy girl. You make me so hard." He slapped my ass, and the sting made me shudder.

I pushed into him and he countered. Three strokes and he was deep. When he'd gone down to the root, he grabbed my hair and pulled.

"This what you want?"

"Harder."

"Touch yourself. Make yourself come, and I'll fuck you so hard you crack."

He planted his hands on my hips. I reached between my legs, for my clit, his dick, feeling the way he moved inside me.

"Cara," he whispered, sucking air in. The tenderness of his call the opposite of the way he fucked me.

He bit the back of my neck as I came, holding me up as I lost control of my body. I bit back his name, turning a scream into a deep breath and a grunt.

He pulled out of me, but held me still by the hair. Then he marked my lower back with his come, softly saying *mine mine mine* as if he was trying to convince himself it was true.

CHAPTER 57

CARA

"I decided something." Brad pushed me against the wall outside the room where Nicole slept. He kissed me and felt my body through the nightgown. We whispered together after midnight, but I still worried about waking someone.

"You shouldn't make decisions right after sex."

"I made it during."

"Even worse."

"I need you. You're staying."

"You cannot pay me and bed me at the same time."

"I'm only paying you for the hours I'm not fucking you."

"Are you serious?"

"Dead serious."

"No. That's—"

"Good. It's decided. I'm going to sleep on the living room floor. See you in the morning."

He stepped back, looked me over from head to toe, and walked down the hall.

"Brad," I said quietly. He slowed. "Do you trust Paula to be at your house while you're here? Since the fight, I mean?"

"Stop thinking about this. You're freaking out for nothing."

I didn't agree with him at all. I thought there was plenty to freak out about. His daily routines. His lists and tasks. Everything she did, which was so very much.

Pushing him was going to get me nowhere though. His breathing had already gotten slow and shallow. If he was letting go, I could let go.

"Good night, Brad."

"Good night, teacup."

CHAPTER 58

CARA

Brad and I had spent two days and two nights together. I met his friend Buddy, cooked with his mother, took Nicole on long walks around town. We took her to the ice cream shop in the afternoon, after the playground, where Brad sat with me and talked about his childhood and his family.

"I can't believe how smart she is," he said of his daughter as she climbed the play structure. "She's reading. And stop telling me it's normal."

"It's normal," I said. "Between five and eight."

He took me by the chin. "She's exceptional."

"She is. But her reading level's in the normal range."

When he held my chin like that I melted into a hot puddle. He was so close to kissing me, brushing his thumb along my jaw, his face softening a little bit. I didn't know when he'd stopped being a star to me, when I stopped seeing his real face and his movie/billboard/magazine face at the same time, but he was more gorgeous without the mental backdrop of celebrity.

"No touching in front of the little one," I said softly. "Later, you can finish that thought."

"I'll finish that and a few more." He dropped his hand.

The past few days had been perfect, and I knew it was because I'd allowed them to be. I let Brad be Brad, and I let myself drop any pretense that I was upholding a standard of behavior. He didn't treat me like a nanny, and I didn't act like one. I just let it go.

Maybe being outside Los Angeles made it easier. Maybe it was his determination that whatever we had wasn't a fling. Maybe he just wore me down. But I didn't pretend I didn't have feelings for him. I didn't get suddenly stupid or unrealistic. I knew we had to go back. I knew people were going to talk, and my job prospects were about to shrink to the size of a studio executive's attention span.

Late at night, after he took me in the garage night after night, lying in the bed next to that beautiful little girl, I worried so much I shook. My heart skipped and twisted, and the pain in my chest seemed unbearable. I couldn't breathe. I didn't want to go back home, and I couldn't stay. How many more days would this last? How long before I was in the cold with no job, no Brad, and no Nicole?

I'd done everything I could to avoid this happening, and here I was, in Arkansas, falling in love with a celebrity daddy and his daughter.

Late at night, with the crickets and the breeze outside, and Nicole's breathing next to me, I panicked.

But in the morning, whether I'd slept or not, I felt at peace. I was living a lie, but it was my lie and if I didn't live it, who would? I dressed Nicole and brought her downstairs. I let myself be affectionate with her. I smiled at Brad with the fullness of our shared secrets. I lived the way I wanted to live, realizing finally that even when this all ended I'd learned something. I learned what I wanted. I wanted a home, a family, and a man to call my own. And when I was with him, I could pretend that life was with Brad Sinclair, not the movie star, but the man.

The only boundary I maintained was with Nicole. She couldn't see the physical affection. We needed plausible deniability to protect her from hurt.

"As long as we have her back for school, I have no objection." I stroked his face in the garage. He'd set blankets out over the desk and fucked me on it in the dark. We'd taken the questions of our relationship in small bites, hammering out a plan in pieces.

"I may be in Thailand a month after you leave."

"You won't. It's monsoon season. Two weeks tops." I held up two fingers and he kissed them. "If we make it that far—"

"We will."

"*When* we come to that bridge . . . I can't even say it."

"I'm going to call you my girlfriend. You're going to find another job if you want. You're going to see Nicole every night when you come over. Everything's going to be normal."

"You're a real optimist."

"Only when I'm with you."

CHAPTER 59

BRAD

I'm dyslexic. Seriously dyslexic. It would be funny if you could see what I saw, but you'd never laugh. I'm sorry I never told you, but outside my family, no one knows but Paula and Mike. I wasn't ready, and now I am. Because I love you.

And I hid your phone because I was trying to keep something else from you.

You can hate me for this shit, but I love you, and I'm not letting you go.

Everything sounded ridiculous and hammy. I played the admissions over and over, trying to make myself look good, then look bad, then more honest and self-effacing. In the end I was just going to say what needed saying, and I'd see how she reacted.

But Paula, she was a loose end. I had to put some ointment on that. She'd been good to me for a lot of years, and yeah, she'd had ideas about me, and said things that weren't particularly true, but I wouldn't hold them against her.

With Cara, Nicole, and Susan's youngest in the front yard blowing soap bubbles, I texted Paula from the porch, speaking softly but clearly into my voice dictation app.

—Are you all right?—

—You led me on a lot of years—

Led her on? Not even a little. I didn't touch her, didn't wink at her, didn't do anything. I'd put a lot of effort into *not* saying a single sexy thing or flirting even a little because I needed her to work for me, and here she was turning that into the exact opposite.

—You know that's not true—

—I am not a stupid woman. I know how to read you—

This was ridiculous. I called her from the front yard. She picked up on the first ring.

"Paula, what's happening? You've gone off the rails."

"I've decided to tell you something, Bradley. I don't care about anything right now but telling you this."

I was sure I didn't want to hear it, and I was sure I had no choice but to listen.

"All right."

"I've been with you for years. Since everyone learned their letters in first grade and you just didn't. No one knows you like I do. All these people in the business, like you call it, they don't know who they're talking to. I do. And all that time ago when we split up, I let it happen because I thought you needed time to sow your oats. Now I think you've sown enough. I think it's time for you to just settle down."

And there it was, on the line, person to person. Shit-and-butter-covered-biscuit . . . I was not prepared for this at all.

"No," I said. "I love you, Paula, but not that way. You're loyal and steady. I respect you. But I don't feel what you want me to feel. I'm sorry."

I wanted to crawl into a hole like a little brown gopher. Just disappear into the dirt. I didn't want to hurt her. She didn't deserve to be humiliated. I stayed on the phone for what felt like the longest pause in the history of awkward pauses, and I just prayed Nicole would be amused by the bubbles long enough not to interrupt that horrible pause.

"Paula?"

"I stayed by you," she answered.

"I know."

"I was waiting for you to wake up. Grow up. All that time. All the things you did."

"What did I do?"

"I smiled through all of it."

"Paula. What is it you think I did?"

I heard her take a deep breath, and I didn't interrupt.

"We were on a plane to Dublin to shoot *Everly*," she said.

"Sure. The Delta flight. What's the—"

"No." She cut me off. "The one after. The first time you flew first class and you were a smiling fucking rube when they gave you a hot towel. The flight attendant performed oral sex on you in the galley."

Right. I was that guy. I was the guy who thought he needed to rack up conquests and movies. I hadn't been the guy in Redfield watching my daughter and my girlfriend (could I call her that?) blow soap bubbles with my nieces and nephews.

"I don't remember what you're talking about," I said, watching Nicole jump for a huge bubble and miss.

"I do," Paula said. "You barely paid attention, which was exactly what Ken wanted. You were looking at her bottom, and I gave you the letter. I told you to read it, but I knew you'd barely try, like always."

Her voice was a soup of rage and hurt. I'd ripped the rug of her life right out from under her. She was already off balance from Nicole, and I'd been a shitty friend.

"What did it say?"

"I told you to read it and you pushed it at me and said, 'Can you just tell me what it says?' so I did, I read it to you and I told you to sign off on what Ken said was best and you did. You signed where I told you to and you went right off to get the stewardess to be disgusting in the bathroom."

"What did it say?"

"I told you exactly what it said."

"Tell me again."

CHAPTER 60

CARA

Brad worked every day. He locked himself in the office/sewing room and worked on his script. I'd nannied for plenty of actors. I'd never seen one work that hard. The hours he put into preparation were far and away the most intense.

Susan came around a lot. She lived around the corner, and her mother babysat most days. The street was like an extended Sinclair campus.

I was sitting on the porch playing a matching card game with Nicole when a delivery truck pulled up.

"Hey," the guy said, carrying a box under his arm.

"Hi." I stood up.

"You must be the girl Brad's been taking around." He had dark skin and a crisp white smile. Six two. Rippling muscles. In Los Angeles he'd be an actor or a model.

"I think you're talking about Nicole."

"Her too." He smiled at the girl and handed me the clipboard. "How are you, Nicole?"

"Good." She looked up from the memory game long enough to say, "I like your head."

He laughed and put his hand on his bald skull. "Thank you."

I signed for the package, and we traded the box and the clipboard, saying our good-byes. I looked at the label as I walked into the house. It was for me. I didn't expect that. The return address was West Side Nannies, but no name. Also strange.

"What did he bring us?" Brad's dad asked when I got to the kitchen.

"It's for me, apparently."

He pulled out a knife, wielding it with three fingers. "Let's see." He slashed the tape, popping the box open. I looked in.

Books.

Dealing with Dyslexia

The Dyslexic Adult

I found a white letter-size envelope and opened it.

> *Cara:*
>
> *I'm sure Brad has told you about his problem.*
>
> *Now that I'm no longer his assistant, it's important that someone take over helping him memorize his lines. These books will help you learn how.*
>
> *I hope you're happy with him.*
>
> *Good luck,*
>
> *Paula Blount*

His problem. I should have seen that coming a mile away.

The way he was so happy Nicole could read without trouble.

The way he never read anything in front of anyone.

The slow, rote memorization of the script.

Paula taking care of everything.

More papers inside. Marked scripts. Flashcards with phonetic spellings.

"Paula," I said to myself, identifying the sender to his parents. "Brad's dyslexic?"

They exchanged glances. "He didn't tell you?" his mother asked, incredulous.

I didn't have a moment to answer. Brad walked in wearing a T-shirt stretched over his perfect chest and jeans that made me want to get him naked. My brain spun off its axis for a second.

If I'd been thinking straight, I would have said something about the books right away. Told him it didn't matter. Or hid them. But all I could do was stand there holding *Phonetics for Dyslexics* staring at him because he was beautiful and that was the book I had in my hand at the moment.

He saw me, the books all over the counter, his parents looking meek, and walked out.

CHAPTER 61

BRAD

Five minutes after Paula hung up, six minutes after she told me what was in the letter I signed, I was back at it. Trying to work, because that was all that kept me sane, but my concentration was shot. I'd just figured out how to tell Cara I was dyslexic only to find out that was a teeny tiny little fib in the face of the incident on the plane Paula had just reminded me about.

Shit, I was just walking to the kitchen for a Coke, trying to decide whether to hide it from Cara or just spit it out. Wondering if Paula could be bought off with money or compliments. I didn't have the testicular fortitude for bribery or flattery, but I didn't have any other options.

I never got that Coke.

When I got to the kitchen, my dad had this shrug on. My mother was kind of shaking her head, and the one who mattered? The one who hated lies? She was just staring at me, holding up a book. I didn't know what to make of her expression.

Ken, my personal PR pith-maker? He had an expression for information that got out.

The toothpaste was out of the tube.

Was I supposed to apologize?

What did someone do right out of the gate?

Was I supposed to defend myself? Tell her I hadn't gotten around to mentioning it?

I didn't care what anyone thought of me, but I cared what she thought.

If you don't care what people think, why didn't you tell them you were dyslexic?

Flooded. I was flooded with my own contradictions and needs. Cara put the book down, and I knew whatever was going to happen was going to happen now. I was going to have to answer for my ambition. I was going to have to tell Cara everything my drive had done to her, to me, to us, to Nicole, and I wasn't ready.

Nope.

Because Paula had just told me the one lie I'd forgotten I'd told. The big one. I hadn't even had to hide it because I'd zipped it, locked it, and tossed it out the window, never to be recalled. Now what? Now that I loved Cara and I wanted to find a way to make her part of my life? Now that I'd figured out how to tell her the first big lie, a second presented itself just as she figured out what a liar I was.

This party boy needed a drink.

CHAPTER 62

CARA

Nicole licked her ice cream bowl and handed it to her grandmother.

"It's clean now. You don't need to put it in the dishwasher."

She had chocolate streaks across her cheeks, on the bridge of her nose, and under her chin. She was as funny and cute as ever, but two hours after Brad left the room, I was uncharmed. I wiped her face as she tried to wiggle away.

"Ow! Hey! I don't like that!"

"No five-year-old likes getting their face wiped." I put the paper towel down, and Nicole gave me the stubborn-child-look-of-death.

"I. Do. Not. Like. It."

"Well," Grandma said, "why don't you show Miss Cara how to do it." She handed the paper towel back to Nicole.

"Come here," she demanded, waving me to her level.

I resigned, leaning down. Nicole gently wiped my face, patting so lightly she wouldn't have gotten a speck of ice cream off me if I'd decided to lick the bowl.

"You're upset," Erma said.

She was right. I was distracted and unhappy. I must have broadcast it with every gesture and word. I felt as if I was dangling. I didn't have a phone so I couldn't call him, and calls from his parents had gone unanswered. I just wanted to talk to him. Nothing more.

"I don't know why he thinks it would matter to me."

She put Nicole's ice cream bowl in the dishwasher while she wasn't looking.

"When he first moved out there he had a lot of people telling him what to do. People who wanted to help him. And things happened so fast for him, he couldn't get his feet under him, so he listened to them." She wiped the counter pensively. "One of the things they told him was that if people knew it took him so long to read, they wouldn't hire him. He didn't go all the way out there to not get work." She pointed to my face and said to Nicole, "You missed a spot, sweetheart."

"Thank you, Grandma." Nicole wiped a spot on my forehead and put the towel down. "See? That's how you're supposed to do it."

"I want to tell him it's all right."

"He's probably down at Buddy's," Milton grumbled, walking in from the living room. With his phone to his ear, he shouted a second later. "Yeah! Buddy! It's . . . Yes! I'm fine! Is my son in there! . . . When?! . . . All right! Thank you!"

He clicked off. "Left an hour ago."

What followed was a good half hour of calls, shouts, a few segues into gossip as Erma and Milton Sinclair tried to track down their son. Calls came in. Calls went out. Susan came in with suggestions and made more calls. Brad had been to Buddy's, peeled off with a couple of high school friends, bought dinner for everyone at Jack's Chicken and Fries, hung out in the parking lot of the Chevron convenience store drinking beer with his friends before Deputy Froman had gotten his autograph and told them to move on. Apparently, he went back to Buddy's and put Theresa Crump on the Harley because she was too drunk to make it out of the lot, much less three miles to Hensley.

And that was the last we heard from him. Theresa Crump didn't answer her phone. Brad didn't answer his.

I wasn't worried about Theresa Crump, though I felt sympathy for her hangover. I wasn't worried Brad's dick was going to find its way into her. I should have been, but I wasn't. I was worried that he was running around town because he thought I was angry at him. I was worried he was partying to cover up some grand hurt I'd exposed.

"He's there?" Susan shouted into the phone. "Tell him not to move. Keep him. Tie him down."

She put the phone away from her face and mouthed "Em-and-Pee" to her mother.

"Find out who he's with," Milton said.

"Sherri—hang on." She put her hand over the bottom of the phone. "No one. He's getting a bottle of water. Talking to Winch Welton."

"So he's on his way back." Erma threw her hands up as if it was decided. "He can sure make us crazy, and we love him." She pointed to me. "But he owes you an apology."

"If he was coming back, he'd get water here," I said to myself but loud enough for everyone to hear. "Theresa Crump's home. She can get her own water. He's going somewhere without a sink and he's staying there."

Where had we been in these few days? More importantly, where had we *not* been? Who had he avoided?

"Can she get him to stay there?" I asked Susan.

She rolled her eyes and took her hand off the mic. "Sherri. Is he still there?" She nodded to me. "All right . . . tell Winch to keep talking . . . it's his field of expertise . . . I know, honey . . . see you . . ."

Milton tossed me the keys to the Buick.

"You know how to get to the M&P? Left out the driveway. Two lights. Right on Wolfe. Can't miss it."

"Thank you."

CHAPTER 63

CARA

I didn't think I'd make it to the M&P supermarket in time to catch him, but I went anyway. A flyer was stuck between the doors. When they *whooshed* open for me, they released the paper. I grabbed it.

REDFIELD LUMBER'S GOT WHAT YOU NEED!

It was a sign from the heavens.

"I'm so sorry, Miss." Sherri rushed out of the manager booth in a blue, zip-front pantsuit. "Winch and Barn tried to chat him up, but he said he had to go." She tripped on a neat stack of just-delivered newspapers. When they fell they fanned out in a multicolored spray of rectangles.

"It's fine." I put the flyer to the side and kneeled with her to pick them up. "He was on the bike?"

"Buddy's Harley. Yeah."

The papers were slick with wax and full-color ink. They'd fallen front down so all I saw were weight-reduction ads and classifieds. Sherri took a stack and slapped them down to make the edges even.

"We see him all the time in these papers." Sherri smiled ruefully. "Perks up the whole town."

Meg Birch was on the cover of *Hollywood Magazine* with her soon-to-be ex, looking as if she'd been under the knife ten too many times.

"You should go catch him," Sherri said, blonde hair escaping from her clips. "I got this."

"Thank you."

I got up and walked toward the automatic sliding doors. They slid open and as I went to step through, I saw the stack that was under the one Sherri had knocked over.

I was on the front page with him.

I stopped.

His face was huge, midsentence, eyes half down, unprepared. He looked drunk or angry. Not gorgeous. The picture from the middle of the roll a friend would have discarded was the front page of the paper. And I was cut and pasted right behind him. They'd reddened my lips and made it look as though I was about to kiss him.

DADDY SINCLAIR TAPS THE NANNY
Right in Front of Sweet Nicole!

Behind that, in a separate rectangle, was a picture of us on the teacups. The camera angle made it look as though we were in the middle of a lip-locked embrace.

I'd imagined a moment like this a few hundred times and recoiled, blocking out the horror of it with other thoughts, other visualizations.

Anything but that.

Anything but what happened to Blakely.

"Can I grab one of these?" I asked Sherri.

She stepped over to me, slipping on the papers, righting herself, and looking at what I pointed at.

"You're prettier in real life," she said.

"Thank you."

"I guess he dropped Paula Blount." She shrugged. "Maybe she'll stop harping on it now."

"I think she dumped him."

Sherri let out a *pfft* as if I was talking crazy, then handed me a paper. "Go ahead. Take it."

I reached into my purse to pay for it, but she waved away the idea.

"Just take it for helping me clean up."

I thanked her again and tucked the paper under my arm, then I picked up the lumber flyer.

The parking lot was dark and empty. There wasn't a soul around, but I felt eyes on me. People were going to see me. They'd know where I was and when. I'd never felt so exposed. Not since I was caught in the backseat of a car with a boy from school and everyone knew. Not since the thoughts of my classmates were written all over their faces.

I was angry at Brad, but not really. I was angry at the world. I was angry at myself for dancing on the edges of celebrity. What else did I expect?

I hurried into the car, slammed the door, and locked it quickly.

Nothing could protect me, and it was my own fault.

This is just a feeling. You're safe. No one is here.

Would I ever believe this again?

I was of two minds. I wanted Brad. I'd feel safe with him, yet he was the cause of my feelings of vulnerability.

My mouth had gone dry and my breath had gotten hard and shallow. I breathed in through my nose and out my mouth five times. It didn't help. I put the light on so I could find the bottle of water in my purse and saw my reflection in the glass.

Blakely talked about changing her face. Would I have to?

I took a deep breath and looked at the paper in the car's dome light.

There I was, far from home, staring at my worst nightmare. They didn't know what was between me and Brad. They didn't know about the late nights talking with Nicole between us, or how we shared love for one little girl.

They didn't know I loved him. Not the shell of a man they'd photographed, but the real man. Where was he in the picture? Nowhere. He wasn't on the page at all. Neither was I.

My armor was all the things the camera couldn't see.

CHAPTER 64

CARA

Redfield Lumber squatted on the main road behind a huge parking lot. Beige with green doors and letters, daylight-bright under floods. And closed. Dark inside, without a sign of life.

But he was here. I knew it. This building was the storage space for his greatest fears.

The traffic light flicked to green, as if anyone wanted to leave the lot at that hour. I got back in the car and went down the side road. I turned left onto a narrow road I could barely see in the dark. The car bumped on the scrappy asphalt. Trees and bushes encroached on each side.

The road opened into a small, well-lit lot behind the lumberyard. Brad was stretched across the concrete floor in front of the loading dock's roll-up door. The Harley was parked by the dumpster and when he turned his head to see who was coming, he was still the most beautiful man in a ten-galaxy radius.

I grabbed the tabloid off the dash and got out.

"I see that thing in your hand," he said, looking back up at the roof of the dock. His fingers dangled a bottle of iced tea off the side of the loading dock. "You were already mad before you found it."

"I wasn't mad."

"Yes, you were."

I hoisted myself onto the dock, sitting by his head.

"Bullshit," I said. "You saw Paula's box and flipped out. You didn't give me a chance to say or feel anything."

I put my face directly over his. Was he drunk? His eyes were clear. He wasn't slurring or spitting. Maybe the iced tea bottle just had iced tea in it.

I put the tabloid on his chest.

"I cannot believe how fast they got this to press," he said, looking at it quickly before sitting up to open it. "It's going to take me fifteen minutes to read it. Give me the log line."

"You're fucking me because you're confused. I'm a whore. Nicole is rotten and spoiled already."

He didn't react right away. Just let the floodlight wash the color out of his eyes. Like a shot, he straightened himself and let the velocity push him to the ground. He spread the paper over the hood of his dad's car. The pictures were crystal clear in the floodlight. I hopped onto the ground with him.

He pointed to my photo so hard the hood under the picture made a hollow sound.

"You look beautiful in this one."

"Brad." I crossed my arms. I hated seeing myself in print. Hated him looking at this flattened version of me. I felt out of control.

"And this one too? A little blurry, but—"

I snapped the papers aside. I couldn't bear it.

"Stop."

"I can't read what they're saying about you!" he shouted. "I don't know what they said about my daughter. I want to choke someone, and I have to calm down to read this fucking shit. And now you know I'm stunted. Developmentally delayed. Re-fucking-tarded. Yes. I was called retarded. Now you know. And it fucking kills me that on this day, when *this happens,*" he indicated the paper, "this is the day you find out Paula's been reading to me like a kindergarten teacher my whole career. I can't even be mad about what they said because I'm too upset to read it."

He grabbed the pages, ripping and pulling them apart. I took his hands in mine to calm him down.

"Let them go. Please," I said, but he held them firm and I held his hands just as tightly.

"I'm not stupid," he said. "He said . . . my father's boss said he'd do me a favor. He'd take me on full time after junior year. It was his way of giving back. Paying it forward. Hiring the retard."

"You know you're not," I said, avoiding the word that had hurt him. "You finished high school. Went to college for acting."

"With a special dispensation for talented idiots."

"You know you've proven them all wrong."

"But what did I prove to you?"

He loosened his grip on the paper, and I took it.

"You've proven you're a little crazy," I said, opening the dumpster. I threw the crumpled tabloid in it and slammed it down. A page escaped. I snapped it up. "You're a passionate guy, and you care what people think."

I went to put the loose page in the garbage, but he took it from me.

"This isn't what you wanted."

"It's not. I hate it. It makes me uncomfortable in my own skin. My parents taught me to protect my security clearance, can you believe that? They drilled it from the minute I could speak. *Protect yourself.* So this? This hurts me in places I forgot about because they don't matter anymore."

"You can't be with me and have security clearance."

I laughed. My clearance hadn't mattered for so long, and here I was talking about it.

"We're always children," I said. "Everything we do, everything we love, hate, fear, it's all the child in us reacting to our adult problems.

No, it doesn't make a difference if people see me in the paper. Not really. But it scares me because it made my parents mad. It scares me because I'm afraid I'll lose someone close to me the way I lost them. When do we get to decide what matters to *us*? Not our parents?"

"When you find out, let me know."

"As long as I have you, it's all right." I put my hand on his chest. "Do I have you?"

He took my wrist and brought it to his lips, kissing the tender inside. "How could you want such a fuckup?"

"I don't," I said. He looked at me with surprise, and I let it hang there. "I don't want a fuckup. I want you."

He snapped open the tabloid and held it up.

"This is what you want?"

"What is that, even? I don't know those people."

I reached for it to take it away, but he held the paper out of my range and took me by the waist with the other hand, pulling me close.

"You're going to make me crazy about you," he said.

"I have that effect on people."

He kissed me long and hard. He tasted like cold water and chips. While we were still locked, I reached for the paper, and he held it away. We laughed, kissed, and fought for the paper at the same time.

Finally, he took his lips off mine and held me at his side. We looked at the picture together. He inspected it closely. I didn't know what he was seeing.

"It's all little dots," he said.

"Yeah. You're not that handsome in dots."

I put my hand on it and pushed it down. He crunched it up.

"You're a sexpot in dots," he said. "But in real life?" He tossed the last of the paper away. "You're still a sexpot. But more. You turned this bombshell from six years ago into a family. You're a magician. Do you know? I wasn't ready for that little girl, and now I am. I can still be me and have a family. I'm never going to read this article, but I bet there's nothing in here about what you mean to me."

"You're probably right," I said. I took the paper and threw it away, letting the lid of the dumpster land with a *slap*.

"This town, those kids, my fucking family," Brad said. "That house I grew up in. I feel right when I'm here. All that stuff I was doing, the parties, the . . . the women . . . was because I didn't feel right. And you make me feel right, and I know that means you and I are going to be on the cover of magazines, but I want you to tell me you can live with it. Tell me you don't care. Say you'll deal with everything they say."

"I only care about you."

He pulled me to him.

"Well, Cara DuMont, people are going to think you don't have a heart of ice."

"I don't care what people think."

"I do." His palm cupped my face. "I want everyone to know what kind of person you are." I thought he was going to kiss me, but he stopped himself an inch away. "Except in bed. That dirty little mouth is my private business."

"Then kiss it," I said. "Just kiss it."

His kiss was defined by what he didn't do. He didn't crash into me or devour me. He appreciated me with that kiss. He brushed his lips against mine as if he valued every place they met. The entirety of what he wanted to say was in that kiss.

His tongue flicked against mine, and I drew it in, opening my mouth for it. He pushed me against the car, and in a burst, my body burned for him. He breathed through his teeth, pinning my arms to the passenger window.

"I want to fuck you right here, teacup."

"The engraved invitation's in the mail." I raised my leg over his waist and he tucked his hand behind my knee. "It says, 'Your dick is cordially invited to come inside.'"

He laughed, but not for long, because the hand that was behind my knee trailed over my thigh and went right under my underpants. We both gasped at the same time. I was wetter than I thought, reactive to his touch. I felt as if lightning had struck where he moved.

"I can't fuck you fast enough," he said, yanking at my underpants. I got them down, pulling a leg out while he got his fly open.

"Go." I got my leg around his waist again. "Take it. Take it hard."

I barely had the last word out before he took my breath away, entering me in two fast strokes.

He pushed forward, and I wrapped my legs around him, digging my fingers in his hair.

Sometimes, not very often, but sometimes I looked at him and couldn't believe he wanted me even once. Sometimes he was even more gorgeous than a human should have been allowed to be. Sometimes I felt broken and unwanted, and his desire didn't match how I felt about myself.

This wasn't one of those times.

He was as beautiful as ever, but starkly human. Flawed beyond belief. Emotional and broken. He needed me to fill his empty places and in letting me do that, he filled mine.

My heart almost spoke through my lips, but he moaned in my ear first. I thought he'd give me pure filth, but his heart was doing its own speaking.

"I never . . . Cara . . . I never wanted a woman like this before."

He kissed my neck, fucking me standing, and I couldn't hear myself think past the roar of emotion and pleasure.

"I just want to get inside you," he said, lip to lip before he rammed into me again with his dick wedged between my legs and his tongue in my mouth.

I felt as if I was getting fucked on both ends, fast and hard, as deep inside me as possible.

Never. I'd never been fucked like this.

My lungs emptied when I cried out. His tongue was still in my mouth when I came. He held me up when my legs stiffened and my back curved like a cat's. He sped up his motions, hitting my center over and over. I pulled away from his mouth and gulped air in his rhythm.

"Coming inside you," he grunted, then got just a little deeper inside me and whispered, "Cara Cara Cara. I'm sorry, Cara."

I thought he was apologizing for what he'd done in the past, but he wasn't. He was apologizing for what he would do in the future.

CHAPTER 65

BRAD

Cara's phone came in the mail with a dead battery. She plugged it into the outlet by the toaster and didn't say a thing.

"Cara?"

"Yeah?"

"The phone?"

"It'll take just a couple of hours to charge."

"I left it in the hotel." I cleared my throat, because she wasn't getting what I was trying to say. "On purpose."

"Why?"

"The pictures. If you were connected, you'd see them. It was fucked up. Very fucked up. I'm sorry."

Fists on hips, she leaned on one foot.

"Is there anything else you need to tell me?"

Mom and Nicole came in before I had to answer.

But yes. I had more things to tell Cara. One thing. The thing I'd forgotten because I was preoccupied with an airplane-bathroom blow job. But there's only so much a guy can do. Only so much a girl can hear. I was getting to it. I swore it. But not now. Just not now.

Before I'd gone to the kitchen to discover the box of dyslexia books, Paula had gone over the details of my youthful stupidity in fine detail, sending me a letter from Brenda Garcia's lawyer five years before.

It took me an hour to decipher words that seemed created just to confuse my scrambled-egg brain.

> Mr. Sinclair,
> You have been named the father of Baby Garcia. The mother, Brenda Garcia, would like to offer you the opportunity to take a DNA test to prove paternity. Should the test prove positive, you will be held responsible for child support and have the right to visitation as set out in family court.
> You also have the opportunity to decline paternity filings, and in doing so you understand you relinquish any and all parental rights, including visitation rights to the child in perpetuity.
> Sincerely,
> Carlina Cruz, Esq.

There had been a voluntary relinquishment form. I'd signed it with my big stupid signature. Couldn't even pretend to deny it.

So, I'd known. But I barely read the thing because I was distracted and Paula had just told me the deal in a sentence. Something on the order of, "You knocked up some girl and if you don't want to have your wages garnished forever, just sign here."

That sounded ridiculous even in my own head. Maybe I remembered it that way, but blaming Paula wasn't going to make me look like a saint. Not to Cara, and she was the only woman I wanted to canonize me.

With Nicole upstairs with Cara, I tried to tell myself the story in a way that would excuse me, but nothing worked. I'd given her up. I'd said "no" to being her father, then forgotten about her before the plane even landed. I made millions while her mother had to keep her in a cabinet at Coffee Chain when she couldn't get a sitter.

Who does that? What kind of person? Amazing how I could decide not to think about something for so long. Maybe I'd put it out of my mind because I'd signed a hundred different pieces of paper I couldn't understand, and that was just another in the pile. Or maybe I didn't want to see the letter for what it was. A statement about my fitness as a father and human being. I'd been so worthless that Brenda Garcia would rather be a single mom than let me claim her daughter.

Ken answered the phone.

"Hello?" He sounded as if he'd swallowed a ball of yarn.

"Dude, are you in bed?" I asked from the porch. The block was dark. No streetlights, no floodlights on front porches. LA was never this dark. "It's midnight there."

"I'm in bed. Like an adult."

"You knew about Nicole. You and Paula. You had me sign papers on the way to shoot *Everly*."

"Yeah. You got away lucky for five years."

"You couldn't remind me?" My heels rocked the porch swing. The hooks in the ceiling groaned same as they did when I was twelve.

"For what? So you could blab to the press that you signed her off? You were on the edge of becoming something or nothing. And that edge? About as thin as net returns. We decided to control the damage."

"We?"

"Paula. Who do you think?"

"Jesus."

"Don't Jesus me." He seemed more awake. I thought I heard the sound of a refrigerator opening and closing. "She would've killed any chance you had. You would've moved all the way to Los Angeles to become an out-of-wedlock father. You could've stayed in Buttfuck Alabama and done that."

"Arkansas."

"Whatever. It wouldn't matter, because mother and daughter would be in Los Angeles and you wouldn't be able to move home. You would've been stuck in Hollywood, worse than nothing. With baggage. No time. No energy. Nothing. Brenda Garcia was a saint. She had it under control."

"How much did you pay her?"

"You paid her fifty grand. On loan. I've been taking it out slowly as expenses. Interest-free. You're welcome."

"Fifty-fucking-grand?" The amount seemed inconsequential to the responsibility of taking care of Nicole.

"Fifty large. She was thrilled. She paid off her debts and got a bigger apartment."

I was playing the part of a father. All the backstory had been taken care of. I was a fraud going through the motions while other people took care of the props.

"Is there anything else I need to know?" I asked.

"That's the last of it. You're writing the rest of this story on your own."

I didn't know if I hung up first or if he did. I looked at the sky and asked Brenda Garcia for forgiveness. I asked her dimples, her smile, her cheap apartment, her lousy-paying job, her discipline, and her little girl. All the things I knew about her. I'd been stingy with her, and the fact that Ken and Paula had conspired to keep it under wraps was irrelevant. They'd done me the favor they knew I'd want.

The living room was dark. I could hear my father snoring upstairs. My mother had learned to sleep through it. And a few years of public drunkenness. And through his loyalty to the lumberyard. And letting the back of the house go to termites before he did anything about it. She'd forgiven him plenty, but she'd never had to forgive anything like this. He'd never denied his own children.

Before Nicole, before Cara, before I became a man, that wouldn't have meant anything to me, but now it did, and I didn't know how to make it right.

CHAPTER 66

CARA

We were leaving for Thailand right from Arkansas. I would be Nicole's studio teacher and nanny, but she and I would return home when school started. When Brad joined us in LA to do the green screening, we would transition into our new version of normal.

Whatever that was.

"Can I wear my twinkling shoes?"

She still asked even though we never said no.

"Yes," I said to Nicole, "you can wear your twinkling shoes. Now just put them on please."

I'd plugged my phone in that morning. It started dinging, bleeping, vibrating when I turned it on as three days' worth of messages came in.

Nicole sat right on the kitchen floor and got her shoes on. She could tie them herself, but it took forever. I scanned my screen, answered messages. Scanned again.

Laura at West Side. Four e-mails and three texts. One long voice message.

Jobs.

Texted back to postpone until I got back from Thailand.

Blakely.

Texts and voicemails.

Her callback had gone well.

She got a second callback.

Then her happiness turned to concern.

Where are you, Cara? Are you okay?

Quick text back of congratulations, comfort, and a good-bye.

"Miss Cara!"

Nicole yanked my shirt and pointed her toe.

"Wow," I said. "That's a perfect bow!"

She smiled coyly. "Double knot!"

"The car's outside!" Susan called from the front. Milton picked up two suitcases and Brad bounded down from the stairway to take them from him. We were going to Memphis International Airport an hour and change away, too far for his parents to drive.

Erma picked up Nicole and kissed her cheek. They extended loving affections while I scrolled through. Junk. Spam. I thought I should call Laura back and explain about Brad and how it wouldn't happen ever again. Maybe meet up when I got back.

And Paula had texted, as if she hadn't caused enough trouble.

"Come on, Miss Cara!" Nicole called out.

Susan tapped my shoulder. "Good-bye Cara," she said, hugging me. "I hope you come back."

I didn't know what to say. I didn't want to hope with her, because I'd committed myself, and hoping meant I thought we could fail. I didn't feel that anymore.

"I will," I said, taking her by both shoulders. "We won't be strangers, I promise."

"Good."

Erma crouched down to hug Nicole. She picked the girl up and swung her. I wrapped my arms around both of them.

"Bradley!" his father yelled from the other room. "Let's get a move on." He came into the kitchen before he was finished with his sentence. "Like middle school all over again. Aw, sheesh, now what are the women doing? All this hugging. Where are we? California? Get in the car before you all turn us into hippies."

I hugged him and despite his fear of hippie-dom, he hugged me back.

"Thank you," he said into my ear. "You take good care of my family. Thank you."

"I love them," I said without thinking.

Brad was right behind me. He draped his arm over my shoulder when I pulled away from his dad.

"Hands off my girl."

Milton put his palms up, all eight fingers spread in surrender.

"Out," his mom shooed us. "The front door's wide open. We're gonna be overrun with bugs in here."

We piled into the limo, which had been sent all the way from Fayetteville.

Erma stood at the porch steps, Susan next to her. The driver held the door open for Brad. He put his arm around his mother, and she broke out in tears. Real, honest tears.

"Why is Grandma crying?" Nicole asked suspiciously. "What's Daddy doing to her?"

"She's sad he's leaving."

"Grandma!" Nicole called out. Erma wiped her eyes and faced the open limo door. "Come to the airport with us!"

"Oh, I can't have him drive all the way back."

"Sure you can," Brad said. "We have an hour in the lounge to kill. You can kill it with us."

"Need a ticket to get in the lounge."

"I'll get you a ticket. Go get your ID and come on."

"The expense!" Erma protested.

"I'll get it," Susan said, running into the house.

"Come on, Grandma!" Nicole patted the seat next to her.

Brad pushed her to the back of the car. "No one says no to my daughter."

"He made three mill on his last movie," Milton said. "He can buy another limo ride. Go with them. I gotta clean up the mess around here. It's like an army ran through the house."

Erma was not impressed. "You never cleaned a thing in your life, Milton Sinclair."

"I will if you git!"

Seeing she had everyone's approval, Erma Sinclair got into the back of the limo, next to me. Brad shook hands with his dad and Buddy, then slid in next to Nicole. Susan came back with Erma's purse. The door closed and we were off to Thailand.

CHAPTER 67

BRAD

I played with Nicole on the limo ride to the airport. She kneeled on the floor and used the seat as a table, drawing herself and her new school, her impressions of a long airplane ride, the pony I was apparently getting her, and her name. The whole name. Nicole Garcia-Sinclair. All the letters, facing the right direction, in order, right side up. We hadn't legally changed it, but she was telling me something.

I picked up the paper and held it up.

"Hey, Cara," I said. "These letters are all in the right place? Right?"

She didn't answer.

She was looking at her phone.

A plane screamed in the sky above. We were almost at the airport.

"Let me see," Mom said, taking the page. "They're perfect!"

Nicole smiled and put her head down to make more letters. And Cara slid her hand over the glass of her phone, eyes wide, chin jutting and tender at the same time, as if she wanted to weep but couldn't.

"Teacup?"

She didn't answer. She put two fingers on the glass and spread them to make an image bigger. I swallowed but nothing went down.

Mom and Nicole chattered about the drawings. I could barely hear them through the scream of Cara's concentration.

She put her phone in her lap and looked out the window as Arkansas farmland whooshed by. Did she know? Was it the truth? A lie? Had Paula embellished? Made it sound worse?

How could it actually be worse?

I texted her.

—Teacup? What's wrong?—

Her phone dinged. She looked at it, then at me. She put the phone back in her lap and looked out the window.

Okay. This wasn't working. I wasn't sitting there wondering what the fuck was wrong with her. I didn't do that. I didn't sit and wait for things to happen. If she was going to be mad, she was going to do it now.

I rapped on the driver's window. It slid down.

"Pull over here, would you?"

"Sure thing."

"What's happening, Daddy?"

I looked at Cara when I spoke. "Miss Cara and I have to make a pit stop."

Nicole went up like a shot, peering out the window. "Can we get a hot dog?"

"There's not a rest stop in sight, Brad," Mom said.

"Not that kind of pit stop."

Gravel crunched under the tires, and the limo came to a stop. A car blew by so fast the limo jolted. I didn't wait for the driver to open the door. I yanked the handle and went to the side of the heat-baked road. Cara didn't follow. I leaned into the car. Her phone was still sandwiched between her hands, which were folded between her legs as if she wanted to protect her device or shield herself from the information on it.

"You coming?" I said. "Or do I have to carry you?"

In the sunlight her eyes were bluer. Less like the deep ocean and more like the color of running sea water.

"Maybe we should discuss this in front of Nicole?" I suggested.

I stepped out of the way and finally, she followed.

"Give us a minute," I said to my mother, whose look of disapproval was cut off when I closed the door.

I decided, as I scanned for Cara and found her leaning on the back of the limo with her arms crossed, that I wasn't going to pretend this could be about anything else. It couldn't be, and if it was, I was just going to bring it up anyway.

I stood across from Cara and crossed my arms so we were a matched set.

"Can you hear me?" I asked.

"Yeah." She handed me her phone. I immediately recognized the documents I'd signed, refusing my parental rights, and Paula's name at the top of the screen. I handed it back. "I don't want to talk about it yet. I'm confused."

Yeah. I wasn't confused. I was real clear. I was going to man up, and she was going to deal with my apology.

"She was better off without me."

Which wasn't exactly what I was planning to say, but that was what came out. The truth.

"How convenient, golden boy." She finally looked at me. The wind blew the hair off her face, and it trailed behind her like a black flag. The opposite of surrender. "Everything just goes your way."

How was I supposed to answer that? I couldn't even tell if she was insulting me or giving me a shot in the arm for being lucky.

"I wonder, sometimes." She moved a rock with the tip of her shoe. "Am I just the last thing that you fell into? Get a daughter and find her a mother right after? Perfect. Home run. Brad Sinclair steps in shit again. Rejects his kid. No consequences. Parties like a teenager for years. No consequences. Suddenly a single dad? Easy. Sinclair doesn't miss a beat. Lies about knowing he had a daughter? What's going to be the consequence?"

I bristled from her summary of my life. She knew damn well it wasn't that easy.

"You don't have to worry about my consequences. You're not God."

Her head shot up as if pulled up by shock. She blazed. Even in the Arkansas sun, her anger was the hottest thing for miles.

"No. I'm not. God forgives. I can only stand so much lying. I'm not a saint. I'm a human and so flawed . . ." She looked away for a second. Trying to gather her emotions. I put a hand to her face, and she slapped it away. "I've copped to every mistake I ever made, and you just make a show of it. You rejected her. You left her."

"I was living in a studio in Silver Lake."

"For how long? A year?"

I was on a trajectory at that point. One low-paying, SAG-waivered critical darling in the can. Shooting another with a major director, and a summer tentpole scheduled. Significant money hadn't started rolling in and wouldn't for another year. But my path was lit like a runway.

"I didn't even remember signing it. I was handed a paper in the middle of a flight."

"Anything else on the list of excuses?"

And you know what? Fuck her. She was betraying me, right there. Stabbing me in the back with my own decisions.

"You know what, lady? I'm trying my best. I took this on. I didn't try and get out of it. I've had to change my life all around for Nicole, and I'm glad I did. But I don't need the self-righteous judgment from you. I don't need to look over my shoulder every second because you might not approve. Here's the deal. I'm in the paper all the time. I'm a dude. I do dude things. Deal with it. And I didn't tell anyone I can barely read. That would have ended me before I started. And I'm not admitting it now. I'm not taking that risk. Deal with it. And the last thing you can deal with is that I have a past just like you and I made decisions in the past you're not gonna like."

Well, that felt good. Real good. Laid it out right there. I didn't know what I expected from her after that, but I held on to that good got-shit-off-my-chest feeling because the goodness of it was about to disappear. Nothing I said was deniable. I knew I was right on paper. But life wasn't on paper. Life was on the side of the road in Arkansas, on the way to Thailand with my daughter and a woman I needed.

"I'm disappointed," she said, the wind blowing hair over her face. "I'm disappointed in myself for trusting you. I thought you were honest. I don't even know who you are."

How could I tell her she did? When we were alone with Nicole in the dark, I was complete. She had to know who I was. She had to see me because I'd opened myself to her. I hadn't opened up to anyone, and I realized how much I needed her to see that. To know that she stood inside the open door of my heart.

I loved her. I needed her. She couldn't turn her back on me over this. I wouldn't allow it.

A minivan came down the highway, slowed. The side door slid open and two girls, no older than twelve, waved and called out, holding up their camera phones.

"Brad Sinclair!"

I waved, but I wanted them to go away. My first reaction was to flip them two birdies, but they were too young. So I turned my back on them and when I faced Cara again, my defenses were up.

"This is what I am," I said. "I'm not deep. I'm just trying to hold this job together."

She shook her head ever so subtly.

The minivan driver got the hint and sped away as the girls squealed.

Cara and I?

We were just locked in a wordless battle.

I didn't know what was on her mind. I couldn't read past the anger. I couldn't look away. Couldn't move. The stillness of our bodies was a lie in my case. My mind was on fire. Should I apologize? Should I say it was a mistake? I could grovel and spend hours dismissing the decision as the worst yet in a series of bad decisions. I could beg and plead for the case of love.

But I wasn't going to.

I'd done what I had to do, and I didn't lie about it. I just kind of more or less chose not to think about it.

The cord between us snapped when the car door opened.

"Daddy?" Nicole stood in the dirt with her legs crossed.

"Yeah?"

"I have to pee."

"Can you make it fifteen minutes?" Cara asked.

"I think so?"

"Let's roll," I said, happy to be away from that shitty scene at the side of the road. I had no idea it would get worse. I didn't even think it was possible.

CHAPTER 68

CARA

Nicole made it. What a kid. The best kind of kid. The kind of kid you met in a bathroom and said good-bye to in a bathroom. The kind of kid you loved face-to-face and had to leave when her father's assistant sent you screenshots of documents denying he wanted a child. I could have forgiven him. I don't know how, but maybe if he'd admitted it. He didn't need to apologize, but pretending those documents didn't exist and getting self-righteous about them made me want to hit him over the head. I was going to run away instead.

It took me the entire ride to the airport and the seven minutes to the first-class VIP lounge to absorb how angry I was.

I couldn't handle this relationship.

I couldn't handle Brad Sinclair. I couldn't handle his fame or his dishonesty. I couldn't trust him. Today it was lies about rejecting his daughter. Tomorrow? Who knew? How deep was I going to get before it got to be too much? And how much closer to Nicole would I be by the time I had to leave?

Nicole flushed the toilet herself. She wiggled her pants up with the seriousness of solving the world's problems. I crouched by her and watched as she moved her shirt out of the way so she could tie the bow on her waistband. She did it slowly so she wouldn't make any mistakes.

I'd fallen in love with a man and his daughter and it was a disaster.

She looked at me through her hair.

"Should I double knot it?"

"No. I think it's fine."

She pulled her shirt down.

"Okay! Let's go fly high in the sky!" She clapped once and sent one hand far into the atmosphere with a breathy *whoosh*.

I grabbed her around the waist and pulled her so close I could feel her heartbeat. I held her longer than I should. Until the hiss of the toilet tank stopped and my knees ached. I held her until she wiggled so hard I had to let her go.

"I love you," I said. "I love you, and I'm always here for you. Please always remember that."

She put her hands on my cheeks.

"Okay," she whispered close to my face. She poked the inner corner of my eye. "Why are you crying?"

"I'm afraid you'll forget."

"I won't." She put her fingertips to my lips then twisted them. "I'll take it, lock it." Her fingertips went to the breast pocket that wasn't there. "Put it in my pocket."

I laid my hand over the place where she'd put my love. "Keep it forever."

"I will. It's pink. I don't throw away pink things." She ripped a square of toilet paper off the roll. "Here."

"Thank you." I dabbed my eyes, but I still cried inside, because I loved her and she wasn't mine to love.

CHAPTER 69

CARA

The private lounge had leather couches and a dedicated bartender. The concierge had set aside a corner for us and placed subtle barriers between Brad Sinclair and the rest of the world. He sat with his back to the rest of the room, and his mother read last month's *YOU* magazine. She folded her magazine, stood up when she saw me, and met us halfway across the lounge.

"Grandma, can I get a donut?"

Before I could say no, Erma did what grandparents do.

"Of course!"

Nicole bounced to the buffet of sweets. It was for the best, anyway. I had no say in the matter.

"Is everything all right?" Erma asked.

"Yeah. Just tired."

Nicole leaned over the metal table and tapped her chin. So many possibilities. So many colors.

"Kids will do that to you."

"I can't go to Thailand," I blurted out. "I don't know what to do."

"Oh, no no no . . ."

"Yes, I'm sorry but—"

"This is last month's!" She held up the magazine.

"What?"

She flopped it open to show me the date, but all I saw was Brad's picture with the costar of his last movie. She was whispering in his ear and he was smiling.

"See?" Erma said, gleeful. "No, wait. These come weeks before the date on the front. So it's the month before last!"

I took the magazine. When that edition came out, I was still working with Willow and Jedi Heywood, who I loved. Always. He hadn't even met me when he was dating Geraldine Starrck. They were beautiful together.

He'd replace me in a minute. Was I all right with that?

I had to be.

"I want the sprinkles!" Nicole called out.

"Yes, dear," Erma called to Nicole before turning back to me. "It's hard to see this, but he cares about you."

I folded up the magazine.

"Get a plate and use the tongs to pick it up," I told Nicole, then brought myself back to Brad's mother. "Have you ever been to Thailand?" I asked.

"No. Why?"

Her brows knit together and she tilted her head. With every word, every expression, every breath I let pass, I got closer to the point of no return.

"Do you have a passport?" I asked.

"I had to show it to get the ticket."

I was going to cry again. I felt my mouth contort and tasted the salty rush of tears in the back of my throat. Erma put my hand over hers.

"I'm sorry to do this to you," I choked out. "I'm putting you in the middle and inconveniencing you terribly. But I can't go to Thailand. I don't want to send Nicole with a nanny who's a stranger."

"It's not the magazine, is it?"

"No. I don't care about that."

I wasn't going to tell her why I was leaving. What would I say? Her son was a liar? He'd denied his daughter and never admitted it? I couldn't trust him. He was her baby. I was nobody but the first woman he was with when he started the process of changing his life. I was the one who was too mad to forgive him.

Nicole came from the buffet with a donut in each hand. One chocolate. One vanilla. Both with rainbow sprinkles spotting the paper napkins they sat on. She had a dot of chocolate cake on her cheek and a blue sprinkle on her chin. She'd obviously already sampled the sweets while standing at the buffet.

"I brought you donuts. Grandma gets to pick first because she's older."

I cleared my throat. Some of the gunk rattled down, only to be replaced by a fresh lump to remind me I could cry any second.

"I'll take the white one." Erma plucked up the pastry and the napkin. Nicole held out the chocolate.

"You can save it for the plane if you're not hungry. Or you can give it to me if you want. I can wait until we're on the plane."

I never saw a kid want a donut more. But it wasn't about the donut. Not for me. It was about the plane.

I crouched in front of her.

"I don't think I'm going to be on the plane with you."

"Why not?"

Because I did something stupid. I did exactly what I avoided doing with every other father I've worked for. I fell in love, and that's going to impact you.

"I have to stay home."

"I can stay home with you." She shrugged. This was easily solved, of course. "I don't want to go to Thailand anyway."

I was doing this backward, and it was going to suck. I had to go talk to Brad and—

"Hey. What's going on?" Brad asked from behind me. Perfect. He'd heard me talking to his daughter, of course.

Erma glanced at me, then at her son and put a big fat southern smile on her face.

"Let's go look out the window, honey! I think that big plane's taking off!"

"Wait!" She handed me the donut. I took it. Nicole and her grandmother walked away to see the planes in the big window.

"The concierge said we're boarding in fifteen minutes." He said it suspiciously, relaying information he'd seemingly lost interest in. "What is this? You're not coming? You all right? You afraid you're going to puke or something?"

He was going to make me say it. He knew damn well I wasn't going to puke. I tried to be mad at him so I could really cut him and leave, but he'd taken his jacket off and I could see his arms. I remembered how they tensed when they held me. How the hard biceps felt under my hand when I gripped them.

It was his eyes that almost took my resolve. He trusted me. He knew I was angry, but he trusted it was a bump in the road, and I was betraying him.

"I think it's best if I stay behind."

"With Nicole?"

"You should take her."

"I'm working all day."

"Your mother will go. She ag—"

"What *the fuck* is going on?"

This was bad. Very bad. I was bailing, and I was the worst kind of coward. But as perfect and beautiful as he was, as much as I admired what he'd gone through in life to get where he was, I couldn't see past the lies.

"You denied her. It's just going to eat at me. And you know what? Keep it a secret. Never tell her. Let Paula put it in the papers now before Nicole can understand it, then never mention it again. By the time she finds out, she'll love you so much."

He straightened his hand into a plane and thrust it in my direction.

"This is bullshit."

"I'm sorry."

"You do this *now*? We got one foot on a plane and this is what you come up with?"

The world got quiet, and he was at the end of a long, dark tunnel. Nothing existed but the hard words between us.

"Just take her," I growled. "She'll be fine. She'll get used to it without me. I'm not necessary here—"

"No, you take her. The two of you wait for me. I'm sorry, teacup. You're not turning your back on us. Maybe she'll be all right without you, but I won't. We're smack-dab in the middle of something good, and I'm not gonna let you go so easy. I fucked up too much already. I fucked up when I denied her the first time, and I fucked up not telling you my trouble. I fucked up taking your phone. I fucked up trying to hide the newspapers. I'm going to fuck up again. I know I am. And I'm asking you to stay with me and let me fuck up. Let me try again and again. There's no one else I want to fuck up with. There's no one else I want to apologize to. There's no one else I want to be better for. It's you. I'm going to be better for you, and if you leave I'm afraid I'll never have a reason to stop being a fuckup."

"Nicole has to be your reason to stop."

"She is, I just . . ." Hands out, as if handing me an explanation. "I'm afraid. With her I'm afraid I'm going to screw up. I'm not afraid with you. I can do it with you. You make it possible."

In his outstretched hands was my power. I could accept it or deny it. I could trust him and myself. Trust that I had the power to build something with him that I'd always wanted. A family of my own.

Or I could do what I'd always done. Run from the difficulty. The vulnerability and discomfort and stay on the outside looking in. I was safe there, but if I was being honest with myself, I was also miserable.

"I know I'm a shithead," he said. "But this shithead loves you."

He did. He loved me.

I had a physical reaction. My heart expanded to fit the room. It grew to fit a feeling of worthiness and belonging. He loved me and he knew it.

His love changed nothing. I loved him and I knew it, but I wouldn't be able to fit myself into his life or understand the lies he'd told. And my heart shrunk back down, folding into itself like a bird tucking its wings in after a short flight.

"I love you," I said. I didn't have to say it. I shouldn't have, because it was irrelevant. "But I don't think that's enough."

He was still in the tunnel. The rest of the world, the airport, the VIP lounge had fallen away. So when Erma's voice cut through the tunnel, I was startled.

"Where's Nicole?" she asked.

Brad's attention snapped away to his mother, then around the room.

"What do you mean?"

"She was right here looking at you. Then I went to put the napkin in the garbage and—"

"Shit." He scanned the room from window to window, and I did too, checking behind the buffet, around the donuts, at the floor where a trail of crumbs and sprinkles ended a foot away from where Brad and I had been standing.

"Not here," I said.

"Nicole!" he called. Everyone looked, but no little girl came.

"They have to close the lounge," I said, pointing to the concierge. "Now."

Brad ran to him. I pointed to Erma. "Check the bathrooms."

"Okay." She went to the bathrooms, and I went through the swinging doors to the kitchen.

She was probably fine.

But Brad was famous and wealthy. He was the target of crazy people for simply existing. His security team didn't come to Arkansas with us because he felt safe, but that didn't mean word of his location didn't get out. The right opportunity with the wrong person nearby could spell disaster.

"Did a little girl come through here?" I shouted to the kitchen staff. The banging of pots and shouting of staff ground to a halt. I didn't wait for an answer. They'd let me know if they saw anything. I scanned the floor, paced to the back exit. It was open. There were elevators. A stairway with an alarm. Huge hampers with linens.

She could be in a hamper or two stories below. Shit shit shit . . .

I upturned the hamper. It was too light to have a little girl under the tablecloths, but I checked anyway.

"Hey!" A male voice from down the hall.

I stood and looked. Security.

"Did you close the lounge?"

He got close enough to see me. "You're the nanny?"

"Yes."

"It's on lockdown. The elevators are shut. Please join your party in the lounge."

"There are low cabinets in the kitchen. She might be hiding in one of them."

He held one hand out to me and with the other he opened the door back to the kitchen. "Please join your party, miss."

I walked fast through the kitchen, taking the long way in case she was there, and entered the lounge where all the first-class passengers were now standing, looking distressed.

I stood between Brad and his mother, catching another security guy with gray hair as he put on his most authoritative tone.

"We cannot lock down the entire airport," he said. "The way we do it is—"

"Fuck your concentric circles," Brad said.

"I know this is stressful, but—"

"You need to lock it from the outside in, not the—"

"No child has been lost on my watch, sir. I promise you. This happens more often than you think."

His radio hissed and burped. He held up his finger and excused himself to take the call.

"This is my fault," I said. "It's my job to watch her."

"Let's not get into that." He spoke to me, but his eyes were all over the room, as if he was looking for a dropped cuff link. I couldn't blame him. My attention was on every nook and cranny a little girl could fit inside.

"We were talking about our relationship," I said, reaching under the buffet and opening the sliding doors. No kid. "What I should have been doing was watching Nicole."

"Your relationship with me is important to her."

"Do you think she heard us?"

"I'm sure of it." He turned to me and took my chin in his hand to get me to look at him. I felt safe and solid when I had his attention. "She's not in the lounge."

"How do you know?"

"I don't know how I know. But we need more eyes out there." He broke our gaze. "Mom." He waved her over.

"I think we should pray," she said.

"Yeah," Brad said. "Do that. We're gonna look in the terminal."

"The lounge is locked."

"Let's pray then." He grabbed the gray-haired security guard, who had just clipped his little radio back to his belt. "My mother needs to get to the chapel. She needs to say a prayer we find her."

"Yes, sir. Over there are people leaving to board their planes. You can get out that way."

We didn't wait for another set of instructions. This lockdown was bullshit. I was sure they were trying, but I was also sure they didn't want anyone to miss their flight.

"You can't cut the line," Erma protested when Brad pushed through the crowd to get out. So many camera phones were pointed in our direction it was a wonder anyone was looking where they were going.

Except Brad, who was unfazed. "Hell I can't."

We were out in the terminal in another minute. Erma wringing her hands, Brad holding one of mine. How long had he been holding my hand? Publicly?

I didn't even care. He needed to hold my hand as tight as he could.

"What were we saying when she was near us?" I asked, hoping there was a clue there.

Brad shook his head, looking over the crowded terminal. People saw him and tittered, or stared, or elbowed their friends. A couple of security guards passed us, all eyes on the corners and walls, looking for a little girl.

"We have to keep moving. Mom, you go that way." He pointed the same direction the security team went. "Keep your cell phone on. Cara and I will go this way."

Erma complied, and Brad and I walked. I let go of his hand, but he grabbed it back. He was shaking. I didn't think I'd ever feel him shake, but for the first time he looked powerless and out of control.

I couldn't blame him. I felt the same way.

CHAPTER 70

BRAD

I had everything I wanted, but everything I needed was getting torn away. I was trying to hold on to a career I'd fought for, and I was losing something I didn't even know I needed. Cara was leaving, and Nicole was gone.

I'd never felt so alone. I'd never panicked so hard. I'd never felt so out of control.

"We'll find her," Cara said. We weren't looking at each other, but everywhere, past everything, everyone, watching for a moving object in a sea of movement.

"Sure." I said it just to say something, but I didn't know what right I had to be confident. The terminal was endless.

"She's a survivor. She'll probably find us." Cara scanned corners. What would I do without her if I lost my daughter?

Her mother, Brenda, didn't have a staff. Didn't have a security detail or tons of time to teach Nicole anything. She'd been an overworked coffee shop employee who sometimes couldn't find child care. With all that against her she did a great job. She never lost Nicole. She raised a girl who was healthy, smart, and well mannered.

And what had I done? Nothing. Denied her. I never even asked how she was. Never told Brenda what a good job she was doing. If I could do it all over again, I'd make it so Brenda didn't have to work. I'd free her from her job so she could take care of our daughter full time, and I'd step in and be a part of her life.

Too late for all that.

Maybe not. Maybe if I found her, I could change things. Maybe I had the power to give Nicole everything Brenda couldn't. Maybe I could finish the job right.

"It's just that she's used to small spaces from her mom taking her to work," Cara said. "So if she's mad or scared, she could be in a freaking cabinet."

I stopped, yanking Cara's hand back.

"What?" she asked.

"You know. When her mother couldn't get a sitter?"

Eyebrows up, chin raised, in a split second Cara and I were on the same page.

Cara, being the woman of my dreams, had been on the same train of thought. Once we found Nicole, I was making changes, and she was going to be a part of it.

CHAPTER 71

CARA

"Ah! Coffee Chain!" I said. "Do you think?"

"No, but we don't have any better ideas." Brad stopped a woman in her twenties holding a paper cup with a blue logo in one hand and a wheelie suitcase in the other. "Hey!"

Her face registered annoyance then shock.

"Oh my God, are you—"

"Yes, I am. Where did you get that coffee?"

She swung her arm back in a general direction, speechless.

He kissed her on the cheek and pulled me away. We got to the end of the hall, looked left, then right, and found a Coffee Chain almost immediately. The sign was big, but the shop seemed eternally distant. We ran. That coffee shop was our only hope. If she wasn't there, we didn't have a next part of the plan. We'd have to start searching all over again.

So we ran, crashing into travelers, hopping over suitcases, dodging when we could. Brad was fast, and he pulled ahead. When I got to Coffee Chain, I walked into pandemonium. Brad was behind the counter, bulldozing through the objections of the manager, slapping open cabinets. Someone was calling security. A dozen people were photographing the entire thing.

Despite the chaos, I could tell one thing. Nicole wasn't drawing ponies in the cabinets.

What had Brad and I been saying that made her run away?

You take her.

No, you take her.

She was five. She had no way of knowing we weren't trying to get rid of her. She thought she was being pushed off again. She'd get yet another home.

Which was what I was consigning her to if I left.

I put my hands over my mouth and looked at the floor.

I was breaking up a family.

My family.

I looked at my shoes and considered what that meant. How much of a commitment that was, and how the rules changed when the stakes were so high.

A slight pink glow flashed against the floor and one side of my left sneaker. It happened so fast I should have missed it. But I didn't.

I looked left, to a standing three-panel ad for frothy autumn drinks. And down, to where the panels lifted two inches from the floor and I could see the flashing lights of a certain little girl's favorite sneakers.

I pulled back the partition, and my heart dropped down while my breath flew up.

Nicole Garcia-Sinclair crouched in the space where the floor met the wall with her arms wrapped around her knees. She picked her head up when the partition disappeared.

"Brad!" I shouted at the top of my lungs. She started crying. I scooped her up in my arms, one arm under her knees, one under her arms.

I didn't care if she was crying. She could cry all day and night.

"I love you, Nicole." I held her close and spoke with her tear-soaked face near mine. "I love you. I love you so much."

Brad came to us and ladled her with kisses, reaching around the both of us, helping me hold her and pulling us all together at the same time.

"Thank God," he said. "Thank God, and Cara. Thank you."

The relaxed guy without a care in the world was back, but different. The relief and joy in his smile were as real and honest as another person's could be. All the other stuff? Well, that was just stuff. That smile was the man I loved, and it was for me and Nicole.

"Daddy," she sobbed. "Who's going to take me?"

He didn't look away from her, but his hand squeezed my elbow.

"We'll figure it—"

"We both are," I interrupted.

I cringed at my own words, hoping Brad hadn't changed his mind. Had I overstepped? Was I promising her something I couldn't deliver?

But his chest expanded and his shoulders dropped as if he'd taken a deep breath, and I knew I hadn't overstepped.

Nicole choked back a sob. "Really, Daddy?"

"Yes," he said. "You belong to both of us."

The big lump in my throat finally went down when I swallowed.

I'd run away from this, from him, from Nicole, from every child I ever loved, and at that moment the running was done. I'd run right home.

He turned away from his daughter and looked at me. Only me. Joy in his face. Relief. A victory dance and I was the ultimate prize.

For a second his gaze went foggy, as if he was looking inside instead of outside. He squeezed his daughter and kissed her forehead, then took out his phone. Assuming he was calling security to call off the search, I held my hands out for Nicole. He shook his head.

"I have her."

He put the phone to his ear. Security found us. Radios squawked and sharp voices called off the search. Travelers dropped their suitcases to take pictures of us, and I was concerned about Nicole's reaction. She had her cheek on her father's shoulder.

I was going to suggest he get out of the way of the impromptu paparazzi, but the knee-jerk fear of exposure got very far away when I heard who he was calling.

"Gene," he said into the phone. "You sitting? . . . Good, because you're about to fire me."

What the heck?

"I'm not doing *Bangkok Brotherhood.*"

"Brad!" I shouted louder than I intended.

He winked at me. Was he joking?

"Never . . . yes, I'm sure. I tried, but I'm not dragging my family onto a movie set right now. I need time to get to know my daughter."

"You can't!" I said, probably echoing his agent's sentiments. "It's a hundred-million-dollar movie! They can't shoot it without you! You'll—"

"—never work again," he said into the phone and to me at the same time. "I can live on what I have for the rest of my life. I don't care . . . No," he said, stopping himself. Nicole looked up at him and their eyes met. "I do care."

He took the phone away from his ear and held it up for me.

"—the studio? They won't even make the bond. Overland is going to make sure you're over. Do you know what *over means?* You won't get a line in community theater in Buttfuck—"

I grabbed the phone before Nicole heard any more foul language.

"Hello?"

"Who the fuck is this?"

"This is Cara."

"That answers nothing. Nothing. Whoever you are, you're standing next to nobody. He's flipping burgers in three months. Three *weeks.*"

"Wait—"

Brad snapped the phone out of my hands. "And tell Roger his project is a maybe. Me going to a shoot in Argentina during the school year isn't happening. I'm reassessing all my future projects against how it affects my daughter."

He held the phone to his ear as Gene ranted and raved, but Nicole was telling him a secret in his other ear, and he seemed to be listening to that with real interest.

"Why don't you ask her?" he said.

Nicole nodded.

"Miss Cara?"

"Yes, Nicole?"

"Are you coming with us?"

"Where are we going?"

We both looked at Brad.

"We'll talk later, Gene." With that he hung up the phone and looked from me to Nicole and back. "Where do you want to go?"

Nicole shrugged and looked to me for corroboration.

I didn't know what to say or think. His agent had said it all. He'd sunk his career with a phone call. "You're freaking me out."

"Kinda freaked myself out," he said. "But I lost everything today and got it back. I might not be so lucky next time."

"Mr. Sinclair," the gray-haired security guy said, "your flight is boarding."

"Wherever you go," I said, "I'll go with you. But I'm confused."

"Well," he said, lifting Nicole onto his shoulders. He held her ankles, and she covered his eyes. "Why not take a family vacation in Thailand? I hear it's nice and relaxing. Away from it all."

"We need to renegotiate our agreement," I said, moving Nicole's hand off his eye. He leaned down and kissed me. I let him.

I let Nicole see it because I wasn't going anywhere. She could depend on us. Not me. Not Brad, but *us*. I was there, with her, with him, forever.

CHAPTER 72

CARA

"How do you fly to heaven if you're old?" Nicole asked. This latest salvo in her attack of unanswerable questions had started as soon as she got up in the morning. "Does someone come and fly you?"

Actually, the barrage had begun the moment we entered the monastery with men in saffron robes. She'd tapped a little gong at sunrise and asked questions we couldn't even answer for ourselves.

"What is exist and not exist?"

You try explaining what "exist" means to a five-year-old.

"Her grandpa's not gonna like it," Brad said over breakfast on the patio. There always seemed to be chimes and bells in the little Buddhist resort.

"He's going to be thrilled." I sipped my tea. Little sticks swam at the bottom of the cup. I missed coffee. "He can answer all these questions the way a good Southern Baptist would. She'll believe her grandparents. Trust me."

Milton was about to have a month to revel in his lovely granddaughter too. We were spending all of August in Arkansas. Then we were back to Los Angeles, and reality. Nicole would be off to school, her father would be unemployable, and her nanny would be in limbo.

"Is there a last number?" Nicole asked, lining up sweet dates and picking them off one by one as she counted them.

"One," Brad said. "The last number is one."

She screwed her eyebrows into a knot and tightened her lips.

"No," she said. "Not one. That's first."

"Not if you count backward."

"Silly Daddy." From the garden we heard the tap of a gong. Her eyes went wide, and her mouth opened with excitement. "They're doing the little gong!"

She threw her napkin on the table and scrambled off the bench. A monk who was reportedly 113 years old approached the steps to the deck. His gait was painfully slow, and his body had little muscle mass left, but he always smiled at Nicole. He must have been the reason for the question about how old people flew to heaven. It was hard to imagine this man in flight.

"She can come?" The monk held out a crooked hand to Nicole, who bounced to him without a thought. "Morning prayers?"

"I can do the little gong? The red one?"

"Go on," Brad said.

She went into the garden with the monk and didn't look back, chattering up a storm.

"We need to get her a gong for her room."

"No way." He brought his cup to his mouth, looking at me over the edge. His eyes were awake, and his skin was flush again.

The hardest day had been the first, when he told his agent he was indeed quitting *Bangkok Brotherhood* and reassessing his schedule. He had been in the middle of contract negotiations on two roles and lost them before the sun set over the mountains. Another smaller picture fell through when he became unbankable because he'd lost the other two. His March picture? Let go when the insurance company doubled his bond.

He laughed it all off and told *Variety* he was dyslexic. He met with the director of *Bangkok Brotherhood* in a nearby riverside café to explain. I didn't think it would help, and he assured me it didn't. He was finished in the business.

Nothing kept his body from mine at night. Nicole was in an adjoining room, and she didn't cry for us to be in bed with her. Maybe she knew we were together on the other side of the wall.

"Home tomorrow," he said on the monastery patio. "I never thought I'd want to see Arkansas twice in a month."

"And then Los Angeles."

We weren't talking about who we were or how we were arranging our relationship when we got back. It was easy in Thailand. I was his, and we were both Nicole's. Back in Hollywood we had questions over whether or not I'd be a nanny or a live-in girlfriend who took care of his daughter. Whether or not I'd work and he'd hire someone else. Whether or not Nicole would be confused, and how much. There was no easy answer.

But the breeze was so perfect, and the humidity hadn't gotten sticky yet, and the chimes and gongs echoed through the mountains.

"I've been thinking about going home," he said.

"Really?" I leaned back and crossed my legs, resting my teacup under my breasts as if it would protect my heart.

He put his elbows on the table. That meant he was serious. "At first I thought we should all just move to Redfield. If I ever work again, I'll just travel."

I tried not to react. I adored his family and even Redfield, but my dismay at being away from him must have been all over my face, because he held his hand up for a moment as if he wanted to calm me down.

"But I'd end up keeping the house in LA and without you guys in it?" He shook his head. "It would suck. So here's what I got. You ready?"

"Probably not."

"I think we have to define what this family is for us. Not for everyone else. And you have to define what you are to yourself."

I was the most complicated piece of this puzzle. We knew that. If I was a caretaker for children, what did that mean for Nicole? And if I loved Nicole as much as a mother could, was I still her nanny? Would she feel abandoned if I got another job?

"I still don't know anything."

"I know."

"Except that I love Nicole," I said, "and I love you."

"Let me ask you. Would this be easier if—"

"Daddy!" Nicole cried from the garden, the exact opposite of a meditative sound. The monks didn't seem to mind. They said they rented out their huts to families because they loved children. Thank God. Because enlightenment was tough enough without a five-year-old's demands.

"Yes, pumpkin?"

She'd stepped away from the circle of monks chanting and held up the little gong with one hand and the mallet with the other.

"Listen! I'm going now!"

"Okay. Go ahead."

She sat cross-legged in the circle, looked back at us, and tapped the gong.

We gave her the thumbs-up.

"No matter what I say," he said, still looking onto the garden, "it's going to sound like it's about convenience. But it's not."

"What's a matter of convenience?"

The gongs vibrated, sending their harmony to the blue sky and the frothy clouds.

"I was happy before I met you, you know." His eyes went to the table between us. "I was perfectly fine. But she came. She came first, and that's a fact. She blew it all apart, and I held my life together with spit and chewing gum." He looked up at me and smiled. "You know, if you break a vase and glue it back together, it's bigger after it breaks? The glue takes up space. The cracks add to it."

I put my cup down. He took my hand before I could put it back on the arm of the chair.

He continued. "You're my glue. You've made me bigger. Better. And you hold it together. All my life. I'm nothing without you."

I squeezed his hand.

"You were a good man before you met me."

"I was worthless."

"You said you figured out something about going back home?"

"I was just saying it's not about convenience. What I figured. It's not me doing the easy thing."

"Can you get on with it?"

"You have to marry me."

Surprised, I tried to pull my hand back. I tried to curl up so I could think for a minute. But Brad wasn't about deep thoughts. He was about action.

"I mean it," he said.

"Brad. It's soon."

"So? You're not going anywhere, are you?"

"No, but—"

"Good, because I'll chase you down."

It was yes. Of course it was yes. I didn't really have a choice. He gave me purpose. He made me happy. I wasn't going to choose misery over him because we hadn't known each other long enough. We'd bonded over the well-being of another person.

Maybe that was my worry. I didn't have to worry, but I always did. I squeezed his hand and looked him in the eye.

"Promise me you're not doing this for Nicole."

"What do you mean?"

He knew exactly what I meant. He was making me articulate it.

"If she wasn't around, would you have asked me to marry you?"

"You mean if I met you . . . where? At a bar? In the SAG waiting room?" He leaned back. "I can't imagine you without her. My life changed, and you were a part of it. Without the life change, you wouldn't want me."

He picked his ass off the bench and leaned over so he was that much closer to me, tugging my hands closer to him. I knew I was going to say yes, because he was right. The man he'd been wasn't a man I'd take seriously. But the Brad Sinclair who quit the best job in the world to make room for his daughter? That was a guy I took seriously.

I half stood off my chair so my face was close to his.

"You know no woman can resist you."

"You're not just any woman. You're mine."

"I am. Always."

Our lips met only briefly.

"Don't kiss on the lips!" Nicole cried on her way back from the garden. "It's germs!"

I pulled away, but Brad grabbed me by the back of the neck and pulled me closer, sealing the deal. He tasted like the salt of the earth and the breeze brushing through the trees. I was safe with him.

No matter where we were, we were home.

EPILOGUE

CARA

It was the one-year anniversary of Nicole's arrival, and we had a huge surprise planned for her. A pony. We didn't have a minute to fuck. Not even a quickie.

Nope. Not a second to spare.

"Hush," he said. "Not a sound."

Brad's voice was no more than a breath in my ear. We'd left Nicole by the pool with Blue, Bonnie Greydon, and Perla, her nanny. We had so much to do that sex had to be quick, but I never promised quiet.

"No way," I breathed back. Brad jerked his hips.

We were in the second guest bedroom, which was dangerously close to the play area. I'd started it. I could be getting dressed already, but when he picked Nicole up and threw her in the pool, laughing, his taut forearms called me. I figured I had ten minutes to get him off.

I'd closed the blinds, dimming the room into a few strokes of light that got in between the wall and the curtains. I'd got on my knees in front of him and took him in my mouth, running my hands all over him.

I couldn't ever get enough.

He was barely in my mouth a minute before he threw me on the bed and took me with nothing louder than a gasp. I was on my back, sweating in the unreasonable early summer heat, sliding against him, my legs wrapped around his waist.

"They'll hear," I said, holding his face in my hands.

"Not if you hush." Push, roll, a gentle thrust. He was going slow on purpose. "And when you come, you come for just me."

My fingers pressed into his back as my body vibrated in a heated throb.

I looked him in the eye, nose to nose.

"Faster. Fuck faster."

"No. You're too sexy like this."

His mouth said no, but he thrust inside me again. Hard. Slow. I was heated to a boil on simmer.

"I'll be quiet."

"You will. Yes, you will."

Slow and steady, he coaxed an orgasm out of me, teasing it higher and higher. I bit my lips between my teeth as he whispered how much he loved me.

———

Family first.

Brad didn't invent the phrase, but it would forever be associated with him getting out of his car in the pickup line at Nicole's school to confront the umpteenth pack of paparazzi with the umpteenth battery of questions.

Why'd you back out of the Brotherhood?

What do you think of them casting an unknown?

We hear you're being sued by Overland Studios.

"You guys want to know why I backed out on *Bangkok Brotherhood*?"

Brad had slapped the car open and the angle of the camera changed as the paparazzi taking the video backed up. He'd been mad. He'd come home mad and when I saw the video, I knew he only came home with a fraction of the rage he'd expressed an hour earlier.

"Because the guy who signed up for *Brotherhood* didn't have *(beep)* to do with his time but work and *(beep)* around. The guy who almost got on the set had a daughter. That changed things. It changed who I was, and it changed how long I could be on *(beep)*ing set. She lost her mother. She needed me. She was first then, and she's first *now*. Not when I get around to it. Okay? *(Beep)*ing *first*. Family first. Now get the *(beep)* out of here. I'm nobody. Git!"

Watching him lose his temper on the entertainment news that night, I took his hand. It was the only way I knew how to support him. Ken had warned about the blowback, finally resigned to the fact that there was nothing he could do to stop Brad's impossible fall from somebody to nobody.

"I'm proud of you," I'd said.

He'd believed in what he'd done. Nicole was first in his life. But as unstoppable as any actor seems, their livelihoods are dependent on factors that are invisible to the public. His career really was over, and he had to realign his idea of himself. That night, we'd slept all three in a bed like the old days.

"I'm scared," he'd said. "I don't know what I'm going to do. I don't want to do infomercials for juicers."

"Give it a week," I said. "Don't make any decisions. Just decide not to worry for seven days."

He'd reached over and took my hand. "If I didn't have you, I'd be nobody. I'd be lost in the sauce."

"You'd be her father."

"All I'm saying is, don't go anywhere. I'm hanging on to you. I need you."

"I'm here." I squeezed his hand. "We'll get through this."

Twenty-four hours after the video went public, the public responded.

My father worked fourteen hour days #familyfirst #Bradvsmydad

I'd rather be Nicole Sinclair broke than have a rich daddy #familyfirst #ImWithSinclair

My father left and got another family #familyfirst #Bradvsmydad

Check out my blog post on the real meaning of fatherhood. #familyfirst #ImWithSinclair

How many dads would give everything up for their kid? One that we know of #familyfirst #ImWithSinclair

My father missed my piano recital because he was drinking. #familyfirst #Bradvsmydad

My father never hugged me. Not once. It was like he was scared of me #familyfirst #Bradvsmydad

He didn't get paid for the talk shows or the appearances, but he did them because he felt that if his fans were supporting him, they deserved an explanation. He became the poster boy for giving it all up for your family. He spoke for women and men all over the country who had made the same choice. He validated them. He let them know they weren't the only ones, and their pain and their identity crises were his too.

I'd gotten so wrapped up in tomorrow, the next day, the incremental progress he made in people's eyes that I never planned the wedding. It never seemed important in the face of his ever-spiraling career. Upward. Downward. We could never tell, and I didn't want to distract him.

Truth be told, I'd been afraid that if I started planning a wedding, something else would go wrong. But nothing went wrong. He just got more and more popular.

Celebrities came forward to talk about the sacrifices they made either for their families or their careers. Michael Greydon first, with heartfelt stories of his children and why he only took movies in Los Angeles. Then others, until a national conversation about career and family became impossible to get away from.

The bubble grew and grew, and when it popped, so did the perception in the business that he couldn't be trusted.

———

Paula had come back just as the internet was exploding with #Bradvsmydad. She didn't contact Brad, who had changed his number by then, but me. I'd agreed to meet her at a coffee shop, expecting she'd demand something or another. But what she wanted to meet about was worse.

"I sent the parental rights form to DMZ," she'd said in her butter-yellow linen pants suit.

"Jesus, Paula. What do you want? Is this blackmail?"

"I don't want a thing. I feel like a first-order Judas." She'd covered her eyes with her hands, and I noticed for the first time that her nails matched her suit. "The devil came over me and after I sent it, I tried to undo it but it was too late." She took her hands away. "I know he can't forgive me, but can you tell him I'm sorry?"

"But why would you do that?"

"I loved him."

She said it and snapped her mouth shut. Closed her eyes. Took a long breath and continued.

"I was jealous. And threatened like a cat in a corner. I felt filthy when I sent it. I just had to come and talk to you and tell you I was the one."

I snapped up my phone and dialed an old number.

"That was shitty," I said while it rang.

"I know . . . I—"

"It's not like it matters. He doesn't have a career to ruin right now, but if Nicole finds out, she might not understand why her father rejected her."

"My father wrote us off when I was just little," she said pensively. I was mad as hell and had a few choice words for her, but the phone had been picked up on the other end.

"Hello?" I said. "Ray? It's Cara."

"Funny you should call," he said. "Something just came across my desk."

"I heard. I was wondering if we could work out a trade." I was about to overstep by a mile, but the tabloids would cross-check with the county and get those documents out in under an hour.

"I'm listening."

"Access." God, I was in such trouble when Ken found out. "Exclusive access to the new Brad Sinclair."

———

Nicole was not good at surprises. She wanted to know what they were before they happened. So we didn't tell her we'd planned anything for the one-year anniversary of her arrival on Brad's doorstep. We distracted her with a playdate with Blue and Bonnie, and planned a pony behind her back.

Her grandfather carved Nicole's new pony's nameplate from the lumberyard in a few hours, sanded it, and got a coat of shellac on it. She was a calm roan mare. After a bottle of wine and a long conversation about our lives and where we wanted them to go, Brad and I had named the horse California Pie.

Brad brandished his father's work. "Gorgeous," he said.

"She's going to love it," I squealed, taking the plate from him. It was still sticky and it needed another coat of lacquer, but I wanted it on the stable when we gave Nicole the pony.

We had a pre-interview with David from DMZ about Brad's upcoming animation voice-over and his newly-packed-but-not-too-bad acting schedule, then David got in his car to meet us at the stables and we blindfolded Nicole for her surprise.

"Why are we going the wrong way?" Nicole asked from the back-seat. She'd tipped up the bottom of her blindfold so she could see.

"Put that down, young lady," Brad said, looking at her in the mirror.

"Okay, but where are we going?"

"It's a surprise!" Brad and I said at the same time.

When we got close I crawled into the backseat and covered her eyes with my hand. Unfortunately, I didn't think to cover her nose.

"I smell horse poop!"

Brad shot a look back as we went past the gate. Behind the beautifully kept clubhouse and manicured lawns sat a functioning stable grounds for training horses and riders.

"Where are the horses?" she cried.

"Keep the blindfold on," I said when Brad pulled up to the front and handed the valet the keys. He sped around the front and opened the door while I leaned back and unbuckled Nicole's safety belt. Dave was there with his assistant, camera rolling. Ten months into their year of exclusivity, they'd used the time wisely, telling the story of the Sinclair family's fall into anonymity and the rise to normalcy. The public had been hungry to hear something positive.

"You got this?" Brad asked Dave.

"Got it."

"Is that David?" Nicole asked. "Hi, David!" She waved at where she thought he was.

"Hi, Nicole. You excited?"

"Yes. How's Buster?"

Buster was Dave's bulldog.

"He's good. You should come visit again."

We led her off the paved road to the dirt road of the stables. The horseshit smell got stronger.

"Do you like surprises?" he asked.

"I like ones where I know what it is."

Even with Brad's career "over" we figured Nicole was going to have to get used to people taking pictures of her. Turned out that if she got comfortable with the person behind the camera, she was comfortable with the camera.

We went into the stables. That was when I sensed something wasn't going to go as planned. I didn't know what about the room seemed different. The same horses were there. The same smell. The same white paint on the stalls and the same wooden nameplates by each one.

Then Nicole giggled and Dave said, "*Shh.*"

And a chuckle from behind a wall.

Why did I smell a little sugar behind the horseshit?

"Brad?"

He flashed a devil of a smile, and I knew something about this picture was as wrong as wrong could be.

"Happy anniversary, teacup."

"What? I—"

"SURPRISE!"

I jumped, oh, ten feet in the air as dozens of people poured into the stables.

"Wait! What?"

Nicole was jumping up and down, clapping, blindfold long gone. Brad picked her up as Blakely hugged me.

"Congratulations," she said in a pink satin dress and heels.

"For what? I—"

Brad's parents hugged and congratulated me too. And Susan and her kids. Buddy. Willow Heywood. Ray and Kendall.

"Brad? What the h—"

"Don't say a bad word!" Nicole shouted.

"It's your wedding," he said.

He pulled me out, and the crowd followed, laughing and talking, until we got to the clubhouse. I dropped his hand when I saw an easel with a flourished sign.

"The Wedding of Cara DuMont and Brad Sinclair."

"A surprise wedding?" I exclaimed, looking for my soon-to-be and not finding him. "There's no such thing as a surprise wedding!"

"Yes there is!" Blakely said. "We got a dress. That makes it real."

"Where's Brad?" I craned my neck to look for him, but only saw David. Jedi Heywood reached up to hug me, and I gave him a hard squeeze before looking over everyone's head for my . . . well, my fiancé.

"Come on," Blakely said, yanking me away. "We have half an hour to get dressed."

"What? I—?"

I was pulled into a dressing room.

———

Blakely and a gaggle of nannies from the parks and parties got me into a white gown and gussied up in thirty-four minutes. *Whirlwind* didn't begin to describe it. I'd gone to the stables to surprise Nicole with a pony and came out in a long white gown with a handful of white roses.

"The wedding's on the lawn overlooking the canyon," Blakely said absently, pulling me out the door. She'd done nothing but pull me from surprise to surprise for half an hour. Surprise, it's your wedding. Surprise, here's your dress. Surprise, long white ribbon on your bouquet. Surprise, Nicole is the most perfect flower girl ever.

"But the pony," I said. "Does she know about the pony?"

"No, I don't think so." Pull down a carpeted hall. Pull around a corner. She pulled me until I was at the top of a stone stairway and—

"Blakely!" I yanked my hand away.

"What?"

"I can't walk down the aisle. I have no one to give me away. Who thought of this? It's like a big missing piece. I can't go alone with everyone looking at me. It's depressing."

I anticipated Blakely recoiling in horror when she realized her massive embarrassing mistake. But she kind of smiled a little, then she smiled a lot.

"Surprise," she said quietly, holding her hand out to the side. I followed the line of her arm to a gray-haired man in a tuxedo. He stood perfectly still, a vision of diplomacy and courtesy. His eyebrows were still dark brown, and blue and brown coexisted in his eyes like dual mood rings.

"Dad?"

"Hi, button."

That was his voice, his stature, his posture. It was him. His presence cracked through the barriers I'd built around him.

"Dad?" I repeated.

He held his hand out for me. My father. He hated me. I knew he did. But he was here, at this ridiculous surprise wedding.

"Let's walk a straight line together," he said. "Then let's dance. Then you, me, and your mother—"

"Mom's here?"

I was reduced to simple thoughts and sentences. Nicole could have gotten deeper sentiments out.

"Of course we are. We love you, button."

Past him, down the stone steps, and over a short flagstone path, a hundred people waited. Past those hundred people stood Brad Sinclair in a tuxedo. With full-length pants. The whole getup. Even the tie.

"Can we go already?"

I had forgotten about Nicole at the top of the steps in her poufy white dress and basket of rose petals. She wore light-up pink sneakers that were never meant to be paired with a flower girl dress. Her brow was knotted, and she looked like a holy terror.

"She has your mouth," my father said.

"That's impossible."

He looked back at me dryly. "I was talking about what comes out of it."

His mouth twitched with a smile, and he gave me his arm. I slid my hand around it at the elbow, and he led me down the stairs. In front of us Nicole liberally covered the center aisle in white petals.

"I'm glad we came," he whispered to me. "You look beautiful."

"Thanks, Dad."

Nicole got impatient in the last three steps. She held out her basket and dumped the remaining flower petals at her father's feet. Everyone laughed, and when she hugged his legs, he laughed with them.

"He seems all right," my father said.

Brad picked up Nicole and held her to one side as I got closer. He waited for me with his daughter and my father patted my hand. I wanted to thank him for giving me the wedding I was afraid to create for myself. For completing wishes I didn't dare have. I felt a tightening circle around me. A bond of family that protected me from harm. A bond I would use everything in my power to protect. We completed a cycle of love and protection passed from father to daughter, generation to generation.

Brad took my hand and I was whole.

EPILOGUE TO THE EPILOGUE

NICOLE

My pony is the best pony in the entire world.
Her name is California Pie.
I love my pony and new mommy and daddy.
All four of us are very happy together ever after.

ACKNOWLEDGMENTS

So many people.

I have to mention my husband first. His help with this book was in his quiet support of whatever I'm doing. My daughter inspired Nicole and rounded out my life the minute she was born.

I have to mention Jana Aston, who read *Shuttergirl* and, in a Facebook post, suggested Brad needed a baby. The second her comment appeared on my screen, I knew she was right.

I had a great time working on the outline with my agent, Amy Tannenbaum. Without her guidance, I never would have gotten it together.

My content editor, Angela Marshall Smith, is completely brilliant at finding the things that work and making sure I turn the volume up all the way on them.

Jean Siska, as always, helped with the verisimilitude of the legal issues in the book.

Kayti McGee, with her sharp, quick-thinking brain, created the tone for the celebrity blog posts.

Jenn Watson poked me with a stick to get me to the finish line. She fed me avocados and cheese. I would have been late without her.

My girls Lauren, Laurelin, and Kristy—thank you for giving me a safe place to talk about all the bookish things I can't share anywhere else.

Thank you to Charlotte and Chris at Montlake, and the entire Amazon team for landing me my first publisher contract after 24 years of trying.

Everyone who supported me, thank you.

ABOUT THE AUTHOR

© 2014 Erin Clenendin

CD Reiss shot up the *USA Today* and *New York Times* bestseller lists with sizzling works like *Hardball*, *Shuttergirl*, and *Marriage Games*, but she still has to chop wood and carry water, which was buried in the fine print. Her lawyer is working it out with God, but in the meantime, if you call and she doesn't answer, she's at the well hauling buckets.

Born in New York City, Reiss moved to Hollywood to get her master's degree in screenwriting from the University of Southern California. Unfortunately, her screenwriting went nowhere, but it did give her enough confidence to write novels.

Today she's adoringly referred to as the "Shakespeare of Smut," which she thinks is flattering, but it hasn't gotten her out of chopping a single piece of wood.